The Three Hour War

Fredrick Hudgin

Novels

The End of Children Series:
    The Beginning of the End
    The Three-Hour War
    The Emissary
Ghost Ride
School of the Gods
Green Grass
Sulfur Springs
A Rainy Night and other Short Stories (My Short Story Collection)

Short stories

A Rainy Night
Ashes on the Ocean
Being Dad
Get Them OFF!
Gina
Green Grass
Nice Day for a Ride
Sowing the Seeds
The Chair
The Last Salute
The Longest Ride
The Mission
The Second Chance
The Wiz
They Don't Have Christmas in Vietnam
When Is a Kiss Not a Kiss

Poetry Collection

Four Winds

Fredrick Hudgin

The Three Hour War

Book Two of
The End of Children Series

This is a work of fiction. Names, characters, places, and incidents either are the product of the author's imagination or are used fictitiously, and any resemblance to actual persons, living or dead, business establishments, events, or locales are entirely coincidental.

All names, measures of distance, time, temperatures, and math have been converted into their common English equivalents for ease of understanding. There are not English words for many of them and in their native languages, pronunciation would be impossible for human vocal cords.

The list of contest submissions in Chapter 18 was created by my stalwart proofreaders. I included them there as they were presented to me, correcting only spelling, punctuation, grammar and tense. I figured that this would be similar to what President Robbins would have received.

No aliens were hurt in the production of this book.

The Three-Hour War, Book Two of *The End of Children* series

ISBN: 978-1539386384

Printed in the United States of America

For my friend and editor, Gina Farago, who said,
"I think you're on to something here."

"A war regarded as inevitable or even probable, and therefore much prepared for, has a very good chance of eventually being fought.
Anais Nin

Prolog

What Has Gone Before

Lily had a dream about how to make the transmitter. It wasn't a complicated device—they'd made far more sophisticated circuits in the physics lab at Stanford University. She tried to ignore it, but her dream had said, "It will change the world forever." For Lily Yuan, Kevin Langly, and Douglas Medder, three graduate physics students, it did indeed change their lives. But the rest of the world? Forever? Really?

What they discovered turned out to be the most important invention since the beginning of mankind—more important than antibiotics, more important than gunpowder, and more important than even the wheel. Lily, Doug, and Kevin had created a device that opened a wormhole, a hole in our universe that goes from one place to another, bypassing everything in between, including the distance. The device gave off a rose-colored glow when activated, so Lily called it the Rosy effect and the device generating it became the Rosy Generator.

When the students opened their first wormhole, an alert was sounded by the detectors that were planted on the moon fifty thousand years ago by the species mining conglomerate, Grock Corporation, after they raised humanity from apes. The alert went to two separate destinations: the communications center at Grock Corporation and the Galactic Species Control Board. The GSCB was the enforcement arm of the New Species Administration branch of the Ur, the loose government of the sentient species of the galaxy that regulated free trade between the member worlds. It was the GSCB's job to determine if a new species had advanced enough socially to allow them to begin mixing and trading with the other civilizations in the galaxy.

Grock Corporation dispatched a starship to investigate the alert and determine if it was real. The captain brought the three students onboard and questioned them. The evaluation team quickly came to the realization that someone had planted the dream in Lily—the scientists on Earth had made none of the discoveries that normally precede a species' first wormhole opening.

The only reason someone would have performed the dream plant was to have humanity evaluated (and failed) before they were ready to join the Ur. The suspected reason for the dream plant was that someone on Earth had discovered something from which another galactic corporation or species was making large amounts of money. The Ur had a rule that, if a newly admitted species had the same technology from which another species was profiting, the two species must split the earnings evenly from that point forward; this cut in half the profit the other species had been making from the device previously. The ship searched Earth's technology but did not find anything to connect the planting of the dream to any being, species, or corporation.

The problem facing Grock Corporation and the GSCB was that wormholes enabled the people of Earth to begin exploring and expanding into the rest of the galaxy. It didn't matter that someone had planted the dream; it didn't matter that humanity wasn't ready; all that mattered was that they could, and probably would, begin leaving their solar system within a year or two. Before the GSCB evaluation team could allow that to happen, they had to verify humans had accomplished five milestones: ending war, controlling capitalism, ending pollution, ending resource depletion, and ending overpopulation.

The GSCB team performed an evaluation and, of course, humanity failed. It had accomplished only the control of capitalism and that one only partially. Of the five criteria, it was our warlike attitude that was the deciding factor in our failure.

Since there was no way to prevent humanity from building starships and leaving their solar system, the GSCB instructed Grock to initiate the elimination of the species. Grock did this by releasing a virus—benign, as viruses went—with no side effects at all, beyond that the infected people could no longer reproduce. The virus identified the target species by using a sample of their DNA inserted into the virus before it began incubation; the starship used DNA collected from Lily Yuan while they questioned her. The infection was successful, and over the course of one week, the virus spread into every corner of the world. Only people, completely out of contact with the infected atmosphere and other infected people, remained uninfected—there were less than five thousand of them worldwide, most in nuclear submarines in underwater patrol and almost all male.

Kevin's father, Dr. Paul Langly, worked for NASA at the Jet Propulsion Labs (JPL) in Pasadena, California. Kevin told his father about Rosy and sent him the plans and lab notes. Dr. Langly built his own copy of the wormhole generator and demonstrated it to the management at JPL. The president of the United States declared Rosy technology a National Secret, and the FBI arrested the three students—ostensibly for their own protection—and brought them to JPL, where they participated in the development of wormhole technology to further its peaceful uses.

Rosy allowed almost cost-free launching of satellites into orbit, almost cost-free transportation around the world, and construction of starships and space stations at a small fraction of the cost of chemical rockets.

The students told JPL management about giving a copy of their notes to their advisor, and the FBI showed up at his house, confiscating all notes and papers about the wormhole generator. They didn't find the plans. All that their searching and questioning really accomplished was to give the students' invention massive credibility to their advisor, who decided to retire by selling the plans to the Chinese, Russians, and Israelis. The Iranians got wind of the invention and killed the professor before taking his last copy of the plans. Rosy quickly proliferated around the globe.

The students participated willingly, even enthusiastically, in the research at JPL until the Department of Defense, the CIA, and the NSA showed up. The US government took the wonderful invention—the thing that was going to change the world for the better—and perverted it into yet another tool with which to kill people. Rosy became a way to deliver bombs and bullets anonymously and for secure spy technology.

One of the students, Douglas Medder, decided he didn't want anything to do with the wormhole generator and how the US government had defiled it into a weapon. He escaped from JPL using the Rosy satellite launcher NASA had built.

On the way back to Palo Alto to find his girlfriend, Doug accidentally connected with the anti-government underground. He met with three professors at UC Berkeley who helped him design and build a Rosy detector. Their detector displayed where each wormhole began and ended, how big it was, and how long it was open, making anonymous bomb delivery impossible. Their hope was that, if everyone could trace a bomb to who sent it, no one would send any with Rosy. Doug took part in a radio interview announcing Rosy to the world, what it could do, what the US government had done with it, and how to build a Rosy detector.

Protestors calling for Lily's and Kevin's freedom and a stop to the weaponizing of wormholes immediately blocked all entrances into JPL. The ACLU presented a writ of habeas corpus demanding the students' release.

Two months after the virus delivery, the world finally realized no women were becoming pregnant. President Klavel convened a summit of surgeons general from around the world to begin the search for the reason and the cure. The virus became known as the Baby Stopper Virus or just BSV.

Doug contacted his girlfriend, Clara, who had left Palo Alto after he was arrested to return home to Montana. They agreed to meet at her grandparents' house in a village in British Columbia, Canada. Doug had to avoid the police and the FBI as he made his way from San Francisco, and when they met, they decided to marry. When they applied for a marriage license in Canada, the clerk realized Doug was on the FBI's Ten Most Wanted list and the Canadian police arrested them. Doug asked Canada for asylum in exchange for showing them how to build a Rosy generator with the condition that they use it only for peaceful technology. Canada agreed since the US would not share Rosy technology with them, and Doug and Clara got married and took up residence in Calgary.

The US moved all Rosy research to a secure area within the Nevada National Security Site, which the residents immediately dubbed Rosyville.

In addition to showing information on wormholes originating on Earth, the Rosy detector Doug created showed three small wormholes opening on the moon every time a wormhole was opened anywhere on Earth. NASA realized these were what tipped off the aliens when Lily, Kevin, and Doug opened their first wormhole. The president tasked NASA with investigating one of the sites and, if possible, retrieving whatever was there. He also told NASA to find a new home for us. This was one of many different efforts underway by the governments of the world as they struggled to find a cure for the virus and build sterile habitats to house uninfected people.

China, Russia, and Israel began building starships using Rosy to send the materials into orbit. The US did the same thing and began plans to establish a new colony for mankind. Kevin and his father worked side by side to help create probes that would examine nearby (less than fifty light years away) stars for habitable planets.

Some momentous discoveries were made by the NASA scientists examining the alien device retrieved from the moon. The technology inside the device would change humanity forever, again. The first discovery was dark energy, which makes up seventy-two percent of the mass of the universe—energy was always leaking into and out of the dark mass. This dark energy portal allowed almost free energy without pollution of any form or consumption of any resources, and NASA utilized it to power the US starship and the probes of the nearby stars.

From the wormhole activity passed to them by the detectors on the moon, the aliens realized Earth was building starships. They returned and sent the four under-construction starships into the sun. Captain Xanny announced to the Earth on all television and radio stations that *he* had released the infertility virus and why the GSCB had selected the people of Earth for elimination. He would allow no one to leave the planet; it was in quarantine until humanity died.

Lily had gotten pregnant two days before the infertility virus spread around the world and gave birth to one of the last babies created via normal man-woman relations. Lily named her child Lan (pronounced "Lahn") after her mother.

The Nobel committee awarded Lily, Doug, and Kevin the Nobel Prize in Physics. Doug declined it but accepted the Nobel Peace Prize for developing the Rosy detector and giving it to the world for free to prevent wholesale use of Rosy portals to deliver bombs.

Earth's quarantine had also trapped the alien pirate Fey Pey, who was responsible for the dream plant inside Lily. His starship *Easy Wind* was still on Earth, hiding underwater in the South San Francisco Bay, as they waited for a window of opportunity to leave.

... ...

In the two years that had passed since the end of Book One ...

The Russians tried to be heavy-handed with the aliens and Rosied a nuke at the aliens' starship. The nuke exploded, but the starship narrowly escaped. Captain Xanny's retaliation was fast and irrevocable—he sent both the launch site and Moscow into the sun.

All three of the students finished their PhDs. Lily, Kevin, and Doug refused to do any more work on the weaponization of Rosy and began working solely on new, peaceful uses for Rosy technology. They exchanged emails at least once a week.

Clara got a job in Calgary at a legal firm and was taking night courses online to finish her law degree.

Doug worked at the Canadian Aerospace Research Centre as chief architect of a Rosy transportation infrastructure that, within Canada, would replace long-haul trucking, train cargo, and air cargo transportation with Rosy portals. Countries all over the world began asking for help with setting up their own systems. A major new industry sprang up in Canada overnight—creating the freight portal system and selling it to the world. Phase two was to replace human long-distance transportation (airplanes, cars, buses, railroads) with Rosy portals.

Kevin and Lily settled into life at Rosyville.

Chapter 1 – The Escape

Two Years After the End of Book One

Fey Pey floated back and forth across the bridge of his pirate starship, *Easy Wind*. The cocoon of water surrounding his marine mammal body was moving constantly, an indication of his inner turmoil. "Are the decoys in place, Byteen?"

"Yes, Captain," his executive officer answered.

"Launch them on my mark."

Pey looked around the bridge. He wouldn't miss this shithole of a world. He had been under the waters of the South San Francisco Bay for almost three years, waiting for an opportunity to escape and continue his lucrative career as an outlaw species miner. Three years they'd been stuck here, and the contract that brought them to Earth had only specified one year. Eleven months into it, the goddamned Ur had arrived and put a quarantine around this planet so tight you couldn't squeeze a gnat's ass through it.

So, here they sat, half-buried in mud, living on fish, and waiting, while *Easy Wind* slowly rusted away in the salt water. Twice these stupid primates had tried to blow through the cordon and had their sorry excuses for starships sent into their sun. Once, they even tried to send a nuke up the ass of the Ur command ship! He still chuckled at that one. All it had bought these silly beings were two big holes in the ground—one where the launch site had been and the other where the country's capital had been. Dumbasses.

But enough was enough—he was determined to bust out of here and no goddamned quarantine was going to stop him. It had taken two years to acquire or build the necessary hardware to cover his launch. He had escaped from tighter spots than this one— you just had to know how to do it.

"Is the Hore energy portal at full power?"

"Yes, Captain."

"Are the energy portals in the decoys armed and at full power?"

"Yes, Captain."

"Sound the launch alarm."

Throughout the ship, the sound everyone had been waiting three years for came through the P.A. system.

"When I give the command, launch all decoys at the same instant we do."

"Yes, sir." Byteen raised his hand to the button in anticipation.

"On my mark. Three, two, one, launch."

... ...

Carl Markovich was fishing in his small boat above where *Easy Wind* was hiding under the water. Nearby, four drunk men were also fishing in another, much larger craft. Their loud music and laughter irritated him more than fingernails on a blackboard. He fished to escape from the noise of people just like them.

"I wonder who's driving *that* boat," he muttered in disgust. "Where's the effing sheriff now that it's not me getting crocked this time?" His rod gave a jerk. "About damn time," he said aloud.

Based on the strength of the hit, it felt like a big one, maybe a sturgeon or a halibut. He began to reel in the line. Whatever he'd hooked, it was big, no doubt, but it was coming up.

"Come on, baby. Come to papa," he coaxed, his fishing rod bent almost double.

The water began to rise like some gigantic sea creature was emerging out of the depths. His boat tipped dangerously as the water flowed away from the rising starship. He threw the rod onto the bottom of the boat and jumped to his outboard, where he pulled on the starter cord like a madman. A huge, slimy, algae-covered sphere began to appear through the water below. To Carl, it was a reincarnation of the *Nautilus* from the Disney classic movie, *20,000 Leagues under the Sea*. Whatever it was, he didn't want to stick around to find out.

The motor roared to life. He gave it full throttle as the rising ship capsized him. Carl hit the water and then rolled over and over. As the sphere rose out of the bay into the sky, a rosy glow surrounding it, the water rushed in to fill the pit, dragging him along. The turbulent water spun him around with the mud and seaweed the departing starship had torn loose from the bottom. Carl panicked and clawed at the water as the air burned in his lungs. He had no idea which way was up.

... ...

Around the world in fifteen separate locations, a chunk of dirt, rock, and water, four hundred meters in diameter lifted into the air. Each ball accelerated away from the earth for two hundred yards and then was suddenly gone, disappearing in a rosy twinkle. Each one left in a different direction. *Easy Wind* disappeared along with them.

The atmospheric pressure at sea level is fourteen pounds per square inch, and the wormhole Fey Pey opened was a quarter mile across—almost two hundred million square inches. That created a 2.76 billion pound battering ram, blasting the water, mud, fish, algae, and air that had been around *Easy Wind* into the vacuum of space at the other end of the wormhole with the force of an F-5 tornado. The winds easily passed four hundred miles an hour, and the maelstrom continued for five seconds after the ship went through.

When the glow faded, a hole remained in the murky waters a quarter mile wide that went four hundred fifty yards into the silt on the bottom. The two fishing boats that had been above the *Easy Wind* had been blown through the wormhole into space, along with the water and the starship.

The other end of the wormhole was five hundred light years away from Earth near the center of the constellation Cygnus. The arrival point was in clear space, a light year from the nearest star.

A massive wall of water rushed in to fill the void left by the ship, meeting at the middle, exploding a thousand-foot column of water into the air. The column collapsed down on itself with a roar, creating a tsunami wave that spread out across the bay, ripping docks off their foundations and destroying hundreds of small watercraft as they rolled in front of the crest like dice on a gaming table.

A new energy source, unlike anything the Earth had seen before, glowed in the depths where the starship had been. The water began to flow into it, increasing its size and hunger.

... ...

The last thing Carl Markovich would ever see was the vast array of unblinking stars among which he found himself floating weightlessly. The nearest star was a red dwarf named Kepler-186 by the astronomers on Earth. His boat drifted away from him as he died in agony. He tried to scream, but he had no air left in his lungs. The gases in his blood boiled, and his eyeballs popped out of his head. Carl's cooler, life vest, and fishing rod joined the rapidly-expanding cloud of air, water, fish, mud, and algae that had blown through the wormhole into the vacuum of space.

Easy Wind accelerated in a different direction and then disappeared in another rosy twinkle.

Chapter 2 – Living on the Rez

"Lan! Get off that ladder!" Lan looked at her mother, giggled, and continued climbing up the ladder in the pantry. Lily began to push her chair back from the breakfast table.

"Stay put," Kevin told her, getting up. "I'll grab her." He snatched Lan off the ladder, threw her up into the air, and blew a raspberry into her belly—she screeched in delight. He spun her around him like a satellite and then dropped her into her mother's lap.

Lan reached for a slice of orange on Lily's plate. Lily broke the slice in half and popped it into her baby's mouth. Kevin collapsed the ladder, put it on its hanger, and closed the pantry door.

"Do you think you'll have time to finish the playhouse this weekend?" she asked him as Lan finished off the last of the orange slices on her plate. She put the child in her highchair, snapped the belt in place, and put some more orange slices on the tray. "Lan really needs somewhere to play where I can keep an eye on her."

"I will finish it this weekend, Lord Vader," Kevin said solemnly, dropping to one knee and bowing his head. He peeked up at her with a twinkle in his eyes. "Unless something interferes, like the trip to Vegas to visit Dott we promised her a month ago."

"Damn. I forgot all about that."

Kevin snickered. "Well, I'm glad one of us still has a memory that functions."

"When are we supposed to be there?"

Lan had unsnapped the highchair buckle and was in the process of climbing out. Lily picked her up, gave her a kiss on the cheek, and stood her on the floor. Lan walked over to Tommy, their cat, and scratched his back. Tommy cautiously arched into her hand, ready to bolt as soon as she grabbed a handful of fur or reached for his eyes.

Kevin pulled out his phone and checked the time. "Ten o'clock. We'd better start movin' that way."

... ...

Leaving with a kid was never a quick thing, but they had it down to a science: check the diaper bag for three of everything, make sure there were bottles of water and juice, a baggy of Cheerios, a couple of cut-up apples and oranges, a few changes of clothes for Lan, a roll of paper towels, the stroller, and the baby backpack.

In fifteen minutes everything was loaded into the all-electric SUV that had replaced Kevin's old Camry. Toyota had made its new dark energy vehicles (DEVs) available to the people of Rosyville before they were available to the general public. Toyota made all DEVs, from bumper to bumper, in the United States, employing only people who had lost their job to the dark energy revolution. That marketing coup and the fact that the vehicles had every electronic gadget and gizmo you shoehorn into a car had allowed Toyota to capture eighty percent of the US DEV market.

Lan was strapped into her seat and the heat was on. One of the "cool" things about DEVs was there was no warm-up period—the heater was instantly on and off, like an electric heater in a house. In November, in the high desert of southern Nevada, that was a definite plus.

They pulled out onto Einstein Street with no exhaust or engine noise—not even a whine from the electric motors driving the wheels—and headed toward the main guard station and the exit from Rosyville. Las Vegas was an hour away. Kevin figured they were only fifteen minutes late—pretty good for them.

"Some difference from the old days, huh, Lily?"

"You mean the old days at Stanford, the old days at JPL before Lan was born, or the old days before we could leave Rosyville together?"

"All of the above," Kevin said, laughing.

Dr. Lowell, the previous head of JPL, had not allowed them to leave together. After he resigned to take over dark energy research and development for Exxon, the director of NASA had promoted Dr. Doogan to be in charge of wormhole research and the administration of Rosyville. The first thing Dr. Doogan had done was allow them the freedom to leave together. All he had asked was for them to be chipped so that, if they were kidnapped, any exit portal out of the United States would scream blue murder when they passed it. The chips became a standing joke between Kevin and Lily.

The marine at the gate recognized the couple and nodded in greeting as he began a thorough check of their van.

"How's Jane doing, Corporal Billingsly?" Lily queried, handing him their IDs.

"She's fine, Lily. Thanks for asking. She gets home tomorrow."

"Tell her I'll come over for a visit when she feels up to it." She leaned over to the retinal scanner next to the passenger window and got a green light. Kevin did the same on his side.

"I will, thanks. The doc says it will be about a week before she can start walking for exercise again. Hysties are a pain."

"Better than the alternative."

"No doubt about that."

Corporal Billingsly's wife had undergone an emergency hysterectomy after her gynecologist discovered a cancerous ovary. Even though women could no longer get pregnant, they were still subject to the same diseases of the reproductive system as they had been before the Baby Stopper Virus (BSV) had struck. The post-operation CT scan had shown no subsequent cancers.

Lan made a face at the corporal as he checked under her seat. He grinned and made one back at her. Two minutes later, he handed them back their IDs, the gate slid back, and he waved them through. Kevin weaved through the tank barricades, and then they were out onto US Highway 95. The high desert surrounding the Nevada National Security Site (NNSS) rolled past them as they headed south toward Las Vegas.

Twenty minutes into their ride, the triple rows of twenty-foot high, razor wire topped, chain-link fences veered away to the east. Between those fences lay motion detectors, sound detectors, laser tell-tales, cameras, and anti-personnel mines. A well-used road ran inside the inner fence, testimony to the number of randomly-timed patrols that searched the fence line for a breach. Another set of fences, similarly configured, encircled Rosyville as well. The guards had standing orders to use deadly force without warning on any trespassers. Rosyville was one of the most secure installations in the United States.

The traffic was light on Highway 95. Kevin touched the radio console and linked to Pandora via the onboard internet connection that supplied the feed. The Shins started playing through his Bluetooth headset. Lily chose a Disney musical cartoon streaming from Netflix for Lan to watch on the high-def display built into the back of the front passenger seat, and then she started surfing the news websites on her screen to see if the oil riots were coming under control in Saudi Arabia.

As dark energy portals proliferated around the world, fossil fuel consumption dropped precipitously. The revenue stream the oil-producing countries thought would never end was rapidly diminishing. The price of a barrel of light Arabian crude oil had descended below ten dollars. Fracking across North America had stopped completely and would probably never start again. State and federal taxes now made up fifty percent of the price of gasoline at the pump. A gallon of gas in Georgia was $1.12.

OPEC was falling apart as the member countries fiercely competed for the customers who still wanted to buy their crude oil. People within the OPEC countries, who had never worked, were realizing they had no education, no money, and would soon have no food. After a hundred years of semi-peaceful coexistence, Sunnis and Shias, the two main sects of Islam, were at each other's throats again across a wide swath of Southwestern Asia and Northern Africa. With the supply of oil no longer a concern to the rest of the world, none of the industrialized countries stepped in to calm everyone down. The Middle East descended into a blood bath that didn't have an end in sight.

Chapter 3 – An Improvement

"How was work, honey?" Doug asked Clara, as he sat down at the table.

"Canadian law is a lot different from US law," she said. "I have a lot to learn."

"How you learning that?" Mindy asked.

"How *are* you learning that?" Clara corrected her.

Mindy rolled her eyes. "Yeah, that's what I said. How *are* you learning that?" When Mindy came to live with them, she'd asked Clara to teach her how to speak correct English. Overcoming eighteen years of living in the ghetto in Oakland, California, as she scratched out a living as a prostitute and drug addict, was an ongoing battle.

Clara chuckled. "I'm taking some online classes through the University of Calgary. How's your English Comp class going?"

"That teacher ain't got the sense God give a flea." Mindy paused, took a breath, and started over, speaking slowly. "My teacher and I disagree on some important issues."

"Which issues are those, Mindy?" Doug asked, trying not to crack up at her careful rephrasing. "I hated that class when I was at Purdue."

"He thinks 'center' is spelled c-e-n-t-r-e. I tried to explain it to him, but he won't budge."

"That's a Canadian thing. He's using the British spelling, not the American one."

"I wish you white folks would decide how y'all want it. Then jus' tell me when you work it out. Doin' it one way for Canada and another for the US is jus' too damn much work for my poor black brain."

Doug had great empathy for Mindy's struggles. He was running into the same thing in his work at the Canadian Aerospace Centre. Whenever he meant to type "centre," he typed "c-e-n-t-e-rbackspace-backspace-r-e." His fingers refused to learn the new spelling.

"Mindy, I can't tell you how proud we are of your studies. You earned your GED last year and now you're working on your associate's degree at college. You've come a long way in two years."

"When you start from nothin', anywhere you go an...anywhere you go *is* an improvement." She got out of her seat and started collecting the dishes; then she stopped and decided to say the words she'd been practicing in private all week. "Clara and Doug, I want to thank you both again for taking me in—for taking us in, Martin and me. I don't know where we'd have ended up if you hadn't agreed to let us stay with you."

A wistful expression played across Doug's face as he remembered how he'd been adrift in California on the FBI's Ten Most Wanted list. He had escaped from NASA's Jet Propulsion Labs, where the government had illegally incarcerated Lily, Kevin, and him. He still remembered how wonderful it felt when someone had offered asylum and help when he had needed it most.

"Well, I owed Mona and the Sunshine Ranch more than I could ever repay, Mindy. When Mona asked if you could live with us while you got your education, Clara and I never hesitated. After you finish your degree, we'll help you get a job and your own place."

Clara reached over to Mindy's hand and squeezed it. "The way I see it, she did us the favor. I can't imagine not having you and Martin as part of our family. Martin may be the only baby I ever hold." Clara's eyes filled with tears. She had aborted her only pregnancy after Doug disappeared from Palo Alto without a trace. She hadn't told anyone she was pregnant—Doug hadn't known. When the FBI arrested him without her knowledge and kept him incommunicado at JPL for six months, she had assumed Doug abandoned her. She couldn't face the prospect of raising a baby by herself on welfare. Then BSV hit, Doug escaped from JPL, and he told the world about how the US government had weaponized the Rosy wormholes. When he'd met her in Canada, she'd told Doug about the abortion. They never had a second chance at making another baby.

Living with Mindy was a struggle at first. She was to earn her keep by doing the cleaning and cooking for Doug and Clara while the two worked in Calgary. They didn't really need someone to help cook and clean, but they'd agreed when Mona asked. The problem was Mindy did not know *how* to cook *or* clean. She had been living on the street since she was ten years old, and just three years ago, she had been a prostitute in Oakland on a downward, drug-infused spiral that couldn't end anywhere but in a six-foot-deep hole. Mona at the Sunshine Ranch in Big Sur had rescued her after she'd tried to get an abortion and the doc had persuaded her not to. Mona had detoxed Mindy and supported her through her pregnancy. Now Martin, her son, was almost two and a half and part of Doug's and Clara's extended family. They had shown Mindy what to do around the house, and she'd been a quick learner.

"Martin, where are you?" Mindy called out. He'd finished his breakfast long ago and had gotten down from his highchair to play.

He crawled out from under the table and stood. "Here, Mama." His skin was a lighter brown than Mindy's and he had blue eyes instead of her brown ones. Already he was the best-looking baby boy Mindy had ever seen.

Sometimes she wondered if his father would even care that he had a son. She didn't know which one of the Johns had fathered Martin, but it didn't matter. All he'd gotten was a quick piece of ass; she'd gotten Martin. Her son was her lifeline to the future—a future she had not dared to even dream about while she was working in Oakland. Mindy touched his cheek with a loving caress and smiled gently. "How's your diaper, Martin?"

"It dry. I use potty."

"Good boy. One more week of dry mornings and you get to wear those Spider-Man underpants at night." Spider-Man was Martin's favorite superhero character. "Go wash your face and bring your clothes to me, my handsome Spider-Man. They're on your bed."

"Yes, Mama." He turned and ran toward the bathroom, shooting Spider-Man webs at the walls as he ran.

Today was laundry day. Martin loved to "help" her sort and fold clothes. It took twice as long with his help, but she wouldn't ask him to stop for anything. They had even more fun putting the folded clothes away into the dressers.

... ...

"Dr. Hehsa from the CDC is on the phone, sir."

President Robbins lifted his head from his desk. He'd just closed his eyes for a moment...ten minutes ago, he realized after glancing at the antique grandfather clock in the Oval Office. "Thank you, Maria. Give me a minute."

"Yes, sir."

He rubbed his temples. Being president wasn't quite what he'd expected. There was never enough time to do anything right and sleep was the consistent loser. He picked up the phone. "Sridhar, good to hear from you. How are the Baby Machines coming?"

"The Baby Machines are fully in production, sir. Pfizer has completed its second plant. They will go into production on Monday."

"That's great news. What can I do for you?"

"Sir, I would be liking to get back to our research on a cure for the virus."

President Robbins paused. He knew what was coming next. "What will that cost, Sridhar?"

"I am needing ten million dollars, sir. At your request, we have exhausted our budget creating the Baby Machines."

"What are your prospects for finding a cure? Money is pretty tight."

"Very promising results were experienced in the last batch. I would like to be continuing that line of research."

"I'll see what I can find. I'll call tomorrow."

"Thank you, sir."

President Robbins was preparing to enter his third year in office. He had made five promises to the country when he was campaigning:
1) Find a cure to BSV
2) Make the USA PATRIOT Act more palatable to the American public
3) Calm down the world and stop the fighting among ourselves
4) Stop Congress from spending the country into poverty
5) Find a way to get our species' death sentence reversed.

There was still no cure, or even a glimmer of a cure, for the virus. The only new babies being born came from the Baby Machines. A collaboration between the CDC and five huge pharmaceutical companies had created the machines, but they were too slow and expensive to make much of a difference in the decline of the worldwide population.

Congress had amended the USA PATRIOT Act over the howling of the FBI, NSA, and CIA. It no longer allowed the government to imprison people indefinitely, citizens or aliens, without a trial. The only thing that really changed was that the justice department tried and convicted a number of inmates in Guantanamo on terrorism charges; the rest of the inmates were sent back to their country of origin for prosecution there. The Department of Defense closed the terrorist containment at Guantanamo for good, as had the CIA to their "black" prisons around the world. With the oil riots going on in the OPEC countries and the raging war across Islam between the Sunnis and Shiites, no one could say President Robbins had brought about a reduction in worldwide conflict.

As far as reining in Congress's overspending, Congress had fought President Robbins bitterly. Six new amendments had been put into the US Constitution by doing something no one had ever done before. The president and the ACLU had gotten the legislatures of forty-one states to demand the Senate convene a national constitutional convention. When the states announced they were going to have a convention, with or without Congress, the Senate had finally relented.

Almost a third of the incumbent senators had been thrown out of office two years ago. A second third was looking at the same thing happening to them this November. They wanted the populations of their states to view them as part of the solution instead of part of the problem.

The proposed amendments were:

1) Congress may pass no law that does not apply to them as well.
2) Congress may pass no law that applies only to them.
3) No person may serve in Congress for more than twelve years.
4) The general population, by referendum, must approve all pay and benefit increases for members of Congress.
5) Congress may pass no law that grants special privileges and benefits to members of Congress and their staffs.
6) The president of the United States has the authority to do line-item vetoes on bills passed by Congress.

The last amendment allowed the president to stop Congress from adding pork barrel earmarks to bills that had nothing to do with the earmarks themselves.

The national convention convened in April in Los Angeles— one of the only convention centers in the country large enough to hold the number of people and reporters who wanted to attend.

At first, the convention was chaos. Every individual with an idea of something they wanted to change in the US Constitution descended upon Los Angeles. The most popular were proposed amendments for gay marriage, elimination of the Electoral College, legalization of various recreational drugs, and abortion rights. The television and radio airways were flooded with paid announcements from various special interest groups.

President Robbins held several primetime press conferences stressing the importance of staying focused on the issues at hand. The LAPD and then the California National Guard were called in to keep everyone except the validated delegates out of the convention center and keep the demonstrations peaceful.

Protests went on continuously outside of the convention hall with the various proponents and opponents competing for the attention of the reporters.

The convention met for two weeks. When it ended, they had produced the list of six amendments. For them to become part of the US Constitution, two-thirds of the state legislatures had to approve the amendments by a simple majority. Twenty-three states put them on a special advisory ballot. Only number three got less than fifty percent in seven states. Besides number three, the lowest passage was by sixty-two percent.

Amendment number five was the most popular of the amendments, getting over ninety-percent approval in over half of the states. The population of the United States apparently felt Congress had been lining their own nests with their special benefits and budgets, treating themselves like royalty at the expense of the average worker.

So, of the five things President Robbins had promised to achieve while he was in office, he had accomplished only two. The world was still in chaos, no one was having babies, and the goddamned aliens still wouldn't talk to him.

The octopus alien, Captain Xanny, had announced on global television that Earth was in quarantine and there was no way out—that, like it or not, humanity was going to die as a species. Twice he had thrown Earth's under-construction starships into the sun—once from space and once from the covert silos in five separate countries.

President Robbins decided it was time to get serious about opening peaceful lines of communication between the aliens and Earth. He pressed the communication button to his chief of staff.

Patty's voice came through the speaker instantly, "Yes, sir."

"Hi, Patty. Please set up a meeting with my cabinet—the subject is establishing communications with the aliens. Today or tomorrow. Check our calendars. I expect it to take an hour."

"You are a hundred percent committed for both days."

"Bump something. This is more important."

"Yes, sir. Uh, sir?"

"Yes, what is it?'

"The people from the Iowa Apple Growers Association are here waiting to meet with you."

"Tell them I'll be right there."

Chapter 4 – The Warden

"Captain Xanny, please come to the bridge!" Commander Chirra's voice was tight with tension.

The captain floated in, a gray-green octopus covered in tattoos and supported by an anti-grav device that also propelled him through the air. "What's happening, Yidee? What's the emergency?"

His executive officer was also an octopus. "We have had sixteen simultaneous off-planet wormholes beginning from separate locations going in different directions."

The comm link next to Chirra's seat came alive. "Commander Chirra, this is Sergeant Shaia in Analysis. Mass readings are indicative of starships. Each one had its own Hore energy portal powering it and left a gravity disruption singularity as they entered the portal. The exits of the portals are out of range of our detectors."

"Thank you, Zarqa. Good job on the turnaround."

Xanny groaned, rubbing his head with a tentacle. "Shit! Not again! Won't these bastards accept that they're going to die?" He settled into his captain's chair and considered his options, hoping to find some way to explain the portals that wouldn't make him call for the Ur stormtroopers. There was nothing to do but report the escape. He sighed again and turned to Lieutenant Nussi, his communications officer. "Nola, alert Grock Central and the GSCB. Tell them we've had a jailbreak." He pressed his shipwide comm button. "Lieutenant Fibari, please attend me on the bridge immediately."

Fela Fibari padded onto the bridge before Captain Xanny had finished his announcement. She'd heard the stress in Chirra's page for the captain and figured it was the kind that would require her services. She sat next to his chair. Fibari was feline with gray and black stripes, about fifty kilograms, and one-and-a-half meters from her whiskers to the tip of her tail. Half of her left ear was gone and she had an old scar—actually, three parallel scars—beginning on her right shoulder, continuing diagonally across her back, and ending on her left flank. She moved with peace and grace, belying the ferociousness that had earned her the position of ship sergeant-at-arms.

"Send a sniffer after each of them," he told her. "Maybe the sniffers can find out where they went and how many people escaped. We might be able to retrieve them before the combat troops arrive."

"It'll be a blood bath if we don't. Grock won't like it."

"Tell me something I don't know."

Fela paused, deep in thought. "The gravity singularities will make following them almost impossible. Where the hell did they get them?"

The captain cocked his head, wondering about it as well. "Yidee, check with Analysis on whether they've found any research or technology that would show these monkeys how to build a gravity singularity. Nola, have you sent those messages yet?"

"No, sir. I was still preparing the encryption."

"Hold off for a few minutes."

"Yes, sir."

"Fela, evacuate the singularities into clear space a million light years from here, before they can do any more damage, and send a sniffer to each departure point—they may be able to find a general idea of where their ships went."

... ...

Forty minutes later, Xanny watched the sniffers go, each one winking out of sight in a rosy ball as it descended to the beginning of the wormhole of its assigned starship. The sniffers would find the direction the wormhole departed and skip down that path, one million kilometers per skip. At each stop they would scan the area, looking for a trace of the starship that departed Earth. If they found anything, they would do a linked-hore transmission telling his analysis section what it found. A linked-hore transmission was a special radio communication between a transmitter and a receiver using a tiny wormhole to connect the two. This allowed instantaneous, secure communications across vast distances. Only the transmitter and receiver were able to access the contents of the transmission.

"Nothing to do now but wait." He sighed and floated back off the bridge.

Chapter 5 – Message in a Capsule

"Could I have everyone's attention for a minute?" Mayor Carver looked out over the assembled crowd. Over two hundred people had collected in the central square of Dobyville, Maine. The audience grew quiet. "We have come here today to create a time capsule—a message to a future that we hope will be there for humanity."

A ragged round of applause came from the audience.

"I would like to thank Hardy Building Supply for providing the lumber and nails to frame it, Ferguson Portland for the concrete, Killian's Funeral Home for the waterproof containment, Montana Contracting for the excavation, the Dobyville Chamber of Commerce for the bronze plaque that we will put in the concrete that seals the capsule today, and a thank you to everyone who made a personal contribution to this project. Before we close it up, you may now put something in that you would like to pass on to whoever is here in a hundred years. If containment for one hundred years underground might damage what you are contributing, there are Ziploc bags and desiccant tablets available to protect it. Feel free to use them or not, and please include a note saying who you are and why you donated your particular item. If you don't have a pencil and paper of your own of your own, there are some on the table behind the podium."

Each person with a contribution passed the opening, handing down to the workers the things they had chosen for inclusion: a favorite doll from a little girl, today's issue of the local newspaper from the editor, a copy of *Moby-Dick* from the librarian, a football and game rules from the high school athletic director. The local credit union president presented a solar-powered DVD player and full set of DVDs containing the *Encyclopedia Britannica*, *Webster's Unabridged Dictionary*, and fifteen different translation dictionaries translating English to the other language and back. He called it the Rosetta gift.

They filed past silently and added the things they hoped would remind the people of a hundred years from now who and what this little town in Maine had been.

After the last person had delivered their artifact, Mayor Carver announced, "Cover it up!"

The gravediggers slathered tar around the lip of the lid and a crane lifted it into place where it settled with a solid-sounding *thunk*. The concrete truck swung its chute around; a pull of a lever and concrete flowed down, filling the hole and covering the capsule. Two men smoothed it and placed the plaque, sinking it down into the surface until it was flush. On the plaque were the following words: "To the people of the future, welcome to our past. The people of Dobyville, Maine. Do not open for one hundred years." The last line contained the date and corporate logos of the contributing businesses.

Everyone who had contributed a gift put a hand down on the soft cement and then printed their name, leaving their handprint as a personal signature on their message to the future.

... ...

The annual porpoise slaughter in Iwate, Japan, ran into a problem this year. Around sixteen thousand Dall's porpoises, which look like half-size orcas, were harvested annually by Japanese fishermen. The tradition of the hunt went back before recorded history. The Sea Shepherd Conservation Society objected to it to anyone who would listen, saying porpoises have a larger brain mass and higher tissue complexity than humans and are intelligent and caring. As much as they could legally, their ship and launched boats hampered the whaling ships' hunt by putting themselves between the whalers and the Dall's. The whalers responded by splitting the hunter packs into smaller groups which were able to bypass the Sea Shepherd blockade.

This year, the harvest was much lower than in previous years. A group of bottlenose dolphins appeared after the first Dall's was harpooned. Much to the irritation of the hunters, the bottlenoses seemed to be herding the Dall's away from their boats. The confrontation escalated when a concerted effort by a pod of ten or more dolphins capsized several of the hunters' boats and killed some of the whalers as they floated in the water, waiting for rescue. No one understood why the bottlenoses were doing this—they had never interfered before. The bottlenoses appeared to be juveniles, possibly two to three years old. The fishermen were angry enough to say on camera they would be eating bottlenose meat instead of Dall's for dinner, but the bottlenoses consistently avoided capture, as if they could predict the whalers' behavior and circumvent it, using the boats of the Sea Shepherd as a shield.

... ...

As Doug drove into work at the Canadian Aerospace Centre, he stopped at a traffic light. A man with a cardboard sign stood by the side of the road, looking for handouts. They made eye contact for a second.

It's awfully late in the season for panhandlers, he thought, refusing to acknowledge the man. *They usually head south long before November.* Night temperatures were going below freezing in Calgary.

Doug stole another look. The man's clothes were threadbare and he had a worn, filthy backpack laying beside him next to the road. A dirty knit cap kept his greasy hair pulled back from his face, and he had clearly not shaved in months. His hollow cheeks and eyes filled Doug with painful memories of his own journey to Canada. What would he have done without Pastor Evans coming to his rescue with clothes, an ID, and money?

He made a point of never giving anything to street beggars, knowing it would simply fuel their drug addictions and delay their reentrance into society. He felt torn between his Christian beliefs and his hard-won street wisdom. Just so he wouldn't have to look at the beggar's skeletal face anymore, Doug read his sign and a cold hand gripped his heart.

"Lost my trucking job to Rosy. Will work for food."

He grabbed his wallet, pulled out the cash, lowered the window, and handed it to the man. "Go get warm."

The man gaped at the wad of money. "Sure thing, governor. I'll stay warm a couple of nights with this, eh? Thanks." The man picked up his backpack and turned toward Calgary, a hungry grin on his face.

Chapter 6 – You Have to Trust Someone

Chief Petty Officer Freddie Harris picked up Wilson Rabinowitz and changed his diaper. It was his first diaper change since he'd started his shift twenty minutes ago, and he didn't expect it to be his last. He had eight toddlers to nurture and raise—an equal distribution of boys and girls. The children were the same age, plus or minus a couple of weeks, and were slowly going through the mess of potty training. The babies mirrored all the races and skin colors of the world. His favorite was a bright, pain-in-the-ass, red-haired girl named Shannon McGhee.

To some, it may have seemed incongruous for Freddie to be a caregiver to infants. He was taller than many of his peers, and tattoos covered his heavily-muscled arms and torso. So he wouldn't have any problems with the Navy's haircut regulations, he kept his head shaved. To anyone who didn't know him, he appeared to be a skinhead or a gang-banger, but nothing could be further from the truth. He had a BA in English Composition and had written three very funny books on life in the Navy. He loved his job with the babies, and they trusted him completely.

He was also a corpsman, the Navy term for a medic. He'd tried out for the Seals, but they had washed him out. When another candidate had lost consciousness during a deep dive, Freddie had brought the pair of them up too fast. He had burst a blood vessel in his lungs, and gotten the bends, but the other man had survived and recovered completely.

Freddie was one of the four hundred fifty-three submariners who had volunteered to be nursemaids to the children at one of the Sterile Heritage Protection Sites (SHIPS). The government had built them to house and protect uninfected babies representing the gene pool in the US. The six SHIPS were distributed around the country, built in areas of low seismic activity and designed to last four hundred years. At last count, twenty-eight other countries around the world were creating the same kind of facilities inside their borders. Two of the US SHIPS were covert, hidden from the rest of the world and kept top secret in case another country decided they would be the only survivors of BSV. The general consensus among scientists was that, if there were no humans to infect for a hundred years, the virus would die out. Freddie's SHIPS, not one of the hidden sites, was in Montana.

The submarine crews were under water on active deployment when the aliens released BSV. Because nuclear submarines on patrol do not surface for months at a time, the virus had not had an opportunity to infect them. The government chose them to staff the SHIPS. Since they'd volunteered, the crews had been housed in the sterile facilities next to the construction sites. Unfortunately, these volunteers were almost entirely male. If they had been female, the SHIPS could have been populated much more quickly. The eighteen females onboard the subs had produced twenty-six uninfected children so far.

Before the release of BSV two years ago, fertility clinics across the nation had created and stored many fertilized embryos for couples who, for a multitude of reasons, didn't want to use them right away. The Future of America Act, passed soon after the discovery of the virus, allowed the US government to seize those embryos and use them in any way they felt was in the best interest of the United States. Scientists had used them for research into a cure for the virus and to create the population of uninfected babies for placement into the SHIPS.

The first surrogate mothers had been the three species of primates genetically closest to humans; rigorously cleansed chimps, bonobos, and orangutans kept in sterile environments. The virus did not infect or live in any other species, and this allowed the surrogates to gestate uninfected human embryos. The babies who survived the surrogate process were given the same name as their genetic mother or father, depending on the gender of the baby.

Now that the artificial uterus, created by a joint development team from the CDC and several large pharmaceutical companies, was fully functional, the primates were no longer needed. The task of birthing a new generation of uninfected human babies had fallen to the Baby Machines, as the press called them.

The embryo confiscation policy was very unpopular and one of three things causing ex-President Klavel to lose his reelection bid. In addition, most of the seats in Congress up for reelection had been filled with people with no connection to the Klavel administration. The new Congress had repealed the Future of America Act after President Klavel was defeated, and the researchers returned the unused embryos to their original donors.

Without a source of uninfected embryos to put into the Baby Machines, the government had fallen back on Plan B: harvesting DNA from the graveyards across the country and using it to clone copies of people who died before BSV was released. However, the cloning process was imperfect—only fourteen percent of the cloned babies turned out well. The rest were physically or mentally flawed—most had enormous defects and died soon after implantation. Some defects were more subtle and didn't appear until well into the second or even third trimester. Those were terminated before the forty-week gestation period completed.

During ABV+1 (the second year after BSV had been released), the babies from the cloning process began to increase the numbers in the SHIPS. As with the surrogate mothers, the names of the babies were the same as their DNA donor, and no single donor was used for more than one baby, keeping the gene pool as diverse as possible. Each potential donor was carefully researched to prevent genetically-passed diseases and to prevent a propensity for depression, as well as ensuring the intelligence of the clones was far above the human average. Other than the above criteria and a desire to keep the ratio of male to female children equal, the selection of donors was random—unless a higher power intervened. With enough bribery in covert meetings at the highest levels, some exceptions were made. High-dollar political supporters were allowed to submit their deceased, uninfected relatives for evaluation at the head of the line. For the largest contributors, the selection bypassed the evaluation process entirely.

The pharmaceutical corporations, participating in the development of the Baby Machines with the CDC, had invested billions into the project. They had done so while operating under an agreement that they would be able to license the manufacture to subcontractors and provide baby-creation services to the general public. The babies created for them would not be BSV-free, but that did nothing to slow the volume of applicants. Within five months of the services going online, the queue of customers desiring access to the Baby Machines had filled all possible time slots for ten years into the future. As specified in their contracts with the US government, these services were available to any US citizen on a first come, first served basis, costing the customers no more than twice the actual expense of running the service. After an initial period of uncertainty, the cost settled to about ten thousand dollars per baby, which the government reduced or waived entirely, on an income-based sliding scale.

As their contract with the US government specified, the manufacturing companies were selling their US-made machines to US gestation companies. However, every one of them had built offshore manufacturing plants, as well. They were selling five times more to other countries, large corporations, and rich families than to the US Baby Centers, and at a considerably higher profit. The one percent of the world who controlled ninety percent of the wealth were buying machines for their personal genetic survival. A million dollars per machine was, to them, a small investment with a huge return.

For the wealthy upper middle class—the people who couldn't blow a million bucks to purchase their own machine—a very lucrative and very illegal offshore business had sprung up, putting people willing and able to pay an enormous fee at the front of the line in a foreign country. No country allowed it publicly, of course—there would have been massive riots if their citizens discovered that wealthy foreigners sat at the top of their Baby Machine queue while the indigenous population had to wait for possibly decades.

Some of those wealthy people wanted clones of dead children or beloved ancestors. Some wanted clones of themselves. Some just wanted a baby from the same gene pool whom they could raise as a normal child of their own. Movie stars and entertainers began offering a milliliter of their blood for up to a million dollars, and many baby gestation services had acquired a certified inventory of famous people's DNA from which, for the right price, they offered to make a clone.

After Rita Hayworth's grave was broken into in Culver City, California, and part of her leg removed, the descendants of many famous people hired armed guards to protect their relatives' gravesites. Of all the famous people DNA available, the sex symbol movie stars seemed to be the most sought after. Some descendants had harvested tissue from their famous ancestors and offered it for sale. You could buy DNA from Greta Garbo, Elizabeth Taylor, Brigitte Bardot, Jean Harlow, and Mae West.

Although Marilyn Monroe's crypt in Westwood Village Memorial Park, Los Angeles, was never disturbed, there were many offers on the internet for "certified" samples of her DNA.

… … … … … … …

"And you're sure you can clone my daughter?"

Samantha Evers had never talked to anyone like this person before. He looked like someone out of a B-detective movie, and not one of the good guys. He was fat and balding with a triple chin and garlic breath.

"You get me some of her DNA and I'll get you a copy," the man rasped quietly as he looked around the dimly lit bar.

Samantha hated bars, and this one held the prize for the sleaziest one she'd ever been in. Her trim runner's body, dark blue business suit, and expensive honey-streaked haircut didn't fit the place at all. "How do I obtain some of her DNA? She's been dead ten years. Will hair work?"

"Nah, hair won't work. It's gotta be a tissue sample."

"How do you do it?" she asked. "How do you turn tissue into a child?"

"I don't know nothin' about *how* it's done or even *where* it's done." He laughed his raspy laugh. "All I know is, if you pay me the money and give me the tissue, I'll give you a baby in nine months. That's what you want, right? Another chance at raising your little girl?"

Her daughter, Kayleen, had committed suicide when she was fifteen. She had left no note—no Twitter announcements or Facebook posts—and hadn't told anyone why. One day after school, she'd gone into her bathroom, turned on the shower, and slit her wrists. Samantha had found her four hours later with the water still running.

There was only one place she could obtain some of Kayleen's tissue, and that was in Forrest Lake Cemetery, about five miles from where they sat.

She already knew the answer, but she still asked, "How much does it cost?"

"Ten grand in cash gets you a position in the queue. When your turn comes up, it's another ninety grand and then ten thousand per month with the last payment made before you get the baby. And that's in cash—no credit cards, checks, money orders, stocks, or bearer bonds. Cash only and only US bills. You get updates every week from an anonymous email account, complete with pictures of the developing fetuses. They create twenty of them because some of the clones don't work out so good. By the end of the forty weeks, only one's left. That's the one you get."

She didn't want to think about the other nineteen copies of Kayleen being thinned out like radishes in a garden. "How do I know you won't disappear after I pay you the money?"

He shrugged and glanced at his cell phone. "You have to trust someone, lady. I have another appointment in half an hour. Whaddaya wanna do?"

She wavered. She was forty-one years old, and the government-sponsored queue was now eleven years out and growing daily. If she went that route, she'd be fifty-two when Kayleen's clone showed up. She'd be almost seventy when Kayleen graduated from high school—old enough to be her grandmother or even great-grandmother. This was her only acceptable option and she was going to take it!

"Okay, sign me up. Here's ten thousand dollars." She pulled out a bundle of new hundred dollar bills, the bank band that said "$10,000" still around the bundle. As he slid it into the inner pocket of his cheap, wrinkled suit coat, she asked, "How do I contact you?"

"You don't. I contact you when your place in the queue comes up—it's running about seven weeks out. When I call, you have twenty-four hours to come up with the ninety grand and the tissue sample. If you don't show up, you lose your place and have to start over again with another ten grand. Give me your contact information."

She handed the man her business card. On the back, she wrote her personal address and phone number.

"Okay...Samantha," he said, looking at her card and turning it over a couple of times. "Looks like I'll call you in about seven weeks. Here are the instructions for preservation of the tissue." He gave her a sheet of paper. "See you then."

She got up and then, not knowing what else to do, held out her hand. He shook it limply and laughed, his triple chin wiggling like an old breast.

Later that night there was a knock on her door. Samantha invited an unkempt man in dirty coveralls into her living room and explained what she needed. He agreed to deliver the tissue to her the next evening. She pulled an envelope out of her pocketbook.

"Here's a thousand dollars. When you bring me her finger, I'll give you another thousand. I'm going to check her fingerprints to make sure it's her."

He pocketed the money. "Don't worry, lady." He flashed his rotten-toothed grin. "What with nobody being able to make new babies, we're gettin' a lotta people askin' for this shit these days. I'll see you tomorrow night."

... ...

Dr. Hehsa watched the ovum in dismay through his microscope. The acrosomal reaction changed the chemistry of the wall to make it impervious to a second sperm penetrating after the first succeeded, which was necessary to prevent two or more sperms from penetrating a single ovum. Somehow, BSV had short-circuited the process by triggering the acrosomal reaction when the first sperm *attempted* to penetrate the ovum, *preventing* penetration and subsequent fertilization. After weeks of work, he had delayed the acrosomal reaction long enough to allow the sperm to penetrate its wall, as it was supposed to do. He looked at the ovum again. At least four spermatozoa had penetrated, with more doing so as he watched. It would live a day or two and then die.

Dr. Hehsa took a deep breath and let it out as a sigh. As he stood for the first time in several hours, the clock on the wall of the lab displayed "2:23 A.M." in bright red numbers and letters. Sridhar walked to the door of the lab and flipped off the lights. The couch in his office was calling to him.

He laid his head down and closed his eyes, but his mind wouldn't turn off. *I have spent all this time figuring out how to keep the acrosomal reaction from triggering too early. Now I have to figure out how to keep it from triggering too late. It has to be the release of hyaluronidase. What did the damned aliens do to disrupt the process so effectively? It has to be the carrier protein that activates the hyaluronidase generation gene.*

He fell into a fitful sleep, dreaming of a video game in which hyaluronidase molecules tasered sperms as they swam toward an unfertilized ovum in a miniskirt and bra hanging at the top of the screen, wiggling, waving, and blowing kisses.

Chapter 7 – Eleven Worlds

"Only one of the 'starships' was a starship," Lieutenant Fibari told Captain Xanny.

"What were the rest of them, Fela?"

"Chunks of rock someone yanked and launched to cover their escape." She said it deadpan, already having worked out what happened. She was waiting to see how long it would take Xanny to come to the same conclusion. Games like this were part of their friendship.

"So, someone obviously not from this planet wanted to leave without us being able to follow." The captain stretched his legs in thought. "The perps? Could they have been down there for three years without us knowing it?"

"That's what I figured. I've been all over the site in the bay where they launched. It's a couple of kilometers from where the female primate you brought onboard had her dream planted three years ago. I went back and checked the scans. No Hore energy emissions from there until yesterday. We didn't notice them then because there are so many vehicles, boats, and buildings with active Hore energy portals nearby."

"They must have been existing on cold fusion...for three years . Damn. I bet they're glad to be gone."

"I have the general direction of their departure but not a distance—could have jumped one light year or a thousand. But look at what else I found." She'd been waiting to share the last tidbit. She pressed the hologram display button on his console and linked to her personal storage. A starship sphere, about half out of the water, appeared in it. "This is the starship leaving its hiding place."

He chuckled. "I knew if I waited long enough, you'd get around to telling me what you were holding back. Where'd you find it?"

"It wasn't hard. The news feeds on their communication network and news channels all over the world were showing pictures of the departing starship every five minutes. I clipped those and had Analysis search the natives' personal communicators in the area. They even found a couple of movies. Let me show them to you."

Everyone on the bridge watched the images in silence.

"Let me see the second still shot again." The ship was about three-quarters out of the water. He reached up with two tentacles and stretched the image, enlarging it, and then he did it again. Next to the main entrance portal was a logo—faded and chipped almost beyond recognition. It showed a fish squeezing a world while the money from the world flowed into a pile of gold.

"Son of a *monkrus*!" he spat. "That's Fey Pey's ship, *Easy Wind*. He's been here the whole time! He's the one who planted the dream!"

Fela just stared at the logo. She had been Fey Pey's second in command until he lost her in a card game to a pirate dealing in exotic sex slaves. A week later, the pirate who'd won her had fled the solar system, leaving her behind in a barely-functioning escape pod. Six months after that, she had signed on with Xanny. No one had ever found out what occurred on the sex trader's ship—she wouldn't talk about it. The incident was a source of endless speculation by the crew.

"I've waited most of my life to cross paths with that *monkrus* again. *Please* tell me I can go after him."

"Let the stormtroopers do their job, Fela. They have a lot more resources than we do, and we still don't have proof that he planted the dream. There are a hundred different and not nearly so serious reasons that would explain why he was on the planet. Once we set up the quarantine, he couldn't leave without setting off the alarms. It must have chapped his ass something fierce to know I was running the operation."

"You know he did it," she said coldly. "You know he planted that dream. Fey Pey is just the kind of low-life who would do something like torpedoing a whole species for profit. I wonder how much he was paid and who paid him."

"Those are the big questions, aren't they? I hope we'll find out someday. Until then, Fey Pey and *Easy Wind* will have trouble finding a place in this galaxy where he can resupply or hide."

Xanny started counting to himself the places they would be able to refit; he got up to eleven before he ran out of possibilities. Other ports existed farther out in the fringe, but none that could refit an entire starship. After three years under salt water, many exposed parts would have to be repaired and soon. Before he began his career as a licensed captain of a licensed species mining ship, he had been a pirate, just like Fey Pey. Well, maybe not *just* like Fey Pey—even when he was a pirate, Xanny still had *some* morals. Some lines he would not cross and killing a species before its time was one of them.

"Analysis!" he called into his comm link.

The response came back in less than a second. "Yes, sir."

"Did you pick up an electronic signature on that ship before it entered the wormhole?" Every starship emitted its own unique electronic signature.

The tech paused. "Well, kind of, Captain. Only one of the launches *had* a signature beyond the Hore energy portals, and that was the only one that began underwater."

"That's the one I want. Send it to Lieutenant Fibari and Lieutenant Nussi."

"Yes, sir."

"Nola, send all this to Grock Central and the GSCB. Tell them the ship is *Easy Wind* and the captain is Fey Pey. Also include holograms from my private gallery of Fey Pey and his ship."

"Fela, I want you to put three watcher drones in place around each of these worlds." He listed them, but he hadn't needed to—she'd already come up with the same names.

"No Captsius?" she asked in mock seriousness.

"Captsius is just a first aid station. You might get a salvaged magnet or thruster if you're lucky, but you can't get a refit. Have the drones hide and watch; program them to look for that electronic signature. If *Easy Wind* shows up at any of them, have it send us an encrypted, linked-Hore signal of the detected electronic signature, the image of the ship, and where it was sighted. The drones are to take no other measures against them. Clear?"

"Crystal." She would deploy three drones around each world, overlapping their scan zones so no approach or departure could be hidden. They would find an orbit around the planets, far away from parking zones and other satellites. They didn't produce any emissions, didn't reflect radar or anything else, and were powered by solar energy—no one would even know they were there. When one of them spotted Fey Pey's ship, it would alert Xanny's ship within seconds.

All they had to do was wait. Eventually, that monkrus would show up at one of the pirate havens—there wasn't anywhere else it could go. In one day, the images of *Easy Wind* and Fey Pey would be in every port, chandler, and law enforcement agency in the Ur-governed galaxy with a reward made doubly fat by Grock Corporation. He would come to one of those eleven planets and, when he did, Captain Xanny wouldn't be far behind. Time to settle this thing by pirate law—pirate to pirate, knife to knife.

... ...

"I saw someone on the way to work this morning," Doug said to Clara as he put their dinner dishes into the dishwasher.

"Who was that?" she asked without looking up from her textbooks spread all over the kitchen table.

"I don't know what his name was. He was a street person, begging at the last stoplight before the entrance to the Aerospace Centre."

"You didn't give him any money, did you? All he'd have done was buy drugs."

"Yep, I did. I gave him all the money in my wallet."

Clara closed her Canadian justice textbook and stared at him, curious. "Why did you do that? Did he have a gun?"

"No, nothing like that." Doug coughed nervously. "He had a sign."

"What did it say?"

"'Lost my trucking job to Rosy. Will work for food.'"

The catch in his voice as he told her what it said got her attention. "It's not your fault he doesn't have a job, Doug."

"Yes, it is...kind of. Even when I use Rosy for peaceful things, someone gets screwed." Doug's chin quivered a little as he tried to control his emotions. A tear ran down his cheek.

"How much did you give him?"

"I don't know...whatever was in my wallet—a couple hundred dollars, I expect. I went to the ATM yesterday."

"Why didn't you hire him? There's plenty of work around this farm just waiting for you to find time. A job would have to be better for him than money." It was his turn to cock his head and look at her. "And another thing, Douglas Medder: what about all the people the new Rosy transportation industry *has* hired? Engineers, scientists, manufacturers, construction workers? What about the reduction in fossil fuel consumption and reduced carbon footprint Canada is seeing? If you're going to blame yourself for the negative side of Rosy, you have to commend yourself for the positive, too."

"None of that good stuff matters to the poor bastard standing out on a street corner in Calgary in November."

"Then go find him—offer him a job. I'll bet he turns you down. It's a lot easier to beg than it is to work."

Doug closed the door to the dishwasher and left the kitchen in silence. He sat in the chair by the fireplace and opened his Bible. It was time to ask a higher authority. Whenever he needed guidance he would put the book in his lap and let it fall open. Invariably, the page that presented itself to Doug led him to a new understanding of the situation at hand and how to deal with it. Today his Bible fell open to the beginning of his favorite book, chapter, and verse: Ecclesiastes, 3:1. "To everything there is a season, and a time to every purpose under the heaven ..."

Doug continued to read, although he had memorized Ecclesiastes long ago. Reading the words out loud gave them the rhythm that was his touchstone to peace. By the time he finished the chapter, he knew what he must do.

... ...

It took longer than two days to arrange the nonemergency meeting between the president and his cabinet, but they were finally all together. President Robbins explained why he'd asked them to meet.

"We need to talk to the aliens and get them to reconsider our death sentence. Does anyone have an idea of how we can do that?"

There was complete silence around the table. They had discussed it with their staffs and no one had any new ideas.

His secretary of state was the first to answer. "Mr. President, we've tried every way we can think of. Let me recap what we and the other governments around the world have tried. We've put you on TV and radio, asking the aliens to talk. We've sent satellites to the moon with radio and TV beacons on them. The Russians tried a nuke." He sniggered a little. "Lord knows that didn't work. About the only thing we didn't try is an airplane with a banner towed behind it, circling the moon."

Robbins stared out the window for a minute. "Do we have anything they want—something we could perhaps offer for a second chance at the evaluation?"

"They have more technology than we can imagine," his secretary of commerce replied. "What could *we* offer *them*?"

"How about art?" the president suggested. "They don't have a Monet, Rembrandt, or Picasso. Could we market them?"

"So you want to sell them paintings of water lilies?" his secretary of defense asked disparagingly. "Yeah, I bet they line up for that."

President Robbins was losing patience. "I don't need an idea that *won't* work; I need ideas that *will*. The survival of our species depends on us finding an answer. No one else is going to solve this, people. It's up to us—me, you, the people in this room. Go back to your departments and ask everyone you can. Americans are the most creative people in this world; surely someone can think of a way to make those bastards talk to us."

The secretary of health and urban development held up her hand. She was a diminutive black woman named Harriett Lincoln. With her white hair pulled back into a bun and wearing one of her signature high-collared blouses under a plaid wool suit, she looked more like someone's grandmother or an elementary school principal than she did a presidential secretary in the most powerful nation in the world. "Sir?" she said softly.

Everyone in the room turned to look at her in shock. She had not said three words in these meetings since the Senate had approved her to be HUD secretary two months ago. Her predecessor had died of a stroke.

"Yes, Harriett? Do you have an idea?"

"You could make it a contest, sir—turn the entire country loose on the idea. Announce a prize of a million dollars, even ten million, to the person who comes up with an idea that works. That money isn't a fly speck compared to what this country has already spent trying to get around the quarantine."

The president did not react while he absorbed her idea. He then smiled his famous huge smile—the one that had, in part, gotten him elected. "Well, finally! An idea that might actually work." He turned to the rest of his cabinet sternly. "Find me some more ideas as good as Harriett's. One of them will have to work. We'll meet back here in one week."

Chapter 8 – What the Hell

"Could we stop for a potty break?" Lily asked Kevin.

They'd spent all afternoon at Dott's in Las Vegas. Lan had a ball playing hide-and-seek with Matt and Miranda, Dott's son and daughter-in-law. They had been married a little over a year ago but, of course, had no children of their own. Lan was ecstatic, happily filling in for the children they never had, and the three of them had worn themselves out. Lan was asleep in her car seat.

"A potty break sounds wonderful. I was thinkin' the same thing."

He checked out the road ahead of them: an empty highway fading into the darkness. There was not an exit or gas station in sight—nothing but desert and mountains—and twilight was almost ending. He pulled over on the shoulder.

She couldn't believe him. "You don't actually expect me to use the side of the road, do you?"

"We don't have a lot of options out here, Lily, my love. The next exit is twenty miles. My bladder won't make it."

She looked outside the car, crossed her legs, sighed, and turned around to see what was behind them. Only one car was visible way back down the road. Kevin got out, went around the car, and started doing what was so easy for men to do on the side of the road. His wife pursed her lips and realized she really had no choice; she sighed again and got out as Kevin was finishing up.

"Stand so you block the view." She squatted down.

Lily had just finished when the car that had been so far back, pulled in behind them and stopped. The driver and passenger got out.

"You guys okay?" the driver asked, walking up to their car.

"Yep, just stretchin' our legs a little," Kevin told him.

"Hey, is that one of those new electric cars?"

"Sure is," Kevin told him proudly. "We got it about a year ago."

"Mind if I check out the interior for a second? I heard about 'em but never saw one."

Lily got back in, ready to finish their drive home, and Kevin opened the driver's door and began to show the man the controls.

"It only has a couple of gauges, a speedometer, of course, but beyond that it has a temperature gauge for the dark energy unit and some sensors for the motors at the wheels."

"There's no gas gauge."

"Nope. No gas."

"What's this?"

He turned to see where the guy was looking. The knockout spray hit him full in the face. *"What the hell!"* Kevin shouted, rubbing at the sting in his eyes. He collapsed against the steering wheel as the world went fuzzy.

Lily reached across the driver's seat, grabbing for the man's arm, but her seat belt held her in place. The man laughed and sprayed her, too. She forced herself to not take a breath, released her belt, and pushed open the door of the van, but the passenger from the other car was waiting for her. He tackled her and they went down together.

She twisted around before they hit the ground, and the man land underneath her with her elbow directly against his solar plexus. As the air went out of his lungs with a whoosh, she kneed him in the crotch. The man let go, curled into a ball, and vomited. She looked up for the second person, the one who had sprayed Kevin, and he was suddenly over her. The last thing she felt as she prepared to launch herself at him was the spray hitting her face as she took a deep breath.

... ...

"Kevin, *WAKE UP!"* Lily shouted, shaking him. *"They took LAN!"*

He gave a gasp and then struck out where he'd last seen the guy who sprayed his face, just missing Lily in the process. He realized the guy wasn't there anymore and sat up groggily. "What happened? Where are we?"

She looked around. "On the side of the road where we stopped, I think. But Lan's not here. *They took her!*" No lights were visible except for the black sky and stars from the Milky Way, spray-painted from one horizon to the other. The moon had not risen yet.

He still wasn't thinking clearly and rubbed his face. "Where's the car?"

"GONE! Get *UP!*" She pulled on his arm. He was still trying to clear the effects of the knockout spray from his brain.

"Where's Lan?"

"Aren't you *listening*? *They took her! GET UP!*" She could barely control her voice enough to speak.

Her words finally penetrated the fog. "WHAT!" he screamed. "They *took LAN*? Where did they *take* her?"

Lily struggled to say the words instead of screaming them. "I don't know. I was unconscious, too, Kevin. GET UP! We have to get the police."

He blinked then rubbed his eyes, trying to make them focus. "Lily, did you call them, the police?"

"With *what*? Don't you *get* it? They took our car, our cell phones, *and our baby!* We're out here in the middle of bumfuck nowhere and someone has *stolen Lan!* DO YOU GET IT NOW?"

"Those *BASTARDS!*" He got to his feet a little unsteadily, wiped his face with his hand, and shook his head back and forth, like he had just entered the *Twilight Zone*. "Let's start walking. Which way do you think is closer to a phone?"

"Back the way we came. Remember that crossroads with the Texaco station about five miles back?"

"Yeah. Let's get going. It'll take over an hour to walk there."

"Someone will come along. We'll get a ride from them."

He reached out for her hand and pulled her to him, trying to hold back the tears that filled his heart. *Lan, my baby girl is gone! How could she be gone*? "We'll get her back, Lily. And those bastards will pay for this. Give me a second for the world to stop spinning." He took a deep breath, and then he began to shuffle-walk-stumble south with as fast a pace as he could maintain. Lily was in front, pulling him along like a sled dog.

A car approached them from the north but wouldn't stop even though Kevin tried to wave them down and almost got hit.

Lily threw a stone at their disappearing taillights. "Why didn't they *stop?*"

Kevin shook his head. *Like, we'd so pick up a couple of people in the desert walking by the side of the road at whatever god-forsaken time of the night this is,* he thought. *Yeah, that would happen—and Elvis is alive in Wisconsin somewhere.* "She'll be alright, Lily. They won't hurt her. She's the reason they hijacked us."

"Kevin, *SHUT UP!*" She was on the verge of hysteria. "I can't think about Lan with someone else. If I do, I'll *LOSE MY MIND!*" She dropped his hand. "I gotta go. I'll see you at the station," and started running south, leaving him walking by the side of the road.

She'd started jogging a month after Lan was born. Over the two years since her birth, Lily had gotten her speed up to where it was before she got pregnant, about five-minute miles. She should do the remaining four miles to the Texaco station in about twenty minutes.

... ...

The police cruiser pulled up next to Kevin. He had walked maybe another mile since Lily took off running. "Are you Kevin Langly?"

"Yep."

"Your wife is waiting for you at the Texaco station. Get in."

He started to open the back door thinking about the other times he'd had a free ride in the back of a police car. Usually his hands were in cuffs and he was more than a little drunk.

"Not in the back," the cop laughed. "You can ride up here."

"Did anyone find Lan?"

"Don't think so. I was on patrol. They dispatched me to come get you. I haven't been to the Texaco yet."

Five minutes later they pulled in to the Texaco parking lot, where three other police cars had their light bars flashing. Lily ran to him as he opened the door.

"Kevin, they found our car! It was burned, but Lan wasn't in it!"

"Do they know where she is?"

"No. They've issued an APB for her and for the two men fitting the description I gave them. Her picture has been sent to the police, the FBI, airports, bus station, train station, and taxi companies."

"Where did you get a picture? Our cell phones were in the car."

"The night shift guy at the Texaco let me use their computer. I downloaded a picture from Snapfish. Remember all those we sent to my mother after Lan's last birthday party?"

"How about the chip Dr. Plumber put in? Can they use that?"

"Yes, if the kidnappers try to leave by mass transit, but nothing so far."

"Can they trace our phones?"

"There's no signal from either of our phones. They were probably still in the car."

"Shit, and no fingerprints in a burned car."

"But get this: the same guys have kidnapped three other children from around Las Vegas in the last week. The descriptions of them were the same and they used the same knockout spray technique."

"Did the police recover any of the children?"

"Not yet."

"Were they chipped?"

"Two were."

"Were there any ransom requests?"

"Not that I know of."

"How did they know we had a child?"

"They probably saw her car seat while we were driving around Vegas. The other people were stopped in the desert too, but they had stopped for a fake wreck the other three times."

"This sounds way too organized to be a couple of idiots stealing children on the side of the road." He was quiet for a moment, trying to figure it out. "I wonder if they had a wreck waiting farther down the road from where we stopped."

They had a moment of silence, looking into each other's eyes. He reached out for her, knowing if he started to cry, the flood would never stop. Lily cried silently, gaining some comfort from just holding each other—both of them trying not to let missing the little girl who had filled their lives for two years overwhelm them. Was she cold, hungry, crying, or in pain? Who was holding her? Did she need to be changed? Was she scared? Was she being physically or sexually abused?

Kevin released her, cleared his throat, and wiped his nose on his sleeve. "Where the hell is the FBI? Kidnapping is a federal goddamned offense. I think I'll check with the police." He walked over to the detective in charge of the investigation.

A van with the logo of a local Las Vegas TV channel pulled into the Texaco parking lot and parked beside the police cars. A guy grabbed a camera from the back of the van and followed the driver, a woman in a windbreaker with the channel name across her chest. They walked over to Lily.

"Hi. I'm Emily Blake, reporter for Las Vegas News Channel 4. What happened here? We heard someone's baby has been kidnapped."

Lily realized this was a way to put Lan's face all over the news, and she stepped up to Emily. "Someone knocked us out, hijacked our car, and kidnapped our baby."

"Let's start at the beginning. What's your name?"

"I am Lily Yuan." She pointed at Kevin. "That's my husband, Kevin Langly."

Emily recognized their names as two of the inventors of Rosy wormholes, Nobel Prize recipients, and she was the source of the DNA in BSV. This story was going to put her into the big leagues! She signaled her cameraman to come over.

Once he was ready, Emily held the microphone to her mouth and said, "Dr. Lily Yuan, tell me what happened to you tonight."

Lily went through the whole night until she got to when the news truck pulled up. She ended her story by holding up a picture of Lan and looking straight into the camera.

"Lan is the fourth child who has been kidnapped in Las Vegas in the past week. If you have any knowledge of her whereabouts, contact the Las Vegas County Sheriff's Department or the FBI. Kevin and I will pay anyone one hundred thousand dollars for information leading to the return of our baby, no questions asked. If you are the person who took Lan, please bring her back."

Emily listened to Lily's story without comment. When she was done, Emily continued the interview. "Lily, you are one of the co-inventors of Rosy wormhole technology. Is that true?"

"Yes, it is. Douglas Medder, my husband, and I invented it while we were graduate students at Stanford University."

"And you three were awarded a Nobel Prize in Physics for your invention?"

"Well, Kevin and I did. Doug declined his."

"And it is your DNA in BSV. Isn't that also true?"

Lily was puzzled at this questioning. "Yes, it is. It was collected from me when the three of us were brought to the alien starship where we were questioned about how we invented the Rosy transmitter."

"Do you think the kidnapping of your child is karma for being the source of the DNA in BSV? That this is your repayment for taking babies away from everyone around the world?"

She stared at the reporter in shock, as though she couldn't fully understand the words. No one could be that unfeeling. A cold anger filled her. "No. I don't think that at all, Ms. Blake. I think the aliens took babies from mankind because we won't stop killing each other. We had a chance to leave this world and begin peacefully trading with the rest of the galaxy, and we blew it. They decided they didn't want any part of our warring, greedy ways. If you want to find a reason for the end of babies, take a good look in the mirror." Lily stalked away from the interview, so angry she was shaking. Kevin caught up and pulled her into his arms. She resisted, at first, and then grabbed him and began to cry.

Chapter 9 – She's Gone

The panhandler to whom Doug gave the money wasn't there when he got to the traffic light. Instead a woman was standing where the man had been yesterday. Her sign simply said "Broke. Please help."

He rolled down his window, and she walked over expectantly. "Where's the guy who was here yesterday? Do you know where he went?"

As soon as she realized Doug wasn't going to give her any money, she looked at the next car. "How should I know who was here yesterday?" She started toward the car behind his.

He pulled a bill out of his wallet. "It's worth twenty bucks to me."

She walked back. "Why do you want it? You some kind of pervert?"

"I gave him some money yesterday. He said he wanted a job. I have one for him if he wants it."

"Doing what? Takin' off his clothes?"

"Working on my farm. I'm too busy at the Aerospace Centre to take care of my place."

She looked at him for a few moments, considering what to do.

"His name is Bill." She lifted the twenty out of his hand. "He got admitted to Rockyview last night—he spent the money you gave him on meth and crack. He overdosed. He may be dead."

"Bill what? What's his last name?"

"We never use last names, mister." She walked away.

The driver in the car behind him honked his horn—the light was green. Doug put his truck in gear and finished the drive to work. When he got to his desk, he called the hospital.

"I can't tell you if we admitted a Bill last night," the receptionist told him.

"Look, I just want to offer the guy a job when he gets out. Can't you bend the rules a little? It might turn his life around."

There was a pause. The receptionist started to speak several times, each time stopping before she'd said even two words, and then she began in a whisper, "What I *can* tell you is no one named Bill died here last night. If you want more than that, you need to come down here and explain why to the hospital administrator."

... ...

"Lily, I am Special Agent Lattimer of the FBI. We are taking over the investigation of Lan's kidnapping from the Las Vegas County Sheriff's Department."

"Well, it's about goddamned time!" She tried to find her husband in the crowd of people around the gas station. She spied him coming out of the restroom. "Kevin! This is the FBI. Come over here." As Kevin hurried over to them, Lily pushed her exhaustion away and faced the agent. Her tear-stained mascara gave a haunted aspect to her face. "What are you doing?"

Agent Lattimer continued when Kevin arrived. "Hi, as I said before, I am Special Agent Lattimer. First, I want to caution you to not discuss any details of our investigation with anyone outside the FBI team. The less the kidnappers know about what we're doing the better."

"Okay. What are you doing?" Kevin asked.

"We've expanded the search to every major transportation hub in the country. Our facial recognition software is examining the face of every child who passes through an airport, train station, bus station, and public place. Lan's picture is at every ticket agent's desk."

Lily laughed scornfully. "Agent Lattimer, don't you think the kidnappers know that? Do you think they will let her face be seen by one of those cameras? These guys are pros—this is the fourth kidnapping in the Las Vegas area in a week, all with the same MO."

"That's just the first step, Lily. We have roadblocks on every road and interstate leaving town. We think we've found the car they used during the kidnapping."

"Was Lan's car seat in it?"

"Yes, we think it's the seat from your car."

"I can identify it—there's a blueberry stain on the upper right corner, next to where her head would be."

"The car was burned, Lily. All we have is a puddle of melted, burned plastic. The owners reported the car stolen five days ago. She wasn't in the seat when the car was burned."

"How about going after the source? Someone has to be buying these children and paying a lot for the privilege. Who's buying them? Who's supplying the children? How are the suppliers connected to the buyers? Where's the money trail? Isn't the FBI trying to break into this?"

"We're pursuing this investigation on many fronts; I can't tell you about most of them. This is going on nationwide."

"Should we expect a ransom demand?"

"That isn't how these people have been operating. Apparently the kidnappers are filling orders placed by customers in advance. There has not been any attempt to contact the original parents in any of the previous kidnappings."

Kevin decided to ask the question burning in his mind. "Why is this new information to us? If this has been going on for a week here—if this has been going on nationwide for months—why haven't you made this public? If we'd known this was happening, we would have taken measures."

Lattimer waited patiently until he was finished. "What would you have done, Kevin? Carry a gun? We've got three dead families from people who did just that."

"We wouldn't have left Rosyville," he snarled. "We damned sure wouldn't have stopped on the side of the road to pee—and we wouldn't have stopped for a wreck either."

"How did you hear about the wrecks?"

"The sheriff told us."

"If you are contacted, please notify us immediately. Your phone lines are being tapped to record and locate any calls. We don't expect that to happen, but in case it does, we want you to run with it. Your offer to pay one hundred thousand dollars for information leading to Lan's return may turn up something, or it may cause them to ask for more. None of the families of the kidnapping victims have offered that much before."

Kevin gasped. "Did you do that, Lily? Did you offer to pay a hundred thousand dollars?"

"Yes, I did." She turned to him, looking him dead in the eye. "Do you have a problem with that?"

"Not at all—I'd have offered more. The Nobel Prize money is just sitting in a CD."

Lily continued questioning the agent. "How about closed-circuit cameras and license plate readers along the path we drove? We must have passed fifty banks and fast food places before we got on US-95. Did any of them see the car following us on their closed-circuit TVs? Could they have taken a picture of the people in the car?"

"We are trying to access them. Most of the businesses are requiring a subpoena. Since the Bush and Obama administrations went so far over the privacy line, everyone's pretty sensitive about government intrusion into their private data. Even if we are able to access them, I'd be amazed if they show anything. These guys know where the cameras and readers are and stay away from them. We think they have at least one and maybe several different cars with different people following the target until they leave town."

"Did you examine the road between where Lan was kidnapped and Rosyville? If they were true to form, there would have been some tracks in the shoulder where the wreck was ready to be set up."

"That's being done, as well. We may get lucky and find they left something behind that we can use to identify the people or the vehicles—a cigarette butt, some spit, pee on a bush, tire tracks...something."

"How about the puke?" Agent Lattimer looked at her blankly. "When the passenger grabbed me and we went down together, I landed on top and kneed him in the crotch as I got up. He puked all over the side of the road—you should be able to get a DNA sample from it."

He pulled out his radio and passed that on to someone on the other end. After he ended the call, he turned to Lily. "This may be the break we've been waiting for. Those guys haven't left a clue until now. Good job!"

She was quiet for a while.

"What happens next?" Kevin asked.

"We'll give you a ride back to Rosyville, if you'd like, or we could take you into Las Vegas if you don't want to return home yet. Have you called your insurance company about your car? They may rent you another one until they pay you for the one that was destroyed."

"I haven't contacted anyone," Lily told him.

"I called Dad a few minutes ago. He said he's on his way."

Agent Lattimer handed both Lily and Kevin a business card. "Okay. Call me any time if you want an update or think of anything else. We will call you if we uncover anything. The composite drawings you created are excellent; maybe someone will recognize them, but don't get your hopes up. Most of the kidnappings have produced composites as good as yours, but each person is different."

"How could that be?" Lily asked. "How many people are doing this?"

"In this area, we think they are the same people using makeup or latex masks."

"Could we have copies of our composites?"

"Sure. I will email them to you."

"How about the other ones? Can I get copies of them, as well?"

He paused, considering her request. "I don't see why not. They're posted all over Las Vegas."

Kevin led Lily to a bench next to a picnic table on the side of the Texaco property. It was the middle of the morning, and people drove by the station, some with child car seats in the back. As they stared at the collection of police cars and unmarked FBI sedans, Lily. looked at them, wishing for the first time in her life that she could have their normal, boring lives of taking the kids to school, picking them up afterward, going to soccer practice, and fixing them a snack. She turned her face into Kenin's shoulder and began crying softly, hoping Lan was being treated well, wherever she was. Lily desperately wanted her arms around her daughter and her mother—her mother would tell her what to do.

Twenty minutes later, Dr. Paul Langly pulled into the station in his beat-up Taurus wagon. The two walked up to him and he didn't say a word; instead, he pulled them both into his arms. That was the split in the dam for Kevin. He'd been strong for Lily and she'd been strong for him. Now they didn't have to be.

"Dad, she's gone," he said between sobs. "Lan's gone."

A car screeched into the parking lot and the driver flung open her door. Four FBI agents drew their weapons simultaneously. Dott got out with her hands in the air.

"This is the beginning of the Mothers' Brigade," she announced, shouting the words so everyone would hear. "Get out of the way if you don't wanna get hurt!" She then walked up to the group, pulled Lily away, and gave her a huge hug. "We'll find her, Lily, and we'll get the bastards who did this. No one takes a baby from my friend and gets away with it!"

Within five minutes, eight other cars arrived at the station. The women who exited the vehicles inundated Lily with a whirlwind of attention and activity. The picnic table filled with sandwich ingredients, potato salad, macaroni salad, iced tea, cups, paper plates and cutlery.

Dott handed Lily a roast beef sandwich. "I know you aren't hungry, but you aren't helping Lan by starving yourself. You need to stay strong, Lily. Lan needs you to be strong."

She blinked at Dott. Her mother's words? Those were the words her mother had said on the night before Lily was smuggled out of China. "Be strong, Li Li!" How had Dott known to say that? She looked at the sandwich like it was made of sawdust. Somehow, her mother *had* felt how badly Lily needed her—her mother *was* here with her now.

Lily considered her actions over the last twelve hours in a cold, hard light. This crying, helpless woman wasn't the Lily her mother had raised. That Lily was never weak. That Lily never cried.

That woman was *Lily the Strong*! Strong enough to flee China in the middle of the night and begin a new life in the United States, strong enough to flourish in this strange, foreign land, and strong enough to get her baby back!

"One bite," Dott told her. "Take one bite. If you don't want more after that, I'll take it away."

Lily took a bite and then another. *When you are furious enough, sawdust isn't too bad.*

Chapter 10 – Where Babies Come From

Gloria Griffasi, the news anchor on *Questions and Answers*, pointed to a curve that showed the world's human population over the past three years. "The government has released new figures on the decline of the human population on Earth since the beginning of the BSV pandemic.

"You will notice the first year after BSV there was a normal population increase of about ninety-four million people. This was due to the babies conceived before BSV. That increase stopped nine months after the release when the last of those babies was born. I call that point the End of Babies. Starting there, the line begins a gradual decline that continues unabated.

"Since the End of Babies, the worldwide population has decreased by two hundred and fifty million people. About sixty percent of those were sixty years of age or older.

"The Baby Machines created by the Centers for Disease Control and Prevention and a coalition of pharmaceutical companies became active a year and a half ago. Since then, they have 'birthed' around fifty-three thousand babies worldwide. While this is wonderful for the lucky parents of those cloned children, the numbers created by this process have not made much of a difference in the population decline.

"We go now to interview one of the manufacturers of the Baby Machine in the US, Dr. Jonathan Lubbuck, chairman and chief executive officer of Lubbuck Pharmaceuticals."

The screen split into two sections, one with the news anchor and one with a smiling man in a handsome charcoal suit, white shirt and pale blue tie.

"Dr. Lubbuck, welcome to *Questions and Answers*."

"Hello, Gloria."

"Dr. Lubbuck, would you explain to our audience why more Baby Machines have not been made to offset the decline of our worldwide population?"

"Sure. It all comes down to money. The gestation of a single child costs about five thousand dollars across the whole forty weeks. Our agreement with the government states that we can charge people who use our service only twice what it costs us for the facilities and personnel."

"And the rest of the ten thousand that you charge?"

"That is used to repay the cost of building the machines."

"I thought the government funded most of that development research."

"They did pay the lion's share—sixty-five percent of the development costs. The rest was split across the partnership of private companies who participated in the effort. We anticipate the machines' life to be about ten years. Each machine actually costs us about five hundred thousand dollars to make. If we split the machines' cost of manufacture across their ten years projected lifespan, we have to make fifty thousand dollars per machine per year. Each baby takes 40 weeks to gestate. That means we make about sixty-five hundred dollars per machine per year. The government reimburses us for the difference between what we make and the cost of the machine. Without the government's reimbursement of the development and operational costs, we would have had to charge more like seventy or eighty thousand dollars per baby, depending on how much we had to pay back to our investors."

"With an eleven-year queue of people seeking your services, why don't you build more machines?"

"There are two reasons. The first is that our manufacturing facilities are already running three full shifts, seven days a week. We are committed to creating machines that will function without problems for their full projected life, so we will not reduce quality control. The result is that we cannot produce more than ten a day at either of our plants. However, we have broken ground on two new sites, and those plants should be functional by the first quarter next year.

"The second reason is that we have almost exhausted the money Congress made available to us to pay for the Baby Machines. Unless Congress increases our allocation, we will have to stop production, and that would prevent our new Baby Centers from opening their doors at all. If we charged the American clientele what it actually costs to make and run the machines, that eleven-year queue would shrink to almost nothing."

He paused so she asked another question. "Lubbuck Pharmaceuticals also has an overseas presence in Vietnam, Mexico, and India. Do you build Baby Machines at those sites as well?"

"Yes, we do."

"Are any of them being imported into the US?"

"No. They are being sold to other countries, corporations, and private individuals around the world."

"Do you charge the same price for the machines made at your offshore facilities as you do for the US-made machines?"

"No. The contract we have with the US government specifies that we supply the US market for ten percent of what it costs us to make them, and the government makes up the difference. We have no such agreement with any other country."

"How much are you selling the offshore machines for?"

"The current price is three-quarters of a million dollars each."

"And where does the quarter-million dollar profit per machine go?"

"That repays our investors for the billions of dollars they fronted to fund the portion of the development costs that the government did not cover."

"And how much are the offshore Baby Maker services being sold for?"

"I don't know. I expect it will vary by country and facility."

"Are you currently building any more offshore manufacturing facilities?"

"Yes. We have eight under construction."

"How many other companies are manufacturing them?"

"There are five US companies in the CDC development partnership, and all five are building them as fast as we can, both onshore and off. At Lubbuck's plants, a display on our manufacturing floor counts the number of babies Lubbuck Baby

Machines have grown and delivered to their parents; that number was 9,392 this morning."

"Where are you selling your offshore machines?"

"In almost every country in the world, except China."

"Why not China?"

"China has expressed no interest. They have developed a Baby Machine of their own and have started marketing them internationally as well."

"You said you sell your machines to private individuals. Could you elaborate on that?"

"Sure. We sell our offshore machines to countries, corporations, and people—whoever will pay the fee."

"Can you give me some examples?"

"No. That information is very confidential."

"Do you anticipate the cost per machine dropping in the future?"

Dr. Lubbuck paused for a second to consider this. "That's possible, Gloria, even probable. We're getting better at making them, and as we make refinements, I expect the cost for a machine will slowly come down. I would hope that within five years we can make a machine that lasts a lifetime for under one hundred thousand dollars. We would be the first to shout Amen when that happens."

"Thank you, Dr. Lubbuck."

... ...

Kyle Daugherty was going to be ten years old in one week. When his father, Daniel, asked him what he wanted for a birthday present, he had repeated the same request he had given for the past five years. "Dad, I want to go blue water sailing. I've heard you tell us all about how many stars you can see a hundred miles offshore. I want to see it for myself."

Daniel repeated to Kyle what he'd said when his son first asked. "You're too small—it's too dangerous. The Pacific Ocean looks calm and tranquil from San Diego Harbor, but a hundred miles offshore, everything is different. I'll take you when you're twelve. We'll take the American Sailing Association's offshore sailing course, we'll live on an offshore boat for a week and be part of the crew. We'll set and trim the sails, and we'll spread your mother's ashes in the blue water, like she wanted."

Kyle tried to hide his disappointment from his father. This year would be the fifth anniversary of his mother's death from pancreatic cancer, and he was having trouble remembering what she looked like. He wanted to spread her ashes before the face in his memories disappeared entirely.

"Two more years? You promise?"

"Son, I promise. We will spread your mother's ashes on your twelfth birthday."

His father turned back to the Padres game he was watching. It was the bottom of the seventh inning against the Milwaukee Brewers. Daniel opened another beer and sat on the edge of his seat. "Strike this bum out, come on!"

Kyle knew the game would distract his dad for at least another hour. He got a gallon-sized, heavy duty Ziploc bag from the pantry in the kitchen and slipped into his dad's bedroom. The box with his mother's ashes was in the back of the closet. He emptied it into the bag, and then put it in his backpack.

"WHAT!" Daniel screamed from the living room. "You gave him a hit? You IDIOT! Come on, catch it! OH NO! It's over the fence. DAMMIT!"

The screaming crowd covered the sound of Kyle leaving. He got on his bike and rode toward the marina where his dad kept their little Laser sailboat. He was sure he could sail it out far enough to spread his mother's ashes and return home before dark. He'd been sailing that boat since before his mother died—all he needed was to get far enough out to sea that he lost sight of land.

There was a steady offshore breeze. The Coast Guard web site on his cell phone said the wind was ten knots from the east-northeast. It blew Kyle straight out of San Diego Harbor and into the Pacific Ocean. The water was smooth with a one-foot swell rocking the Laser like a cradle in a tree. Kyle enjoyed the sunshine and the soft movement.

Downwind sailing was mesmerizing. When the swells ran the same way as the wind, you didn't have to pay much attention—the wind was mild, since you were running with it, and the swells just pushed you along a little faster. All a sailor had to do was keep the boat aimed in the same direction and watch the trim of the sails. Mostly, you slid through the water and daydreamed.

Kyle adjusted the tiller keeper until the Laser sailed a consistent line due west and spent the time remembering everything he could about his mother. She'd had blonde hair, blue eyes, sparkling white teeth, and two dimples that showed every time she smiled. She'd loved to sail. She had made him pancakes, drawing with the batter whatever cartoon characters he asked for, and she'd always had peanut butter cookies for him when he scraped his knee.

He pulled out the scuffed, cracked picture of his mom he carried with him at all times. She was smiling back at whoever took the picture—probably his dad—and sitting in *this* boat at the front of the cockpit. The place she had been sitting now had his backpack with her ashes in it. Kyle looked at the backpack wistfully, as though she were there now, smiling back at him and then he turned around and watched the shoreline. The mountains east of San Diego were disappearing into the afternoon haze. It wouldn't be long now.

He closed his eyes and tried to sense all parts of the little sailboat as it moved through the water—he'd heard solo sailors could feel their boat like it was an extension of their body. The swell steadily increased as he went farther from shore, rocking the Laser as it glided cleanly through the clear blue water.

... ...

The crew on the container ship never knew they had run over the Laser. Kyle tumbled head over heels as the ship swept past him. He had fallen asleep. The bow wave of the ship had pushed the Laser almost far enough to port to allow it to escape damage, but not quite. The mast had snapped off and the hull broke in two.

The side of the ship slid past at twelve knots, only inches from him. When the stern finally passed, the wash from the propellers turned him over in somersaults again. Pieces of the Laser bobbed near him, and his backpack disappeared into the depths.

"Well, that's what you wanted, Mom!" Kyle shouted, looking down. "I love you. Goodbye!"

He was wearing his PFD (personal flotation device), as his mom had made him from the first day she took him out on the water. She never let him call it a life vest—life vests didn't have a harness or ring for a safety line when the weather got rough. It had inflated automatically when he hit the water. The Laser was not set up for blue water sailing. It didn't have a VHS radio, flares, or an EPIRB (the Emergency Position-Indicating Radio Beacon that would call the Coast Guard automatically when it was submerged). His cell phone was soaked with salt water and wouldn't turn on. No one knew he was here or where to look for him. He had no fresh water or food, and the California Current was carrying him south, toward the Mexican Baja California Peninsula at about four knots. He pulled himself onto the front half of the hull.

A dorsal fin appeared an hour after the crash. It circled Kyle and the bits of the Laser still floating nearby and then came to within a foot of him. If he hadn't been so terrified, he could have reached out and touched it, but he kept remembering the scene in *Jaws* when the shark swam past the little girl who didn't move. The dolphin's head broke the surface next to Kyle and squeaked a greeting.

"You aren't a shark!" he laughed in relief. "You're a bottlenose dolphin! I was ready to shit my pants!"

Kyle spent a lot of time at SeaWorld in San Diego and knew bottlenose dolphins had been friends to sailors since the first sailboat made its maiden voyage. The dolphin swam around him again, blew, and stopped next to the hull fragment that supported the boy. It leaned its dorsal fin toward him. Kyle reached out and held the fin—it was warm! They began to move toward land, but Kyle let go, unwilling to leave the relative safety of the hull. The dolphin put its nose through a life ring bobbing nearby and came back, the short rope attached to the life ring in tow. Kyle decided it wanted him to hold on, so he did.

They left the Laser behind and began to make their way to the mainland. Kyle was ecstatic. He'd seen bottlenose dolphins play with their handlers at SeaWorld and had always wished he could do the same—and now he was! He could feel the muscles of the dolphin beside him work as it pulled him through the water. Every ten seconds or so it would take a breath, covering them both with mist from its exhale.

As the dolphin pulled Kyle through the water, he told it all about the trip and burying his mother's ashes. He told it about all of the good times he could remember and even about his mom spanking him for disobeying her rules. He decided his friend needed a name so he named it Willy—*Free Willy* was his favorite movie.

"I know you aren't an orca, but I don't think he'll mind."

Two other dorsal fins appeared and swam around them; they turned out to be two more dolphins. Periodically Willy would pass Kyle off to one of the other ones. All three of them took turns pulling him through the water. He noticed small differences between the three—one had a ring of pale skin around its head like a halo and the other one had fist-sized dark spot on its left side, next to its dorsal fin, that looked like a baseball. The dolphin with the halo he named Mary, after his mother, and the one with the baseball mark he named Daniel, after his dad.

Sometimes the two who weren't pulling him would leave for a few minutes and then return. Several other dolphins joined the three but didn't come close enough for him to study. Kyle realized with a shock that some of the dorsal fins he was seeing farther out were sharks, not dolphins, and they would have made him the main entrée on their lunch menu, if the dolphins hadn't kept them at bay. One of the smaller sharks, a young mako maybe, tried to come closer. Two of the dolphins rammed it hard, one on each side. It didn't try that again.

"Thank you, Willy's friends," Kyle called out, even more glad they were escorting him.

It was way after midnight when Willy pulled Kyle into Ensenada Bay in Baja California, Mexico. The group had traveled almost seventy miles down the Pacific Coast, carried by the current, as they swam toward shore. Kyle had tied the rope from the life ring to his PFD after his arms grew too tired to hold on anymore. That put his whole body into contact with the one pulling him and kept him warm. He had fallen asleep at some point during the trip. Willy was pulling him when they arrived and the boy awoke to the sound of the surf as the dolphin swam as close to the beach as it could.

Kyle tried to stand but fell back into the surf; his legs weren't working yet after the hypothermia of being in the water for over fourteen hours. Willy nudged him toward land.

"Relax, Willy. I'm okay. You can go back now. You saved my life." He leaned over and hugged the dolphin. "I'll never forget you. Say thank you to Mary and Daniel for me."

Willy swam a little distance out and then turned around, made some squeaky dolphin sounds, and dove into the water. *How cool is that!* Kyle thought to himself. *That sounded like Willy said 'Bye Kyle'.* Willy popped up twenty feet farther out, executed a perfect double flip, and began to swim away.

A voice above Kyle spoke out from the dock, "I never seen a porpoise do a single flip, let alone a double."

"It's not a porpoise," he told the voice. "It's a dolphin—a bottlenose dolphin—and his name is Willy. He just saved my life."

A flashlight shined down on him. "I'll be damned...it's a kid! Where did you come from, little guy?"

"San Diego," he said, trying to stand again. "I need to call my dad."

... ...

"How many can you deliver?" the man asked, chuckling at his pun.

"I can guarantee you a steady one hundred full-term babies per month, sometimes more."

"And they will be healthy and normal? Not ones with an arm growing out of its forehead or a hole where its brain should be?"

"No culls. These are the ones that go full term with a brother or sister. The company gives the parents the one they think is most like what the parents want and kills the extras. There's nothing wrong with them. Maybe the parents want a girl and the other one's a boy; maybe one's blonde and one's redheaded. It breaks my heart doing that when so many people want a healthy baby."

"How much do you want for each?"

"A thousand dollars."

"I'll give you five hundred, and only if they're normal."

"Eight hundred. I've got to pay off some people to get them out of the plant."

"I'll go eight hundred, but don't give me any you wouldn't want for your own or I'll shove 'em right back up your ass. When can you get me the first one?"

"Be here tomorrow night; I'll have the first four. Are you going to have facilities to care for 'em? These're newborns—you can't just give 'em a bottle and go have a beer."

"You bring the babies; I'll have the cash. Don't worry about what happens to 'em after that."

Chapter 11 – Thanks for Caring

"I'm not sure I can do this, Lily."

Lily and Kevin sat outside their house in Rosyville; the insurance company had rented them a car while the payment was being processed for their burned vehicle. Neither of them could muster the courage to walk to the front door. They'd waited until almost midnight at Kevin's father's so they wouldn't have to deal with their well-wishing neighbors.

"It has to be done," she said, opening the driver's door.

He sighed and pursed his lips. "Yep."

They walked to the front door, hand in hand. He opened it and entered the house that wasn't a home anymore. The toys Lan had left on the living room floor were still where she'd let them drop before they loaded her into the car for the trip to Dott's. Everywhere they looked was some reminder of their little girl: a sippy cup on a towel next to the sink, a book left next to the recliner where Kevin had not finished reading it to her, a child's sweat shirt on the back of one of the kitchen chairs because she hadn't wanted to wear it.

Lily walked around the house picking up all of the "Lan things" and putting them in a laundry basket. She put the basket inside Lan's bedroom and closed the door, promising herself she wouldn't open it again until her baby came home. They both showered and got into bed. Kevin started snoring before his head was even on the pillow, retreating from the stress of the day to a place where children were always within eyesight and people never squirted knockout spray in your face.

Willing her mind to stop, Lily lay in the silence of their bedroom. Every creak and pop in the house sounded like a gunshot as the events of the past twenty-four hours played back and forth in her memory. *What could I have done to stop it?* Anger filled her again with its white-hot glow. *How dare they take my child from me!*

Her thoughts returned again to Lan. *Where is she? Is she safe? Is she cold? Is she hungry? Did she miss me as much as I miss her?*

Kevin's snoring irritated her beyond reason. She couldn't escape to the Land of Nod while he blithely embraced it; she wanted to shake him awake and make him suffer with her. She thought about recording him and playing it back through the stereo at warp volume. *That would teach him to sleep when I can't!*

She got up and walked down the hallway to Lan's bedroom. The room was dark when she opened the door. The toys piled on the bed looked like her little girl asleep under the covers. Lily moved toward it without turning on the light. She tripped over the laundry basket she'd put there when they'd gotten home, pushed the toys off the bed, and climbed under the covers. Lan's favorite toy, Mr. Mumbles, looked askance at her from the floor, his button eyes and smiling face hiding how much he missed his playmate. She lifted him off the floor and pulled him under the covers with her. Finally, with the smell of her daughter wrapped around her and Mr. Mumbles in her arms, she fell into a fitful sleep filled with faceless people trying to pull Lan out of her arms.

"Mama! Help me!" she cried out as she was pulled away, just out of reach of Lily's grasping fingers.

"Hold on, Lan! I'm coming!" she shouted. But she wasn't. Something held her while Lan drifted away, calling out to her, "Mama, save me!" No amount of kicking and hitting would make the evil, invisible thing let go. At last, she screamed in frustration.

Lily woke with a start, her scream was still ringing in her ears. She clasped Mr. Mumbles so tightly that her arms had fallen asleep. The covers were soaked with sweat and wrapped around and around her like a snake.

Kevin ran through the door, naked. "What happened?"

"I had a bad dream."

He took a breath and let it out, and then took another and tried to will the cold fingers around his heart to let go. Lily looked so pitiful in Lan's bed with the covers twisted around her. He unwound her from the sheet and crawled in beside her, putting his arm around and pulling her to him.

"Kevin, I couldn't reach her." Lily started sobbing. "She was just beyond my fingertips and, no matter how hard I tried, I couldn't get to her. She cried out to me to save her, but nothing I did helped."

He didn't know what else to do but hold his wife while she cried. After a while she stopped. The eastern sky started to brighten with the coming dawn, and her breathing grew regular and deep. It was his turn to listen to her sleep while he couldn't.

Sometime later he fell asleep also. The gremlins that caused nightmares must have been busy somewhere else that morning, because both of them slept without dreams.

… … … … … … …

Dr. Sirandohu, the hospital administrator had listened to Doug's explanation of his meeting with the homeless man and then the woman. "Dr. Medder, I would love to help, but there's nothing I can do. I can't give you his name or even let you talk to him. Canadian health law is very clear about that."

Doug was quiet for a moment, and then an idea came to the surface. "Well, can you do this? Can you give him my phone number and tell him I would like to meet him to offer him a job? He can throw it away, but I'd at least like him to know he can work, if he wants to."

It was Sirandohu's turn to be quiet while he pondered Doug's request. "I suppose I can do that, but I wouldn't count on him calling. People are homeless because they want to be. No one has to be homeless in Canada—especially not someone who worked his whole life and built a retirement for himself. What he wrote on the cardboard was most likely a lie. From what I understand, no one working in the transportation industry was let go involuntarily. There were so many new jobs created by the Freight Portal buildup, that there are still positions going unfilled. Companies closed, to be sure, but more started up. He must have known most of our Rosy research was being done at the Aerospace Centre—he figured on cashing in on the guilt of its employees."

"Looks like it worked." Doug shook his head in chagrin but wrote down his phone number anyway and handed the piece of paper to the administrator. "Thank you for doing this."

Dr. Sirandohu stood and shook Doug's hand. "From the Americans I've seen, not many would have gone to the trouble you have, Dr. Medder. Thanks for caring. I hope it works out for you. But be careful with this guy. If he's not a trucker, he's a liar and a thief."

"I appreciate your help, sir—and I'm not American anymore. I am a Canadian citizen and proud to be one."

... ...

President Robbins looked around at his cabinet. "Okay, people. Amaze me." As they went around the table, his secretaries presented what their staffs had come up with to get the attention of the aliens.

"An Alien Day...really?" The president was incredulous. "And that was your *best* idea?"

Secretary Quierro was a little put off by the president's reaction but not ready to give up. "I thought we could do something like a cross between Mardi Gras and Halloween. We could combine it with something like the Macy's parade and New Years at Times Square. Have giant helium balloons of benevolent aliens, floats showing the aliens and humans trading and living together, make the ball an octopus when it drops ..." Secretary of Defense Hagland was looking at Quierro like *he* was an alien. "Every city could do something with their own theme," he added a little defensively.

The general shook his head in amusement. "So these guys show up and give us a death sentence, and then we throw them a parade? Why?"

"General Hagland, what did Defense come up with?" the president asked.

"We thought we would all hold hands and sing Kumbaya," he said in his gravelly voice. "After that, we'd have tea and crumpets."

President Robbins looked at him coldly. Hagland shrugged and looked away. He was in the killing business, not the make-friendly-with-people-who-want-to-kill-you business and was feeling pretty impotent. That wasn't a feeling he liked at all. It was his job to defend the country and keep it safe, and they had no defense against either the virus or the aliens. Even the biggest club in his arsenal, nuclear weapons, wasn't useable. The Russians had demonstrated that very clearly.

The ideas went downhill from there. State suggested they solicit letters from ordinary citizens to the aliens and send them to the moon. Energy wanted an energy off day, hoping they would investigate. Interior wanted to present a tour of Area 51 and show them how we'd been using the alien technology gleaned from the flying saucer.

General Hagland snorted. There was no flying saucer. Area 51 was where the NSA kept their underground super computers and server farm. They had created the rumor to justify the top-secret status without telling anyone why it was really top secret.

Labor wanted to invite the aliens to participate in a nationwide sit-in and tailgate party. Agriculture wanted to write huge letters in the wheat fields all over the country welcoming them to Earth. Commerce wanted to use one of the Hawaiian Islands to create an island recreation resort for them to visit on R & R. His thinking was they would have to be tired of living on the moon, and once they were on the island, humanity could start interacting with them.

Robbins wasn't sure what to do. "Thanks for your efforts. I will decide and let you now."

Chapter 12 – More Fut

"You're late. She's all yours. I gotta get outta here." Louise put a cigarette in her mouth and walked to the door, lighting it as she went out.

Lan watched her leave, got down from the bed, and walked to the chair where Ernest had plopped down. "Unca Ernie. Potty"

He threw her up in the air. "Come on, little Lan. Let's go potty." As they walked to the bathroom, he spun her around. She laughed and grinned.

Not only did she need to go potty, she had poop all over her bottom. *The lazy bitch couldn't even wipe the kid's ass!* When she finished peeing, he tried to wipe the dried-on poop but realized this cleanup needed a bath. He started the water running.

"Bath!" Lan squealed again, clapping her hands. She loved baths.

Ernest got the bath toys he'd made her from Styrofoam plates and tape, tested the six-inch-deep water to make sure it wasn't too hot, and then stripped her down. She had bruises on her legs and stomach.

"Lan, how did you get these?" He pointed to the bruises.

She hung her head. "Aunt Louie. She say I bad. Can't get off bed. Can't ask where Mama or Daddy. Can't cry. Can't ask for Big Bird."

She climbed into the tub by herself, and he mixed up some motel shampoo with the water to make suds. Lan began playing with the foam, making shapes.

"Birds, Unca Ernie!" she said happily as they floated away. She reached up to his face with a handful of suds and put them around his chin line. He added a big glob on top of his head, and she laughed and did the same with hers.

He got up while she was busy with the suds and washed the crap out of her underwear. There were only three changes of clothes. That was all there had been in the diaper bag when they snatched her. She went through all three outfits almost every day.

He was the only one who took the time to wash them and hang them in the bathroom to dry.

Ernest sat on the toilet while she played, fascinated with how she could entertain herself with chunks of plastic. Fifteen minutes later, she was clean and the water wasn't. He dried her off, dressed her in clean underwear, and drained the tub.

"Come on, little girl. I bet you're ready for breakfast."

"Bekfist! Want fut!"

"Fruit, Lan. Say *fruit*."

"Fut." She giggled. She knew how to say the word fruit—she was just playing with her new uncle.

He laid her towel on the floor next to the table, put a chair on it, put her in the chair, and opened the to-go box he'd brought with him when he'd arrived. In it were scrambled eggs, toast, and, of course, a heaping pile of cut-up oranges and apples. She grabbed for the fruit, but he pulled the box away from her.

"Here's your spoon, Lan. Eggs first."

She held the child's spoon with her left hand, carefully loaded it with scrambled eggs using her right, and then lifted the spoon to her mouth with both hands. She only spilled a little into her lap.

And that's why I never dress her until after breakfast. He opened the newspaper while she continued to feed herself. He took a sip from his Styrofoam cup—at least the café made a decent cup.

"Tirsty, Unca Ernie."

"Thirsty," he corrected her.

"Yeah, tirsty." She held out her hands toward his coffee.

He knew better than to give her a Styrofoam cup—it had taken an hour to clean up *that* mess the first time. He got her sippy cup from the bathroom and poured some of his coffee into it. Lan slurped it greedily. No one had thought to buy some milk before they snatched her. Coffee or water from the tap—that was all they had—and his was the only coffee she would drink. He figured it was the cream and sugar. He used three teaspoons of sugar and four creams. So, he always got *two* twenty-ounce cups when he got one for himself.

The newspaper described the search for Lan. Tips were coming in from all over Vegas. Everyone wanted a piece of that hundred grand reward her mother had offered. The tourists, businesses, and truckers were putting a lot of heat on the FBI to stop the roadblocks, but the Feds wouldn't budge. They believed she was still being held somewhere in the area around Las Vegas. The governor of Nevada announced this morning that he was starting an anti-kidnapping task force with the Nevada Bureau of Criminal Investigation, and Lan was their poster child. The president of the United-fucking-States was having a meeting with the leaders of Congress today to see what *they* could do about it.

He'd told Julio snatching the kid of someone famous was a bad idea. No one gave a shit about some blue-collar schmuck from Fresno or a migrant with too many kids to begin with—you could snatch those babies all day long and it wouldn't make page seven of a local newspaper. But take a baby from someone famous—someone with friends who go all the way to the White House and enough money to garner the whole nation's attention—then hell breaks loose. Plus, the people who had hired on to receive the little girl had backed out, giving up the ten grand they'd paid as a deposit. "She's too famous. We can't take the chance, and we found someone who can get us a newborn."

So, here they sat in two motel rooms at the end of a single-story mom-and-pop, twenty miles from Vegas. They couldn't leave; they couldn't go out; and they couldn't even let the owners in to clean. Just Ernest and Louise playing tag team while they babysat Lan and waited for Julio to decide what to do.

He heard a noise from next door. *She must have finished her eight or ten cigarettes and is ready to crash.* A man's voice came through the wall, followed by a feminine giggle.

Louise's voice said, "I *love* your cock!"

How did she do it? She left this room a half an hour ago and already picked up a john. The headboard on the bed started bumping against the wall.

Shit. Now I have to listen to that for an hour. Louise started her fire engine whine after only a couple of minutes. *This one won't take very long.* It usually took fifteen minutes before she got to the fire engine. Sometime in the next five minutes would be, "Fuck me harder," and then came the huge moan, and then "Oh, baby, that was great!" Sometimes she'd stretch it out for a full hour; sometimes it only took two or three minutes. You'd think she'd find some new lines, but the johns didn't seem to mind.

"More fut, Unca Ernie."

"Here you go, Lan."

… … … … … … …

President Robbins appeared on prime time on every television channel in the US. He gave the camera his trademark smile and then began. "Two years ago I was elected by you to be president of the United States, in part, by the promise that I would talk to the aliens and persuade them to give us a second chance. To date, they have ignored our every attempt to communicate with them with the exception of when Russia sent a nuclear weapon to blow up their starship. That attempt resulted in the death of millions of Russians and did nothing but confirm their reasons for selecting humanity for elimination.

"I still believe we can open a meaningful dialogue with them; we just need to think of a way that will cause them to listen. I believe the United States is the most creative country on Earth. We invited the poor, the weak, and the downtrodden to America. The people who came were dissatisfied with their lives and hoping to do better in a new land—they came here to start over. It is exactly that initiative that led me to appear before you tonight.

"I am announcing a contest with a prize of one hundred million dollars for an idea that would cause the aliens to talk to us. Let your imaginations run wild. There is no cost to enter, and you can enter as many times as you want. There are three ways to enter; they are displayed on the right side of your screen now. Be sure to include your name, address, and phone number. Thank you."

The right side of the screen displayed:

Send an email to:
> TalkAliensTalk@Whitehouse.gov

Tweet to: @talkaliens

Mail your idea on paper to:
> Talk Aliens Talk
> The White House,
> 1600 Pennsylvania Avenue
> Washington, DC 20500

The full rules are posted at:
> www.whitehouse.gov

The reporters attending the announcement were on their feet, shouting questions. "Mr. President, is the contest open to noncitizens living in the US?"

"Absolutely. In fact, if they make the winning suggestion, an offer of citizenship for them and their immediate family would be included as part of the prize. This is not about politics; it's about saving humanity."

"President Robbins, is this contest open to people in other countries?"

He had been expecting this question. "Let's see what the people in this country can do first. If other countries want to run the same kind of contest, let them. But I believe in America—I believe someone here has the answer, and now is the time for that person to come forward. Tell us how to contact the aliens so we can ask them to reverse their decision to eradicate us."

Chapter 13 – Full Time

"I hear you can find me a baby."

"Who told you that, lady?" The man took another sip of his whiskey without looking at Dott.

"Don't matter who told me. Is it true?" This was the fifth bar she had visited today, the thirty-ninth of the week.

"Why do *you* want a baby? You should be having *grand-babies* by now."

She could see he was skeptical. His eyebrows were up, his eyes were a little squinted, and his lips were pursed with a slight smile—but skeptical was *way* better than dismissive. "I don't want just any baby. I want Lily Yuan's baby."

"Shit, lady! Get away from me. That baby's so hot, it glows in the dark."

"I'll split the reward money with you and I'll take all the heat."

He took another sip of whiskey and shook his head. "Even if I knew where that baby was—I don't, but even if I did—how would you do it? How would you collect the money and how would you give half to me?"

This was the first guy who didn't ask, "Lily who?" While his response wasn't a resounding "Yeah, I've got her," it wasn't an "I don't know what you're talking about," either.

She began her prepared speech. "As soon as I have the baby in my hands, I call the number on the flyer and arrange the drop. She gets the baby and we get the money. You give me a number. When I get the money, I call the number and arrange a pickup for your half."

He took another swallow of whiskey. "Lady, that plan has so many holes in it you better never go near the water."

"What do you mean?" Dott was a little offended. She'd been proud of her plan.

"First, the number on the flyer has a tap on it, courtesy of the FBI. Second, the money is bullshit. There ain't no money, never is. It's just a come-on to grab the baby and lock up whoever's stupid enough to try to cash in on it. Third, why would you call me when you have all the money, your freedom, and no baby?"

She wasn't sure how to respond. Maybe he could tell her. "So how *should* I do it? I wasn't involved in the kidnapping. I got an airtight—they can't put me in jail for doing it. And yeah, the money is real. Lily got a Nobel Prize two years ago; they paid her and her husband a little over a million dollars for it. They're also living in Rosyville for free. The government paid off their student loans and the remainder of their PhDs."

"You know an awful lot about her," he said suspiciously. "You a Fed? A cop? You wearin' a wire?"

"I'm no damned cop and I don't have a wire. All that info was on Channel 5 news last night. While I was watching it, I got this idea. Everyone's trying to claim the reward on little Lan, but no one's a winner. I figured if I could find the right guy, I could be that big winner. I been looking all over today for someone who knows where the baby is." She motioned the bartender down. "Joe, tell this guy I'm no cop."

Joe walked to where they sat, finished drying a martini glass with a towel, and put it with the other ones. "I've known Dott for thirty years. She used to wait tables in here and sold nickel bags of pot when she thought I wasn't lookin'. She's not a cop."

"Don't move, lady." The man got up and stood behind her chair. He expertly ran his hands down her back, under her breasts, between her legs, and down each leg to her shoes, feeling for a recorder or transmitter. He picked up her purse and dumped the contents out on the bar. He opened her wallet, fanned through the pictures, and pulled out her driver's license. "Okay, Dott," he said, holding it up so he could compare the photograph to her in the flesh, "if I hear anything, I'll let you know. How would I contact you?"

She wrote her name and phone number on a napkin. "So how should I do the exchange?" The man squinted at her with his eyebrows together, like he didn't understand her question. "The baby drop? You said I shouldn't call the number on the flyer, so how *should* I contact Lily to get the money?"

"Let me think about it. If I can find someone who knows something, maybe I'll figure out a way. Until then, it's not a problem. See ya around, Dott." He set her license next to her purse, threw down a ten-dollar bill, and left.

Joe watched him go. "Dott, I don't know what you're doing, but that is one bad hombre. If I were you, I wouldn't walk, I'd run away from that SOB...as fast as I can."

"Thanks, Joe. I'll keep that in mind."

... ...

"Captain Xanny, we have received a transmission from one of the snoop satellites around Taramon."

Taramon was one of several planets on the edge of the Ur-controlled portion of the galaxy infamous for embracing the quasi-legal business of welcoming pirates for rest, relaxation, and refit.

Xanny slid into his anti-grav device and left for the bridge. "What have you got, Nola?" he asked Lieutenant Nussi when he arrived.

"Satellite two picked up this." She pulled up a hologram of a starship approaching the planet. Chunks of dried mud still clung to many of the magnet enclosures on the hull. "The ship had an electronic signature with several cloaking transmitters running. I told Analysis to remove the cloaking. Once it was gone, this is what was left." The display changed to a digitized analysis of the signature. "This is the signature that *Easy Wind* had when she left Earth." A second display appeared. She put it beside the one from the ship at Taramon. They were identical.

"I've got you, you son of monkrus!" the captain chortled. "Great job, Nola." He reached for his shipwide comm button. "Commander Chirra and Lieutenant Fibari, please attend me in my quarters." He hadn't been to Taramon in fifty years—not since... Maybe it was time. This would certainly qualify as being drawn.

... ...

"You pinch Lan again, and I'll knock you out."

"Fuck you. I don't work for you." It was the beginning of Louise's shift.

"She's two years old, Louise! She misses her parents. Surely you have enough feelings left in that dried-out heart of yours to remember what that's like."

"I don't need this shit. I'm no goddamned nursemaid. If you think you can do better, you can stay with her full time. *Fuck off!*" She went back outside, slamming the door for effect.

Lan looked up in trepidation at him from under the covers. He grinned at her. "Ready for dinner, Lan?"

Lan smiled back. "Fut!"

Ernest picked up the phone and dialed the café next door.

Chapter 14 – I Hope It's That Easy

"Kevin, come in here a minute."

He walked into the study where Lily had been working all day with the composite drawings of the perpetrators in the four kidnappings from around Las Vegas. She'd scanned them into her computer and used some morphing software to develop a composite of the composites.

"My assumptions are that all four kidnappings were done by the same two guys and that the two guys were using a latex buildup to camouflage their real features. With that in mind, I used their estimated height to separate the eight composites into two groups of four images, one for each perp. Then I made the faces in each set the same size. After that, I created a three-dimensional projection of each composite." She brought up the images. They slowly rotated on the screen. "Next, I created a three-dimensional point mapping of each projection. About an hour ago, I realized that by using the points closest to the skin, the result would look most like how their real faces appeared, so by merging the point maps of all four composites and extracting the points that were closest in, I created a single point mapping, and did a morph build using the result. Here they are." Two faces rotated on the screen in front of them. She'd never seen either person. One appeared to be about forty-five, the other somewhere around thirty-five. "I have labelled them Abel and Baker."

"They had long hair. You're showing them with short hair."

"The hair was a wig. Their real hair may be longer than this, but the longer the hair is, the more work the latex application would be. Since these guys are criminals, I anticipated they would go the easy route."

"Let's send them to Dott," he suggested. "She knows more people than anyone in Vegas."

"Should I send them to the FBI, too?"

"I'd think we'd have better luck with the Vegas PD. Agent Lattimer said we should hang tight and let them do their job, but Lan disappeared a week ago and they haven't done jack shit but cause massive traffic jams with those damned roadblocks. Let's see what Dott has to say about them first."

She thought about that. "We can't send them over the internet—they read everything going out of Rosyville before they allow it through, and that wouldn't happen until Monday."

"That means we drive down there."

... ...

"I know this one," Dott said after studying the pictures. She held up the image of the older guy, the one Lily had labelled Abel.

"You know him?" Lily was surprised and a little shocked.

"This part's a smidge too fleshy,"—she indicated the area under his chin—"and his under-eyes needs a touch more, but that's him. Know might be a stretch. I met him in a bar two nights ago."

Kevin looked at her in disbelief. "In a bar? Really? You were hanging out in a bar with a kidnapper/murderer?"

Dott filled them in on how she'd spent her evenings for the last week.

"Are you *crazy*?" He shook his head. "These guys have *killed* people! Did you tell the police? The FBI?"

"Nope; I don't have any real evidence yet. No one has admitted to anything. If one of these people panned out, I assumed you were good for the money. You are, aren't you? Would be nice to know that before I have my ass hanging in the wind."

"Of course we are," Lily told her. "If someone showed up tonight with Lan, I'd pay the money and say *thanks*!"

"That's what I thought. I also assumed they would find a way to keep all the cash. The whole point is to return Lan back to us where she belongs."

"Unharmed," Kevin said tensely. "Unharmed, please."

"Of course, unharmed." Dott agreed. "I think there's a good chance this guy will contact me. When he does, how can I get holdda you on a moment's notice to have you bring the money to my house?"

"You want to do this away from the FBI?" Lily asked doubtfully, wondering if she had misjudged Matt's mother.

"If the FBI tries to SWAT these kidnappers, I think Lan will end up dead in a hole somewhere. This is the only way we bring her back alive."

Lily glanced at Kevin, and he nodded slightly. She considered what to do next. "I'll withdraw the money and have it ready. If he contacts you, call my cell phone—I'll have it on me 24/7. When you call, say: 'How about lunch?' If we can leave immediately, I will say 'How about in an hour?' If we can't leave right away, I will say another time when we *can* get there. If I don't answer, leave a message and I'll call back with our expected arrival."

"I don't pay him until I have Lan in my arms," Dott told them.

"I hope it's that easy."

Chapter 15 – The City of Angels

"Dr. Medder?"

"Yes. Who is this?" Doug had been sitting at the kitchen table, checking emails on his iPad, when his phone rang.

"It's Bill Lewis. I was the guy on the side of the road you gave all that money to."

"How are you feeling, Bill? The hospital wouldn't let me talk to you."

"I feel a little embarrassed. I never done nothing like that before. No one ever gave me that much money."

"I'm glad it turned out the way it did. Could have been a lot worse."

"Yeah. Dumbass thing to do."

"Your sign said you wanted a job. Do you? Do you still want a job?"

"What are we talking about here? What kind of job?"

"I have a farm and don't have enough time to do the things that need doing around the property. I need someone to help out. If you're interested, it would include room and board and a salary."

"What kind of things need doing?"

"Repairing the fencing, feeding the horses, putting them in and out of their stalls in the barn, mucking out the stalls every day, doing repairs around the property when something breaks—you know, farm stuff. Are you interested?"

"Yeah. I could do that. Room and board, you say?"

"Yep, part of the deal. We're kind of far from town—getting out here when the snow flies would be a problem. And Bill, we don't allow any drugs on the property. Is that okay, too?"

"Yeah, no drugs is fine. I'm done with that shit."

"I'd like to bring you out to meet my wife and our housekeeper. They get a vote too."

"When?"

"Tonight?"

"What time?"

"How about I pick you up at the same corner where I gave you the money? I get done working at the Aerospace Centre about 4:30."

"I'll be there."

"See you then, and thanks, Bill."

... ...

"Welcome back to *Shark Week* on the Discovery Channel. This show will begin with an interview with a young man many of you have heard about. He survived for almost fourteen hours in the Pacific Ocean after a container ship ran over his sailboat. He had no food or water, no radio or flares, and was twenty miles from shore when a shark fin appeared in the water next to him. We are at the dock in Ensenada, Mexico, where he finished his journey. Please welcome Kyle Daugherty!"

As he walked onto the set, Kyle told the interviewer, "It wasn't really a shark fin."

"Tell us what happened, Kyle. Start from the beginning. How did you happen to end up twenty miles offshore in a fourteen-foot sailboat in the path of a monstrous container ship?"

He told them the whole story. About his mother dying of pancreatic cancer and wanting her ashes spread at sea. About his dad saying he wasn't old enough to do blue water sailing.

"And what happened after the ship wrecked your boat?" The interviewer turned to the camera. "You won't believe what happened next."

Kyle told them about the dolphin approaching him and he thought it was a shark at first, how it offered its dorsal fin to him and then the life ring, how he'd tied his PFDt to the rope when his arms gave out, and how the two other dolphins showed up and took turns pulling him toward Ensenada while their friends kept the real sharks away. He told them about naming the dolphins, and how, for the last half of the trip, he'd fallen asleep.

At the end of the story, the interviewer looked into the camera again. "Don't believe it? I've got one more person who witnessed the end of this amazing, incredible story." He turned off-camera. "Mr. Russel Gall, please come tell us what *you* saw."

The man who had let Kyle use his phone walked onto the set smiling. "Hi, Kyle. We meet again." They shook hands and Russ sat down.

"Russ, please tell us what you saw in your own words."

"I was having a glass of wine ..." A moment of panic crossed his face. "Am I allowed to say that?" he whispered.

"Sure, Russ."

"Like I said, I was having a last glass of wine before turning in. Earlier that afternoon, after my wife, Wanda, and I sailed down from San Diego, I had moored our sailboat nearby. It was about four in the morning and we'd been enjoying the entertainment in Ensenada. Wanda had already hit the sack and I was about to turn in, when a dolphin jumped out of the water and did a double flip—and I am not exaggerating, it did a full two-and-a-half. It was dark and I mistook it for a porpoise.

"I said, 'I never seen a porpoise do a single flip, let alone a double.' Then I heard a boy's voice tell me, 'It's not a porpoise. It's a dolphin—a bottlenose dolphin—and his name is Willy. He just saved my life.' I looked down at the beach, where the voice came from. Under the dock was a boy who was struggling to stand in the surf. I hadn't seen any American kids around the marina all day, so I asked him where he'd come from, and he told me 'San Diego. I need to call my dad.'

"By the time I got down to him, he was shivering badly. He had a life ring tied to his inflated PFD. I got the PFD off him, wrapped him up in my jacket, and let him use my phone. He called his dad. When we got to my sailboat, Wanda took over. She wrapped him in blankets, made him some hot chocolate, and warmed us up some chili. He drank the chocolate, a couple of quarts of water, and ate more chili than I did and I've got a pretty good appetite." Russ rubbed his ample belly at the camera and gave a contented sigh. "Two hours later, Kyle's dad showed up and he left with him." He motioned off-set for someone to come in. "Wanda and I have something we thought you'd want to have."

Wanda walked onto the set with Kyle's PFD with the life ring still tied to it. "After your ordeal, we thought you would like to have this back as a keepsake. We fished it out of Ensenada harbor the next day. And here is the recipe to my chili. You said you wanted to know how to make it. I have renamed it: Kyle's Rescue Chili, in honor of your journey."

The interviewer spoke up. "The supervisor of the marina Kyle sailed out of in San Diego remembered the exact time he left; he had sent a text to Kyle's father at 12:01 P.M., to make sure he knew his son was taking the boat. Daniel Daugherty alerted the harbor patrol at 12:04 P.M., but they didn't find the boy. According to the National Weather Service, the winds on that day at that time were constant from the east at 12 knots. To go twenty miles in the fourteen-foot Laser sailboat with those winds would have taken a little over two hours. That placed Kyle's sailboat at the collision point at about 2:10 P.M.

"We checked maritime records, and only one container ship was passing San Diego Harbor twenty miles out. We called the ship's corporate offices and asked if the ship had reported the collision. They transferred us to their legal offices, where they told us their company takes offshore collisions very seriously, but that there had been no report of one at the time and place we described. We asked for a picture of the ship's bow to see if there were any scrapes on it. They said it would take a court order."

The camera panned back to include the interviewer, Kyle, Russ, and Wanda. "So, did it happen? Did Kyle get run over by a container ship? Did three dolphins pull a ten-year-old boy from San Diego to Ensenada for fourteen hours and seventy-five nautical miles as the California Current swept them along at four knots? Did a troupe of dolphins keep the sharks away from him? If it didn't, what happened to the sailboat? How did Kyle get from the collision point to Ensenada, where he came out of the waves wearing a PFD with a life ring tied to it? I, for one, think it did. Willy, if you're listening, THANKS!"

... ...

Rebecca viewed the inside of the cabin with disdain—it couldn't be more than eight hundred square feet: two bedrooms, a living room, and a kitchen. They'd left their beautiful four-bedroom condo on the beach in Malibu for *this*?—no running water, no electricity, no furnace, and a fucking outhouse!

"Are you out of your fucking mind?" she asked her husband, Jeremiah.

"When the collapse happens, this will be safe. LA will be a war zone."

"You expect me to go outside in a snowstorm to take a shit? Where's the fucking washboard and tub of hot water? I might as well start doing laundry."

Jeremiah walked outside and began unloading their Lexus SUV.

"*Guns*! Are those *guns*? When did you buy guns? We haven't had a gun in our house in the twenty-two years we've been married."

"Rebecca, not only do I have guns, but you will also have to learn how to shoot them and maybe kill with them. You've never been at war—you don't understand what will happen without law or anyone to enforce it. I have. When I served in Somalia, I saw babies raped in front of their parents, men tortured for amusement, and cannibalism—no law, no police, no military."

He paused again, collecting his thoughts. "Our government will collapse. It won't be able to support the infrastructure as the population ages and the trillions in national debt that they have accumulated. The tax base will dwindle. They'll print more money to fund the government just like the Germans did in World War II. Inflation will go through the roof and that will crush the middle class. Their hard-won savings will be worthless. The government will cut back, and then eliminate social services. All those people who are used to being on the government's dole will have to start making it on their own, but the jobs, food, and money will be gone. So guess what? They'll turn to crime. And the crime won't stop with robberies, looting, and vandalism. They will take over the military outposts and all their weapons. Our Land of the Free and Home of

Page 91

the Brave will crumble into chaos. The criminal underground, who pretty much ignored the laws of the land before, will become warlords and organize those gangs into militias."

Rebecca wasn't listening—she'd heard it all from him a hundred times before. He decided to try a different way that might make this transition a little less traumatic for his wife. Her idea of "roughing it" was flying to Cabo San Lucas and having dinner delivered to them on the beach.

"Up here, we will be safe—and we aren't alone. Five other families are within a mile of us up here, doing the same thing we. Within five miles, there must be a hundred families who have read the writing on the wall and decided to escape from the jungle before the collapse."

"I can't wait to see who else would live in these woods. The Sons of Sasquatch? The cast of *Deliverance*? Men in bib overalls with three teeth?"

"Well, Amy Johansson is a writer. I think you have one of her books. Her husband, Liam, is a chemist. They have two kids whom they home school; one was a National Merit Scholar this year. Harvard accepted him for this fall without his parents having to pay a hundred-thousand dollar "helper" fee. Marvin and Lucy Schroeder are musicians. They can play anything with strings or keys. Kimberly Kirkpatrick is an RN. She and her grandson moved up here to escape his step-dad—seems he liked to climb into little boy's beds."

Rebecca's head snapped around at those words. She still fought her own demons from a childhood filled with memories of a predatory priest.

"None of these people are losers who live here because they can't live anywhere else. These people are educated professionals. They've made a conscious decision to live out their days away from the chaos and bloodshed they are sure will come to the urban areas of our country."

She was looking out the door at the Lexus.

"Look, Rebecca, in two days, I'll have the dark energy generator hooked up and lighting installed. I'll put the pump in the spring and get you water at the sink in two more days. By the end of the week the furnace will be here. Can you give me a week before you decide?"

"One week, Jeremiah. If I have to use that outhouse in one week, I'm outta here."

"Deal!" He held out his hand.

She looked at it like he was a Martian, turned on her heel, and walked back outside. The Sierras wrapped around the horizon like snow-covered teeth; the smell of pine was so thick you could cut it and box it; and the sky...the sky was a shade of blue that never made it to the streets of Los Angeles. One week—she could live here for one week—and then it was back to the City of Angels. Jeremiah could play mountain man of the Sierras if he wanted, but she wasn't going to have anything to do with it. The night lights called to her with a siren whisper that wouldn't be ignored.

Chapter 16 – See You in an Hour

"You are in command, while I'm gone, Yidee."

"Yes, sir." Commander Chirra obviously wanted to be the one going instead of staying behind.

Captain Xanny turned to Lieutenant Fibari. "Fela, is the shuttle ready?"

"Well, it's as ready as it ever will be. Are we really going to jump a thousand light years in a landing shuttle?"

"No choice. We can't take the ship and I'm not going to risk losing that monkrus to an informant in the GSCB. How is the armament fit-out going?"

"It'll be done in about an hour."

"What did you select?"

"Two class-B laser cannons, two gravitational field disrupters, two photon torpedoes, two smaller fusion devices, and two large area evacuators."

"Two photons?" One could blow a planet into asteroids.

She raised an eyebrow and shrugged. "This is Fey Pey. I'd rather have 'em and not need 'em than the other way around."

He studied her, wondering if she had a private agenda. She'd been Fey Pey's exec for two years, a long time ago. As he remembered, her departure from him hadn't been a happy occasion.

"Provisions?"

"Enough for two weeks."

"Small arms?"

She looked at him like he was stupid. "Yeah, a few." Of course she'd brought small arms—she was sergeant-at-arms. They could fight a small war with what she'd loaded.

"Who are you bringing on your team?" he asked.

"Flug."

"Good. I want to bring Sergeant Shaia from Analysis, too. As soon as the fit-out is done and the navigation charts are loaded, we launch."

… … … … … … …

"Louise is gone." Ernest had dreaded making this phone call.
"Shit."
"She told me she couldn't do her shift last night—that she had a headache. She showed up in the other room around 2 A.M. with some guy in a Ferrari. She sounded drunk as hell—wore out the bed with the poor bastard. They were pounding on the walls all night. They left about dawn and headed east. All her stuff is gone from the room."
"She's gonna rat on us. We have to leave that motel. I'll pick you up in an hour. I think I got a nibble on unloading the kid."
"We could just leave her here. Someone'll find her."
"Yeah, I thought about that, but I got a line on cleaning up that hundred grand."
"Ransom? You never do ransom. You're the one who told me that people who do ransom get a free room at the gray bar hotel with a sign over the door that says 'Stupid.'"
"Times change."
"Since when? What's changed? They still got the FBI. They still got courts. They still got prisons."
Lan woke up. "Potty, Unca Ernie."
"I gotta go; Lan's up. We'll be packed and ready in an hour."

… … … … … … …

"Clara, Mindy, Martin, this is Bill."
Bill gave a little self-conscious wave. "Hi."
"I've asked him to work here. He'll be doing all the chores I don't have time to do."
Clara held out her hand. "Hi, Bill. Welcome."
Mindy wasn't quite so welcoming. Her prostitution days had made her an excellent judge of people, and she'd seen men like him

before. There it was, in his eyes as he scoped out the entrance hallway—he was a taker, not a giver. "What did you used to do—before you were homeless?"

"I drove a truck, long haul." He saw the scars of the track marks on her arms and smiled knowingly. "I see you done some long haulin', too."

She pulled down the sleeves of her sweater self-consciously. "Everyone got somethin' they don't want to remember."

"I wanna drive a truck when I grow up!" Martin started running around the hallway making truck noises.

Doug was watching the interaction between Mindy and Bill, wondering if he'd made a mistake by bringing him here.

Clara broke up the apparent confrontation by saying, "Let's eat." As they sat at the table, she picked up the mashed potatoes, put some on her plate, and passed the bowl to Bill. He took a huge portion and put it back on the table instead of passing it to Mindy. The mixed vegetables ended up next to the potatoes, soon joined by the sliced roast.

"I'm hungry, Mama," Martin said.

Mindy reached to the center of the table and retrieved the potatoes, glaring at Bill. "Some people got no manners at all."

He shook his head and grinned at her with his mouth full. "Sorry. Don't know what I was thinkin'." He passed her the vegetables and then the roast. "Been a while since I ate at a real table."

Doug and Clara looked back and forth between Mindy and Bill with the same question on their minds: where was this going?

... ...

"He gives me the creeps!" Clara told Doug as they got ready for bed.

"He's just been homeless for a while. He'll be okay after a few days. It took me a while to get over my trip to Canada."

"I don't know, Doug...this might be a mistake. You never looked at me like he does. It's like he's peeking under my clothes."

"Let's give it a week. If you still feel that way, I'll tell him it isn't working."

"You're going to leave us alone with him while you go to work? Have you talked to his last employer? Do you have any idea why he really got fired?"

He was surprised. "No. Do you think I should?"

"Yes, Doug, I do. And until you do, I'd like you to work from home. I don't want to be alone with him in the house."

... ...

"Hello?" Dott answered the phone in her kitchen as she dried her hands on a kitchen towel. She was making some spaghetti sauce. Her children were coming for dinner that evening.

"Do you know who this is?"

She checked the caller ID: Blocked. "No. Who is this?"

"We met at Fernan's a couple a days ago. You said you were lookin' for Lily Yuan's baby."

"Did you find her?" She was covered with goose bumps. This was happening!

"We need to meet. I found something you might like to hear. I don't wanna talk over the phone."

"When and where?"

"Fernan's in ten minutes."

"I'll be there." The call ended with a click. She turned off the sauce and reached for her pocketbook.

Ten minutes! No time to call anyone. She ran out the door, got into her car, and streaked out of her neighborhood.

Halfway to the bar, a ratty Chevrolet pulled up next to her at a stoplight. The driver waved at her and tapped his horn a couple of times. She looked at him impatiently and then at the red light, wishing it would change. Suddenly she realized who the driver next to her was; it was the guy from the bar, Lily's Able.

"Change of plans," he told her through the open window. "Pull into that parking lot." He led them to a deserted corner of the lot and got out of his car and into hers.

"I found someone who says he knows where she is."

"Where is she?"

"He wants the hundred grand before he'll tell me. He's scared of the people who have the baby."

"No money until I have her in my arms."

"It doesn't work that way, Dott. Here's how it will work. I'll give you a place to put the money, and you put it there. Once I have it, I'll call the guy. I'll give him the money and he'll tell me where to find the baby. I'll tell you."

"I need to talk to the baby to make sure he has her and she's alive and well."

"You want to talk to a two-year-old?"

"That's the only way he'll get the money."

"Let me see what I can do." He got out of her car and into his.

As he drove away, she sat in her car and pondered what to do. On her cell phone, she selected a number from her Favorites. Lily answered. "Hi, Dott. What's up?"

"How about lunch?"

Lily's voice caught in her throat. "Sure. How about in an hour? What can I bring?"

"That green salad you said you were making. I've got everything else."

"See you in an hour."

Chapter 17 – I Probably Wouldn't Either

The shuttle popped into real space, about a million kilometers out from Taramon. Captain Xanny was smug. "All those years and I haven't lost my touch, Fela." They'd made the thousand light year trip in just eight jumps.

Lieutenant Fibari was busy checking in. "Taramon Traffic Control, this is unregistered starship *Black Swan*."

"What is your cargo, *Black Swan*?"

"Mining equipment. We're on R & R. We heard Taramon could make us welcome for a week or two."

There was a chuckle on the other end of the line. "You are assigned orbit 35E-15. After you land at the spaceport, look up Pirate's Alley in Spelie Cove. I expect you'll find everything you're looking for there."

"I acknowledge orbit 35E-15. Maybe we'll meet in Pirate's Alley. *Black Swan* out."

It was so easy to swing back into pirate-speak after all those years of being legitimate. *Unregistered starship* was synonymous with *pirate vessel*. *R & R* meant they had been successful in their pirating and were ready to spend some of what they had stolen. Places like Taramon existed to allow the pirates to do just that. *Mining equipment* was a generic cargo description for *don't ask—you don't want to know*.

Fela downloaded the coordinates for 35E-15. The jump alarm sounded as she prepared to place them in their assigned parking orbit.

Sergeant Shaia spoke up from her console. She'd been examining the electronic signatures of all parked starships. "*Easy Wind* is still here. They are in orbit 17K-01. According to the ships-in-port list at the TTC, their name is *Russell Shoal*. They are queued for a refit scheduled to begin next week."

"Can you access their computers, Zarqa?" the captain asked.

She tried three different ways to hack in, but none worked. "No. They are either off, offline, or shielded. The chandler's list is public, though. Let me check what parts they are scheduled to use in the refit." She paused a moment. "Corrosion repair in nine places on the hull, three jump magnet replacements, lots of conductor replacements, and cold fusion generator replacement."

"Living under saltwater for three years will do that." He smiled coldly. "Zarqa, before we go down to the surface, leave a marker buoy here in orbit. I want its electronic signature to be the same as the shuttle. Anyone scanning it will think an entire starship is parked here."

"I can do better than that. I can have the buoy create a hologram of a generic starship; that way, if someone looks at us, they'll see what looks like a fully functional and armed vessel."

Xanny coughed, trying hard not to laugh. "You might have missed your calling as a pirate, Zarqa. Please put the hologram in place, as well. Fela, I know how much you'd like to repay Fey Pey for the way he treated you when you were his exec, but we have to capture him alive. As much as we both want to, we won't accomplish anything if we kill the monkrus. We have to find out who paid him to plant the dream and why. If we can do that, we can get the GSCB to cancel the failure of primates and give them a second chance."

"I understand." She stretched and bared her claws. "Capturing would be better, actually." He understood her meaning. Being captured by a blood enemy was the worst thing possible for a pirate. They earned respect from other pirates much more by who hated them than by what crimes they had committed. Being captured by an enemy meant the enemy was stronger than them. It was embarrassing—far worse than being killed.

"Fela, call approach control for Spelie Cove and get into the queue. We're about to jump to the planet. No uniforms. We're all pirates now—dress like it."

Flug raised an eyebrow at that. He was a big primate, something over two hundred kilos, and not much of it fat.

Lieutenant Fibari whispered to him, "Worn-out civilian clothes, the dirtier the better, and lots of weapons."

"I hear the mating call of a bottle of queetle," the captain said happily as they got ready. "My name is Captain Zeeg, if anyone asks—but people don't ask many questions around here. The answers are usually cold, sharp, and metallic."

"When they aren't explosive," Fela said as she slid her laser sidearm into its holster, next to her knife. She put a pair of flash-booms into a hidden pocket in her vest and another knife in a quick-release holster on her right front leg.

The rest of the crew dressed and armed themselves similarly.

"Flug, I need to show you some pirate hand signs in case we get into trouble." Five minutes later, the big man had them down.

Fela checked each person. "Corporal Flug, you take the armor-piercing machine gun. You're the only one big enough to carry it. Don't let anyone else touch it; they command a high price here. Don't hesitate to kill to protect it. What kind of ammo load do you have?"

He picked up the weapon and checked. "Four hundred rounds."

"Bring another hundred."

Flug hid a small grin. When he'd been a senior sergeant in the Ur Combat Corps, he'd carried three times that. He checked the cycling and cleanliness. Fela watched him carefully. The weapon was spotless and in perfect condition. It cycled smoothly. The power and propellant reservoirs were full. He nodded in approval to her. Flug considered this particular model a special friend. He had used it successfully for five years in the Corps, keeping himself and his squad alive. That she took such good care of it raised her credibility immensely in his eyes; that he saw the beautiful condition of the weapon raised her appreciation of him, as well. She would see how he comported himself when the bullets began to fly, because it *was* coming—she could taste it.

Clearance to jump to the approach path to Spelie Cove came through. Xanny reached for the jump button. "Zarqa, once we arrive at the spaceport, I want you to remain with the shuttle. No one comes in or near it while it's parked. They will test you. Don't hesitate to aim the laser cannons, but try not to kill anyone unless you have to."

"Yes, sir." She sounded a little disappointed. She was the smallest and youngest of the group, and although everyone had heard about the pirate havens, not many had been to one.

"I'll take you on our next visit, Zarqa," the captain said gently. "It will be a great story for your grandkids. But beware of the dark corners down there. There aren't any rules in a place like this. Don't look if you don't want to see."

... ...

"Do you have any clothes for a one-year-old?" The Second Chance consignment store was also her last chance consignment store. Lola Barkely had searched all over Odessa, Texas, for clothes for her baby.

The woman behind the counter paused while she thought about Lola's request. "I don't think so, but let me go check."

She returned five minutes later with a small box, about a foot square. "This is all we have left."

"How much for the whole box?"

"Don't you want to know what they are? Boys or girls? Colors?"

"She's a one-year-old—she doesn't care. This stuff is getting impossible to find."

"Did you try the internet? I would think eBay or Amazon would have something."

"Those people want a fortune for their clothes; and it takes forever to be delivered. They don't make them until someone places an order, and then it has to be shipped from Vietnam, Malaysia, or some other sweatshop country."

"Gimme five bucks for the box. I think the owner was ready to throw them out. We have some eighteen-month and two-year-old things, too. You want those, as well?"

"Sure. Might as well buy 'em now."

After the clerk retrieved the boxes, she said, "If I could find some more one- and two-year-old clothes, would you want me to call you?"

"Absolutely!" Lola told her. "That would be wonderful! Girl's clothes if you have them."

"I'll look in my mother's attic. She never throws anything away. There's still stuff up there from when we were kids. If I find something, could I ask you a favor?"

"You can ask." Lola cocked her head, waiting.

"You got one of those Baby Machine babies, right?" Lola nodded. "Would you bring your daughter in next time? I'm on the list for a baby, but I'm twelve years out. I'd just like to hold a real one again."

"Of course I will"—Lola checked the clerk's nametag— "Maggie. I don't travel with her very often because of all the kidnappings."

"I don't blame you. I wouldn't either. Have you heard about the break-ins? Babies gettin' stolen right out of their cribs?"

"I've got seventeen reasons why that would be a very bad idea," Lola told her grimly, "and they're all sitting right here in my holster." She patted the lump under her jacket. "My husband and I go to the range every weekend. Little Bridget is getting so she likes the noise."

"I'll give you a call if I find anything. I'll need your number."

"Here's my email instead. I don't give my number out—too easy to trace." Lola wrote it on one of the shop's business cards. "Thanks."

... ...

"Sridhar?" his wife's voice came from his iPhone sitting on the lab bench at the CDC.

"Yes, Lavanya, what is it?"

"I am outside with your dinner. Come eat with me."

"I can't stop. Please leave it in my office." There was an extended silence, but the end-of-call click never came. "Is there something else?"

"Today is our anniversary, Sridhar. I made the meal we ate when we were married. Please come share it with me." She said the last few words in tears. He had not been home in a week.

He sighed again and looked one last time at the failed reaction under his microscope. Either the sperm wouldn't penetrate at all, or the little bastards gang-raped the poor ovum. Spending an evening with his wife on their anniversary wouldn't change anything.

"I'll be right out, my love. Please forgive me."

... ...

"When did he say he'd call back?" Lily paced back and forth in Dott's living room. She'd given up trying to sit still.

"He didn't. All he said was he'd see what he can do."

They'd been over the whole conversation three times. Dott knew Lily was on overload. Kevin sat on the edge of the sofa, wound about as tight as a piano string.

The phone rang. Dott grabbed it. "Hello?"

"Hi, Mom. Do you need me to pick up some wine before we come over?"

Dott took a breath and mouthed, "It's Matt," to Lily and Kevin.

"Yeah, some wine would be great—something red, but not too oaky. And get enough for Kevin and Lily. They're here, too."

"Cool. How's the search for Lan going? Any leads yet?"

"Not yet. Gotta go. I love you."

"Love you, too, Mom."

She hung up the phone. They waited. The refrigerator turned on and off. The sunlight coming through the window overlooking the backyard moved across the floor.

"How do you think he'll want the money delivered?" Kevin asked.

Dott cracked up. "A locker in the bus station! That's how the movies always do it."

Lily wasn't paying attention; she was looking into the backyard where her daughter had played the last time they were there.

Matt and Miranda showed up around six o'clock. Dott's daughter, Evelyn, arrived soon after. When they sat down to dinner, the only sounds were of people eating. No one talked much.

The phone rang. Dott answered. "Hello?"

"This is AT&T calling. Please stay on the line for an importan..."

She hung up. "Telemarketers."

After another five minutes of silence, Matt decided he had to ask, "Mom, what's going on?"

She looked at Lily and Kevin. They looked back. Lily nodded.

"Someone contacted me today. He said he knew someone who knew where Lan was." Dott told the three of them about meeting the man in the bar and about the phone call today.

"That sounds like bullshit to me. He just wants the money. Did you tell the FBI?"

"No. You don't have the whole story. Lily created a picture of one of the kidnappers. She built a composite of the drawings the victims created. He's the guy I met in the bar. If we tell the FBI, we think, the whole thing will go sour, and either we'll never find her or we'll find her dead."

"She's probably already dead," Matt said almost to himself. When Lily caught her breath, he realized he'd spoken out loud. He reached for her hand. "Lily, I'm so sorry. That was a stupid thing to say. I would give anything to have it not be true."

The phone rang again, and everyone looked at it. Dott picked it up. The caller ID was blocked.

"Put Lily on," a muffled voice said. She pressed the speakerphone button and passed the phone to Lily.

"Hello?"

Everyone in the room heard Lan's voice come over the line. "Mommy? Wanna come *home!*"

Lily burst into tears. "You will, sweetheart," she managed, "in just a little while."

"Wanna come *NOW!*" Lan started wailing.

The first voice came back on the line. "A map is taped to the steering wheel of your car. Put the money where it leads you and leave. When I retrieve it, I will call you with directions to where she is. No cops or Feds—I will know, and she will disappear."

The line went dead.

"She's *alive*, Lily!" Kevin shouted as he hugged her to him and spun around. "Our baby's *still alive!*"

... ...

The map led to an abandoned mining shack built against the side of a mountain about forty miles northwest of Las Vegas. Kevin and Lily searched, from top to bottom, which took maybe one minute, but there was no sign of Lan or even occupation. The dust on the floor had not been disturbed in years.

He put the small suitcase of money on the table in the middle of the room. "Nothing to do but leave."

"Do you think they'll let her go?"

"Yes," he lied. "Why would they kill her if they have the money?" They walked out to their car and began the drive back to Las Vegas.

The FBI had heard the entire conversation via their wiretap on Dott's phone. High above them, a drone with fuel for three days circled slowly. It had followed Kevin's car all the way from Las Vegas and created a real-time video feed in natural and infrared light, wide angle, and narrow angle, which it transmitted to the FBI command center. The drone pilot studied the images. About a mile south, several pronghorns were grazing, and a colony of prairie dogs was busy collecting food a hundred meters south. The drone stayed in position at an altitude of six miles as Las Vegas air traffic control kept all commercial aircraft away from it.

The Blackhawk helicopter, ready to take an FBI SWAT team to the shack, squatted on the helipad outside the FBI headquarters. The pilot sat at a poker game with the SWAT members. Unmarked Nevada Highway Patrol units arrived at diners and gas stations in a circle about ten miles away, ready to block all highways leading away as soon as the FBI gave the word.

The bait was placed—the trap was set.

Chapter 18 – EnduroCross

The next morning at breakfast Doug was alone with Bill. Mindy was in the kitchen with Martin, and Clara had not come downstairs yet. Doug decided this would be a perfect time to ask about his past job.

He sighed and started. "Bill, who did you work for when you were a trucker?"

"An outfit in Toronto."

"What was their name?"

Bill was suddenly suspicious of where this was going. "Why? Aren't I workin' hard enough?"

"You're working very hard. You did a wonderful job fixing the fences around the pastures—I couldn't have done as well. I'm glad you finished before the really bad weather started."

"Then who cares who I used to work for? Those people were assholes—a bunch of Chinese cocksu—" He paused and then started again. "Chinese sons-a-bitches who tried to use us drivers as slave labor."

"So you won't tell me?"

"Jinha Trucking. Their headquarters is in Mississauga, outside of Toronto."

"Thanks, Bill."

Clara came down the stairs. Bill glanced at her and continued. "If you call them, this is what they'll say: I was lazy, I didn't maintain my truck, and I missed my pickups and deliveries. That's what they say to everyone who calls about an ex-driver. What really happened was I asked for my vacation. I was supposed to get two weeks a year, but every time I asked for it, they had something that had to be delivered yesterday and couldn't afford to give me the time off. After two years, I asked for all four weeks. They said I only had two coming—that I didn't use the two from my first year, so I lost them. They offered me the two weeks from my second year, and I told 'em to kiss my ass. I left their truck at a truck stop on the other side of Calgary. That's why I'm here. They wouldn't even pay me for the last week I worked so I could hitchhike down to the States."

"Wow. Did you complain to the authorities?"

"Why should I? Wouldn't do no good. The government never helped me do nothin'—those bastards are in bed with the transportation companies. All Ottawa is good for is takin' money out of my wallet to support them damned immigrants what come to Canada for a free ride. None a them migrants was with me in Iraq during Desert Storm. I wore Canada's uniform and was proud to do it. Someone had to pull fuel to feed them tanks and choppers while we kicked Saddam Hussein's ass. I didn't see no one with brown skin from Canada."

His face was angry and red, and he realized he'd been ranting. He took a breath, stood, and carried his dish toward the kitchen. "The manure spreader threw the impeller chain again. It needs a new one," he said from the kitchen. "I've fixed the old one four times now."

"I'll pick up one tomorrow. Can you make the old one work for today?"

He walked back into the dining room. "Yeah. If it pops off again, I'll just put it back on."

"And Bill, if they tell me you were lazy, I'll know they're lying. You work hard for me, and I appreciate that. Payday is tomorrow. Will you be needing some time off?"

"I'll do the morning chores, and then I'd like a ride to town— got some debts I have to repay. I think I'll spend the night in town. Are you alright bringing the horses in tomorrow night and turning them out Sunday morning?"

"Sure. No problem."

"Don't bother with the stalls—I'll do 'em before I leave and when I get back. And I'll need a ride back out here on Sunday sometime."

"Give us a call. Someone will come for you."

"After church would be nice," Clara offered. "We could meet you around 11:30"

"Works for me. I'll be at the corner where we first met."

Mindy walked in with two plates of bacon and scrambled eggs, put them down where Doug and Clara sat, and left without a glance at Bill. She had started feeding Martin in the kitchen.

Bill walked into the kitchen behind her, rinsed his dish, and set it with the others to be washed. He blew a raspberry at Martin; the little boy laughed and made a face back. He put on his coat and walked outside toward the barn.

... ...

The drone operator pressed the alert button that rang on the on-call officer's desk. "Hey, Jerry. Something's happening!"

The agent walked over. "What do you see?"

"Motorcycles—at least twenty of 'em—converging on the shack. They are beatin' feet. Man, look at the guy in front go! He's flyin'!"

"I'll let the state police know the balloon is up."

... ...

Tommy came over the ridgeline in the lead on his Kawasaki. The new muffler he'd put on was working great; it must have added five horsepower. He'd found five of the six waypoints. Colby had beaten him to 2 and 3. Dan had tied him to 4.

He led everyone through a prairie dog colony on the way to the last waypoint, knowing how much dust his bike would kick up. It made the rest of the group slow way down, and if a couple of prairie dogs got hurt, who cared? There were millions of 'em out here.

This waypoint had turned out to be on the backside of an old shack. The bike was running great! An hour from now, he would be at work at the NAPA Auto Parts store in Vegas with three hundred bucks in his wallet!

He crested the last hill before the highway, got some big air, and then saw the four state troopers with flashing light bars on their cars and rifles pointing at his chest. A fifth trooper was in front of them and held up his left hand. In his right hand was a pistol and it was aimed directly at him. Tommy landed, downshifted, slid sideways, and stopped about ten feet from the cop in a cloud of dust.

"Turn off the bike and dismount slowly," the officer shouted. Tommy laid the bike carefully on its side—competition bikes didn't have kickstands. "Lie on the ground, face down, with your hands behind you." Another officer cuffed him.

"I'm sorry!" Tommy wailed. "They were just prairie dogs!"

The rest of the group showed up in ones and twos as they came over the hill. They got the same treatment as Tommy.

... ...

The FBI analyst who had been talking to the state police came into Special Agent Lattimer's office. "The troopers say all the bikers were local kids from a motocross club. None of them had the money. All their stories were the same. Some guy asked their club to run a waypoint course. He gave them GPSs with the waypoints programmed in, and the riders put them on their handlebars. He told them he was trying out new technology for a Pro Competition EnduroCross course, and if it worked out, this would be a whole new race circuit for them to compete in. He taped a barcode to both their gloves; each waypoint had a reader and the competitors had to present their barcode to it to get credit. When they finished, the guy running the course was going to meet them and he would give each one who completed the course fifty dollars. First, second, and third place would get an additional three hundred, two hundred, and one hundred."

"Let me guess—the guy wasn't at the finish line."

"You got it. The troopers went there, and the guy was long gone—not even tire tracks in the dirt."

"Could the bikers create a composite of the guy?"

"Yeah. They're bringing them in to do that now. The troopers want to know what to do with the bikes. Should they impound them or what? The bikers were pretty upset about leaving 'em lying on the ground—they said a lot of 'em are getting stolen out there."

"Tell one of the troopers to watch over them."

"I'll tell them, but they won't be happy. They think the FBI should take over the scene, so they can get back to work."

"Is the money still in the shack?"

There was a pause. "Don't know. We were focused on the bikers. No one's out there."

"You might send someone to check.

"Will do."

... ...

"The shack's on fire."

"Shit!" Lattimer rolled his eyes. It kept getting worse. "Who's out there?"

"Nichols."

"Tell him to stick around and watch the bikes until the kids return. Let the troopers go. Don't forget to say thanks."

"Will do."

"And send a search team. Someone had to get in and out; I want to know how."

"Yes, sir."

"Get them moving within five minutes. Whoever took that money is only half an hour away from the shack. See if they can at least get a direction to look. Tell them to bring the dogs—they might be able to pick up a scent trail."

"Yes, sir."

Lattimer walked into the drone control center. "Did you quit watching the shack after the bikers left?"

"Of course. I followed the bikers."

"How about the wide angle? Did it still cover the shack?"

"Nope. Out of view."

The agent sighed. "I figured. Do a scan of the surrounding area. Look for anything moving."

"It'll just be natural light—infrared won't help during the day. There isn't much out there that isn't over a hundred degrees. And smoke from the grass fire that spread from the burning shack is obscuring the whole valley for natural light."

"Do what you can. Maybe we'll be lucky."

"Yes, sir."

The search team arrived as the forest service was finishing up with the grass fire. The area was red with dye from the fire retardant airdrop they had called in to put out the bulk of the fire.

When he was told about it, Lattimer was furious. "Why the hell did they use fire retardant on a little grass fire? It wasn't more than ten acres!"

"They said that, with the wind, that little fire could be five hundred acres in an hour and five thousand by tomorrow. Apparently, it's standard procedure this time of year when a fire is close to the mountains."

The search team led the dogs around the perimeter of the burn, but they didn't pick up anything. In the smoking remains of the shack, there was no trace of the money or the suitcase.

... ...

During his morning staff meeting, President Robbins asked Patty Kendricks, his chief of staff, "What's come in on the contest mailbox?" A week had passed, and each morning he wanted the highlights of what the country had come up with.

"Well, we've gotten something on the order of fifty-seven million entries so far, between the emails, tweets, and letters. The filter program the Caltech kids created is doing an excellent job now that the bugs are sorted out. The suggestions fall into eight categories. Here's how the more interesting ones are breaking down." She handed the president three sheets of paper with the following text:

A. Draw the aliens to Earth
1. Create a group very diverse humans—racially, ethnically, physically, and socially. Maybe a married

couple, two singles, and a same-sex couple, all from different racial or ethnic backgrounds. Send the group on a camp-out where they'll roast meat over an open fire and sitting around chatting or singing, like a Scout evening gathering. The aliens' curiosity will draw them in to investigate this strange human behavior in the face of a death sentence. The humans will welcome the aliens to the camp-out and casual chatting. Hopefully the informal route will lead to more formal discussions about Earth's problems.

2. Have a big party like Woodstock. Music is the universal language. Give them marijuana and they will give us a cure for the virus.
3. Have some humans volunteer themselves as a type of vicious pet to be sold across the galaxy for companionship and entertainment.
4. Hold a worldwide love-in. Include the aliens.
5. Invite the aliens to holiday celebrations, such as Thanksgiving, Christmas, etc.
6. Write giant messages of kindness that can be seen from space, such as "we love you" and "make peace, not war."
7. Have space shuttles cover the alien spaceships with flowers.
8. Turn Earth into a brothel, offering whatever passes for sex with the aliens in return for continued existence.
9. Find out what brings them pleasure and attack that weakness. Pleasure is always the downfall of dictatorial powers.

B. Contact the aliens on their starship or moonbase
1. Recommission the Space Shuttle and send representatives from Earth's population with an envoy to the quarantine ship or moonbase, broadcasting the message that we'd like to talk on its way.
2. Use a psychic to persuade the aliens to talk to us

C. Explain to the aliens what is good about humanity and hope they listen

1. The aliens would understand and trust the innocence of an unjaded child who still believes in the innate goodness of humanity. They could continue to quarantine the adults while gathering the Earth's children in a safe place, perhaps taking them to another galaxy to be raised with the values we once cherished and practiced. This would prove to the aliens humans are not born warlike.
2. Offer to share something good mankind has created, such as the cure for cancer or some other catastrophic illness.
3. Share the blueprints for McDonald's Golden Arches for the gateway to the alien world to greet travelers.
4. Offer the recipe for curly fries!
5. Disband all militaries and melt down all ships, missiles, tanks, military aircraft, guns, bombs, and bullets. Build a monument to galactic peace.

D. What gives POTUS the authority to negotiate for Earth?

1. I don't buy that the president of the United States has the authority to negotiate for humanity. Why would the UN or other international unions agree the POTUS has this power? Why would other countries, governments, or citizens agree to this? Who gave us the authority?

E. Attack them

1. Have the 1.2 million lawyers in the United States threaten to bring a collective galactic lawsuit against the GSCB, alleging discrimination against the human race. Compensatory and punitive damages sought will be 1.7 googolplex dollars (a sum larger than the number of atoms in the known universe). If successful, the lawsuit will bankrupt the GSCB and all the other species permitted to trade via wormholes, who will be named as codefendants of the lawsuit. This would result in the

destruction of the entire social and economic fabric of the galactic community. The mere threat of such a lawsuit will force the GSCB to relent and allow the human race to start procreating again. We'll settle for, say, 17 quintillion dollars and everyone will be happy. The lawyers will only be allowed to keep 15.5 quintillion dollars for services rendered.

2. The human body could be a weapon in itself. Technically we are a cloud of bacteria, fungus, parasites, and pathogens. An alien species will probably not be affected by things that have evolved to feed on us, but there must be a correlation if they were able to develop a biological infection for us.

3. Locate GSCB headquarters and send the virus back to them with their DNA in it.

4. Build a virus that attacks the alien immune system and turn it loose on Earth. If we can't have Earth, no one can.

5. Plant small nuclear devices into select seniors who volunteer themselves to the aliens as slaves. Once on board the starship, the devices are remotely exploded.

6. Have them eat at McDonald's!

7. Find out how they reproduce and develop a virus that neuters them; hold the antidote until they free Earth.

8. Send them Barack Obama!

9. Send them Hillary Clinton!

10. Send them Donald Trump!

F. Bypass them

1. Send a probe to Mars, where an organism will be found that can be injected into humans to make them fertile again. The new children would be faster and smarter than the aliens.

2. If we believe Albert Einstein, space and time are the same. Since we have managed to bypass distance by using wormholes, we should be able to bypass time, as

well. This should allow our physicists to travel back before the alien technology was used in the first place.

G. About the contest itself

1. One hundred million US dollars is too small of a prize for saving the humans on this planet.
2. The prize should be at least 10 billion. It's the end of mankind—go big.

H. What to do during the negotiations

1. Discuss ways to make human society more peaceful.
2. Point out that, if the aliens are willing to perform genocide on us, they are no better than what they have condemned us for. What they have done is the ultimate hypocrisy of using violence to enforce peace.
3. Determine a commodity only humans are capable of providing to the aliens. Maybe we have more robust immune systems due to our years of exposure to other types of germs the aliens have not had to deal with in eons (kind of like in *War of the Worlds*) and we can help bring about cures. Maybe there's a disease affecting the aliens that only humans have the ability to cure.
4. Point out that fighting is a positive survival skill. There are events in any civilization that require a violent response to survive. The aliens must know this since they can manufacture weapons such as the birth-control virus and throw entire cities into the sun. They have chosen when not to use these skills in a violent manner; they need to give mankind the ability to choose, too.
5. Tell them we understand why they've us under quarantine and ask how we can find a graceful, acceptable way to seek their forgiveness.

Robbins studied the list for several minutes, chuckling a few times. "I think the American Bar Association might have a little trouble with that lawsuit."

"Do you think they would want more?" Patty asked innocently.

The president shook his head in amusement. He'd been a lawyer before he'd decided to run for office. "There's nothing here that isn't stupid or that we haven't already thought of."

"Nope, nothing."

"Dammit."

Chapter 19 – Go Back to Work

The Honorable Gilford Dulton, congressional representative from New York City, was having a press conference. "I demand a congressional investigation be started into the Baby Machine utilization process. It is my belief that the babies that have been made to date do not represent the racial makeup of our great country. I think this is yet another attempt by the white people who control America to eliminate us, the nonwhite 'problem.' I demand to see the ethnic breakdown of the babies that have been produced so far and the ethnic breakdown of the people in the queue waiting for babies, by month."

A round of raucous applause came from the audience.

"The chart behind me shows the racial makeup of the United States. Caucasians make up sixty percent of the population; Hispanics eighteen percent; Blacks thirteen percent; Asians six percent; and the last three percent are Native Americans, Hawaiians, Inuits, people of mixed race, and people who refuse to identify themselves with one of the groups.

"It is my belief that the babies coming out of the Baby Machines do not reflect this same mix. I believe the numbers will show that almost all the babies that have been produced to date are white because only white people can afford the bribes that will put them at the top of the queue!"

Another round of applause filled the room.

"The whole system of deciding who gets a baby is corrupt. Black, brown, and yellow people are being put at the back of the bus yet again so the white people with money can sit in the front. I, for one, won't stand for it. Rosa Parks wouldn't do it in Montgomery, Alabama, on December 1 in 1955 and I won't do it today in Harlem."

… … … … … … …

"You no hire Bill Lewis. Bill Lewis no good."

Doug was having a little trouble understanding the words through the man's heavy Chinese accent on the other end of the phone call. "Why do you say he's 'no good'?"

"Bill Lewis lazy. Bill Lewis miss deliveries. Bill Lewis no maintain truck."

"He says you wouldn't pay him for his last week of work. Is that true?"

"Bill Lewis leave truck Calgary. Cost five hunerd dolla fly driver there so bring back Toronto. Truck out of gas when driver there—Bill Lewis leave truck running when park. Cost five hunerd dolla to fill tanks. Jinha Trucking no owe Bill Lewis nothing."

"How about his vacation time? He said you wouldn't give him his vacation time."

"Jinha Trucking no owe Bill Lewis nothing. Bill Lewis owe Jinha Trucking."

The line went dead.

... ...

"So, let me get this straight." Lily was angrier than Kevin had ever seen her. "You tapped our friend's phone line and you followed us when we left the money in the shack, which a drone, along with an army of state troopers, was watching, and you still lost the money?" Agent Lattimer had prepared himself for the tongue-lashing. After the one the station chief had given him, this would be a cakewalk. "Did it ever occur to you your efforts at catching the kidnappers might endanger Lan? How many times have you succeeded in getting a kidnapped child back?"

He couldn't tell them that, to the FBI, catching the kidnappers was more important than saving Lan. The political pressure on the Bureau to make some progress on the nationwide outbreak of kidnappings was far more important to the director than the life of one baby. "The statistics on kidnapping are well documented and available for public view, Lily. I'm sure you've seen them. Most kidnappings end with the victim dead. We were trying to keep that from happening to Lan."

"And arresting a bunch of dirt bikers while the kidnappers took our money from the shack was helping how?"

Lattimer decided to try to change the subject. "Have you had any contact with the kidnappers since they retrieved the money?"

"Gee, I would have thought that, with all your phone taps, you would have already known the answer."

"The FBI isn't the problem, Dr. Yuan. We're trying to help you get your child back."

"Time will tell on that one, Agent Lattimer. The FBI hasn't been too friendly to us in the last three years. This is just the next installment."

After Lily, Kevin, and Doug Medder invented the first Rosy transmitter that opened the first wormhole, the FBI had arrested them in the interests of national security and then kept them locked up at the Jet Propulsion Laboratories in Pasadena, California, for months without charging them with any crime. It wasn't until Doug escaped and the ACLU created public outcry that the government moved all Rosy research to Rosyville and gave them something like a normal amount of freedom. Of course, that freedom to come and go as they pleased had led directly to Lan's kidnapping.

He decided now wasn't the time to point out all the things the FBI *had* been doing to recover Lan: the roadblocks, composite sketches, news reports and interviews, investigating all the phony tips received about sightings, and the pressure the agents were putting on the criminal underground of Las Vegas to find the little girl and return her. The phone rang as Lily glared at him in silence.

Kevin picked up the phone from the cradle. "The baby is in room nineteen of the Cozy Rest Motel." He stood frozen in shock, staring at Lily with the phone still to his ear.

"What?" she demanded loudly. "What did it say? Who was on the phone?"

"'The baby is in room 19 of the Cozy Rest motel.'" Lattimer pressed the secure radio comm button on his belt. "Central, this is Lattimer."

"We're on it, sir. ETA at the farthest one in about ten minutes."

"Where the hell is the Cozy Rest motel?"

"There are two within fifty miles of Vegas. We're going to both. One was right across the street from roadblock 5 on I-15. Should be there in about one minute."

Kevin, Lily, and Dott stared at him. They couldn't hear the radio traffic that came through the agent's ear bud. He repeated the message to them.

His earbud crackled to life again. "We have her—she's alive. We are transporting her to University Medical Center."

"They've got her," he repeated to them. "She's alive. They're taking her to University Medical Center so they can check her out. Please come with me—I can drive a lot faster than you can."

"What do you mean *alive*?" Lily asked in alarm. "Is she injured?"

He pressed the talk button on his radio as they got into his black Suburban. "This is Lattimer. I am en route with Lily and Kevin. Could you give me more information on Lan's status?" He pressed the Bluetooth button on the console so the response would come through the car sound system.

A voice came through the speakers. "Roger that. She's upset we took her away from her tray of fruit in the motel room...and she wants her mother."

They could hear Lan in the background. "I want fut!"

"Ten-four. Lattimer out." He turned on his emergency lights, put the car in gear, and began driving toward the hospital with the siren wailing.

"That's our girl," Kevin said, tears starting down his cheeks as he squeezed Lily's hand so hard that it hurt. "Don't get between her and a bowl of fruit."

... ...

Doug searched online for complaints against Jinha Trucking Company. There were many, and several drivers had gotten the government to arbitrate confidential settlements between themselves and the company. In all cases, Jinha Trucking was on the losing end of the arbitration. Denial of vacation, nonpayment of overtime, nonpayment of worked hours, and unsafe operation of vehicles from poor maintenance seemed to be the most common complaints. Eight other cases were still pending—two were criminal indictments brought by the Ontario Provincial Department of Transportation about poorly maintained trucks that had been involved in auto accidents with fatalities. Angie's List showed even more complaints, most by ex-customers, for late deliveries, overcharging for services, and lost shipments. A search on his new farmhand was nonproductive. There were twenty-nine people named Bill Lewis or William Lewis in Toronto alone.

He walked into the kitchen and handed the list to Clara. "Everything he said checked out." She studied the list without comment and then continued making the pie she'd started. "Does that mean I can go back to work at the Centre?"

Clara sighed. "Doug, I know your search supported what Bill said and I have seen how hard he works around here, but I can't shake the feeling in my gut whenever I look into his eyes." She sighed again. "Go back to work at the Centre."

Doug was conflicted. He knew that Clara was uneasy about Bill being on the farm while she and Mindy were alone in the house, but he also felt pulled by his job to be working at the Centre where his daily interaction with the development and research teams was vital to the progress of the projects in which he was participating. "OK, let's do this. You collect your schoolbooks and come with me. I'll drop you at the library in Calgary and pick you up when I finish work. I'll contact an investigator today to do a thorough background check on Bill. We have his ITN. That should allow the person to find anything weird in Bill's history. We'll do this until the report comes back on Bill."

"Give me a few minutes to get ready."

"OK. I'll warm up the truck." He put on his jacket and walked outside. A few snowflakes drifted around the driveway as he started the motor and waited for Clara to come out.

She watched him through the kitchen window and then picked up her phone and did a search for "CFSC Alberta," the Canadian Firearms Safety Course. The closest one was in Calgary, beginning in two days. Taking the one-day course was the first step in the Canadian firearm ownership process. The location was two blocks from the library.

Chapter 20 – I'll Make Some Calls

The smells as they entered Pirate's Alley were awesome. After living on quarantine rations for two years, everyone's stomach was anticipating real food. The name Pirate's Alley was a misnomer. Millennia ago it may have started as an alley in Inshasa, by far the largest city of Taramon, but long ago it had grown out of that small area. The Alley now encompassed over half of the city and, if the construction going on everywhere was any indication, more was being committed to it every day. Any vice you could think of was on display as Captain Xanny and his crew wound through the labyrinth of streets. Whores and pimps of every species worked the crowds and beckoned from storefronts. For the right price, visitors could find almost any kind of drug, delicacy, or self-indulgence. Gold, silver, jewels, antiques, art, and tapestries from a thousand worlds were on display, and exotic pets hopped from cage to cage.

A primate girl with four arms stumbled into Lieutenant Fibari. The girl had reddish skin, almost orange, with white hair. Fela grabbed the girl's arm as it reached inside her vest for her money. "I'm probably not the right person to try that on," she whispered.

The girl tried to pull her arm free, wiggling around. "Let go of me, you *pervert!*" Fela kept hold of the struggling girl, waiting.

"What's going on here?" a uniformed yellow and black arachnid asked, stepping up.

"Your protégé tried to pick my pocket," she told him. Xanny turned around and remained floating nearby, smiling. He motioned for Flug to watch but not interfere.

"I've never seen her before," the arachnid said. "Papers, please."

"Now where did I put my papers?" Fela seemed a little confused. "Oh yeah, I have 'em right here." She reached into her vest and pulled out her laser, pointing it at the arachnid's chest. It froze. "Try those guys over there," she whispered, indicating a group of well-dressed avians on the other side of the narrow thoroughfare. They were gawking and pointing like they were walking down the main street of a carnival sideshow. "You'll have better luck with them."

The arachnid glared at the girl. "I told you they were the ones!" She eyed the avians.

"I'd go for the female behind the one in front. She thinks she's in charge and isn't paying any attention to who bumps into her. Better hurry before those other guys get her first." A boy was following the avians closely, waiting for his chance.

The landing party left the two pickpockets behind and continued down the street.

The captain led the group to a bar with a sign over the door that said "He's Not Here." The inside was smoky and dim. The heavy smell of incense couldn't quite cover the other smells of burning herbs and fungi the Ur had banned across most of the civilized galaxy. A deeply tanned primate with a razor-thin beard line that followed his jaw and then went up over his mouth came up to them.

"Captain Xanny," he hissed, "welcome back to my establishment. It's been many years since you visited last. I heard you went legitimate."

"The only thing constant is change, Girba. How's your wife?"

"She still tolerates me." The proprietor shrugged. "I don't know why."

"Tell Loisha I still think about her stew on lonely nights. It's a memory I cherish."

"You can tell her yourself—she's in the kitchen working her magic. I'll tell her you've returned."

"You wouldn't have a cold bottle of queetle for an old adventurer, would you?"

"For you, my friend, you have only to ask." He held up his hand and snapped his fingers, and an animal scurried out from behind the bar. It was about the size of a German shepherd, perhaps forty kilograms, but its body shape was more like a badger.

"Bottles of queetle for the captain and his crew, Annadel." It rushed away. Girba showed them to a table against the back wall with a clear view of everything, and Annadel brought them four bottles in a carrier strapped across its back.

A shriek came from the kitchen and the doors flew open. A buxom, heavyset, middle-aged, female primate with long red braids ran into the bar, looked around, and then ran directly at their captain. Flug started to pull up his machine gun. Fibari put her paw on his arm and shook her head, trying not to laugh.

The woman pulled Xanny to her ample breast. "I knew you'd come back someday, Irkoo. Being legitimate can only last so long for someone with pirate blood in his veins."

"I have something for you, Loisha."

Her green eyes grew wide. "You don't mean..." He pulled a small packet from the pouch slung next to his anti-grav unit.

Fela nodded, finally understanding. *This* was why they had stopped at Planet Oonam on the way to Taramon—to pick up that little bundle of forbidden herbs. The captain had not let anyone accompany him when he left the shuttle.

"Don't use them all at once. They're getting a little hard to find."

She took the small packet reverently. "No one even knows where to *look* for these anymore. It just takes a pinch, but that pinch is sooo important."

"I was thinking you might find time to make some of your magic stew while we're here," he suggested hopefully.

"It's been a while." She got a faraway look in her eyes. "I'll have to see if I can find all the ingredients. Maybe in two days. Will you still be here?"

"Whether I'll be here depends on if I can find another old friend."

She eyed him speculatively. "And who might that be? As if I didn't know."

"Have you seen him?"

"No, I haven't. I expect he won't come in here again, not after the last time. But the rumor is he's here and"—she peered into the

dark corners of the room and lowered her voice to a whisper—
"you aren't the only one trying to find him."

"Really?" he asked, absorbing this new detail with interest.
"Another old friend wanting to renew their relationship?"

"Well, *friend* might be a stretch," she said nervously, looking
around again. "They didn't seem too friendly when they came in
asking."

"Who were they, Loisha?"

"I would have said Ur until they started talking. They had to
be mercs."

"Mercenaries? Who did he piss off enough that they would
hire mercs to settle the score?"

"No idea, but those sons of a monkrus were evil. At least the
Ur troopers have to follow the law. I don't think those mercs follow
much of anything but money."

"Any idea where they went next?"

"I overheard they were going to the Cauldron and Kettle."

"The witches? Are they still here?"

Fela had been studying Xanny's face as soon as she heard
Cauldron and Kettle. His relationship with the head witch,
Xirandra, had always been a mystery to her. While is voice was
noncommittal, he had a soft smile on his face that looked almost
affectionate.

Loisha continued, "Yep. Xirandra died—or at least that's
what the other witches said. Knowing those people, I'd bet her
death wasn't exactly *natural*."

"Who's running the show now?" the captain sounded
disappointed.

"A young witch named Zuna. Rumor has it she's Xirandra's
daughter."

"Why would the mercs go there?" he wondered out loud.

Two bipedal pachyderms jumped up, knocking over the
table between them. They weren't large as pachyderms go—
possibly three hundred kilos each.

"You take that back!" one of them screamed.

The other shrugged. "Not likely! Your sister is a whore and I had her. She wasn't too bad, as whores go."

The first pachyderm pulled a laser, but the second one was ready. They traded shots. Both missed.

"The next shot will be your last." Girba had his under-the-bar laser out and aimed at the two. He centered his laser dot in low-powered, aiming mode on the chest of the one who'd fired first. "And I won't miss. Pay your bill and leave. Now."

... ...

"Mama!" Lan squealed as Lily ran into the examination room.

Lily scooped up her daughter and held her tightly. "Lan! Lan! Oh, my baby girl!"

"Mama! Stop! Hurt me."

Lily quit squeezing her so hard. Kevin was right behind Lily. He put his arms around them both. Dott hung back, letting the family have their moment.

The doctor who had been examining the little girl waited until they finished. "She's in pretty good condition, actually," he began. "She has some bruising on her stomach and thighs—I think she was pinched. There was no sexual abuse."

"Aunt Louie pinch me!" Lan said vehemently. "I no like her."

"Other than the bruises, she has no damage that I can see. She's been fed and bathed regularly and kept in clean clothes. Someone has taken good care of her. I've seen a lot worse."

"Can we take her home now?"

"Well, you need to fill out the insurance forms at the admissions desk but, yeah, after that you're free to go."

Agent Lattimer spoke up, "We have a psychologist who specializes in child kidnappings. We'd like her to talk to Lan, if that's alright with you. We may be able to glean more details of the kidnappers and how they operate." Both parents stared at him, hostile. Lattimer backpedaled quickly. "Tomorrow! Tomorrow would be fine. I didn't mean tonight."

"We'll talk tomorrow, Agent Lattimer," Lily told him.

Kevin walked to the door. "I'll go do the paperwork. You stay with her. I'll come back when we're ready to go." He turned to the agent. "When I finish, I'll need a ride back to Dott's to retrieve my car."

"Not a problem. Let me know when you're ready to go."

"Kevin, where are we going to get a car seat?" Lily asked. Lan's old seat had been burned with their car. "I'm not leaving without a car seat to keep her safe."

"I have no idea. Everyone has dumped their toddler stuff. I'll check Walmart and Target on the way back. Someone has to have one."

"Check that secondhand shop on West Flamingo," she suggested. "I imagine you'll have better luck there."

Dott spoke up. "Why don't you two relax in here for a few minutes and enjoy having Lan back? I'll make some calls. I'd be willing to bet someone in the Mothers Brigade will have one. A few of our members have kind of a problem with throwing things away."

Chapter 21 – One of Us Gonna Die

Rebecca was gone. She'd taken the pistol she'd grown fond of—the Walther PPK .380—, her clothes, and the Lexus. Jeremiah sighed. He'd both expected her to leave and prayed she wouldn't. She'd stuck around for two weeks instead of the one she'd promised him when they got here, and a glimmer of hope began to grow in him that, once she'd gotten over feeling like she'd been kidnapped from LA, she would begin to like it up here.

The PPK was her favorite of all the firearms he'd brought with them. She'd learned to fire it and then practiced every day with him as they'd both gotten better. She'd named it Sean, after Sean Connery. The Walther was James Bond's signature weapon: easy to conceal, very accurate, and very deadly.

Without her knowledge, Jeremiah had moved almost all their money out of their joint accounts and into a new private account under a different name and social security number. The twenty grand he'd paid for the ID and number had been worth it. There was only a thousand dollars left in their joint account, and if her past spending was any indicator, she would burn through it pretty quickly. Maybe she'd come back, maybe she wouldn't—time would tell on that one. For now, he needed a ride to Sonora to buy a truck.

The Lexus was great in LA for impressing their friends, trips to the bar, or a ride on the beach if the sand was firm enough. Up here, he needed a truck—something with four-wheel drive, oversize snow tires, a winch, a cargo capacity of a ton or more, and a dark energy power plant. Last month, Toyota announced a truck with all of that. The ninety-thousand-dollar price tag had made him gulp, but that was the cost of progress, even with the additional ten thousand on top of the sticker price for the dark energy taxes the Feds and the State of California had added.

Since the dark energy vehicles weren't using gasoline or diesel, the fuel tax revenues to maintain the roads had fallen steadily. The governments had put a new tax on the dark energy vehicles up front to offset the lost revenues. After so many years of the government encouraging people to use less nonrenewable energy, there was a lot of anger from the owners of such sustainable vehicles. To make matters worse, the governments weren't putting any of the dark energy taxes into savings for road maintenance; instead, all the money went into the general fund, where they used it to pay for social programs. It was typical government double-speak: "Quit using so much non-renewable energy, but, my goodness, don't quit paying taxes on the energy you aren't using anymore."

A diesel truck costing seventy thousand dollars three years ago was now selling for thirty thousand at the GMC dealership. Even if he installed a five-thousand-gallon tank of stabilized diesel behind his cabin, the cost would have been less than half of the Toyota—diesel was down to a dollar a gallon. The Toyota, however, was cool with a capital C and he had not completely lost his LA Cool yet. Besides, he told himself, money was going to be meaningless after the collapse, and he still had over three quarters of what he'd made selling their condo. He could buy five of those Toyotas, with money left over.

He'd have to stop at the Guns and Ammo store while he was in Sonora. He wanted another PPK to replace the one Rebecca took, and he had a flyer from the store about a bulk ammo sale. As long as he was down in Sonora anyway, it wouldn't hurt to stock up a little for the deer rifle and the very illegal AK-47 he'd bought in the city before they left. They might even have one of the Desert Eagle .50 pistol combos they said they would stock. It had the same leather shoulder holster Vinnie "Bullet-Tooth Tony" Jones had used in the movie *Snatch*. It even came with a bullet tooth stick-on to complete the effect. They also had a huge stockpile of military surplus Meals Ready to Eat he could buy, now that he didn't have to worry about his wife bitching at him about there being no room to move around inside the cabin.

He walked to the bedroom to retrieve his wallet from the locked drawer in the nightstand where he kept it while he was up here, and his heart skipped a beat. The drawer was unlocked and open. He grabbed his wallet; his new ID and credit cards under his new name were gone. Also missing was the slip of paper with the new bank account numbers and PINs. He grabbed for his phone. A message saying "No SIM Card Installed" displayed on the screen. He jumped to the laptop; the battery was gone along with the AC adapter.

He ran outside the cabin. "REBECCA! YOU *BITCH!*" he screamed.

Far below him, at the mouth of the valley, the Lexus turned onto the road toward Sonora. The echo of his scream came back to Jeremiah again and again, fainter each time, almost as if it were mocking him.

… … … … … … …

Clara prepared to aim her new .40 caliber H & K subcompact pistol. She mentally talked herself through the steps on target acquisition. *Make sure it's something you want to shoot. Take a breath. Let half of it out. Raise the pistol. Sight it. Squeeze the trigger, keeping the target in the sight.*

The gun jumped in her hand.

"A little low and to the left," the coach said beside her.

She went through the motions again.

"High and left—closer than before"

Her grouping was slowly becoming smaller. She spent her entire lunch hour every day at the range two blocks from the law office where she worked. She had not told Doug about her training. She could now load, fire, and clean the little pistol, and she kept it in her locked briefcase when she was home. She'd been concerned little Martin would find it and hurt himself or someone else.

She sighted again and squeezed.

"You nicked the bull, Clara. Good job! Let's run it out another ten feet. I want you to use the upper left bull."

Each target contained six bull's-eyes printed on it; she shot three rounds at each. Once she finished with the stationary phase, she would graduate into the flip phase. One of six targets on her firing lane would flip into view when the coach pressed a button.

One or more of them would be something you didn't want to shoot—a little girl, an office worker, or maybe a cop.

Once she mastered that, she would graduate into the holstered phase. It was on the same range as the flip phase, but she began each session with her gun in its holster. The last phase was walking. She would walk through a SWAT training range with her pistol holstered and have to acquire and shoot each target as it appeared, first making sure it was something she wanted to kill. There were more targets than bullets in her magazine, which meant she would have to reload and continue.

... ...

Bill came in from his chores for lunch and sat at the kitchen table. Mindy ignored him. He decided to try to break through to her one more time. "So, where did you grow up, Mindy?"

She glanced at him and then looked away, keeping silent. Instead of answering, she put a plate in front of him with a roast beef sandwich, a cup of soup, and some chips on it. Bill reached for the sandwich.

"I guess we got off on the wrong foot. I'm sorry if I offended you. This is a big change for me, workin' here. Truckers don't have to be nice or even polite to nobody, and livin' on the street is even worse. I like this job. I like the food you feed me—beats the hell out of dumpster diving for dinner. Can't we try to get along? I mean, I will if you will."

She returned to washing the dishes and remained silent for a while. Bill decided he'd failed again. "Oakland," Mindy said, breaking the silence. "Oakland, California."

"Oakland? How the hell did you get to Calgary from there?"

"That's not a very happy story," she told him. "I'd as soon forget about it."

"I understand what an unhappy story is. Mine started out in Georgia." He told her about growing up in a religious commune with a father who believed he could beat Satan out of his children.

The day he turned fourteen, Bill had decided to beat back. He'd left home with his father unconscious on the floor and never returned.

"Is he still alive?"

"No idea. Don't care. That old son of a bitch can rot in hell; I hope he's already there. Don't you have someone you hate more than life itself?"

The image of Jonah, her pimp in Oakland, rose in front of her. She remembered the last day she'd seen him like it was yesterday. She'd gotten pregnant from one of the johns, and Jonah had given her two days off so she could have an abortion. His parting words to her were clear in her mind, as if he'd just said them: "You get rid a that kid by the time you come back, or I'm gonna do it my own self." To emphasize his point, he'd pulled out his eight-inch ghetto knife and started sharpening it.

"Yeah, I got someone like that. Hope I never see him again. If I do, one of us gonna die."

With no alternative, she'd gone to Planned Parenthood and asked for an abortion. It was there that she'd met gentle, old Dr. Poppalov. Instead of just going ahead with the abortion she'd requested, he'd explained her options, one of which included a placement at the safe haven of Sunshine Ranch in Big Sur, California. His friend, Mona, spent two weeks detoxing Mindy from her heroin and meth addictions. Mona had washed the puke off her face, kept her covered or uncovered through the chills and sweats, and wiped her ass when she couldn't make it to the toilet in time. Six months later, Mona had held her hand while Martin was born.

She heard her son flush the toilet upstairs. He'd been taking his morning nap; he'd be down in the kitchen in a minute, looking for lunch. She got out the plate of chicken fingers she'd made for dinner last night—Martin loved her chicken fingers—and she began to cut up an apple to go with them as he walked through the doorway.

"I'm hungry, Mama," he said, sitting down at the kitchen table.

She put his plate in front of him, followed by a sippy cup filled with milk.

Bill got up. "I got to get back to work in the barn. Doug got some new, heated water dispensers for the stalls. Somehow I got to install 'em and route water to 'em before it freezes in the pipes." He turned to Martin. "If your mama say it's alright, you can sit on the tractor while I clean the stalls."

"Please, Mama? Please?"

She looked back and forth between them. "We'll go out for a little while after I finish the dishes, Martin."

Bill made a face at him and laughed when the little boy made one back. He pulled on his insulated coveralls and heavy jacket and then walked outside, toward the barn.

She watched Bill go, not sure what to think about him anymore.

Chapter 22 – I Would

Advanced Micro Devices announced availability of its new line of Quantum processors, or QP for short. These were the first CPUs utilizing the computer technology that IBM, AMD, and Intel had reverse engineered from the wormhole detector recovered from the moon two years ago. These processors used so little power that they produced negligible heat. They ran happily without a CPU fan in hothouse temperatures and were one hundred times faster than anything previously available by AMD or their competitors. AMD's stock doubled in value overnight with the same expected again over the next twenty-four hours.

Intel and IBM both issued press releases within two hours of AMD's announcement, telling the world about their own versions of the processors, named Wildhorse and BlueDiamond, respectively. Intel's Wildhorse was to be available within two months. IBM was putting its BlueDiamond into its new line of mainframes and servers, due to be available within six months.

NVIDIA announced a graphics controller based on the alien technology that they said would leave everything else in the graphics video market in the dust.

The NSA preordered five of the new IBM mainframes for its Nevada facial recognition and intelligence analysis server farm in Area 51.

Lenovo announced they would have a new line of tablets, notebooks, laptops, and desktops available with AMD's QP within six months. The mobile devices would be incorporating China's new argon-ion batteries that would run them for a full year between charges and reduced the battery weight to between two to five ounces, depending on the machine. Dell, Acer, Apple, and Hewlett-Packard did not respond to repeated requests for comment.

... ...

Air Canada issued a press release about the commencement of its first scheduled portal transportation service between Toronto Pearson International Airport in Ontario and Vancouver International Airport in British Columbia. This service allowed passengers and their baggage to move the thirty-four hundred kilometers between the airports in about twenty minutes. Pets and service animals were subject to the same restrictions as with airplane flights.

The Honorable Jennifer Holcombe, Canada's minister of transportation, was one of the passengers in the inaugural "flight." Canada TV had an interviewer ready as she stepped out of the transportation pod in Vancouver.

"I'm excited to be one of the first people to use this amazing new technology," she said, smiling into the camera. "Imagine, sitting down in Toronto and standing up in Vancouver twenty minutes later. This will allow travel throughout Canada to everyone at a fraction of the cost people have paid in the past for airplane seats. It produces none of the pollution the planes, trains, and cars have created until now. Once again Canada leads the world in creating peaceful uses of Rosy technology."

"Was there a beverage service, Minister Holcombe?"

She shook her head in amusement. "No, that would have just slowed us down. There's no first class either. You just take your seat, open a magazine, and before you finish the first article, you've arrived. It was amazing! When we started, there were a couple of soft bumps, the pod tipped down maybe fifteen degrees and filled with a rosy glow. I felt a gentle acceleration, a gentle deceleration, and then the glow disappeared. There was no noise except for the faint whine of an electric motor, and no jet lag. The only weird thing was how gravity changed when we went through the portal. In Toronto, we left pointing down. In Vancouver, we arrived pointing up. They tell me that's because we went through the Earth's crust in a straight line between the two airports—made my stomach do a little flip-flop. My grandkids will love that part. Some of the passengers put their arms up, like it was a roller coaster.

"You may not have noticed, but we have some pretty severe weather here in Canada. Flight delays and cancellations from foul weather are something all Canadians have suffered through, and inflight turbulence is a constant problem. This portal system will experience none of that.

"The real savings to everyone, though, is in the reduced fares, reduced use of fossil fuels, and reduced production of CO_2. As we expand the use of this technology, we expect the carbon produced by the airline industry to drop as quickly as the transportation industry has in the past two years. Canada is leading the world in reducing carbon emissions and our dependence on fossil fuels.

"Is Air Canada or WestJet going to offer frequent flyer miles for portal travel?"

"You'll have to ask the carriers about that. Thank you for your time. I have to meet some people here in Vancouver, but I hope to return to my home in Toronto this afternoon. My granddaughter has a soccer match that I would have missed before this service was available." She waved into the camera and stepped away from the microphone.

As Minister Holcombe, stepped away from the camera swung arounbd to the interviewer. "A week ago Melissa Mercury of the BBC interviewed Dr. Douglas Medder, the architect of the new system and a Nobel Laureate. We replay that interview now." Doug and Melissa, sitting in a studio, appeared on the screen.

"How long does the actual travel take, Dr. Medder?"

"The elapsed time is about ten seconds—that's how long it takes to open the portal and push the transportation pod through. It takes about a minute to move the pod into the sending station and align it with the receiving station, and another minute to move it out of receiving at the other end. By far the most time-consuming thing is getting everyone and their luggage into and out of the pod."

"How many passengers do the pods hold?"

"They have forty seats in ten rows of four, with a central aisle. Baggage is put into a chamber behind the passenger compartment or in the overhead storage."

"Do they have any windows?"

"Nope. There's nothing to see but the sending and receiving stations."

"When are other airports going to be included in the network of Rosy portals?"

"Eight are under construction. We're using the same technology we've been using with the freight transfer system inaugurated two years ago. Minister Holcombe is rolling out as many as she feels we can, while concurrently maintaining the same level of safety for the passengers and the system."

"Why are you using the airport terminals as launch points? Why not put them on every street corner?"

"The safety of passengers as they travel from one place to another has always been the highest priority for the Canadian government. The airports already have secure transportation hubs in place; we are just building onto that existing security and safety."

"Which airports will be next?"

"In order: Montreal, Calgary, Ottawa, Edmonton, Quebec, Winnipeg, Saskatoon, and Halifax."

"Is international travel on the horizon?"

"That's not up to me, Melissa; it's up to the Canadian government and Minister Holcombe. There is no scientific reason two countries can't put portal travel in place immediately, but like the freight system, the governments involved will have to address many safety, border crossing, and customs concerns before we can implement it. What I can say is we've had many inquiries from governments around the world about buying the equipment for portal transportation from Canada. Portal transportation is the fastest-growing manufacturing sector in our country now, and I expect that to continue into the foreseeable future."

Melissa had reached the end of her prearranged questions and she had one more that was pure curiosity. "Dr. Medder, if Australia and Canada ever allowed Rosy travel between them, what would it be like?"

Doug didn't understand her question. "Do you mean what would it be like to be in Australia? No different from now, I expect."

"I mean what would travel through the portal be like? Australia is on the other side of Earth—we are upside down compared to them. When the pod makes the jump through the portal, it would start by falling straight down and end by falling straight up."

"It would be pretty exciting," Doug agreed with a faraway look. "If that was a problem for anyone, though, they could make the trip by taking multiple smaller jumps, much like the airplane connections of today—jump from here to LA, to Hawai'i, to the Marshall Islands, and to Australia."

... ...

Byteen, executive officer to Captain Fey Pey, pressed the comm button. "Captain Pey, another five crew members have failed to return from Pirate's Alley. The ones who did return are in pretty rough shape. Three are in sick bay."

"Anyone dead?"

"Not that I know of."

"They're just burnin' off some excess energy. You can't blame them. Three years under water will make anyone a little crazy."

"Should I put out the word we're hiring?"

"No, not yet. Give the crew a little leeway—they've been with me a long time." To himself he muttered, "Hard to believe they'd sign on with someone else with me still owing them all their back pay." Then he asked the question he'd been dreading. "Is anyone important missing?"

"Computer Tech Gilliam, Electrician Mate Yardley, and Armament Officer Teech haven't reported back yet."

"Where do their locators show them?"

Byteen touched an app on his hologram. A three-dimensional display of the space traffic around Taramon appeared in front of him. "Gilliam and Teech show as on the *Choona*." He touched the image of the *Choona*; a side-bar popped up next to it. "They filed for a space-available exit path this morning. Yardley's on the *Xerx* along with Bawt, who went missing yesterday. They're supposed to leave tomorrow."

"Bawt, too? Damn. He was a good analyst." He pondered what to do while he watched Taramon in the display. "Dock rats!" he spat. "There used to be a code among pirates." He stopped himself. The "code" meant whoever paid the most, got the best people.

The money he'd been promised in the Earth contract had disappeared while he was stuck there. Instead, a bunch of mercenaries waited for him to show up down on the surface. The funds from his emergency account should arrive today so he could pay the crew and get the refit going. After that was complete, he was going to pay a visit to some people who didn't want to meet him very much. They had sure been in a hurry when they sent him to Earth.

"Three other ships have announced that anyone who wants to leave *Easy Wind* is welcome aboard. Two are offering signing bonuses for anyone in analysis or piloting."

Fey Pey sighed. "I suppose we should see if anyone wants to sign on. Maybe we'll get lucky. Make me a list of positions we need to fill, and announce to the crew payday is tomorrow. That should slow the rats from jumping ship."

... ...

Lily's earbud rang while she was doing the dishes. She tapped it with the back of her hand to answer. "Hello?"

Doug's voice greeted her. "Lily?"

"Doug? Is that you?"

"Yep."

"It's great to hear from you," she said, drying her hands on a kitchen towel. "How's Clara?"

"We're fine. How's Lan? Is she okay?"

"Other than asking where Unca Ernie is every so often, she hasn't shown any adverse side effects."

"Who the hell is Unca Ernie?"

"One of the kidnappers, we think."

"Damn."

"So what's going on?" Lily picked up her cold cup of tea and put it in the microwave.

"Clara and I were thinking about taking a vacation. She has a house in a little village in southern British Columbia her grandparents left her, and we were wondering if you three would like to meet us there. The house is plenty big enough for everyone and we would love to meet Lan. We thought maybe you and Kevin would like to get away for a little while after all the turmoil."

There was a long pause. "I don't know, Doug. We haven't left Rosyville since we got Lan back. I'll have to ask Kevin. When do I need to tell you our decision?"

"We were thinking of leaving Calgary this weekend."

Today was Wednesday. "What's the closest airport?"

"Spokane, Washington, on the US side. Canadian Rockies International on the Canada side."

Lily paused again, trying to make the butterflies in her stomach go away. Even the thought of leaving Rosyville made her begin to tremble all over.

"If you flew to Calgary, we could all drive down together," he suggested, hoping they would agree. He missed his friends.

"Let me talk to Kevin. I'll call you back this evening."

"Okay. Bye."

"Bye, Doug."

... ...

President Robbins had called a meeting of his entire support staff in the press briefing room at the White House. He told everyone from the cabinet secretaries to the secretaries to attend, and this unusual meeting had everyone wondering what the subject would be. The room went silent when he walked in.

"Everyone keep your seats. This isn't a formal meeting. I will ask questions. If you have an idea or an answer, speak up. My contest hasn't come up with any suggestions I like on how to contact the aliens. While many of those suggestions were entertaining, my hope is someone here will have a perspective the contestants don't. I deliberately excluded you from the contest so there would be no question about it being impartial. Here is your chance." The room was utterly silent. "Okay, let's begin. Does anyone have an idea of how to talk to the aliens?"

No one answered.

He thought for a moment and then decided on a different tack. "Okay. Let's go over what we do know about them. General Hagland, please recap for us."

"They have created an outpost on the back side of the moon," his secretary of defense told the group, "but they keep moving its location, making it impossible to attack. Every time someone begins to build a starship, they send it into the sun. If we attack them, they retaliate massively. We know of two different species onboard the ship, but interviews with the three students who were taken to the ship indicated there are many other species as well."

Robbins spoke up again. "I have tried to initiate a dialogue with them since I came into office, but they won't respond to my requests. They divert into the sun anything we send near them on the moon. How can we get through to them? There has to be a way." He motioned to his chief of staff. "Patty, what do you do when you want to talk to your husband?"

She chuckled. "I buy him a bottle of Scotch and then help him drink it." A wave a laugher rolled through the room.

"Somehow I don't think that would work with these guys."

"Couldn't hurt. Maybe they'll like Scotch. I'll donate a bottle of my husband's favorite." The room laughed again.

"How about an unarmed solo envoy?" a voice said from the back of the room.

Everyone turned to see who was speaking, a woman stood. "Sir, my name is Leann Jenkins. I'm an intern here for this semester until classes start again at George Washington after Christmas break. The way I see it, the aliens have weapons that can defend themselves against any type of attack we might mount. We can't make them listen to us by being tough, so maybe we can get them to listen to us by being gentle. The only way to do that is to approach them helpless and defenseless. Just one person in a capsule with no armament and no way back to Earth. Announce what we are doing and why on every radio and TV channel you can think of. The worst that could happen is they would send the envoy home."

A pin dropping would have been loud in the room. No one could believe someone would suggest such a thing.

"What is your major, Leann?" the president asked, studying her while he absorbed her idea.

"Political science, Mr. President."

"Are you going to run for office after you graduate?"

"I had hoped to someday, sir."

"Let me know when you're ready. I'll introduce you to some people."

"I don't belong to your party, sir."

"If what you're suggesting works, it won't matter what party you belong to."

The secretary of homeland security spoke up. "Actually the worst that could happen with Leann's suggestion is the aliens continue to ignore us and the envoy continues past the moon and into deep space. With no way to retrieve them, the envoy would surely die."

"On the other hand, what if they don't ignore us?" President Robbins asked. "Does anyone have a better idea?"

No one raised their hand.

"Okay. Who should go?"

Again came silence. No one was going to volunteer for what would probably be a suicide mission.

"I would, sir," Leann spoke up.

"Okay, that's one person. I will convene a meeting of the National Security Council to see who else should be considered. This may be the most important job in the history of mankind. We want to make sure we send the correct person."

Chapter 23 – I Think She's Hungry

Clara's phone rang as she was studying for a test in her evidence class. It was a number she didn't recognize. She picked up the phone. "Hello?"

"Clara?"

"Yes. Who is this?"

"Clara, this is Lily Yuan."

"Hi, Lily. So I finally get to talk to you?" She got up with her phone tucked between her chin and shoulder and walked toward the coffee pot.

"I understand the feeling. Every time we talk to Doug, he tells us all about you, the farm, Mindy, and Martin."

"Doug has told me so much about you and Kevin and your time together at Stanford that I feel like you're an old friend. How's Lan? Has she recovered?" She poured a cup of coffee and settled into a chair at the kitchen table.

"She's healthy, happy, and driving me crazy. From what I've read, that's normal for a two-year-old."

"I can't wait to meet her. Are you three coming up this weekend?"

Lily took a breath. She didn't think it would be this hard; her hands shook, and her stomach was in knots. "Yes, we are. I have to overcome this fear of leaving Rosyville. The longer I wait, the harder it's going to be. We've rented a jet to fly us to Calgary—I didn't want to chance public transportation yet." She didn't mention the armed guards she'd hired to accompany them to the Las Vegas airport. "We're scheduled to arrive at 6 P.M. on Friday. Can you meet us at the airport? Do they have a bizjet terminal?"

"I don't have any idea, but YYC is a big airport—I'd be surprised if they didn't. We'll find what they have and be waiting for you there."

"We'll still have to go through customs, and I have no idea how long that will take."

"Doesn't matter—we'll be waiting for you when you finish."

"Thanks, Clara."

"See you on Friday."

... ...

The Cauldron and Kettle had changed; it was no longer the brightly lit entertainment bar Captain Xanny remembered. The wood floors, carnival atmosphere, and naked wait-staff were gone, replaced by a quiet bar with dim lights in which everyone was clothed. Randomly placed booths crowded the floor space and aisles wound between them, like paths through an English garden. All four walls of each booth had a floor to ceiling display panel with a fifth display panel on the ceiling, giving the appearance of not being walls at all. Each booth had its own three-dimensional sound system, so when the patrons sat, they entered an alternate reality.

The hostess, a young primate with long black hair, was dressed in traditional witch's garb. She was pretty, pale skinned with huge, dark eyes, and she wore a tight black dress with a low neckline. Xanny snorted. The movie production companies of the galaxy had built the witch standard. This woman was a walking stereotype.

She led the captain and his crew to their booth. As they passed the other booths, they saw each presented a different reality, customized to the home world of the beings seated there.

"My name is Clarrisse," their hostess purred. "Your server will be Shoa. She'll be here in a moment to take your orders. When you're ready, speak the word 'menu' and it will appear in front of you." Clarrisse backed away from them with a faint smile on her face, raised her hands, and clapped once. She dissolved into a multitude of sparkling dots that swirled around the booth, coalesced into a single dot over the middle of their table, and disappeared with a faint pop.

"Damned holograms keep getting better," the octopus grumbled. The apparition had fooled even him.

Their booth walls came to life. They were suddenly sitting on a featureless plain that spread around them to the horizon. It was nighttime, and there was one crescent moon, about two-thirds of the way across the sky. The wind whistled softly past them. Predators of different shapes and sizes would approach them from the plain, snarl, and fade back into the darkness until all you could see were glowing eyes that would blink and then move. The animals were never in clear focus but you got the impression they had massive muscles and teeth. Occasional lightning lit the landscape, revealing a herd of horned beasts grazing nearby. A rocky shoreline with crashing waves went from horizon to horizon. One of the grazing animals came down to drink. As it lowered its head, an enormous sea predator rose out of the water, grabbed the animal in its mouth, driving its huge teeth through the animal's body, and then slid back into the deep with the struggling beast.

Lieutenant Fibari stared at the panels in disbelief. "This is where I grew up. How did they know? My family's dwelling is over that hill."

The world had transfixed Corporal Flug; his eyes darted from one thing to the next. When a voice beside him spoke, he snapped his head around. Another beautiful primate sat next to him. She was as heavily muscled as he. Flug was raised on a gas giant with gravity three times that of Earth and he had twice the mass of a human male.

"Is this is your first visit to Cauldron and Kettle?" the woman asked Flug. He raised his hand to her breast; it passed through. The apparition gasped in fake modesty, her hand to her mouth. "That would get you killed on Aramere!"

"On Aramere, it wouldn't have passed through."

"I am Shoa," she announced to the three. "Would you like anything to eat or drink?"

"I want to talk to Xirandra. Is she available?" Loisha had told him she was dead. This was the only way to be sure

The image blinked, and an ugly fish body appeared for an instant where the muscled woman from Aramere had been. "Xirandra is...indisposed," she stammered, and then Shoa's image returned. "Can I help you?"

"Nah. The information I have is for her ears only. Tell her I'm here. My name is Irkoo."

"As you wish." Shoa disappeared.

The images of the animals on the plain changed to an underwater scene of a reef. You could see the combers passing by overhead and then crashing on the coral, the sound of the surf muted underwater. Fish swam in and out of the reef protuberances, occasionally eating or being eaten. They hid when a shark swam toward the table from out of the darkness; it passed out of one panel, across the middle of their table, and into the display on the other side.

Flug was in awe. "If this gets any more real, I'm going to need a towel!"

An octopus flowed down the side of the reef, settled on a mollusk, pulled it open, and fed on the contents inside.

"Irkoo!" A pink and white hyena with gray hair around its muzzle appeared beside him. A rune was branded into the hair between its orange eyes. "I thought I would never see you again."

"I heard you were dead, Xirandra."

"Not today," she said, laughing. "At least not yet."

"Where can we talk privately? Face to face."

"That would be a problem. Even the air has ears around here."

"Well, I agreed to try. My obligation is done." The captain turned to Fibari and Flug. "Ready to go?"

"You always were in a hurry, Irkoo."

"And you always were a bitch."

"That I am." She chuckled. "Come with me."

The hologram rose from the seat. The captain motioned for the other two to follow, using his left hand to make a pirate signal: be prepared for trouble. Flug flipped the safety off on his machine gun, coughing to cover the sound. The three of them walked behind Xirandra's image, moving slowly toward the back of the bar.

A door opened in a wall where there had been no door a moment before. Xirandra's hologram passed through, and the three followed her. The door closed soundlessly behind them and the hologram disappeared. Another door appeared and a real-looking

Xirandra walked through. She carefully appraised Lieutenant Fibari and Corporal Flug before sitting canine-style, and looking at Xanny. "What have you got?"

"Is that all you have to say to me after all the times I've shared your bed?" He sounded appalled. "Where's my kiss?" A split-second look of revulsion appeared on the hyena's face. "Zuna, quit fuckin' around. Is Xirandra dead?"

"Mother never slept with a *fucking octopus!*" she screamed as the old hyena morphed into a much younger one.

"Whatever you say. Is she dead?"

"Kind of."

"What the hell does that mean? Either she is or she isn't."

"She's in a coma. We can't wake her. She's been that way almost three years."

"So I talk to you or nothing, is that it?"

"Yes," she said defensively.

"I want to see her."

"Don't you believe me?" she asked, incredulous.

"A witch lying? What a concept! Now a witch telling the truth without being coerced? That would be one for the record books!" Zuna started to say something, but he interrupted her. "No, it's not that I don't believe you. I think I can wake her."

She looked at him, a mixture of hope and dread in her eyes. "What will it cost me?" Pirates never did anything for free.

"Some information."

"About a pirate fish and some mercs?"

"Why, Zuna, you really are telepathic! I never believed your mother when she told me."

She ignored his sarcasm. "Come with me." She traced a rune in the air, and a different doorway opened in the wall. They entered a well-lit, deserted corridor that led even farther into the labyrinth at the rear of the bar.

After they had walked for several minutes, she stopped in front of an unmarked doorway. She drew another rune; the doorway opened. Inside was Xirandra on a padded coma maintenance massage platform with the machines and feeding tubes keeping her alive connected to her. She had wasted away to half her previous mass. Much of her hair had fallen out, leaving patches of bare skin where the bones from her shoulders and hips rubbed against the gentle massage of the bed.

He lifted her front paw tenderly. "I need to be alone with her."

Zuna was resolute. "Not gonna happen."

"Do you want her back or should I let her die? She won't live another month the way she is now." Zuna wavered, unsure. "She told me this was going to happen fifty years ago. She knew her rejuv would eventually fail and told me what to do." He saw her make a decision. "*Fine!*" She turned and left the room.

The captain looked at Fibari and Flug and nodded toward the door. They left, and the door to the room slid shut. He approached the bed, remembering the last time he had seen Xirandra. She had said the words then—words he had not understood until today, until just now...

… … … … … … …

They had just finished making love. "Irkoo, I need you to remember something."

"Like how to make you feel like this?" He slid a tentacle over to her and rubbed her in that special place.

She smiled and stretched. "Yeah, that too, but that's not what I mean. Pay attention for a minute." She moved his tentacle away. "I had a vision last night."

"You mean a dream?"

"No, a vision. Dreams are make-believe, or sometimes they are what *could* be. Visions are different; they are what *will* be. Witches can tell one from the other."

"What did your vision say to you?"

"It said I was going to die."

"We're *all* gonna die, Xirandra! They punch your ticket when you're born. The only unknown is when and where it will happen."

She was exasperated. "Will you pay attention? I'm going to die, unless you prevent it."

All the humor left his voice. "What do I have to do?"

"You have to say some words and draw a rune in the air. And you have to do them perfectly. You will only have one chance."

"Tell me the words."

She did and then made him practice them until they were perfect. Next she showed him the rune and made him practice that until she was satisfied. "There's one more thing. You have to draw the rune and say the words at the same time. And you have to do it when I am dying."

Xanny started to do it.

"NO! Not now!" she said, panicked. "If you do it before I need them, you *will* kill me."

"Why me?"

"It has to be done by a person who has no ulterior motive— someone who is pure at heart."

"Well, that leaves me out!"

"You are the only one I can trust with this. Will you remember? Will you do it?"

"How will I know you need it? I don't come to Taramon very often."

"You will know—you'll be drawn here. Listen for the call. Promise me."

"I promise, Xirandra."

She got out of bed and walked to her altar. She picked up her altar knife and nicked her paw. Five drops of blood fell into a little bowl. She walked back to him and did the same with the end of his tentacle. Xirandra then mumbled some words and made a rune over the bowl. There was a flash and a small puff of smoke.

"It is done."

... ...

Captain Xanny studied her. The fur around her muzzle was completely white. As he began saying the words she had made him memorize, the air seemed to thicken. He lifted his tentacles and began drawing the rune in midair. It became visible, glowing

Page 152

brighter as he continued. The room began to rotate around them, but then he realized it wasn't the room that was rotating, it was them. He finished the rune and the last word at the same moment. A bolt of lightning struck out of the center of the rune, striking Xirandra in the chest. She exploded, covering him and the walls with bits of flesh and gore.

Zuna ran back into the room. "WHAT HAVE YOU *DONE*?" she screamed. "You've *KILLED* her!"

Xanny didn't move. From under the blood-soaked sheets, a newborn hyena crawled out. It wobbled to its feet and gave a laughing growl.

He scratched her under the chin. "I think she's hungry. Do you have any mothers with a litter?"

Hours later, Zuna held her mother in her lap. She was asleep with a full belly of milk.

"She knew you wouldn't do it," he told her gently. "She knew you wouldn't say the death spell, even if you drew the life rune at the same time."

Zuna looked down. "She was right. I couldn't have done it."

"That's why she had me do it."

"It could actually have killed her."

"Yep. She knew that."

They were both quiet for a while.

"I'm sorry for what I said about you and Mom being together. I'm glad she chose you. There aren't many males around here—at least males you can trust. I hope you stay around a while."

"What about Fey Pey and the mercs?"

"The mercs came in here about a week ago. They were looking for crew from *Easy Wind*. We didn't help them. No one likes Pey, but everyone hates mercs."

"Have they come in again?"

"Nope."

"How about anyone from *Easy Wind*?"

"Yeah, a couple of them came in last night. Fey Pey had finally paid them after hiding out on some world for three years. They were looking for sex and drugs and thought they would score a witch."

The captain laughed out loud. "How did that work out for them?"

"They should be waking up about now. The memories we planted will keep them warm for years to come. I hope they like their new ship and captain."

"Where did you send them?"

"With the *Xerx*. We got a nice thank-you note and the signing bonuses they would have paid the crew."

"Captain Yolli is a good commander, as arachnids go. They could have gotten a lot worse. What specialty did they have?"

"Analysis and weapons, as I remember. Yolli was ecstatic."

"He should be. Competent analysts are tough to find, especially in places like Taramon. Before I leave, I have one more question." He braced himself. This might not turn out well. "Did any witches sign on with Fey Pey three years ago? Someone who could plant a dream?"

She looked at him curiously. "Why would you ask that?"

He gave her the thumbnail on Earth, what had happened and what he suspected was the reason.

Zuna pondered his original question. "No witch would have anything to do with that. Our first and greatest law is: do no harm."

He knew she wasn't telling him something. "That doesn't answer my question."

She paused again and sighed. "There's a group that has been exiled for practicing what we call the dark arts. They live on Zindarr. It sounds like something one of them might do for enough money."

"Thanks for the info. Take care of your mom. I'll stop by before we depart."

"No, Irkoo, thank *you*." She leaned over and licked him under his chin—a hyena cub's kiss to a trusted adult, reserved for loved family members. "And you might want to take a dip in our ceremonial pool before you leave."

He looked down at himself. Bits of hyena flesh were drying and falling off him. "Yeah, you're probably right. Which way is it?"

Chapter 24 – On Automatic

"Samantha Evers?"

"Yes. Who is this?" She knew who it was—the gravelly voice was unmistakable.

"Your position in the queue has arrived. Do you want to go forward with Kayleen's cloning?"

For the past six weeks, Samantha had been alternating between ecstatic and terrified. She'd tried to convince herself this was a scam—that she should call the whole thing off before she gave him any more money. Kayleen's ghost had plagued her dreams every night, alternately begging to come back for another chance and then promising to kill herself again if she did. Every time Samantha wavered, she looked at her daughter's smiling picture on her fireplace mantel and reaffirmed her decision.

It had been six weeks and two days since she'd paid the ten thousand dollars to be assigned a place in the queue. She'd cleaned out half of her 401(k) retirement account to pay the rest of the fee. It was sitting in a suitcase in her closet—one hundred and eighty thousand dollars, eighteen bundles of hundred-dollar bills, one hundred bills per bundle.

She looked at Kayleen's picture. "Yes, I do." One way or another, she had to find out if she could make her daughter's life a happier one than it had been before.

"Terrific. Do you have the tissue sample?"

"Yes. I kept it frozen, as your instructions indicated."

"Excellent! Your next payment is ninety thousand dollars, in cash. They won't start the cloning process until they receive it. Do you have it ready?"

"Yes. I have it right here."

"Perfect. Meet me in the bar where we first met, say, in half an hour. Bring the cash and the tissue and park outside in their parking lot. It's a Friday night; there should be parking spaces all the way in the back. Don't go into the bar. I will come to you."

"I'll be there."

Twenty minutes later, Samantha sat in her SUV in the parking lot. She waited for fifteen minutes, watching people go in and out of the bar. The cook came out of the kitchen and smoked a cigarette. As he went back inside, a knock sounded on her passenger window. The gangster guy was standing beside her car.

She pressed the unlock button. "Hi. I was beginning to wonder if you were going to make it."

He got into the passenger seat and closed the door. "Just being careful. Where is the tissue sample and the cash?"

"Right here." She reached around to retrieve them from the back seat. She'd put the ninety thousand and the sample together in a paper grocery bag.

He opened the bag and reached into it, doing a quick count of the number of bundles. "You understand that, each month for nine months, you will owe an additional ten thousand dollars. You will receive a picture of the developing fetuses. There will be twenty at the beginning; these will dwindle across the nine months to only one. As long as you continue to make the payments, they will continue to grow. If you stop, the fetuses will be terminated."

"I understand all that."

"This is the thirteenth of March. Your first picture will arrive on the tenth of April. Your next payment is due on the thirteenth of April."

"Got it."

He paused. Besides getting paid, this was what he liked best; they were past the business part and he could now do the people part. He let down his business demeanor and relaxed a little. "So, Samantha, are you excited? Are you looking forward to having your daughter back in your life? Assuming they do the cloning in two days, she will arrive just before Christmas. Some present to yourself, huh?"

She didn't know how to answer that, so she smiled and said, "I better be excited. That's a lot of money to spend if I wasn't sure." She had not done the math yet—Christmas with a newborn! Now *that* would be something to look forward to. Her mind was spinning on overdrive. *It has been almost twenty years since a newborn has been in my house. Good Lord, this is really going to happen! A second chance with Kayleen! Am I going to fuck this one up, too?*

He picked up on her mixed feelings. "Yeah, it sure is, Samantha. This is a big step and you have a lot of planning to do. I'll see you in a month." He got out of the car with the bag, walked across the parking lot, and around the corner of the building.

She took another deep breath, started her car, and drove back home. It was time to start making lists; now *that* she was good at.

... ...

The Cessna Citation rolled to a stop at a gate at Calgary International Airport. The pilot came out of the cockpit. "Welcome to Calgary. Customs will be here in a minute, Dr. Yuan. Just sit tight. You filled out those customs forms I gave you, right?"

"Yes, we did."

"They are coming to us?" Kevin asked in amazement. "Customs is coming to us inside this plane?"

"Yes, sir. Just part of the service."

There was a knock on the door; the flight attendant opened it and lowered the steps. A young Indian woman in a customs uniform with her hair knotted in a bun at the back of her head, came into the cabin. She carried a laptop that she set up on a table. "Passports and customs declaration forms, please." They handed them to her. She held the passports up to the camera on the laptop and then held up the declaration forms. "Are you bringing any fruits or vegetables into Canada?"

Lan was wiggling around in her car seat, trying to release the straps. "Nope. Some crackers for Lan, but no fruit. She ate it all on the way up here." Lily unsnapped Lan.

The agent studied their customs declarations. "Do you have anything else to declare? Over the limit on alcohol? Excessive cash?"

"No, nothing. Just personal clothing and toilet articles."

"Do you have any firearms?"

"Nope," Kevin said. "Left them all at home." Lily gave him a wary look that told him to shut up. He tried to hide the twinkle in his eyes.

"How long will you be staying in Canada?"

"One week. We're meeting some friends and staying at their house."

The laptop beeped. The agent smiled, pulled out a stamp and inkpad, stamped their passports, and returned them to the Americans. "Welcome to Canada, Dr. Yuan and Dr. Langly. Enjoy your stay."

Lily picked up Lan and her pocketbook, Kevin grabbed the car seat and the baby bag, and they followed the agent out of the plane. While customs interviewed them, their baggage had been loaded into the Hummer stretch limousine waiting near the bottom of the stairs.

The agent got into her airport vehicle and left. The pilot shook Kevin's hand, bid them farewell, and then walked through a doorway into the terminal. The limo driver held the door open for Lily. Two other men with ominous bulges under their jackets stood nearby, looking away from the jet. Kevin came in behind her with the car seat.

The driver waited patiently while they got Lan's seat situated and her snapped into it. "Where would you like to go, sir?" The armed guards got in the front seats of the limo.

"We're meeting some friends in the main concourse, so there first"

Clara and Doug were waiting for them outside the security checkpoint. "How did you guys get past us?" Doug asked, amazed. "I didn't see you come through."

"We drove." Kevin smirked. "Lucky Jets had a limo waiting for us. The driver brought us to the drop-off area. He's still outside with all our luggage."

Doug hugged Lily. "How was your flight?"

"Smooth. I could get used to private jets." She hooked her arm into Clara's and they began walking toward the limo. "Tell me all about the farm."

The men followed behind them. "Damned shame your people-mover portal isn't in place between the US and Canada, Doug."

"The US doesn't seem interested in it. Don't know why."

Kevin shook his head. "Probably because it was invented in Canada by an ex-citizen who used to be on the FBI's Ten Most Wanted list."

"That and Homeland Security hasn't figured out how to expand their bureaucracy to cover all the portals," Doug agreed, shaking his head. "Canada actually reduced their security forces because of it up here. There are fewer trucks on the roads, less wear and tear, less maintenance, fewer accidents."

As they walked back to the limo, Doug noticed the armed guards trailing along behind them, paying attention to everyone but them. "Hey, Kevin, are those guys with you?"

"Yeah. Lily wanted them. Don't worry, they'll only be around until the limo drops us off at your place."

"My truck is in the parking garage—a red Ford pickup. I'll meet you where we pay the toll. Tell your driver to follow us to the farm. It's about fifteen kilometers."

… … … … … … … … …

The first bomb exploded at 3:01 A.M., Eastern Daylight Time, on Saturday morning, the fourteenth of March. It landed inside the White House, in President Robbins's bedroom. Over the next several minutes, hundreds more bombs from launch sites all over the world exploded within the District of Columbia and nearby suburbs, targeting Congress, congressional member homes, cabinet secretaries, Supreme Court justices, agency directors, generals, admirals, Camp David, the Pentagon, FBI headquarters, the NSA headquarters at Ft. Meade, and CIA headquarters at Langly, Virginia.

The United States' automatic retaliation software instantly launched counter strikes, and those responses were devastating— any site that had launched at a location inside the US had one or more bombs sent back to it five seconds later and then a dozen more sent at any military targets nearby. No presidential approval was necessary; with a Rosy attack, the National Security Council had decided there wasn't time to ask.

What the US had not anticipated was that the attackers knew this and had hidden their launch sites inside other countries in politically- or economically-sensitive locations. Some of those countries were allies of the US; some were adversaries. If they had a Rosy response system of their own, they returned retaliation fire of their own. Across the United States, every major fort, naval base, and air force base was blanketed.

In the previous world wars, the combatants on both sides performed carpet bombing—dropping hundreds of bombs on a target in the hope that a few would hit something important. Most of them did very little tactical damage.

Each Rosy bomb, however, was precisely targeted and the targeting didn't cost a million dollars each like cruise missiles. Rosy bombs were dumb thousand-pound devices that cost thirty-one hundred dollars each to manufacture. Explosives companies around the world had been manufacturing them nonstop for three years. They didn't have any guidance mechanisms or fancy fuses— ten seconds after they went through the portal, they blew up. None of them missed. If someone targeted a bunker or headquarters, it was hit.

North American Aerospace Defense Command (NORAD) headquarters in Cheyenne Mountain, Colorado, had four separate thousand-pound devices go off inside the command center within seconds of each other. Across the country, the bombs took out the US ability to attack, communicate, move, analyze, and defend itself. Fighters, bombers, submarines, aircraft carriers, motor pools, barracks, computer centers, internet hubs, refineries, conventional and nuclear power generation stations, dams, airports, banks, gold depositories, corporate headquarters, and bridges were destroyed. Since so many governments were throwing bombs, most targets got hit more than once.

Underground bunkers seemed to be favorites. Multiple governments had figured out the locations of each other's special little hidey-holes—the places countries hid their heads of state and critical staffs, in case they were attacked. In the US, the Minuteman III silos with their multiple independently-targetable reentry vehicle (MIRV) warheads were uniformly destroyed, as were the rocket bunkers in Russia, England, Ukraine, Korea, Iran, Pakistan, India, and China. The countries launching the attacks had created accurate enough coordinates to put a bomb inside them all. Most of those silos were built strongly enough to withstand a direct nuclear strike from above. That same strength kept the explosions contained within the silos. While the nukes themselves did not detonate, the solid fuel in the missiles exploded and temperatures inside the silos reached ten thousand degrees. The blast shields contained most of the atomized plutonium, uranium, and tritium.

A month before the attack, the US had completed the implementation of a new, second-generation response system based on the freight mover technology Canada had created. They built ten primary launch sites across the US in massive underground caves that contained from thirty-one thousand to ninety-eight thousand bombs. Huge feeder networks passed the unarmed bombs to one of ten Rosy launch mechanisms. Each device could send one bomb per second to repeater sites, where they were armed and then sent to their ultimate destination. This camouflaged the primaries from attack.

The repeaters contained no bombs until they were Rosied to them from the primaries. Since the repeaters were small, less than the size of a shipping container, they were very easy to conceal, very inexpensive to deploy, and they could target up to five different destinations simultaneously. The US had concealed them all over the world in countries they considered adversaries, at places the defense department considered sensitive. The countries targeted by the repeaters thought that was where the attacks were coming from and attacked those sites instead of the primaries. All that attacking a repeater accomplished was to have another repeater, somewhere else, become activated. China, Iran, and Russia had implemented similar technology and, like the US, had camouflaged their repeaters in *their* adversary's countries in sensitive locations.

The Three Hour War

A few minutes into the attack, friends or foes became indistinguishable. Bombs were flying from almost every country to every other country.

... ...

The sounds of explosions woke Rebecca. *Christ! What was that?* She looked at the clock on the nightstand; it displayed 12:11 A.M. She'd only been asleep an hour. *Not another effing earthquake! We had one last week, for god's sake.* Bright lights were dancing on the wall next to her bed. Another explosion rocked the apartment. She got out of bed and walked to the window, wrapping a robe around her shoulders.

When she arrived in LA, she had rented a furnished third-floor apartment in San Pedro next to the marina. The refineries in Long Beach across Los Angeles harbor were burning, huge flames and smoke ascended into the night sky. As she watched, Seal Beach lit up with a blinding flash. The Naval Weapons Station took five direct hits; the concussions rattled her windows. Secondary explosions began at both the refinery and the station's ammo dumps. The National Guard's 40th Infantry Division armory and motor pool blew up. Targets all over greater Los Angeles began to explode as the rain of bombs escalated. Emergency vehicle sirens began to fill the air in the lulls between the explosions. The harbor container storage facility took two enormous hits.

Rebecca realized this wasn't an accident—this was an attack. She grabbed the go-bag Jeremiah had made her prepare. It contained her PPK, extra magazines and ammo, changes of clothes, food and water, a heat-reflective tarp called a Space Blanket, six liters of water, ten MREs, a first-aid kit, and ten packs of twenty dollar bills, one hundred bills in a pack.

By the time she got to I-110, she was pushing a hundred miles an hour. Police cars, ambulances, and fire trucks passed her, going the other direction; they weren't interested in a speeding SUV.

At the Santa Monica exit on I-405, traffic slowed to a crawl. Bombs were still falling around Los Angeles like rain. The clock on the dash said 12:25 A.M. The overpass she crossed ten seconds earlier exploded behind her with a tremendous concussion that rocked her car. Flames had engulfed LAX, Los Angeles's gigantic international airport. Immense black clouds of smoke and flames from burning airliners, concourses, warehouses, hangars, and fuel depots were billowing up into the sky. Car accidents were everywhere.

A Jeep Cherokee scraped by the side of her Lexus and then continued up the shoulder, its horn blaring. She pulled in behind it, and they made it another mile until a car wreck on fire stopped their progress. All she could see through the smoke was the taillights of the few stopped cars that still had their headlights on. The line disappeared over the mountains toward the San Fernando Valley, and people were walking between the lanes. As the power grid failed, the lights went out across Los Angeles, leaving the city in total darkness.

Rebecca's car was wedged between the guardrail and the car next to her—she couldn't open any of the doors—and she was still dressed in her nightgown and robe. After changing into jeans, a shirt, and sneakers from the go-bag, she retrieved the flashlight from her glove box and pulled on the shoulder holster for the PPK. She pulled back the slide on the pistol to chamber a round, replaced the round from the extra ammo, made sure the safety was on, and slid it back into its holster, pulling her jacket on to hide the pistol.

Before she got out, an issue occurred to her. A steady stream of people were passing by the cars that were blocking her in and not a cop was in sight. If she needed money, it wouldn't turnout well if she dug into her go-bag and pulled out a wad of cash. Rebecca reached inside the bag to pull out ten twenties, stuffed a couple into each pocket of her pants, and then climbed out the passenger window, slinging the go-bag, which was also a backpack, onto her shoulders. She put her head down and joined the herd walking north on I-405.

As she walked, she remembered her wallet with her ID and credit cards were still on the dresser in her bedroom—right next to her cell phone, wired up to its charger.

... ...

It had been a long day for everyone. After Kevin and Lily finished unloading the limo and tipping the driver and guards, Clara had opened a bottle of wine to celebrate. That bottle led to a second.

Lily was enjoying the feel-good of being with her friends without the pressure of the world hanging on their shoulders. "This is just like the old days at Stanford."

Doug agreed. "When we were just three graduate students struggling to wrap our minds around quantum mechanics."

"Before Rosy, the FBI, JPL, and the octopus," Kevin added.

"Before the world went upside down," Clara said quietly. "Let's pray that doesn't happen again."

Just after midnight, Lily and Kevin finally got to lie down in the guest bedroom. Lan, as expected, had fallen asleep before they'd even left the airport. She was still asleep, on a pallet of folded blankets on the floor beside their bed. The clock on the nightstand showed 1:15 A.M.

"I like their house," Kevin said as they got into bed. "It must be beautiful in the summer."

"I'm sure it is." She was quiet for a while and then rolled over, so she was facing away from him. "Hold me. Please."

He spooned her, putting his arm around and cupping her breast. She snuggled in close to him, and they were silent for a couple of minutes.

"Is something wrong?" he asked. While she was always affectionate, she almost never asked to be held.

"I'm all out of sorts," she said after a moment. "I don't know why. Maybe it's because we're out of the safety net of Rosyville. I don't know."

They lay still for several more minutes. Kevin was beginning to fall asleep when Lily twisted around to face him again. "Make love to me."

Suddenly, sleep wasn't quite as alluring as it had been. "Give me a minute," he said, rubbing his face.

"I could help you with that," she giggled, reaching down between them.

He gasped. "Okay...you know...that'll work."

... ...

The intercom next to his bed on Air Force One popped on. "President Robbins?"

He answered sleepily, "Yes, what is it?"

"Sir, we need you in the conference room immediately."

He snapped wide awake. No one ever woke the president for something minor. "What's going on?"

"We've lost contact with Washington. There is substantial radio traffic from all over the country about explosions and fires. San Francisco reported they have taken direct hits on their primary and backup runways; we are diverting to Travis. We think the United States is under attack."

"I'll be right there."

Thirty seconds later he walked into the conference room in his bathrobe. "What's the status?"

General Rheem, his military attaché, spoke up from his console. "Travis just went offline. We are diverting to McChord."

"How bad is it?"

"Don't know yet, sir. It sounds pretty bad. Our Rosy response system has been active for nine minutes."

"Nine minutes!" the president said in alarm. "And they're still active? All of them?"

"Yes, sir."

"General, we are capable of firing a hundred bombs a second! That means we've already sent out..." He did the mental math. "Dear God! Fifty-four thousand bombs! Where the hell did we send them?"

"I don't know, sir. The centers are programmed to return fire at anyone who attacks us. The fact that our response centers are continuing to react means we are still receiving incoming fire."

"Who's attacking us?"

"We don't know yet, sir."

"Can I turn the response system off? Maybe if we stop, they will also."

"Yes, you can, sir, but if you do, I expect we will continue to receive fire. We didn't start this, sir—someone attacked us. If you turn off our defenses, we will be, well...defenseless. There's no telling how many Americans will die or how many already have."

This was the worst nightmare of any president—damned if you do, damned if you don't. He took a deep breath. "Stop the response centers."

"I will need that in writing, sir."

"Goddammit, General, I have given you a direct order! I am commander-in-chief. TURN THE RESPONSE CENTERS OFF!"

The general pursed his lips and started to say something, paused, then said instead, "Yes, sir."

Robbins checked the clock on the wall and watched each second tick off on the display. Each second meant we sent another one hundred bombs somewhere. Each device had a shrapnel blast radius of four hundred yards; it could burst through eight feet of concrete or fifteen inches of steel.

General Rheem spoke up ninety seconds later. "I was able to stop two of them. We cannot turn off the other eight. All communications to them are down."

"Even Rosy channels?"

"We haven't installed them yet. They were scheduled for next year."

President Robbins looked out the window of Air Force One. Every second, each of the remaining eight active response centers was sending ten new bombs out of the United States. Eighty new targets were hit and destroyed, ending lives and ways of lives— eighty new reasons to hate the United States. Those eighty bombs would precipitate at least eighty in response that would kill

Americans and destroy the American way of life, and he couldn't stop it. He was the most powerful man on Earth, and he was helpless to stop the disintegration of life as they knew it.

A tear wound down the side of his cheek. His wife came up behind him and put her arms around him as they watched the world crumble.

… … … … … … … … …

"Commander Chirra, please come to the bridge."

He floated in several minutes later. "What's happening, Shanti?"

"The primates are blowing each other up."

The real-time display of the bomb explosions all over the world was on the large bridge hologram. "Sound the alarm on the moonbase for emergency evacuation! Get everyone on the starship now! I don't want anyone down there if someone sends one of those bombs up here."

It didn't take long to evacuate; they practiced the evac drill every month. Once everyone was on board, the captain moved the starship to the other side of Earth using a cloaked jump.

Chirra continued to monitor the bedlam on the planet. This usually happened during the first year of quarantine; he'd begun to think it never would. "Any fission or fusion devices yet?"

"No, sir. I'm getting some radiation, but it's probably from ruptured fission reactors or someone destroying an adversary's nukes. Lots of Hore portals delivering bombs. They've been busy little primates."

"As long as they don't pop any of those nukes, Grock won't care. This bombing will just speed up their demise a bit. Let me know when it stops; we'll send down a team to assess the damage. We might get out of quarantine duty a lot sooner than we expected."

She sighed. "That would be nice."

"Are they blowing up population centers?" If so, it would mean a major reduction in worldwide population and possibly an early end to their quarantine.

There was a pause while she checked. "No, sir. They appear to be concentrating on each other's military, governmental centers, and infrastructure. Major population areas are being left alone."

"Damn!"

... ...

China was able to zero in on the active primaries in the US and Russia. They were taken out one at a time, causing enormous secondary explosions that left huge craters and started wildfires. While China was attacking the US and Russian primaries, Iran started taking out China's. China countered by targeting Iran's. India took out the last launch site in both Iran and China, right before India's was taken out by Pakistan.

The sun came up over Washington, DC, three-and-a-half hours after the attack began. It showed a vastly different landscape than what had been there the day before. Congress, the White House, the Pentagon, and the headquarters of all the cabinet secretariats were just heaps of rubble. The air was thick with smoke; fires burned out of control across the District. Even if the fire trucks could get to them across the ruined roads and bridges, there was no water to fight the conflagrations.

Over half of the 1.3 million men and women on active military duty in the US were dead—their forts, ships, and bases destroyed and burning. Outside of the two nuclear missile submarines that had escaped annihilation by hiding under the thermocline, America's nuclear arsenal was completely destroyed. In the American heartland, San Francisco Bay, Puget Sound, Houston, Los Angeles, Norfolk, and Rhode Island, areas of radioactivity spread locally from destroyed reactors and nuke storage areas. The aircraft carriers and military ships that were underway had been blown up by targeting satellites. Only the military on deployment in little-known places and planes in the air had avoided the carnage.

In the Three-Hour War, as it would come to be known, the military capacity of Earth was cut by three quarters. More bomb tonnage was exploded than in World Wars I and II, Korea, Vietnam, and the Gulf Wars combined; unlike those previous conflicts, however, almost every bomb hit its target. Not a single country that created a Rosy response system had avoided the devastation. Many non-Rosy countries were attacked, as well, because of the repeaters and remote launchers placed within their borders. Almost all the world's heads of state were dead. The United States had not launched a single nuclear warhead, although people in many countries were struggling to hide from and survive the damage from localized radiation created when nearby nuke storage areas were blown up or reactors had melted down.

At the end of the Three-Hour War, five mushroom clouds, small by multistage nuclear standards, rose from the ruins that had been the capital of the United States. One or more countries had used the cover of the worldwide apocalypse to repay America for making itself the world's policeman. As the explosions ascended into the atmosphere, they pulled vast amounts of water from the Potomac River, turning it into a huge cloud of radioactive gases and dust.

The fireballs faded as the plume of superheated gases and dust reached the stratosphere. Erratic winds began moving the radiation around the coastal plain. At sea level, the winds were directly from the west at ten knots, but depending on the altitude, the winds came from many different points of the compass. By noon, they had turned until they were uniformly from the west-southwest at one hundred and ten knots. If the wind had been from the southeast or east, eastern and central United States and most of Canada would have been inundated with the radiation. As it was, though, the wind blew the radiation cloud across Chesapeake Bay, eastern Maryland, Delaware, southern New Jersey, and then out into the North Atlantic. If the wind patterns didn't change, it would reach Europe in two days, much diminished but still formidable.

The destruction was not limited to Earth. The communication and observation satellites surrounding the world were taken out; the GPS satellites had been destroyed. The internet was down, the news channels were down, the phone systems, and electrical grid were down. The fuel, water, and natural gas supply systems had been blown up, causing huge fires and flooding. To get water to fight the fires, fire departments turned to local swimming pools, ponds, streams, and rivers. Even ham radio operators were having only intermittent success in getting signals through the background radiation from the nukes and generating station meltdowns.

No one ever figured out who started the Three-Hour War— no one denied sending the first bomb or claimed responsibility for it. There was no communication infrastructure left for them to make the announcement. Of course, speculation ran wild among the people who survived. It could have been one of the remnants of ISIS, still active in Iraq, Turkey, and Syria. It could have been Al-Qaeda, although they were falling out of favor and funding across most of the Muslim world. It could have been a thank you letter from North Korea or Vietnam in response to President Klavel blowing up their ship, the *Da Nang*, as it carried to them the Rosy scientist they had kidnapped from JPL. It could have been China trying to take complete control of the economy of the world. It could have been Russia trying to reestablish itself as a superpower after the aliens sent Moscow into the sun. It could have been Iran after all those years of sanctions, repaying the great Satan for its kindness. It could even have been the aliens, trying to seal the coffin of humanity.

At the end of the three hours, though, it didn't matter who started it or why.

Chapter 25 – Land Anywhere You Can

"President Robbins?"

"Yes. What is it Colonel Phillips?" It was unusual for the pilot to enter the main cabin of Air Force One, especially when they were at DEFCON 1, but after watching the US disintegrate while they'd been on what should have been a quiet public relations flight to San Francisco, no one gave it a second thought.

"Sir, McChord is not responding to radio messages. We have to assume they have been destroyed. That was our backup destination; no other US airport capable of landing a 747 is within our range. All their runways have been destroyed. Even Boeing's factory runway in Seattle was annihilated."

"Any chance of a refuel?"

"No, sir. Our last hope was Minot. The tanker with our fuel was taxiing when it took a direct hit. From what the tower told me before they quit transmitting, there isn't much left of Minot. The bombers and SR-71s went first. We could take a chance on a straight portion of the interstate system—President Eisenhower made them put in three-mile straight stretches every so often with no overpasses. If we land on the interstate, though, we'd have no access to refueling and might hit some cars."

"How about Canada?"

"Vancouver, Victoria, and Kelowna are out of commission. We think Abbotsford is out, as well. We could make Calgary—they are reporting no damage. Our computer says we can make it with fifteen minutes to spare. A lot of in-flight jumbos are heading to them. Canadian Rockies International Airport is taking the smaller jets and commuter planes that can reach them. Calgary is the last airport still in operation in North America that can land something this big."

"Calgary it is then. Do we need their permission?"

"No, sir. I mean, yes, sir, but we already have it. Uh, sir?"

"Yes?"

"The F-35s on our wingtips are not going to make it. They don't have enough fuel."

"Tell them to land anywhere they can—and, Colonel..."

"Yes, sir?"

"Tell them thanks. I appreciate their protection."

"I will, sir."

"How about the 117s above us?"

"They're fine for now, sir."

Phillips returned several minutes later. "Sir, the pilots of the F-35s said they will accompany us until they run out of fuel."

President Robbins looked out the window, trying to find the fighters in the night sky outside. After a couple of seconds, he could barely make out the outline of one of the fighters behind the 747. Air Force One and the fighters were running without lights, per wartime rules. He thought back to when he'd flown F-4s in Vietnam. More than once, he'd coasted into Bien Hoa Air Base on fumes. It was a terrifying thing for a pilot to run out of fuel; those fancy fighters turned into flying coffins. The country below them was black. *We should be over the mountains of Montana by now. The chance of landing down there safely at night and out of fuel is zero.* "Is there somewhere they can land between here and Calgary?"

"They can land almost anywhere. I'll find something at the end of their range. Out here, it'll be something local or a private strip."

"We've lost enough good men and women today. Make sure we don't lose those two. I'd like their names."

"Yes, sir."

... ...

"Sparwood Airport, this is US Air Force Jet XK3482, requesting permission to perform an emergency landing."

There was no response.

The pilot's air-to-air channel opened from the second F-35. "Crusty, we need to land. This is an uncontrolled strip. Let's just enter the pattern and land, like we did in the old days."

"Roger, Lucky. Just to keep everyone honest, I will issue the Mayday." She opened the UNICOM channel, used by all unattended civilian airports. "Mayday. Mayday. Mayday. This is United States Air Force jet XK3482. We are out of fuel and landing at Sparwood Airport in British Columbia." Again there was silence. "Follow me, Lucky."

"Rodger."

The UNICOM channel came to life. "Hello?" a woman's voice asked.

Crusty answered. "Is this Sparwood Airport?"

"Yeah, Sparwood/Elk Valley. I mean, my dad runs it. He isn't here right now. I'm doing my homework in the kitchen or I wouldn't have heard you."

"We have an emergency. We are out of fuel and landing at your airport."

"Okay. I'll tell him when he comes home. Park next to the hangars. He charges ten dollars to land."

"Roger ten dollars. Do you have any jet fuel?"

"No. All we have is avgas for the forest service planes. I don't think we've ever had a jet land here. We could order it from the Canadian Rockies International Airport, but the phones are down. I'll turn on the runway lights—we just had them installed."

Crusty saw the lights come on directly in front of her flight path. She touched down thirty seconds later, followed by Lucky. They taxied to the small apron, turned around, and shut down the engines. Four small hangars and a small building that could be a comm center/office were in view. The lights from what could be a farmhouse were on behind the line of birch trees paralleling the runway. The sky above the mountains surrounding the airport was crystal clear with stars filling it from horizon to horizon.

The two pilots jumped down from the cockpits. Captain Gaye Marshall, or Crusty, had strawberry blonde hair, green eyes, and freckles across her perfect nose. Many people who met her made the mistake of thinking her supermodel good looks meant she was lacking in the brainpower department, and then they found out she had graduated at the top of her class from the US Air Force Academy. Lieutenant Gary Owen, or Lucky Seven, her wingman, was wiry with a chiseled Germanic face and blonde hair. He took great amusement in watching the rest of the world fawn around Crusty.

Every fighter jockey had a nickname; they were used to communicate quickly with each other in combat. Captain Marshall had gotten *Crusty* in Afghanistan. She'd made it all the way through flight school without either choosing or being assigned a nickname. After a long, grueling series of sorties, she'd complained about having crusty underwear. From that moment on, she was Crusty.

A person with a flashlight came running down the access road from the farmhouse.

"Hello?" a young woman's voice called out from behind the flashlight. "My name is Margaret Kund. I had to see if you guys were really Air Force." She approached the jets, a little out of breath. "Man, this is great! I tried to call Dad, but the cell phones are down, too. Are those real rockets? What kind of jets are those?"

Captain Marshall was a little unprepared for the girl's questions, given their present situation—stuck in the middle of Bumfuck, B.C., out of fuel, while the U.S. was at war and the president had continued on without them. She sighed, realizing nothing was going to change until morning, and then turned to the young woman. She was probably still in high school, and the girl was all blue-eyed, blonde-haired, swim team enthusiasm.

"Hi, Margaret. I am US Air Force Captain Marshall. This is US Marine Lieutenant Owen. They are F-35s. And, yeah, those are real rockets."

"What are you doing up here?" The girl was staring at the F-35s with undisguised awe. "How fast do they go?"

"They go very fast." Gaye was tickled by her nonstop curiosity. "We were flying and ran out of fuel."

"Wow. I didn't think the Air Force ever ran out of fuel. Can they break the sound barrier?"

"Yes, they can. And they run out of fuel when you fly them far enough and the refueling tanker doesn't show up. Margaret, could you do us a big favor?"

"Sure!"

"It looks like we're gonna be here until morning. Would you happen to have any sleeping bags we could use? We can't leave our jets, and it's going to be pretty chilly up here."

"Yeah. This time of year, we get down to around freezing at night." She cocked her head in thought for a moment. "Let me check—I think Dad keeps some sleeping bags in with his hunting gear. I'll be back in a minute. You can camp in the office. I'll open it up for ya." She unlocked the door to the small building and then started walking toward the house.

"Break out the pistols and ammo, Gary. We're on guard duty. You want first or second shift? I figure four hours each."

"I'll take first. Go get some sleep."

Gaye pulled out her cell phone. "No Service" was displayed on the screen.

Fifteen minutes later, Margaret was back with a wheelbarrow loaded with two down sleeping bags, two cots, a case of bottled water, a thermos of coffee, and a picnic basket full of food.

"How did you make coffee already?" Gaye asked, puzzled. "You weren't gone long enough."

"I had just started a pot when you called on the radio. I figured, if you guys were going to stay out here all night, you'd need it more than Dad. He'll be drunk anyway—he won't know the difference. The rest are leftovers; eat 'em if you like. Dad put a microwave in the pilots' room." She looked back at the fighters. "I'll bet they can do a loop that'll pop your eyeballs out."

"They can pull five Gs positive or two negative. Are you a pilot?"

"*Five Gs*—wow! Blackout city! Yeah, Dad taught me to fly in a Cessna 150 Aerobat when I was ten. He had to sell it last year. God, I miss that plane—I flew it every chance I got. Now all we have is a V-tail Bonanza Dad finished restoring a couple of months ago. He won't let me near it."

"You can do a lot of flying in an Aerobat. What year is the Bonanza?"

"1965. He put on wingtip tanks as part of the restoration. Along with the extra tank where the back seat should be, he says his range is around three thousand miles. I don't know why you'd want to fly that far without stopping—it would take you eighteen hours and there's no toilet, but Dad's a little weird like that. With the Cessna, I could do the most perfect chandelle, but my favorite was the hammerhead stall turn. It made that little plane feel like a fighter."

"Are you going to be a pilot after school?"

"If the US Air Force Academy accepts me. I applied last fall. I'm a senior in secondary school."

"The commandant of the academy and I go way back. I'll tell him about you."

"Really? That would be wonderful!"

Gaye pulled out a small, wire-bound pad of paper and made a note of the girl's name. "Spell your last name, please."

"K-U-N-D."

She put her pad away. "I expect both the Canadian and US Air Forces are going to need a lot of pilots."

"Why's that?"

"Take my word for it, Margaret. Some big changes have happened tonight."

... ...

"Okay, people. Our mission is the same." Dr. Sridhar Hehsa was addressing the gathered scientists and support people at the CDC in Atlanta. "We have a job to do and we will continue to do it. We have power, we have supplies, and we have food and water to last a year."

"I have to go home," one scientist announced. "I don't know if my family is alive."

"The bridge to Jonesboro's down," another clerk said, standing. "Hartsfield Airport is in flames."

Dr. Hehsa looked around the room. "Anyone who feels like they have to leave may do so. Bring your families here, if you can. Marines guard our perimeter—we will be safe."

In his heart, he knew most of the people who left would not return. Greater Atlanta had over five million people—there would be chaos and anarchy. With murdering, raping, robbing, and pillaging, the police would be overwhelmed, as would the military. The people inside the chain-link fences surrounding the CDC campus would be safe, at least until the food outside ran out.

Chapter 26 – Five Hawks

"Something's wrong with the TV reception," Clara announced from the living room.

Doug was in the kitchen making scrambled eggs and bacon. "Did you cycle the DVR? That usually works."

"Yeah, and the internet's down too."

"I'll call them when I finish breakfast. I wish cable was available out here. The satellite internet is so slow compared to what we had in Palo Alto."

She pulled her cell phone out. "You're busy; I can do it." Clara called the number three times. "That's odd. I keep getting a message saying all lines out of Calgary are busy and to please try again later—same thing with the number for DirectTV."

He walked into the room trying his cell phone. "I get the same thing. Let me call work and see if they know anything." He dialed his boss. "Hey, Russ. What's going on? Our internet's down and we can't dial out of Calgary. Even our TV satellite feed is down." Doug's eyes suddenly widened in shock. "*What?*" After another long pause, he said, "I'll be right there."

Clara looked at him with concern, wondering what could possibly have happened.

He was pale when he ended the call, his face registering disbelief. "World War III," he said, emotionless. "As far as they know, Calgary is the only major city in Canada to escape destruction. The US has been annihilated. The Aerospace Centre is calling everyone to work. The cell phones only work for local numbers; the trunk lines to the rest of the world are down."

The shock from Doug's words paralyzed Clara for a moment, and then her practical side snapped into action. "Go pack some clothes. I'll get some food ready for you to take. Lord knows when you'll be back home."

… … … … … … … …

Byteen was collecting resumes. The Cove Bar was more than happy to host the event. "So, you're an analyst?"

"Yes. I am."

"What kind of name is Zarqa Shaia? Where are you from?"

"What difference does that make? You need an analyst and I'm a damned good one."

"What ship did you come in on?"

"Do you need an analyst? I got four other ships that want me. I'm going with whoever pays me the most."

"Thank you, Shaia. I have your information."

The link from *Easy Wind* activated in his ear. "Hire her. I like her spirit."

"We'll give you twenty huz a day. Are you still interested?"

"I want twenty-five. Curz offered me twenty-three."

"Give it to her," Fey Pey's voice ordered.

He made a note. "Okay, you're in. Wait over there with the rest of the new crew."

Zarqa studied the assembled group: a primate, a feline, an arachnid, and a Mellincon—a lion-looking being about two meters tall that walked on its hind legs and growled at anyone near it. She picked up her gear bag and walked over.

"What is your specialty?" Byteen asked the next person in the queue.

Flug looked at him coldly and stretched his huge muscles. "Gee, let me guess...combat?"

"Does that gun come with you?"

"I'd like to see someone try to take it away."

"Can you use it?"

"Been using it, or one like it for forty years."

"Where did you work?"

"Combat Corps."

That made him look up. "What rank?"

"Senior sergeant...until we had a disagreement about the terms of engagement."

"You ever been on a private reconnaissance vessel?"

"Yeah. But not as crew."

"Which one?"

"*Sky Limit* was the last."

The bar got quiet. *Sky Limit* had been robbing merchant starships for ten years until the Ur stormtroopers boarded it and took the vessel by force. The entire crew had been killed. "I had some friends on *Sky Limit*," Byteen said, baring his teeth.

Flug shrugged, unimpressed. "You roll the dice and you take your chances. If I'd been part of the crew, they wouldn't have been taken. No one was in charge, and their defenses were a mess. My team didn't lose a man. It was an easy kill. You need me or not?"

The voice in Byteen's ear came alive. "He's right. *Sky Limit* was a piece of shit. We need him. I like how he holds that gun. He can work for Ursa; she'll keep him in line."

"You got a problem working for a female?"

"I'll work for anybody as long, as they're good."

"Okay, you're in. Wait over there." He motioned to the group where Zarqa was standing.

Flug didn't move. "How much?"

"Standard soldier wages: eighteen Huz."

"I want thirty. I'm no beginner."

The voice in his ear told him, "Offer twenty-four with a review after our first mission."

He repeated the offer to Flug.

"Yeah. That'll work."

"You better be that good," he grumbled.

Flug looked into Byteen's multifaceted eyes with a slight smile that didn't reach his cold stare. "I hope you're around when it starts. I'll show you."

Lieutenant Fibari sat at the bar, watching the interviews. She touched her ear. "They're both on," she whispered.

... ...

Yesterday, the eight children under his protection were virus-free and living in the Montana SHIPS. Now it was after midnight, the SHIPS had been destroyed, the kids were crying, and his shoulder hurt. Chief Petty Officer Freddie Harris had no doubt his two surviving children, Shannon and Wilson, were now infected with BSV, as they were outside in infected air. They wouldn't die of it, of course, but they would never have children; now neither would he, for that matter. The other six children who'd been placed in his care two years ago were dead.

The first bomb had been a small one, just large enough to blow the front door and seals and expose the people inside to BSV. After the explosion, he'd grabbed these two from the nursery and run outside. He'd been the only one who did. The second bomb had been a lot bigger than the first; the entire mountain collapsed on the SHIPS, and then the warehouses were blown up, along with the barracks for the external support personnel, followed by the motor pool with its Humvees, trucks, and tanks of stabilized fuel.

Either the motor pool bomb or the barracks bomb had wounded him—he couldn't remember which. After whichever one was first, he'd dived into the shallow ditch beside the driveway and held both children under him. The concussion from the second one had knocked him out. When he'd come to, his shoulder hurt and the children were crying but unharmed.

Freddie was able to pull the long, thin piece of shrapnel from his shoulder with the pliers in the multitool he kept on his belt and then bound the wound with the sleeve of his shirt. He didn't have any antibiotics or even antiseptic; it would have to do. His makeshift bandage had almost stopped the blood flow.

It was dark and cold outside the SHIPS. The only light was from the fires burning around the compound. Thick smoke, probably toxic, filled the air. Freddie was shivering uncontrollably. He picked up the children and, as he wandered around the destruction of what was left from the warehouses and barracks, stumbled over something in the shadows at his feet; two blankets. When he picked them up, something fell out onto the ground. Curious, he reached down to examine what had dropped—an arm, still warm. He threw it away in disgust, realizing the blankets must have been blown out of the barracks.

By cutting a hole in the middle of one blanket, he turned it into a serape and tied it around himself with the belt from his pants. He was able to make two slings out of the second blanket to carry the children. They liked his warmth and snuggled up to him under the serape. There was nothing left in the compound he could use as shelter and that was becoming important—it was cold; not freezing yet but they needed to get somewhere warmer fast. Nothing to do but walk.

When he got to the end of the driveway, Freddie stopped. *Which way?* he asked himself, looking in both directions. The Milky Way stretched across the sky without any moon in sight, the stars barely twinkling in the clear, cold air. The countryside was completely dark, not a light anywhere. No one had told him what was in either direction when he'd arrived, he'd never thought he would need to know.

In the starlight, he could see the asphalt highway stretch away in both directions with its broken yellow line down the center. To the right, the road went uphill; to the left, it went down.

"Downhill should lead to a town," he muttered before he turned left and began walking.

Freddie was in shock from his shoulder injury and the explosions. The farther he walked, the fuzzier the world around him became. Slowly his mind generated a kind of waking dream and his feet hitting the ground became a hypnotizing mantra. He and the children were wanderers seeking shelter from the storm, and the shelter was ahead of them somewhere.

He started mumbling the Wicked Witch of the West's soldier chant from *The Wizard of Oz*. "Oooh eeee oooh...Eee ooooooh hooh." He then sang Green Day and then The White Stripes. Freddie fixated on the road in front of him and put one foot in front of the other; everything else faded into oblivion. His world began three steps ahead of him and ended after he passed. All that mattered was for him to keep walking, one foot in front of the other. He walked past farmhouses camouflaged in the darkness by trees. Two cars passed him at high speed, but they didn't stop when he tried to wave them down.

He walked until dawn started lighting the eastern sky. When he finally snapped out of his dream enough to look around, he was standing in front of a big, white farmhouse. A herd of cows with tags in their ears stared at him over the fence paralleling the road.

He approached the house shouting, "Hello?"

An old man greeted him with a rifle across his arms. "Get the hell away from us!" he shouted. "We got nothin'!"

"I'm injured," Freddie called out. "I got two babies with me."

"Don't care. Go away or die." The old man cranked a cartridge into the rifle and sighted at them. Freddie turned around and continued down the road.

The next house was several miles farther, in a grove of cottonwoods. It was different from the others he had passed, and he studied it for a minute, trying to get his foggy brain to figure out why. He knew different was important, but he'd forgotten the reason. At last, he got it. This one didn't have barbed wire fences, a barn, and assorted outbuildings. It looked more like the house of a retired couple. A garage with two doors was attached to the side of the house—one door was tall enough for a bus or RV. The driveway was covered with leaves and branches, like it hadn't been used all winter. If no one was home, it was probably safe.

A locked gate spanned the entrance. Freddie climbed over it carefully, trying not to wake the children. When no one answered his knock, he walked around the house, looking in the windows. No one was visible. He broke out one of the small panes on the door to the mudroom behind the kitchen at the back of the house. The door to the kitchen was unlocked.

"Hello?" he called out, not wanting a repeat of the man with the rifle. There was no answer.

The house was cold—not as cold as outside, but still far from comfortable. He laid the children on the sofa in the living room and wrapped them in the sling blankets while he explored. The thermostat wasn't off, but it was set to forty degrees. He turned it up to seventy, and the furnace kicked on in the basement. The electricity was on! He walked to the sink in the kitchen and turned the faucet. The water was on and so was the water heater! He leaned his head over and took a long drink of clean, cold water from the faucet—it helped clear his head. He hadn't realized how thirsty he was. He took another drink, got a glass and filled it up, and then began to explore the kitchen with the water in hand.

The phone on the kitchen wall was dead—no dial tone. The old gas stove didn't light when he turned a burner knob and he didn't hear the hiss of gas. When he lifted up the stovetop, he saw the pilot lights were off. *Crap. Please let the tank have some propane in it.* He went back outside and walked around the house, a propane storage tank greeted him beside the garage, and, sure enough, the valve was closed. He turned it on. The gauge on the tank showed three-quarters full.

Back in the kitchen, after a minute of running the burner on full and using up four matches, it lit. He made a cup of instant coffee and wrapped his hands around the warmth. The house was noticeably warmer. Warm air was blowing out of the heater vents.

The kitchen fridge was empty, of course—blocked open and turned off—but the freezer in the pantry was on and full of frozen vegetables and meats. The shelves in the pantry were stacked in neat rows and filled with canned goods and baking supplies, in labeled plastic tubs. On the top row were perhaps fifty quart-jars of home-canned vegetables, fruits, jams, and jellies, all neatly labeled and dated. The back of the door to the pantry held a wire shelf system full of spices.

From the mudroom next to the kitchen, he descended a stairway to the basement. A dark energy generator sat next to the furnace, squatting like a huge toad on the floor, its green "active normal" light like a beacon of normality across the storm of the previous day. That explained why the power was left on—this house was off the grid. Freddie opened a door off the main room of the basement and flipped on the light. The walls were lined with shelves, crowded with boxes of food and water. The owners had stored enough emergency survival food to last for years. At the end of the room was a gun safe.

One of the children upstairs awoke and called his name. "Sounds like it's time for breakfast." He shook his head and sighed. "This'll be interesting." He hadn't cooked since he went into the navy seventeen years ago."

He flexed his shoulder; it hurt like hell. Carrying the kids had been rough on it. With all this emergency food stored up, the owners had to have some first-aid supplies somewhere. He walked back up the stairs to the kitchen. First breakfast for the kids, and then he would doctor his shoulder and maybe even take a bath.

"I'm thinking oatmeal," he said to himself as he pulled the container off the shelf. "How hard is it to screw up oatmeal?"

... ...

"Calgary Approach control, this is United States Air Force One. We are twenty miles southwest of Yankee-Yankee-Charlie."

Y-Y-C were the airport identification letters for Calgary International Airport, but it wasn't in sight yet. They were reporting cloud layers at five thousand, nine thousand, and fifteen thousand feet, and five-knot winds on the ground from the northwest.

"Air Force One, we don't see you on our radar," a harried female voice responded.

"Our transponder is off, per US Air Force wartime regulations."

"Please turn on your transponder for just a second and squawk 4133 so we can vector you in." A moment later the controller continued. "Roger contact, Air Force One. Please enter standard holding pattern at Zulu at ten thousand feet."

"Negative, Calgary. We have seventeen minutes of fuel left. Request a direct vector to runway 34-Romeo."

"Air Force One, two other planes are in front of you with less fuel than you have. You will have to wait your turn."

"Well, you better get them on the ground. We are coming in. Our escort aircraft will be happy to clear the runway."

"Air Force One, we don't see your escort aircraft on the radar. We cannot keep other aircraft away from them without their transponders on."

"They will stay away from any authorized aircraft. They will continue to provide protection above the airport as long as we are on the ground."

"Roger, Air Force One. Turn to heading 210, follow Air Canada 7541, the A-340 ahead of you, to runway 34-Romeo. Report Air Canada in sight. Once you land, you will have thirty seconds to clear the runway. Contact Ground Control 124.3."

"Roger, Calgary. Heading 210, taily on the Airbus, Air Canada 7541, clear the runway within thirty seconds. Ground Control 124.3. The United States thanks you, ma'am."

Air Force One typically required the entire airspace around an airport to be clear for half an hour before their approach for landing. The normal minimal spacing for heavy commercial aircraft in the air was four minutes apart. That approach control had them spaced at thirty seconds was an indication of how desperate the situation had become. Calgary International Airport was apparently the last functioning airport in North America capable of landing large commercial airliners; they were stacked up in the sky, waiting their turn to land.

The Air Canada flight touched down, went into full flaps, full air brakes, full reverse thrust, full wheel brakes, and then swerved off the runway when it had slowed enough. Air Force One did the same, thirty seconds behind it. Ten other aircraft were visible on approach behind the 747 in two queues as they descended through the lowest cloud layer, one queue for runway 34R and another for runway 34L.

"Air Force One, this is Calgary ground control. Please taxi behind the Follow Me truck to the Canada Air Force jet apron. When you arrive, ground guidance personnel will help you park. We don't have much space left, sir. Captain Mitchem, of the Royal Canadian Air Force, will be waiting for you with a security detachment."

"Roger, ground control. Thanks again for the courtesy." Everywhere Colonel Phillips looked, airplanes were parked, wingtip-to-wingtip. A bunch of tugs were turning around every other plane so they could fit even more of them head-to-tail in their limited space. The colonel passed all this to the president.

"Did the two fighters get down safely?"

"Yes, sir. They landed at a small municipal airport in a little town named Sparwood in British Columbia."

"I suspect the airport manager will be pretty surprised in the morning, with two F-35s sitting on his tarmac."

Colonel Phillips chuckled. "I expect so, sir."

"What are the pilots' names?"

"Air Force Captain Gaye Marshall and Marine Lieutenant Gary Owen."

"Gary Owen? Really?"

"Yes, sir."

"I would have thought he'd be flying for the Seventh Cavalry."

"He probably wanted to drive fast movers instead of Blackhawk's, sir. I suspect you have some empathy for that."

"Yep, I sure do. See if they can get some fuel at that airport. If they can't, check with Calgary Ops; they may have a tanker truck we can send to the fighters. Either way, we need them here with us within twenty-four hours."

"Yes, sir."

"Has there been any contact with the US armed forces?"

"No, sir. We keep trying all emergency frequencies; no one has replied. The satellites are all down. We've received some intermittent transmissions from ham radio operators around the country. There's been lots of damage."

"Thank you, Colonel."

As he left, Leann Jenkins walked into the conference room that had become the US government headquarters in absentia. "President Robbins, Captain Mitchem of the Royal Canadian Air Force is here."

Ever since Leann volunteered to be the emissary in the capsule, the president had been evaluating her covertly—that was why she had accompanied his entourage on the trip to San Francisco. She was poised, cautious, bright, and thorough—and she was twenty-two. He kept running into that. How could someone so young accomplish what the professional diplomats, generals, and politicians of the world had not in two years?

"Thank you, Leann. Send him in."

The captain entered the conference room, snapped to attention, and saluted. "Sir. The Royal Canadian Air Force is proud to help the United States in any way we can."

"We are grateful for your help, Captain. Please, sit. Would you like some coffee or tea?"

"Tea would be grand, sir."

Robbins pressed his comm button. "Please bring hot tea for Captain Mitchem and coffee for me." He settled back in his seat. "Have you had any contact with your government?"

"Yes and no. I contacted my headquarters in Moose Jaw just after this started. They said to remain up here until told otherwise. Communications with them disappeared early on. We still have communication with CFB Edmonton; they were hurt but are still in business."

"CFB?"

"Sorry, sir, Canadian Forces Base; home of the 3rd Canadian Division."

Leann brought in the captain's tea along with a small pitcher of milk and some sugar cubes. While the captain prepared his tea, Robbins lifted his cup of coffee and took a sip. "Have you had any communication with any of the US armed forces?"

"No, sir." Mitchem paused. "How bad is it, sir?"

"We don't know. We're trying to find out."

"I wouldn't be here if I hadn't been on training maneuvers with my student pilots."

"How many personnel did you bring with you, Captain?"

"Ten, sir, including myself, and we have five CT-155 Hawks."

"What kind of range do they have?"

"Twenty-five hundred kilometers, sir."

"That's three hundred more than my F-35s."

"Yes, sir, but I expect the F-35s are a lot more fun to fly."

That made President Robbins laugh out loud. "Yes, they are, Captain!" He grew serious again. "My F-35s are out of fuel and parked at a little community strip in British Columbia. Until I can refuel them, I have a favor to ask the Canadian government. Do you think your students could fly to the Seattle area to try to contact the

US forces there? I also need someone to fly to Minot Air Force Base in North Dakota for the same thing. It's about a thousand kilometers to Minot and seven hundred to Seattle from here."

The captain took a moment to think about it. "If this wasn't wartime, I would say there's not a chance...but it is. Let me check with CFB Edmonton. I'm sure they won't have a problem with it."

"I'd also like to send a liaison officer up there to set up communications with them. If you don't want two student pilots flying that far unsupervised, there must be hundreds of commercial pilots, most with military backgrounds, sitting around the terminal with nothing to do. I'd be surprised if a few of them wouldn't love a chance to copilot one of those shiny blue CT-155s for an afternoon."

"That would work, sir. I'd feel much better about sending my students on a mission if they had an experienced pilot with them."

Chapter 27 – This Is Good

Rebecca had walked all night. She'd made it over the mountain to Mission Hills in the San Fernando Valley. The people she passed might as well have been dead; no one talked, and as many people were going toward LA as away from it. She figured everyone was still in shock from the attack and was pretty sure she didn't want to be around when they woke up.

The sun was coming up over the San Fernando Valley. The air stank, and waves of smoke and ash passed across the highway from fires burning out of control all over the area. The hills around her were either burning or already had. She'd been walking for seven hours straight; it was time for a rest. I-5 in both directions was a parking lot of abandoned vehicles and walking dead.

She went down the Sepulveda Boulevard exit ramp from the elevated freeway to the street below, looking for a quiet, safe place to hide. As she got to the street, she saw five men in a parking lot next to a looted restaurant, hooting and cheering as they looked downward. With saggy pants, shaved heads, brown skin, and tattoos, they appeared to be Latino gang-bangers. Bushes obscured her view, so she crouched down and came closer to find out what was going on.

A man was on top of a girl who didn't yet look fourteen. She was naked, and his bare ass was up in the air, his pants to his knees. The rest of the men were obviously waiting their turn, as the girl made half-hearted attempts to push the man off, saying "*No. Por favor. Alto.*" (No. Please. Stop.) The other men laughed and responded to her entreaties with derision.

Rebecca pulled out her gun, flipped off the safety, and held it behind her back as she walked around the bushes. About fifteen feet away from the group, she shouted, "*Stop! Get off her!*"

"Now why should we do that?" one of the men asked.

"Because, if you don't, Sean will kill you."

"Yeah, right." He starting walking toward her. "Who the fuck is Sean? You're all alone, you dumb cunt. Hey, I got a better idea. Why don't I give you some a the same thing she's gettin'?"

He was about six feet from her when she swung her gun from behind her back and shot him in the forehead, just like Jeremiah had made her do with targets in their firing range. His brains sprayed the rest of the men.

"Let me introduce you to Sean, *asshole*," she told the guy, glancing down at him to make sure he was dead. He had a pistol handle in the waistband of his pants.

She looked at the rest of the men. "Anyone else?" The guy on the ground rolled off the girl and pulled up his pants. "Get her up," Rebecca told him.

"Fuck you, lady."

She shot him dead center in the chest. He fell over backward and died, with his mouth opening and closing like a fish out of water.

"You with the pistol." She indicated a skinny man who had his hands up. "Two fingers. Take your pistol out and lay it on the ground." He did. "Now kick it over here." She pointed the gun at the guy next to him. "One more chance. Get her up." He helped the girl to her feet. Rebecca saw she had a huge welt on the side of her forehead. "Where are her clothes?" No one said anything. Every one of them was looking somewhere else. "Strip!" she told the guy who was closest to the girl's size.

His eyes snapped to her in disbelief and got hard. He leaned over, as if to remove his shoes, bunched his legs underneath himself, and looked up at her. She realized then that he was preparing to leap at her.

"Don't even think about it, Paco, or you'll join your friends. Just shut up and get naked." She paused for effect. "Or not. She can wear your clothes even if they're a little bloody." Rebecca pointed her gun at his crotch.

The guy got undressed to his undershorts and T-shirt, his eyes never leaving hers as he glared at her in hatred. "We're gonna find you, lady, and when we do, this is gonna look like *Romper Room*."

She ignored him. "Now dress her." They helped the girl into his clothes. She fell down a couple of times while they were trying to put her legs in the pants, but she was slowly becoming more aware.

When the girl was dressed, Rebecca told the remaining three men, "You guys got a choice to make. You can leave or you can die. You've got five seconds to decide. Leave and don't come back or stay and die." She started counting.

"We'll meet again, bitch," the naked man said, turning to go.

She smiled coldly. "I hope so."

After they walked away, Rebecca picked up their guns and stowed them in her backpack. She put her arm around the girl, supporting her as she watched to see if the men were coming back. "Can you hear me, honey? Can you walk?"

"Wha happen?" the girl managed to slur. She squinted and blinked, like her eyes were having trouble focusing.

Rebecca was concerned. The men were coming back and they would be armed when they did. The two of them had to get somewhere else in a hurry. "Can you walk?"

"Yeah, I guesso. Whose clothes're these?"

"They're yours now. Paco donated 'em to you." She began pulling the girl up the exit ramp.

"What happened? The last thing I remember is carrying home some groceries. Who's Paco?"

"You don't wanna know. We're gonna walk back up to the freeway. Think you can do that?"

"These shoes don't fit—they're too small. Where're my clothes?"

Rebecca was becoming exasperated. They were vulnerable on the exit ramp, and she kept looking at the corner where the men had disappeared. "You were being raped by a gang," she said a little too loudly. "I think they hit you on the head before they started. Maybe they know where your clothes are. You wanna go back and ask 'em?" As soon as the words were out of her mouth, Rebecca regretted being so hard on the girl.

They continued up the exit ramp, and then the girl stopped again. "I can't wear these shoes." She took them off, tied the laces together, hung them around her neck, and started walking again, barefoot. "Where're we going?"

"I've got a friend with a house in the mountains. We'll be safe there." Rebecca watched the corner, expecting the men to return at any moment; the two men she'd killed were still lying in the parking lot. She wished she and the girl were far away from here.

"What about my family?" She started to cry.

"I don't know. What about your family?"

"They're dead. They're all dead!" she sobbed. "My whole block burned. I left to buy some stuff at the all-night grocery, and when I came back, everything was on fire. I heard my mother screaming. I don't remember anything after that."

"What's your name?"

"Josephina," she muttered, blinking like she couldn't quite focus. "Josephina Sanchez."

"Well, Josephina, my name is Rebecca. These are hard times, honey. The way I see it, you've got a decision to make. I have to go before those guys come back. You can come with me or not. What's it gonna be?"

The girl looked around like she had just realized where she was. Her eyes filled with tears again, and she sniffled a little. She wiped her nose on her sleeve. "I've got an uncle in Santa Clarita. Is that on the way?"

"Yeah. That's on the way. We'll see if we can find him."

They walked for a while in silence, finally putting some distance between themselves and the exit ramp.

"I've never been to the mountains," she said. "Is it cold?"

"Not during the day. Are you hungry?"

"No."

"Well, I am. Let's get in one of these cars, lock the doors, and eat something."

Rebecca tried the doors on a couple of abandoned cars, but they were locked. She glared up at the sky in frustration. "Who the hell would lock their car when they ditched it in the middle of the frigging freeway?" The next car, a beat-up 80s Camaro, was open. It even had roll-up windows and locks that worked.

"What do you have to eat?" the girl asked.

Rebecca chuckled. The appetites of fourteen-year-olds had not changed much since she was a kid. If food was around, they wanted some.

"Nothing but the best: Gen-u-ine M-R-Es!" Rebecca pulled out two MRE packages from her backpack. "You can have corned beef hash or chicken breast with cavatelli."

When Josephina didn't reply, Rebecca glanced over. Her face said it all: both sounded terrible.

"Let's go with the corned beef. Jeremiah seemed particularly fond of that one." She poured water into the bag up to the line, placed it inside her jacket next to her body, and then drank the rest of the bottle. The girl watched her without saying a word.

"Are you thirsty?"

"Yes." Josephina was so pitiful. The bruise on her forehead was turning blue, black, and red. Tomorrow it would be even prettier. Yesterday, she'd probably been her neighborhood's beauty queen; now she was barefoot and wearing men's clothes, her hair matted with blood and dirt, and covered with soot. What makeup was left on her face was smeared and tear-stained.

Rebecca dug another bottle of water out of her backpack and handed it to the girl; there were only four left. "Don't throw the bottle away. We'll have to refill them when we can." The keys were in the ignition. She turned it on and then the radio. All she got was static, until she got to 91.9 FM.

"...massive destruction all over LA. No reports from the rest of the country. The phone lines are down, the cell phone system is down, the internet is down, satellite feeds are down, and the GPS system is down. Electricity is off, natural gas is off, and water is off in many places. If you can, boil any water you use. The water in your toilet tank should be safe—don't flush it. Stay inside your homes and lock the doors unless your building is on fire. Do not admit anyone you don't know. Police, emergency services, and hospitals are overwhelmed, and the California National Guard has declared a state of emergency with martial law in effect. No civilian auto traffic is allowed. Freeways are at a standstill. Looters will be shot. A dusk-to-dawn curfew is in place. Get off the street and stay off. This is UCLA Radio broadcasting on our legacy transmitter at 820 AM and 91.9 FM because there is no internet. We are located in the Ackerman Student Union and are running on generator power until the fuel runs out."

The message repeated after that. Rebecca turned off the radio and the ignition key. She leaned back and closed her eyes, exhaustion threatening to overwhelm her after having been awake for twenty-eight hours straight. She'd walked fifteen miles and just killed two men. As the reality of that finally soaked in, her hands started to shake. Those men had mothers and families—maybe wives and children. What would they think when the other men told them their loved ones were dead? Then Rebecca remembered those men had been raping a fourteen-year-old girl. She took a breath and let her anger wash away her regrets. After whispering another thank you to Jeremiah for teaching her how to shoot her pistol so well, Rebecca pulled out the PPK. She ejected the magazine, replaced the two rounds she had used, re-inserted it, flipped the safety back on, and put it back into her shoulder holster.

Her stomach was talking to her and it wasn't being very polite. The MRE was as hydrated as it was going to be. She pulled the bag out from her jacket, squeezed some of the contents into her mouth, and passed the bag to Josephina.

"Sorry about eating like this, but that's all we have."

The girl held the bag up to her nose cautiously, like it was full of crap. Her expression changed to curious, and she made a tentative taste on the tip of her tongue. A huge smile blossomed on her face. "Hey, this is good!"

Rebecca agreed. "It will be 'til we run out."

"Who's Jeremiah?" she asked between bites.

"My husband."

… … … … … … … … …

"Commander Chirra, please open your comm link." The page sounded through the starship.

Chirra had just gone to bed. He sighed and wished once again Captain Xanny was back on board. He pressed the comm button next to his bed. "What's happening?"

After a couple of clicks and pops, a computer-generated voice came through the link. "Sir, this is Sergeant Zpplt. We've had nuclear detonations on the world. They look to be multistage fusion. We've counted five so far. All are in a small area around the capital of a country named the United States. They aren't very large, as fusion bombs go, approximately one megaton each."

Sergeant Zpplt—that explained the CG voice. Zpplt was a strange being that Grock had hired. They didn't appear to have genders and were spirits that lived in individual blocks of silicon. They didn't need to sleep or eat, and they made excellent analysts; plop them in front of a holistic link to the computers and they were on duty. He had no idea what they did for fun or if they even understood the concept.

Commander Chirra had been expecting nukes. Those primates had too many not to use them in a worldwide war. "Have any other detonations been detected?"

"No, sir. Only the five."

He sighed again. Grock wasn't going to like this. "Where are the winds blowing the radiation cloud?"

"All around the coastal plain, initially, and then into the ocean east of the capital."

"Well, it could have been a lot worse." He pondered his next step and sighed again. He really had no choice—the standing orders were very clear. "Send a message to Grock HQ and the GSCB. Tell them what happened and pass them your assessment of the damage to the world." He suspected Grock would like to say, "Hit them with a SEV-1," but the envoy himself would have to authorize it, and Envoy Gart-Disp had never once allowed a SEV-1 deployment.

A SEV-1 was one of the three Species Elimination Viruses approved for eradicating a species that had been failed by the

GSCB. They were already exposed to the SEV-2—it was the reason the primates were infertile. A SEV-2 allowed the species to live their normal lifespans before dying off. SEV-1, on the other hand, was a little different. It killed almost everyone within a week. It was only 99% effective, though, while the SEV-2 was 100%. They would still have to deal with the remaining 1% of the population that survived the pandemic. This world contained something over seven billion of the primates—a 99% reduction would still leave seventy million of them, and they would be scattered all over the world. What a SEV-1 *would* do, however, was end the quarantine and the costs associated with running it. With only one percent of the population surviving, they wouldn't have enough physical or intellectual resources left to build a starship.

… … … … … … … … …

Captain Mitchem had been flying around the greater Seattle area for the better part of an hour, looking for any functioning military. He had tried to raise Naval Station Everett, Naval Base Kitsap, the naval air station, and the coast guard using the standard and emergency frequencies President Robbins's military attaché had given them. There was no response; either everyone was dead, or they didn't have any functioning communications.

Lieutenant Gribaldi took pictures of each installation as they circled over it. At Everett, a huge aircraft carrier lay half-submerged at the dock with two F-18s still on her steeply-sloping deck. All the other ships at the base were burning, sunk, or both. At Kitsap, another carrier had been blown up in dry dock and was still burning along with all the ships and submarines sunk nearby. At Bangor, two ballistic missile subs were destroyed, one at dock and one at dry dock. The bases were a shambles of burning buildings, vehicles, ships, and aircraft, and they saw no evidence of any organized fire control effort. Mitchem began his approach to Joint Base Lewis-McChord.

"JBLM, this is the Royal Canadian Air Force calling Joint Base Lewis-McChord. Come in JBLM."

"Royal Canadian Air Force, this is JBLM. This frequency is reserved for US military use. What is your business?"

"JBLM, do you have a functioning runway where we can land? We have a message of utmost importance for your commanding officer."

"RCAF, how much runway do you need?"

"Eleven hundred meters, minimum."

There was a pause. "Can you land on a taxi strip? We have a fourteen hundred meter taxi strip still intact at McChord."

"Yes, sir. Could you possibly mark it with colored smoke?"

"We can do that, RCAF, but be advised McChord is covered with smoke from active fires; it may be hard to see the smoke we generate."

"I need something to tell me which taxiway is safe to land on."

"Give us half an hour."

Captain Mitchem circled around the base with Lieutenant Gribaldi taking pictures of the damage and watching his fuel gauge slowly moving toward empty. He no longer had enough fuel to return to Calgary. A lot of smoke still spewed from burning buildings and equipment, but he saw the taxiway he thought they meant; it paralleled what was left of the main runway.

Twenty minutes after the last transmission, his radio crackled to life. "RCAF, do you see purple smoke?"

"Yes, sir." The smoke was visible at both ends of the taxiway he had expected them to mark and was blowing away to the south. He brought the CT-155 around, lined up with the southern end of the taxiway, and brought the plane in for a short field landing.

The devastation at McChord spread out in front of and around him as he landed. On one side of the taxiway, what had been eleven huge planes—cargo or refueling tankers probably—were now just smoking piles of rubble. On the other side of the crater-filled runway were smaller ash piles that might have been fighters or possibly helicopters. He turned the plane onto an undamaged portion of the apron, shut down the engine, and waited. A jeep pulled up a minute later.

Fredrick Hudgin

"I'm going to need a step ladder to climb down," the captain shouted to him.

"Let me call," the driver told him.

Five minutes later a second jeep pulled up with a stepladder in the back. They set it up, and Mitchem climbed out, followed by Gribaldi.

"I have a message for your commanding general from President Robbins."

"President Robbins?" the sergeant asked, surprised. "He's dead."

"Not as dead as you might think. He's on Air Force One in Calgary."

"You'd better come with me."

As they drove back to Fort Lewis, Mitchem saw every major building at JBLM had been blown up. They passed through three checkpoints bristling with heavily armed soldiers and then parked in front of a partially-collapsed warehouse.

"Come with me." He led them through a doorway. Inside was a lieutenant seated at a desk. "We need to see General Wright."

"He's busy," the lieutenant told him.

"I think he'll want to be interrupted for this. President Robbins is alive. He's in Calgary."

"And here I thought he was in Kansas singing there's no place like home." The lieutenant snickered, looking back and forth between Captain Mitchem in his Royal Canadian Air Force flight uniform and the sergeant. Neither of them laughed. "Let me tell him. Wait here."

Thirty seconds later, Major General Timothy Wright burst through the door like a bear. He was a big man with a white hair crew cut and a ruddy face. "Get in here, Captain."

General Wright closed the door. Inside the room were eight other officers: a brigadier general, three colonels, three lieutenant colonels, and a major.

"What's this about? Tell us what happened. President Robbins is alive?"

The captain gave them the whole story Robbins had prepared about Air Force One being on approach into San

Page 199

Francisco when the bombing started—that they had diverted to Travis, then McChord, and then Calgary as each one was destroyed, how Air Force One had showed up in Calgary and the two F-35s escorting him ran out of fuel and landed in British Columbia. He gave the general the packet the president had prepared for him to deliver in case he found a functioning military.

"He has been unable to contact any US armed forces. He included frequencies and encryption codes for you to use to contact him. He also sent a second reconnaissance flight to Minot. I haven't heard what they found there."

General Wright gave the frequency and encryption data to Major Healy. "Joe, can you set this up?"

The major studied it. "Let me check with the 66th TAC. I seem to remember they got upgraded last year. If they did, we can use their equipment to make the transmission. But before we try that, I have another idea. Captain Mitchem, are you returning to Canada any time soon?"

"Well, yes—this afternoon if possible. President Robbins would like someone to come back with me to Calgary for a face-to-face."

Wright turned to Brigadier General Armon, the officer next to him. "Robert, I can't go, so you will have to. Find out what he wants and return tomorrow. It'd be nice to have some direction out of this clusterfuck."

"Yes, sir."

Major Healy spoke up again. "Captain Mitchem, could you carry a STU-15 with you when you return to Calgary? We have four here. That would allow us secure voice between the president and us."

"What's a STU-15?"

"Secure voice radio. Uses Rosy technology."

"How big is it?"

"The size of a shoebox."

"The CT-155 has no cargo storage, sir. It's a fighter trainer. The radio would have to sit on General Armon's lap."

The general sighed. "Yeah, I can do that. Give me some place to put the beverage service when we're in the air," he added with a snicker.

"General Wright, I'll need some fuel before I head back," the captain announced. "I don't have enough for the return flight. Can you top me off before I leave?"

"Don't know." He turned to the only attendee in the meeting with "US Air Force" above the pocket on his BDUs, Lieutenant Colonel Burnette, "Mike?"

"No problem. We have a million gallons, more or less, in underground bladders at McChord. No one throwing the bombs at us must have known about them; they weren't blown up with the rest of the base. I'll have to find a tanker truck that still runs with a pump that still works. That hasn't been too important until now—we don't have anything left that flies. Let me start some of my people working on it." He got up.

"Colonel Burnette, I saw two F-18s that appeared to be intact on an aircraft carrier at Everett. The carrier was sunk, but the flight deck was still above water." Mitchem turned to the General Wright. "Sir, as we flew around the Seattle area, Lieutenant Gribaldi took pictures of the destruction. We flew over Everett, Bremerton, Bangor and the areas between. Would you like us to pass those pictures to your intelligence section?"

"Please give them to Colonel Bennett." Wright nodded to the colonel beside him. "Russell, I want a presentation about what your team can see from the pictures—recovery efforts, damage, what's still intact. I want it by end of day."

"Absolutely, sir." He got up. "I'll have them begin the analysis immediately. Could I have that camera, lieutenant?" He held out his hand. "I'll have it returned as soon as we copy the pictures."

As Gribaldi handed it to the colonel, Mitchem had another idea. "Colonel Bennett, after you examine those photographs, if you find any areas you would like me to photograph in more detail on my return flight tomorrow, tell me where through the secure radios. Or, we could even do a reconnaissance flight."

"Will do, Captain. Thanks again, son. You've been a godsend. Please carry our sincere thanks back to Canada."

"I will. Thank you, sir."

Colonel Bennett walked out the door.

The general thought out loud, "Maybe those pictures will show why, of the thousands of military radios that existed in the greater Seattle area, not a single fucking one but ours is still working." He turned back to Mitchem. "Captain, have you eaten? We have a chow hall set up. Troops keep trickling in from around the state. We've been trying to establish a zone of control; it's pure anarchy outside JBLM. Seattle and Tacoma are having a lot of trouble with gangs and looters. We've been backing up what's left of the local emergency services and the National Guard as much as we can."

"Food sounds great, sir. Thank you. And we'll need quarters for Lieutenant Gribaldi until I bring General Armon back to you tomorrow."

"That is not a problem." He pressed his intercom button. "Lieutenant Johnson, find quarters for one of these Canadian pilots for the night."

"Yes, sir." The voice came back. "It'll be a tent."

"A tent will be fine, sir."

Chapter 28 – See You in a Few

Doug got home at midnight, exhausted. Clara was asleep in her grandmother's caned rocker in front of the TV. She'd put on *The Sound of Music* to stay awake and fell asleep in front of it.

"Guess who's sitting on the tarmac at the airport?" he asked her.

"I don't care, my love." She yawned and stretched. "Come to bed. You need some sleep."

"The President of the United States, that's who."

That made Clara stop. "Really? What is President Robbins doing up here? I'd have thought he'd be in some secure bunker somewhere with the rest of Washington."

"He was on his way to San Francisco when the bombs started. By the time he got turned around, Calgary was the only airport in range still in business."

"All the military airports are out of commission?"

"Not only are they out of commission, but they aren't even answering their radios. The US got hit hard."

"What about the rest of the world? Was everyone hit as bad as the US? Was this the aliens?"

"No one knows. Washington got hit first in a coordinated attack from sites all over the world. The US fired back at the sites and then at the countries containing the sites. Those countries fired back. It went crazy after that. Everyone firing at everyone else."

"Who fired at Canada?"

"So many portals were opening and closing that no one could keep track. The attack computers were running the show."

"How bad was Canada hurt?"

"We don't know yet. Pretty bad, I expect. Ottawa isn't answering. Neither is Montreal, Quebec City, Regina, Winnipeg, Vancouver, or Toronto. Edmonton was hit, but it's still functioning. Halifax is okay."

"I didn't know Canada had any Rosy attack machines."

"They didn't—*we don't!*" Doug said, trying to keep the anger out of his voice. "We think someone planted remote attack portals in our major cities. Once they launched at another country, those countries launched back at us."

"Why would anyone do that?" Clara asked, shocked.

"That's the question on everyone's mind at the Centre. Maybe it was because Canada backed the US in Afghanistan and Iraq, or maybe it was because we were simply adjacent to the US. We just don't know."

"Do they think radical Islam is behind this? Is this an Al-Qaeda attack?"

"We don't know yet. We may never know. The evidence was probably destroyed. For now, Canada's capital is in Edmonton, and the 3rd Canadian Division is still functional up there. They are trying to figure out how to set up lines of communication to what's left of the rest of the country. They asked the Aerospace Centre to build Rosy radios they will deliver to the cities around the country with recovery teams to coordinate reestablishing a provisional government. After that we will have to build and deliver Rosy transportation portals to deliver people and goods. Canada is too big and sparsely populated for everyone to have been killed and all our armed forces destroyed. The Aerospace Centre director is scheduling three shifts to build it all and created a search and pillage team to find all the components."

"Search and pillage?"

Doug laughed. "That was my name for 'em. Those are the scavengers who have to tear apart other stuff to get the materials to build what Edmonton wants. It isn't like we can offer a contract to twenty manufacturers and take the second lowest bid. President Robbins is trying to do the same with the US. He sent some Canadian planes to Seattle and found a half-assed recovery going on at Fort Lewis. He's hoping the other military bases around the country have survived and are recovering also. The Aerospace Centre has agreed to supply him with Rosy radios, too. Once he gets his F-35s up here from British Columbia, he's going to use them to distribute the radios."

Clara started to ask why the F-35s were in British Columbia but stopped. It was after midnight and they were both exhausted.

"Where are Kevin and Lily?"

"They went to bed long ago; Lan was tired and so were they. Come to bed, Doug. There's time to talk about this in the morning. You need some rest so you can get back to work tomorrow."

He closed his eyes and leaned back against the wall of the entranceway. "Yeah, I do. Now if I can just turn off my mind so I can get to sleep."

"Now *that* I can help with." Clara grabbed him by the belt and led him upstairs.

... ...

The oatmeal turned out better than Freddie had dared to hope. He'd found a Betty Crocker recipe book in the pantry that gave what turned out to be bulletproof instructions. A handful of dried, cut-up cranberries, some maple flavoring from the spice rack, a little agave sweetener, and protein powder. The kids had two bowls each. He was pretty proud of himself and ate two bowls, as well.

He'd decided he didn't want to advertise that he and the kids were camping in the house. No other houses were nearby, but he didn't want to take any chances after the guy with the rifle on the way there. They would stay away from the windows and wouldn't use any lights at night. After they'd eaten, Shannon and Wilson played with some boxes he'd found in the attic over the garage. The boxes were from the washer and dryer in the basement, and Freddie had cut windows and doors in the sides. The kids were having a great time playing house while *The Little Mermaid* played on the TV. Either the owners had loved kid's movies or they'd had kids or grandkids of their own because they had a huge collection of children's DVDs.

Four bedrooms were upstairs, and one even had a crib. He moved it to the bedroom at the back of the house, so the kids could sleep in it while he slept next to them on the bed. Thick curtains covered the windows that might allow some nighttime reading; the living room had two bookcases filled with books.

Each of the bedrooms had a closet, an end table, and a dresser. In one of them was a large desk that could double as a craft surface. The closets held no surprises—a bunch of clothes and shoes—and the dresser in the master bedroom contained everything he needed. The clothes were a little big around the waist, but a belt would keep them up. Nowhere in the house were any clothes for the kids. The upstairs bathroom had a magnificent iron bathtub, complete with ball-and-claw feet, and in the hall closet, he found a large first-aid kit.

Time to take a good look at my shoulder, he thought. He wasn't looking forward to this. It was sore and getting sorer.

When he looked in the bathroom mirror, the face that stared back shocked him. Dirt and soot covered him. His forehead was bruised, and scrapes and scabs ran down his left cheek, like he'd had a fight with a wildcat. He pulled off the makeshift bandage and examined the backside of his shoulder in the mirror. The cut was about two inches long. He didn't see any pus, but the cut was definitely unhappy—the edges were inflamed and red—and a little drainage was on the shirt sleeve with which he'd bound the wound. He ran hot water on a washcloth and began to wash the area around the cut. The washcloth felt like it was a thousand degrees, but Freddie ignored the pain and continued gently working the antibacterial soap into the laceration and massaging the edges.

"Come on! Bleed!" he whispered. Blood would flush out the wound. No sooner did the words come out of his mouth than he got his wish. The wound opened up and bled with a vengeance. He let it bleed for a while, continuing to massage the edges to encourage the cleansing flow. He repeatedly soaked up the blood with the washcloth and rinsed it out until the flow dwindled to almost nothing. He patted the skin dry with a clean towel, let it air-dry the rest of the way, and then put Steri-Strips on it to draw the edges together before slathering the whole thing with Neosporin. A clean pad of sterile gauze taped in place finished the dressing. *Stiches would be good, but I'm not going to operate on my own back.* His arms were already aching from what he'd done so far.

He washed the important parts of the rest of his body with the washcloth, put on clean clothes, and walked around the rest of the upstairs, feeling a lot better. In the footwell of the craft desk, he found a sewing machine. *This looks more fun than the oatmeal.* He'd never used one. *I wonder if she has a beginning sewing book, as well. I'll have to try to make the kids some clothes. How hard can it be?*

In the end table beside the bed in the master bedroom, he found a piece of paper with four two-digit numbers on it. He stared at it without comprehension. "No idea," he mumbled. "Maybe PINs to their bank accounts, but who cares? The bank is probably gone, along with the rest of the industrialized world." He put the paper back in the drawer. What he hadn't found was any kind of weapon, in case someone *else* decided this house looked like a good place to break into. "I thought everyone in Montana owned at least ten guns," he muttered in disappointment as he walked back downstairs. *All these survival supplies and no guns. It doesn't make any sense. Maybe they're in that safe in the basement. Now if I only had the combination...*

A screech came from the living room. And he decided it was time to bathe the babies. *They can run around in a couple of T-shirts until I make shorts for 'em. Thank God they're already potty-trained.* Freddie tried to remember if he'd seen any toilet paper in the storage room in the basement. "I'll have to check on that."

He tried to imagine what it would be like to do the third-world thing and use his hand instead of toilet paper—and he'd have to train the kids to do the same. He shuddered at the thought of two two-year-olds walking around a bathroom with crap all over their fingers. *Please let extra toilet paper be somewhere*, he thought, looking up, and then laughed at himself.

He hadn't said a prayer to the Almighty since Father Gilroy had cornered him in the chapel at St. Marks in Philadelphia. Freddie had been twelve years old, and he'd left the good father lying on the floor, unconscious, with his pants down around his knees. A solid right hook was one of the many things he had learned on the streets of Philly.

... ...

Davey Williams pulled his tractor-trailer into Sparwood/Elk Valley Airport. They were really there: two F-35s sitting on the apron next to the little pissant runway. He hadn't believed them when dispatch told him to pull a full tanker of JA-1 up here.

"It has to be a joke!" he'd fumed all the way up that winding highway. The world was going to hell in a handbasket, and he had to take time out of the emergency parking and refueling at the Canadian Rockies International Airport to drive a truck full of jet fuel to this remote community strip that never bought anything but avgas. Now that he was here and so were the fighters, he figured the joke was on him. What the hell were they *doing* here? US Air Force in Canada? And Edmonton had sent the requisition!

He parked the tanker next to the F-35s. "You the guys that ordered some jet fuel?"

"Yep, we need fuel." Captain Marshall walked around the side of her F-35.

The driver's eyes grew wide and he caught his breath. The captain could have been a centerfold—she was gorgeous. Even without makeup, she could make any man with a pulse stare, and maybe even some men without one. He'd never seen anyone fill out a flight suit like the one she was wearing.

"Uh, hello?" she asked him, waving her hands. "Are you going to fill us up?"

Lieutenant Owen walked up to them, finished from his business at the edge of the apron. "Another worshiper to add to the flock, Gaye?"

She rolled her eyes and sighed. The truck driver's name was above the pocket on his coveralls. "Davey, come on! Snap out of it! We need fuel. Let's get 'er going. Whaddaya say?"

Davey rubbed his face, took a breath, and walked toward the back of his tanker. He clipped on the ground wires, pulled out the fuel loading hoses, and dragged them over to the first F-35. He attached the hose to the fuel inlet on the fighter, turned on the pump, and started the transfer. "How many liters do you need?"

"Ten thousand each."

About halfway through the refueling of the first jet, he came around the side of the truck. "Would you guys mind taking my picture next to one of these F-35s? No one's gonna believe it when I tell them about it." He held out his cell phone.

She looked at her watch and the tanker filling the planes. Taking time for a picture wouldn't delay anything. "Sure," she said. "Stand next to the nose wheel."

"Why don't you pose next to him, Gaye?" Lieutenant Owen suggested. "You know that's what he wants."

She handed Gary the cellphone. "Come on, Davey. Let's give 'em somethin' to see." Captain Marshall walked up to him, fluffed her hair, put her arm around him, and gave her biggest smile for the camera. She kissed him on the cheek and Gary snapped another picture.

The pump flipped off; ten thousand liters in one jet and one to go. He rolled up the hose, climbed into the cab, and moved the truck to the other jet. Fifteen minutes later, he disconnected the hose and actuated the retraction motor to roll it up into the truck. "Sign here." He held out a clipboard to Gaye, and she signed her neat signature followed by her rank and duty station. "I need a phone number, too, eh?" He looked at her hopefully.

She glanced at her watch again in frustration. "I don't have time for this, Davey. Here's the number of the ops desk in Omaha." She scribbled the phone number. "I don't know why you want it— none of the phones work. Omaha probably glows in the dark."

"I can dream, Captain." He wrote his own phone number on the receipt and handed it to her. "You guys be careful." He climbed back into his truck and pulled away from the fighters.

"Let's get back on the job, Gary." She had stayed up all night talking with Margaret about the Air Force and flying in Afghanistan. The girl reminded her a lot of herself ten years ago. "Sorry about breakfast, Margaret." She had delivered breakfast just as the tanker pulled up, and the two pilots hadn't had time to eat any of it. "I know you will succeed at the Academy."

"Thanks, Gaye...I mean...Captain Marshall." "No problem about breakfast. Dad will eat it when he wakes up."

Gaye pulled the girl into a quick hug and then ran to her fighter and climbed into the jet, using a ladder from the hangar. Gary moved the ladder to his jet and climbed aboard, as well. Margaret moved the ladder away from the fighters, and the engines of the F-35s whined into a roar. Two minutes later, the countryside around Sparwood was treated to the sight and sound of two F-35s screaming out of their little airport, afterburners on. They took off to the south and then turned back north using a perfectly coordinated chandelle followed by a roll and a loop over Margaret. The Blue Angels would have been proud. Margaret watched the aerobatics in awe, dreaming of the day when she would do exactly the same thing in that exact fighter.

Davey saluted them as they passed over him, hoping Gaye would call someday, and then settled back for the long return ride to his home base at CRIA. At least the tanker was almost empty for the flip side of his trip. Maybe most of the frantic work would be finished by the time he got back. Canadian Rockies had received a lot of the smaller jets and planes that Calgary turned away so they could land the big ones.

The valley echoed with twin booms as both jets went through Mach 1 and they turned northeast toward Calgary, passing twenty thousand feet.

Captain Marshall alerted Air Force One. "Box Office, this is Crusty and Lucky Seven. We are inbound to Yankee-Yankee-Charlie. ETA in two-zero minutes."

"Roger, Crusty. Contact Calgary Approach on 123.8 for vectors. Welcome back. Report to Box Office upon landing."

"Roger, Calgary Approach on 123.8. See you in a few."

Chapter 29 – I'll See What I Can Find

Zarqa threw her bag on a bunk. She was small and slim as primates go: a meter and a half and fifty kilos with platinum blonde hair. Underestimating her was an easy mistake—think spring steel: lightweight but incredibly tough. She looked around the bunkroom in disgust. *Easy Wind* was in a horrible state of disrepair; everything she saw needed fixing or replacement. What wasn't broken had been half-assed patched at least once and sometimes two or three times. She'd forgotten what it was like to be on a for-hire vessel instead of a company ship.

"That bunk is taken," a voice from across the room told her.

The bunk had a rolled-up mattress with netting around it for when they were weightless. No nametag was on it. The other bunks in the rack had nametags.

"Looks empty to me," she said.

A male Mellincon came around the corner. He was at least a head taller than Zarqa, and his lion mane and tail filled the aisle beside the bunk. A scar shaped like a lightning bolt went from his left eye across his forehead to his right ear. She hadn't worked with Mellincons very often. He pointed to the bunk by the entrance to the latrine. "You can have that one over there."

With people going in and out of the latrine all night, no one in that bunk would get any rest. "I think I'll stay here. You can sleep over there, if you want."

"Move your shit, grub," the Mellincon growled. *Grub* was the not-so-affectionate name for a new crewmember.

"Not gonna happen, fuzzy." She got up in his face, as eye to eye as two beings so different in height could be. His whiskers touched her cheeks as he tried to stare her down. "I'm no grub. Save your newbie shit for someone else."

Flug was suddenly beside her. "Is there a problem, Zarqa?" He didn't have his machine gun pointed at the Mellincon, but it could be in a heartbeat.

"No problem—just an exchange of opinions." She didn't break eye contact with her new *friend*.

The Mellincon glanced at the other primate. "And you would be?"

"Flug."

He gave Zarqa a cold stare and spit on the floor. "The hiring pool on Taramon must be the dregs," he growled, padding away. As he turned the corner, he ran his claws across the metal of the bunk, leaving deep scratch marks.

"There's always one," Zarqa said almost to herself as the Mellincon disappeared behind another rack of bunks.

"When there isn't more than one," Flug whispered, watching where the Mellincon had exited.

"When do you start to work?" she asked, changing the subject.

"Waiting on someone called Ursa to find me. How 'bout you?"

"Beginning of the next shift, in"—she checked the ship's clock on the wall of the bunkroom—"two hours. I thought I'd check out the canteen and see what kind of food it has. You coming?"

"Yeah, I could use some food."

That made her laugh. "When could you *not* use some food? You eat more than any five low-gravity primates."

"That's so I can keep my girlish figure. Do you think it works?" He took up a ridiculous pose with his heavily-muscled arms bulging behind his head, his knees crossed, and a lewd grin on his face.

Zarqa rolled her eyes. "Come on, Gorgeous."

As they walked through the bunkroom door toward the canteen, a pair of eyes watched them from the shadows of the next room.

... ...

Doug looked back and forth between Lily and Kevin. "Are you sure you can work in Canada? Isn't Rosyville and the US government going to have a problem with you working up here?"

"I'm not sure Rosyville even exists anymore, let alone much of a government for the old US-of-A," Kevin said. "The way I see it, if we can help the Canadian and US governments recover from this attack, everyone wins. Who cares where we are while we help?"

"Why don't we ask President Robbins for permission?" Lily looked out the window of the kitchen as she held her cup of tea, waiting for it to cool. "I mean, he's right here, and we *are* US citizens. I don't think too many people are clamoring for his attention."

"The Centre doesn't have any childcare facilities. Who will watch Lan?" Doug asked.

"That would be me," Clara spoke up. "I'm sure that, between Mindy, Martin, and me, we can entertain another two-year-old. We might even talk Bill into giving us all a hay ride behind the tractor."

"Martin would love some company," Mindy said as she bounced Lan on her knee.

"Well, let's go to the airport," Doug told them. "I'll call work and tell them we're coming. I'm sure the director won't have any problem with another couple of Nobel Laureates helping out."

… … … … … … … … …

Leann's voice came through on the intercom. "Sir, I hate to interrupt you, but we have an incident."

"What's happening, Leann?" President Robbins' voice was thick with fatigue.

"We have two people inside the terminal asking to see you. They are from Rosyville—a Dr. Yuan and Dr. Langly."

"Christ!" he muttered to himself. "What the hell are *they* doing up here?"

Leann misunderstood; she thought he was talking to her. "They want your permission to work at the Canadian Aerospace Centre while the Rosy radios and transportation portals are being constructed. They say they are friends of Douglas Medder and were visiting him here when the attack came."

"Did Security check them out?"

"Yes, sir. They both have US passports. They aren't on the no-fly list or on the FBI wanted criminal list, at least the latest one we have. They aren't carrying any bags or weapons."

The president sighed. "So much for a couple of hours' sleep." He got up and pulled on his robe. "Tell security to bring them in, Leann. I'll meet 'em in the conference room."

"Yes, sir."

Robbins got a cup of coffee and waited. A knock on the door sounded five minutes later, and Lily and Kevin walked in. "Hi, Dr. Yuan and Dr. Langly. What can I do for you? Would you like some coffee or tea?"

"No, thank you, President Robbins," she told him. "We were here visiting Douglas Medder when the bombs started. He is working at the Canadian Aerospace Centre making secure Rosy radios for the Canadian and US governments. We figured we could help. Doug, Kevin, and I invented the Rosy technology while we were graduate students at Stanford. Doug wanted us to get permission from the US government before we started. You are the only one we could think of to ask."

He considered their request, remembering the turmoil that had surrounded the three when he was running for office. They had been locked up at the Jet Propulsion Labs in Pasadena, California, for "their own protection" because President Klavel had tried to stop the spread of Rosy technology outside the United States. His attempts had failed. Now almost every country around the world had found a way to acquire Rosy, following the lead of the US lead in weaponizing it. Robbins defeated Klavel, largely because of the bad press his rival got from the detention of the students.

"The United States hasn't been very kind to you two, has it?"

"The people of the United States have been wonderful to us, sir," Lily told him with a hint of bitterness. "It was the government that treated us poorly."

"And now you want to help us? Why?"

She turned to Kevin, unsure of what to say. He took over, deciding the only path was truth. "The three of us were disgusted with how our Rosy wormhole generator was turned into a weapon. We feel the destruction of the US was a direct result of that decision. What should have been a boon for the peaceful spread of humanity into the galaxy has, instead, turned into its worst nightmare. But we are Americans, President Robbins, and someone attacked our country. Hundreds of thousands—perhaps millions—of innocent people have been killed because of something we invented. We want a chance to show everyone what Rosy should have been instead of what it was turned into. We want to foster peaceful uses of Rosy technology—uses that will benefit humanity instead of blowing it up."

President Robbins took a sip of coffee as he pondered what to do. "Sure. Anything you can do to help would be appreciated. The Canadians have been more than cooperative with allowing me to impose on them until I establish some kind of government back in the US; this is the least I can do. Thanks for asking. Please don't divulge any classified information you may have carried with you from Rosyville."

Lily responded. "If, by classified, you mean ways to use Rosy as a weapon, you can count on us not to disclose anything like that. I don't believe we know anything else that's classified. Could we have your permission in writing, please?"

"I will have the letter for you in a couple of minutes. Please wait outside."

"Yes, sir."

Robbins pressed the intercom button. "Leann, could you come in here for a moment?"

Lily and Kevin passed the young woman as she entered.

"Leann, please draft a letter from me to Drs. Yuan and Langly stating they have my permission to work at the Canadian Aerospace Centre. State in the letter they are not authorized to reveal any classified information associated with the weaponizing of wormholes while they work there. The duration of their work will be as long as needed during the present crisis of the attack on the United States and Canada. They are waiting for the letter. Please compose it for my signature as soon as you can."

"I'll do it now, sir. It should be ready in a couple of minutes."

"Copy Homeland Security, NASA, the FBI, the NSA, the CIA, the US secretary of state, Canada's minister of state, and the director of the Canadian Aerospace Centre. Thank you, Leann."

"Uh, sir?"

"Yes? What is it?"

"We have no internet access. How can I send copies to those recipients?"

"We have to assume we will resurrect the internet sooner or later. Those emails will sit on our server until then. We are still the government of the United States; eventually this crisis will pass and we will return to the business of running the country. I need to protect the people who will help us in that recovery. The witch-hunt is coming and I don't want those kids to be on the chopping block. We're going to need all our brilliant minds to get through this one. If anyone has to take the heat for this decision, I want it to be me."

"Yes, sir."

... ...

"Taramon Traffic Control, this is *Black Swan*. We request a departure window."

"*Black Swan*, you may leave immediately. Please make sure your jump is at least one light year away from Taramon."

"Roger, Taramon. Thanks for the R & R."

"*Black Swan*, you are welcome back any time. TTC out."

Captain Xanny poised his tentacle above the jump button. It was time to leave pirating behind again and return to the life of a licensed starship captain on quarantine duty: safe, legal, and boring.

Lieutenant Fibari misunderstood his hesitation. "They'll be fine."

"Oh, I'm not worried about Flug and Zarqa. They knew the risks when they volunteered. When they are finished collecting their data, they'll let us know." He sighed and touched the jump button, and a Rosy aura surrounded them.

The alleys and bars of Taramon would still be there the next time he visited. Maybe Xirandra would be grown.

... ...

"Do you remember how to get to your uncle's house, Josephina?" Rebecca asked. The rain culvert where they'd spent the night had provided little comfort. It was the middle of the day when they reached Santa Clarita, and both of them were tired.

Josephina had trouble keeping up; her feet were swollen and bleeding from walking ten miles on the freeway without shoes. Rebecca had tied rags around the girl's feet to protect them, but she was limping badly. Rebecca worried about how much longer she would be able to walk at all.

"Do you have any idea where your uncle lives?" she repeated.

"That way, I think." Josephina pointed across the overpass. "I don't remember the address—someone always took me there. They live in an apartment across from a mall with a Walmart and a barbeque place." A series of pops sounded nearby. "Are those firecrackers?" she asked, startled.

Rebecca grabbed her and dove behind a short decorative wall next to the exit ramp. "I'd say no—those are probably gun shots."

A pickup truck full of men with rifles and shotguns sped by them on Lyons Avenue, shooting at the police car following them with its lights on and siren wailing. A cop leaned out the window and shot back at the pickup with his automatic rifle. When the police car's windshield exploded after a shotgun blast from the pickup, it careened across the street, knocked over a street lamp pole, and came to a stop on top of the wall that said, "Welcome to Santa Clarita." The truck sped down the street and disappeared behind a grocery store. No one came out of the stores to help the officers. The street was deserted.

"What's his name?" Rebecca asked, wishing they had better cover.

"Who?" She was still staring at the police car.

"Your uncle," she said, trying not to get irritated.

"Carlos Sanchez."

Several spurts of automatic gunfire came from a nearby 76 gas station, and then a guy clutching a pistol ran out into the street. Blood covered the front of his white sleeveless T-shirt. He turned and fired two bursts into the gas station he had just left, fired once more into the street in front of him, and then went to his knees. He tried to lift the gun again but instead, leaned over and put his head on the street with his arms to the side and his butt sticking up in the air. He was still clutching his gun in his right hand, but he didn't move again.

A man with a pistol ran out of the 76 convenience store toward the guy in the road and looked up and down Lyons Avenue. He kept his gun pointed at the guy, kicked the guy's gun away, and pushed him over with his toe; the guy rolled onto his side and remained motionless. The man leaned over and took the dead guy's gun, emptied his pockets, and left him lying in his blood pool. Next he checked out the cops—apparently both were dead. Emptying the cops' trunk took two trips, and then he came back for their guns, ammunition, and wallets. He kicked the dead guy in the head as he walked pass him on his last return trip.

"Come on," Rebecca whispered. "We gotta get outta here." She began walking in the direction Josephina had indicated her uncle lived, helping Josephina as she hobbled on her injured feet, very glad they were moving away from the guy in the street and the steaming police car. They walked a couple of intersections to The Old Road.

"There's the Walmart!" Josephina squealed. Someone had crashed through the front doors with a vehicle. People were walking out with cartloads of goods and loading them into cars and trucks. Rebecca kept them on the other side of the street as they carefully skirted the looting at the mall. "And there's the barbeque place!" She jumped and clapped her hands. "We're almost there!"

When they came to the apartment complex, the girl led them up some stairs and knocked on a door. There was no answer. "Uncle Carlos?" she said to the door. "It's me, Josephina."

The curtains opened a crack and a brown face appeared. The door was flung open and the girl was suddenly embraced by the entire family.

"Josephina! What are you doing here?"

"Where is your mother?"

"What happened to your family?"

"Are you hurt?"

A man who looked to be about sixty with a crewcut and short salt-and-pepper beard came outside. "Get her inside," he commanded. He looked around to make sure no one had followed the women to his apartment. "Who are you?" he asked suspiciously, his hand behind his back.

"A friend. And you would be Carlos Sanchez?"

"*Sí.*"

"Well, Josephina asked me to bring her here. So, I guess I'll be on my way."

"She saved my life, Uncle Carlos," Josephina announced from behind him.

He turned back to the girl. "How did she do that, *mi flor?*"

She was grateful for his endearment, which meant "my flower." Her uncle had called her *mi flor* since she was born. Tears started to trickle down her face and her voice faltered. "Uncle Carlos, these men—a gang—they had me on the ground..." She looked into his face, her eyes pleading him to understand—to not make her say it.

His eye grew narrow and his lips pressed together. "Who was it?"

"*Cueva Diablo.*"

The adults in the room gasped as one. *Cueva Diablo*—Devil's Cave—was a violent gang in the San Fernando Valley.

"Are you *sure*?" His voice dripped with hatred.

"I am sure. Mickey Suarez was one of the guys and Rebecca killed him!" Mickey was a lieutenant in the gang, and he'd made his desire to be Josephina's boyfriend well known. Carlos had thrown him out of her mother's house; the bad blood between them was renowned. She continued in a rush, "Rebecca killed Mickey and some other guy I didn't know. She made them stop doing what they were doing to me and made one of them give me his clothes in the middle of the parking lot. If it wasn't for her, I'd be dead or worse. We walked all the way from Mission Hills and slept in a rain pipe last night."

Carlos stared at his niece in silence, considering what she'd said. He turned back to her companion. "I apologize for my rudeness, Rebecca. These are hard times. Thank you for bringing our Josephina to us. You must be tired; please come in." He opened the door wide.

Five other adults and seven children were in the apartment. Rifles and shotguns were lined up against the wall by the door, and all the men had pistols in their hands. When they saw Carlos admitting the other woman, each of them flipped on the safety and tucked his pistol back into his belt. Rebecca took a seat in a chair next to the door. The table in the dining room was loaded with food—they were obviously just about to eat. Her stomach growled. MRE's might be adequate when they were all you have, but this food smelled heavenly.

Josephina was in the process of telling everyone about her trip here. Her eyes filled with tears. "Mom's dead!"

An old woman Rebecca figured was Carlos's wife gasped and held her hand to her mouth. "Juanita is dead? *Aiii, Dios mio! Aiii! Aiii!*" She started rocking and crying.

"The whole apartment building was on fire," she told them through her tears. "I heard her screaming. The next thing I knew, Rebecca was stopping *Cueva Diablo* from doing...what they did."

After Josephina finished her story of their trip to Santa Clarita, Carlos's wife walked over to Rebecca and gave her a hug. "*Gracias*, for bringing my sister's daughter to us. I will pray that Jesus will walk with you and protect you."

"*De nada, señora.* Josephina will be fine. She's a tough little girl."

The old woman smiled at the girl and then at Rebecca. She muttered something under her breath in Spanish, touched Rebecca's forehead, and closed her eyes. "That will keep you safe. *Vaya con Dios.* But for now, come eat. Everyone, come eat! The food is getting cold."

The old woman led Rebecca to the table, and the rest of the family got into line behind her as she filled her plate and sat back down to eat. After everyone had served themselves, she asked, "Would any of you know where I could buy a car? I have three hundred miles to go to reach my husband. I had to leave my car on the freeway in Los Angeles."

Carlos nodded at one of the other men. "José, do you know?"

"*Sí*, there are many cars. What kind of car do you want?"

"Something with four-wheel drive. Jeremiah lives up in the mountains."

"I'll see what I can find." He poured the food on his plate onto a tortilla, rolled it into a burrito, stood, and left the apartment.

Rebecca sat in the chair and simply enjoyed the happy family swirling around her. Josephina was being treated like royalty. Her feet were in a tub of hot water while everyone waited on her. Rebecca got up to wash her plate in the sink and it was gently but firmly removed from her hands by one of the older children. She sat back down and got comfortable in her chair, and the people in the apartment faded as she fell asleep—warm, comfortable, and safe for the first time in three days.

Chapter 30 – You Won't Believe It

"What about all the little airports?" Captain Marshall asked, raising her hand a little self-consciously. For the first time in her life, she had been invited to a National Security Council meeting with the president of the United States. She knew it was only because so few military personnel were on board Air Force One for what was supposed to have been a quiet public relations flight. They were discussing how to contact the surviving military in the US.

"What do you mean, Captain?" President Robbins asked.

Gaye cleared her throat. Everyone in the room—generals, colonels, the president—was looking at her. She swallowed and commanded the butterflies in her stomach to settle down—the butterflies weren't listening. "The big airports are all out of commission, at least until their runways and facilities are repaired, but what about all the little airports? Tens of thousands of them are spread all over the US and Canada. Most will still have functioning airplanes we could use. A lot of them will have longer-range twin-engine planes, like Beechcraft King Airs and Cessna 340's, and the older ones use gasoline instead of jet fuel. Gas is going to be a lot easier to find at the little airports when they need refueling. Plus, the little planes can land almost anywhere."

"And we have hundreds of pilots camping out in and around the Calgary airport," General Rheem added, wondering why he hadn't thought of the same thing. He was the Air Force military attaché who carried the black box with all the missile launch codes, never more than a few steps from the president at any time.

Leann came into the conference room. "The STU-15 General Armon brought has been synced, sir. We have communication with JBLM. General Wright is waiting to talk to you."

"Put him on the speaker phone."

The phone popped. "President Robbins?"

"Yes. Is this General Wright?"

"Yes it is, sir."

"Please record this conversation so you will have a permanent record."

After a short pause, Wright said, "We are recording it now, sir."

"This is George Robbins, president of the United States, talking to Major General Timothy Wright, commanding general of Joint Base Lewis-McChord, in Washington State. General Wright, what is your status?"

"We have approximately five thousand combat-ready troops, including the walking wounded. There are about twenty-five hundred seriously wounded and another seventy-five hundred missing and assumed dead. The units of the First and Seventh Infantry Divisions stationed here have lost about fifty percent of their manpower. The 47th Combat Support Hospital from the Reserves has set up on the base at about half strength with maybe a quarter of their equipment; they have triaged the injured and are attempting to treat the ones they can help, but they are overwhelmed. Many of the seriously wounded are not expected to make it. We have extinguished most of the fires burning around JBLM, and we have set up temporary housing for the troops that survived the bombing. Almost every building on the base was destroyed. We are burying the dead in mass graves. There were too many to do anything else with them."

"Do you have arms and ammunition to secure the base?"

"Yes, sir, we do. That stuff was kept in underground warehouses as a contingency against exactly what happened. We are secure and functioning, sir."

"Have you made any contact with other military units in the Seattle area?"

"No, sir. The pictures Canadian Captain Mitchem gave us yesterday showed massive damage at Bremerton, Everett, and Bangor. There is nothing left of Kitsap command center and no organized recovery going at any installation. None of the bases are answering our attempts to contact them via radio. We plan to send a convoy to them tomorrow to organize any survivors and set up aid stations."

"Do you have any functional aircraft?"

"No, sir. Not a one."

The president glanced at Captain Marshall. "Have you checked the local private airports?"

"Do you mean like the old Boeing Field, sir? They were destroyed with the rest of the commercial fields."

"I mean the small private airports where people fly single-engine airplanes. They escaped the destruction up here. I'm sure you can find something that flies at one of them. You can use those little planes to do your reconnoitering and transportation between the bases."

"Yes, sir. We hadn't thought to use them. We'll do that without delay."

"Send people up to the three naval bases. I'll be willing to bet all three have surviving military. Secure those bases and bring them under your command. There are a lot of weapons on them, including some nukes; we don't want them falling into the wrong hands. We'll be sending you more Rosy radios. Use them to establish zones of control. What is the situation outside of JBLM?"

"There is widespread looting and mayhem. We have declared martial law and established a curfew, but we haven't been able to enforce it or even announce it effectively. The local police and emergency services are overwhelmed and the highways are completely clogged with abandoned vehicles. As soon as we secure the three naval bases, we will assist them in bringing back law and order."

"Have you encountered any chemical or biological weapon damage?"

"No, sir, not yet."

"Be on the lookout for it. From what we've learned so far, both types of weapons were used on Washington, New York, and Los Angeles. I am giving you wartime powers of command and materials acquisition, General. If you need something, take it and give a receipt. And use wartime terms of engagement. Deadly force is authorized when we are attacked, but remember these people are Americans. We don't want to attack people defending their own property; we want to arrest the law-breakers and assist the law-enforcers."

"Yes, sir, I understand. Does anyone know what happened?"

"We were attacked. I wish I had a better answer for you. At this time, we don't know why or who. Based on the lack of radio traffic around the world, we weren't the only ones who were attacked. Our Rosy defense systems were programmed to respond automatically to where we were attacked from. As it turned out, the countries we fired back at might not have been the people who actually attacked us. Those countries were simply where the attackers hid their launch sites. It went downhill from there. Everyone started throwing bombs at everyone else."

"So, this is worldwide?" the general asked in surprise. "It wasn't just us?"

"We think so. We haven't been able to talk to any other country but Canada. The communications satellites were taken out, along with the internet and GPS. I have one more thing to ask. I want to send General Armon to Edmonton as my liaison to the 3rd Canadian Division. They are still in business and may be the last military unit still functioning in Canada. Can you survive without him?"

"You do what you need to, sir. I will continue here with the tasks you have given me. We will get through this."

"I want daily reports of your progress—more often if necessary. If you encounter something unexpected or have an idea we haven't thought of, tell us immediately. We will do the same for you."

"Yes, sir."

"We are in the process of making and sending more Rosy radios to the other military installations around the country. Like Fort Lewis, I expect to see groups of survivors at each one. We are going to use these radios to reestablish our government. We are also making Rosy transportation portals and will be transporting one of those to you. We need you to inventory what supplies you have and send us the list. I will have each base with which we establish contact do the same. Since we can't requisition new supplies yet, we will have to share what we have through the portals. But for now, your primary supply channel is what you can scrounge from the area around your fort."

"My quartermaster will begin the inventory as soon as we finish this call."

"How about McChord? How bad was it hit?"

"McChord is out of commission, sir."

"Can the runway be repaired enough to land a cargo plane like a C-130?"

A new voice came across the radio. "Sir, this is Lieutenant Colonel Burnette. I believe I am the senior surviving Air Force officer at McChord. The C-130 needs a minimum of three thousand feet to land. We have a fifteen-hundred-meter taxi strip that is intact. That should be adequate until we can repair the main runway. The Canadian pilot who visited us yesterday was able to land and take off from it."

"Good to know. As soon as we find a cargo plane, we will use it to bring you a transportation portal. Once it is in place, we can use it to send materials and personnel to support you. Do you have any questions?"

"Were any nukes deployed?"

"Not that we know of—at least not from our end." Robbins thanked himself again for refusing to allow the nukes to be attached to the Rosy bomb distribution centers.

"How about the subs? Did any boomers or attack subs survive?"

"I hope so, but I have no confirmation on either. We have no way to contact them at the present time."

"I may be able to help with that, sir. Bangor had the low frequency encrypted radios that the subs listen to. I'll put that at the top of the list of things we need to find."

"If you are able to contact any of the fleet, please tell us without delay."

"Yes, sir."

The president looked around the conference room at the staff that accompanied him on his trip to San Francisco. "Does anyone have any other ideas of how we can help JBLM?"

Leann Jenkins spoke up. "General Wright, can you find a radio transmitter? One on a civilian band? Something powerful?"

"Probably. Why? What would we do with it?"

"The people are terrified. No one knows what's going on or what's happened. You could start broadcasting on both the AM and FM bands—tell them what you know, that help is coming, and that this anarchy is temporary. Tell them how they can help. You could use the radio to activate all Reserve and National Guard personnel within its range and order them to report to JBLM for the duration of the emergency."

Robbins stared at Leann in amazement. *Why didn't I think of this?* He jumped in. "General Wright, many of them won't want to leave their families because of the violence and anarchy. Tell them to bring their dependents with them. They will be safe on the reservation and you'll get a lot more people you can draw on for help. Ask for all retired military and people with prior service to report. Promise full pay and benefits. Use them to augment your active duty troops. I will send you a daily announcement to run every hour about the status of the country, and I want you to augment that with daily local news updates. We have to convince them that the United States will come through this. If our citizens think we are still in control and they are part of the solution, things will calm down. We will feed you information as we discover it.

"Also ask all able-bodied people to report to Fort Lewis for training as militia. Tell them to bring their own weapons, ammunition, and vehicles. Train the militias in how to calm people down. Start a court system to punish the law-breakers. Try to arrest instead of shoot. Imbed trained soldiers in the militias as advisors instead of keeping them as separate combat units, but hold back some good people to be emergency response units for when the militias get in over their heads. We want the law-abiding militias to view us as a support system, not adversaries. We want the law-breaking militias and gangs to be arrested or killed.

"And we need more than combat troops. Announce that we need every skill and trade to help repair the infrastructure and get things back to normal. Make the fort functional first. We need heavy equipment operators, electricians, plumbers, carpenters, firefighters, nurses, doctors, cooks, mechanics, and anyone who wants to help. Have them come to Fort Lewis, so we can put them to work fixing this country. And you better be ready for them—a lot of people will be showing up. Americans in a crisis are like no other people in the world; they will roll up their sleeves and get to work.

"I want you to establish your command as the go-to people for the Northwest. Create a priority list. We need everything. Purchase, rent, or take whatever construction equipment and supplies you can find. I am authorizing you to use your emergency cash reserves for pay and procurement. Once electricity and water begin to flow again—once people can leave their houses without worrying about being raped, murdered, or robbed—they will start to believe we can return to normal. General Wright, call us if you need us."

"Yes, sir."

… … … … … … … …

"How many units have you completed today?" Lily asked the assembly line supervisor.

"Forty. The changes you showed us have allowed us to double our output."

"Make sure they are delivered to the Calgary airport for distribution."

"We're dropping them off twice a day."

"What are they doing with the radios? None of those airliners can land anywhere but here."

"You won't believe it," the supervisor said. "They are flying 'em out on little airplanes. They collected a fleet of Cessnas, Pipers, Mooneys, and Beechcrafts from the local private airports around here. The pilots of the jet liners parked on top of each other at the airport are planning to fly those little planes all over North America, delivering radios to any military they can find. They are calling themselves the Beechcraft Brigade."

Lily shook her head in amazement. "Have they found any military still functioning?"

"Well, they've found people at every base and fort they've visited so far. Fort Lewis in Washington State was the first. Since then they've set up communications with Minot Air Force Base in North Dakota, Fort Carson in Colorado, Fort Riley in Kansas, and Great Lakes Naval Station near Chicago. They've tried to find someone around the District of Columbia, but no one answers and the smoke is still so thick they can't see any kind of recovery on the ground. What they did see wasn't good. The Pentagon is just a hole; so is Fort Meade and the CIA headquarters in Langly. And they picked up lots of gamma radiation. Looks like someone popped some nukes on our capital."

"My God! Nukes! How about Canada? Have they found anything in Canada?"

"No nukes yet. Outside of the military bases and Ottawa, Canada came through without a lot of people damage. I mean, the bridges are blown; the airports are out of commission; and the electricity, water, and phone systems are shot. But, compared to the US, Canada was a cake walk. Tomorrow, the Brigade is going to try the US East Coast—Maine, Massachusetts, Rhode Island, Connecticut, New York City. They have to do it in hops since those little planes don't have the range to make it in one leg. They've got another crew ready to try the Southeastern United States. Canada's sending their own planes to Vancouver, Regina, Moose Jaw, and Ottawa."

Kevin joined them. "How are the radios going?"

"Great!" Lily told him. "We're producing forty a day."

"How are they going to distribute them? The bridges have been knocked out all the way across Canada." She told him about the Beechcraft Brigade. "No shit! What a wonderful idea."

"And now everyone is clamoring for more radios. A week ago, they couldn't talk at all, and now they want more!"

"What about the transportation portals? How are they coming?"

"We go into production this afternoon. The first one should be ready in about a week. But no one's figured out how we're going to put them where they need to be. The big planes don't have anywhere to land, and the roads are blown to hell. The only portals still functioning from before are the one in Halifax and Doug's development portals here."

Lily sat quietly for a moment, considering the problem. "I wonder why the planes they're sending out aren't reporting where the bridges are damaged. If we knew that, we could figure out a route for trucks to deliver the transportation portals."

"Don't know. I'll suggest it to Doug. He can probably convince the director to ask the people organizing the Brigade."

"How's the radio station repair going?" Kevin had been working on it all day.

"The only thing wrong with it is the power. They had a generator, but they'd never used it. It didn't work. The diesel engine locked up after only half an hour. I'm putting in a dark energy generator. The production line is making one just for this. Should be done today."

"How far will the radio reach?"

"Sixty thousand watts? I would expect a thousand miles on the AM side at night—maybe more, depending on weather conditions. FM will be a lot smaller than that."

"That should help settle people down."

"I hope so. Fort Lewis is setting one up, as well."

"Is that light I see at the end of the tunnel?"

"Unless it's a train. We're a long way from 'out of the woods.'"

… … … … … … … …

"Commander Chirra, we have received a message from Grock." Lieutenant Nussi was on duty as officer of the deck.

Chirra answered, "I'll be there shortly."

He floated onto the bridge. Everyone pretended to be busy as they waited to hear what Grock was going to do about the nukes. "Nola, please play the message—and turn the volume up. I'm sure everyone wants to know."

Nola pressed the play button and the communication software read the message. "Per Envoy Gart-Disp, a SEV-1 is not—I repeat, *is not*—authorized. If you have prepared it in expectation of its allowance, immediately destroy all you have in incubation. It is the envoy's decision that enough damage has been done to the primates' infrastructure to disallow their ability to create a starship. You will continue to monitor the primates and maintain their quarantine. However, to reduce the complications of a large area of the continent becoming uninhabitable due to the nuclear detonations, evacuate the contaminated area to a depth of one kilometer. The crater will backfill with seawater, which will cleanse any minor residual radioactivity. This will allow the next selected species to flourish without worry of radioactive contamination in their gene pool. If you can determine the location of any remaining fission or fusion devices, including electrical generation reactors, evacuate them, as well."

The commander looked at everyone on the bridge. "You heard them. Send the SEV-1 we have prepared into the sun." He turned to Sergeant Bleese, Lieutenant Fibari's second-in-command for weapons. "Sergeant Bleese, prepare the evacuation modules. I want them deployed within a day. Coordinate with Sergeant Zpplt to get the extent of the needed evacuation. For many of the targets, it will take more than one evacuation device. Use as many as you need, but do not penetrate the crust of the planet. One kilometer deep—no more than one kilometer. If you need more devices than we have in inventory, tell me. Grock will send us all we need."

"Yes, sir." He left the bridge.

Chirra pressed his comm link again. "Sergeant Zpplt?"

"Yes, sir."

"Please commence a scan for any remaining fission or fusion devices on the planet. Include the electrical generation stations. Give the coordinates of any device you find to Sergeant Bleese for evacuation."

"Yes, sir."

… … … … … … … …

"Rebecca, wake up."

She opened her eyes and yawned. It was dark outside. Josephina was standing over her. "How long have I been asleep?"

"All afternoon and most of the night. José found you a car." He stood next to her.

"What did you find, José?"

"It was a tough deal, but the owner finally agreed. I got you a Jeep Cherokee."

"That's perfect! What do I owe you? How much does the owner want?"

"The owner donated the car to you after he heard about how you brought Josephina to us—how you killed the *violadores*." He saw that she didn't understand his Spanish word. "How you killed the rapists, Rebecca."

"Donated? Really?"

"He didn't need it anymore. At least, that's what he told me."

"Where is it?"

"In the parking lot. I filled the tank with gas."

Rebecca pulled on her shoes and walked outside with José. The Cherokee was in the driveway, between the rows of cars. It looked almost new. The lights were on and the motor running. Both front door windows were gone, and the car was still dripping water. "And you washed it, too?"

"The owner was a pig. I was happy to clean it for you."

Rebecca decided she didn't want to ask him about paperwork. "Thank you, José. I appreciate you 'finding' this car for me." She hugged him. He was surprised and hugged her back awkwardly.

As she opened the door, Josephina hobbled to her and hugged her tightly. "Thank you, Rebecca. *Please* be careful."

"I will, Josephina. You be careful, too. Goodbye."

"Wait!" the girl said, handing her cell phone to José. "Picture!" He took three pictures with Josephina doing various poses with Rebecca, and then it was time to leave.

As she got to the entrance ramp on I-5, Rebecca noticed a brown paper grocery bag on the passenger seat next to her; it was full of food, and next to the bag was a box of hollow point .380

cartridges, the ammunition her gun used. She pulled her pistol from its holster. It had been cleaned, oiled, and reloaded; the magazine was full, and a round was in the chamber with the safety on. Her backpack was on the floor with six full bottles of water in it. The money was still there, untouched, under a fresh supply of MREs.

Every lane on the freeway was jammed with abandoned cars. She wove through them on her way to Sonora. Many times, a blockage forced her to leave the highway and drive on the grass beside the road. Sometimes she had to cross the median to the other lane or push over the deer fence next to the road and then take local roads to bypass a freeway blockage or knocked down overpass.

As she progressed toward Jeremiah's mountain home, she wondered if he had returned. Would he be waiting for her? Was he still alive? Would he want her back?

Chapter 31 – Blood, Guns, and Hostages

"Let's go for a walk." Freddie and the kids had lived in the house for four weeks. At least once a day, he brought the kids outside. Spring was in full bloom, and bright green foliage was appearing on all the trees and bushes. The weather was clear and in the fifties, and no one was around. Each time they went outside, before they left the security of the mudroom, he studied the area around the house carefully.

He'd made moccasins for the children out of some boot socks from the dresser in the master bedroom with shoelaces woven into the tops to tie them above their knees and some leather from a vest sewn to the bottoms with the sewing machine. "Not too bad for an old sailor." He watched with amusement as the kids ran around wearing them.

Their jackets were made from a pair of thermal vests he'd found in what must have been an older child's bedroom. Some long johns had morphed into pants held up by another pair of shoelaces, and the T-shirts became the kids' primary clothes. He'd cut down two sweaters so they fit the two-and-a-half-year-olds and had another bout with the sewing machine to sew them back together.

"Only broke one needle this time!"

He and the machine were slowly becoming friends—well, more of an armed neutrality, but at least it wasn't fighting him quite as much as it had at the beginning.

"I want red shirt!" Wilson screamed.

"No! MINE!" Shannon screamed back.

"You can wear it next time, Wilson," Freddie told him. "Shannon had it first. How about the Harley shirt? It has a motorcycle on it."

"Yeah! Harley!" That made him chuckle. Wilson had never seen a real Harley, but they'd watched *Easy Rider* last night. The kids had liked the music.

He checked again for anyone else in sight as they went out the back door. A doe and two fawns lifted their heads and bounded away into the forest behind the house, the fawns right behind their mama.

"Well, it's a good bet no one's around. Them deer woulda been long gone."

They walked into the woods. Each time they ventured in, he pointed out things the kids should know about. He figured, if he did it enough times, even a couple of two-and-a-half-year-olds would remember what he'd said.

"That's poison ivy," he told them. "Don't touch it or you'll get blisters all over your hands and they'll itch like crazy. See the three leaves and the glossy green color? When you see 'em, don't touch!"

Wildflowers were coming up everywhere, and Shannon put a blue and yellow crocus behind her ear, as they'd seen the little mermaid do in the movie. He had to laugh—sometimes she was such a lady and the next moment she was pure hellion. A squirrel sat motionless on a branch, watching them pass.

The stream that flowed down the hill at the back of the property and was full of run-off from the mountains that touched the sky to the north. It emptied into a pond next to the house. A trout leapt out of the water as it tried to catch a bug flying over the surface. In the pasture next to the house, a herd of cattle watched them as they munched on the new grass. He didn't see another human.

Wilson picked up a stick and started banging it against a tree, making sounds like a lightsaber. "Take that, Darth Vader!" They'd watched *Star Wars* yesterday afternoon.

"Hold it right there!" a man announced as he stepped from behind a gigantic fir tree, his rifle aimed directly at Freddie's chest.

… … … … … … … … …

"Calgary Approach Control, this is Canadian Air Force CJ7946. We are thirty kilometers north of Yankee-Yankee-Charlie."

"Roger, CJ7946. This is Calgary Approach Control. We see you. Fifteen degrees Celsius. Winds from south-south-east at twelve knots. Visibility twenty kilometers. Turn to heading 185 to runway 17-Lima. You are cleared for landing. Contact ground control 124.3."

"Roger, Calgary. Heading 185, Land 17-Lima. Ground control 124.3."

The C-130 touched down gracefully and rolled up to the air cargo area. This was one of the two surviving Canadian Air Force cargo jets that were in Edmonton when the bombing started. Edmonton command agreed to allow this one to carry the transportation portals to the various US military bases where the Brigade had found large numbers of survivors. Doug accompanied the machines to set them up, and he was waiting with it as the plane pulled up to the loading area.

A brown-skinned man wearing a Canadian Air Force flight jumpsuit and a turban walked down the loading ramp as it descended. "Are you Dr. Medder?"

"Yep."

"I'm Warrant Officer Venkatabhanu Shaik. I'm the loadmaster." Doug didn't recognize him. A different guy had been on the other flights to the Canadian locations.

"What happened to Sergeant McCoy? He was loadmaster on our other trips."

"He had a dentist appointment today. A tooth was bothering him."

"I hate it when my teeth hurt. How do you pronounce your name again? Venkata..."

"You can call me Venkat or Loadmaster. Most non-Indians have trouble with my name."

"Thanks!" *Venkat* he could remember.

"Is this the portal that's going to McChord?"

"That's the one."

He walked around the metal box with a measuring tape, writing down the dimensions on his bill of lading. "How much does it weigh, eh?"

"Fifteen tons..." He paused. "Excuse me, a little shy of fourteen metric tons."

Venkat raised an eyebrow. "American?"

"Was—Canadian now. The airport said we could use their forklift."

He cracked up. "And I was soooo looking forward to muscling it on!" The forklift driver pulled up. "Is the weight evenly distributed inside the box?"

"No." Doug indicated one end. "That end has about sixty percent of the weight."

"Good to know." The loadmaster pointed at the heavy end for the forklift operator. While the driver jockeyed around for position to lift the portal, Venkat wiped the sweat off his forehead. This day was hotter down here than Edmonton had been. "The ones you set up in Edmonton and Vancouver are working great. The other C-130 is going to deliver the next one to Moose Jaw. Got a bunch of soldiers there, too."

"Any word from farther east? Toronto, Montreal, Ottawa?"

"Yeah, survivors were found in every one of them. I guess it could have been worse. No one's detected any nuclear fallout in Canada, besides the blown-up nuke reactors and missiles. Do you know what happened?"

Doug decided he should keep his mouth shut. "Nope. Beyond some wild suspicions, nothing more than you—maybe less. We should have the next portal ready by next week. We're working three shifts."

"If no one has said it, Doc, thanks for being here when we needed you."

Doug watched the forklift jockey the portal onto the plane without expression. He didn't feel like he warranted any kind of gratitude. If he and his friends hadn't invented the wormhole generator, none of this would have happened.

After a minute of silence, he responded, "We're all in this together."

They got the box loaded into the cargo bay of the plane and secured. After the two previous installations, the next part was routine. He pulled down a seat from the side of the plane and put on his seat belt. As the plane engines started, he got out the lunch Clara had made him. Venkat did the same in the next seat. They taxied, took off to the south, banked to the west, and began climbing toward Seattle. The flight was supposed to take three-and-a-half hours.

"Do you like keema naan?" Venkat offered him a piece of the flat bread as the plane climbed to its cruising altitude. "My wife thinks I have to feed my own private army; she always packs more than I can eat."

"I don't think I've ever tasted keema naan. What is it?"

"Fried flat bread with a spicy ground lamb filling."

"Spicy for you or spicy for me?" Doug asked cautiously. He had heard about Indian food from people at the Centre.

"A little spicy hot, but mostly spicy good."

"Why sure then, I'd love to try some." He bit into the bread. "Wow! This is *wonderful!*" He took another big bite. "Have you ever had a corn pone?"

"What is a corn pone?"

He pulled out the cornbread stick and offered it in return. "My wife is a magician with these. She puts in cheese and corn kernels with chopped jalapenos and red bell peppers. They are baked in cast iron molds with melted butter to keep them from sticking."

Venkat took one and had a bite. "Now *these* my wife would love. Can I have another one to take back to her?"

"Sure." Doug handed it to him. "Are you Sikh?"

"Yes, I am. Born in India, raised in Toronto."

"How long have you been in the Air Force?"

"Twenty-two years in the Reserve. I was up in Edmonton on annual training when the bombs started. My home is in Toronto; I'm a computer programmer."

"Is your family alright? Have you heard from them?"

"No word," he told Doug quietly, shaking his head somewhat diagonally. "But it seems like the bombs were targeted at primarily military, government, and infrastructure sites. Residential areas were left alone. They should be fine."

"What kind of programming do you do?" Doug asked between bites.

"Internet infrastructure," he said with a sigh. "Passing signals from one node to the next. I may be out of a job now. The internet has been destroyed."

Doug cocked his head. "Have you ever tried to send a signal via laser?"

"Yes. It's not hard to do—and it's fast. The problem is atmospheric interference."

"What if you had no atmospheric interference?"

"Like in a vacuum? That would work great. In fact, it does work great. I did something just like that in graduate school. Several other graduate students and I were trying to get the Aerospace Centre interested in it for satellite-to-satellite communications. We got a prototype working, but couldn't get their attention. They told us it was cute. Can you believe it? *Cute!*"

Doug was quiet for a while, his mind was running at full throttle. Rosy internet! Absolutely secure and instantaneous. It would have no latency (time delay of the signal going through thousands of miles of fiber optics cables and repeaters or to satellites and back). It could work! And a laser beam would have the same capacity as the fiber optic cables in the old internet backbones. They could rebuild the internet with Rosy! He sighed and put the idea on the shelf in the back of his mind for later work.

"Tell me about India," he said, settling in for the trip. "I've never been there. I hear it's beautiful."

If there's one thing Indian people love to talk about, it was India. Venkat gave Doug a three-hour description of where he was born and all his trips back to India since his father moved his family to Toronto when he was six years old. He had met his wife on one of those visits.

… … … … … … … … …

The right front tire of the Cherokee went flat with a rush of escaping air that sounded like a gasp.

"*Dammit!*" Rebecca screamed in frustration.

She was trying to escape a gang of teenagers who had pelted her car with rocks as she swerved around their makeshift roadblock on Highway 99 outside of Visalia, about two hundred miles north of Los Angles. This was her third day on the road since she'd left Santa Clarita. One of the rocks had smashed her windshield, and she drove another mile on the flat before the tire left the rim. She jumped out and jerked open the rear door to access the jack. Maybe she had time to change it before the kids caught up to her.

The nine teenagers arrived as she was putting on the spare. "You shoulda stopped, lady," a tall boy with dreadlocks announced. She tried to ignore them as she spun the lug nuts onto the studs.

"Now you got to pay a fine on top a the passage fee," another told her.

"What's the passage fee?" she asked, beginning to tighten the nuts with the lug wrench.

"Fifty bucks is the fee. The fine is a piece of ass," the boy in dreadlocks smirked.

"For each of us," a redheaded boy added, reaching out to stroke Rebecca's hair.

She smiled up at him as she tightened the last lug nut. "Fifty bucks? Yeah, that's fair. As far as the sex, well, you might think twice about that. The doc says I only got six months to live. But I don't mind giving it, if you don't mind getting it."

"Shit, lady. What you got?" They stepped away.

"Some new thing the aliens sent down to speed up the cleansing of us humans from Earth. It eats you from the inside out." She paused and grimaced a little, like she was in pain. "But with men, it's worse."

"Damn, what's worse than that?" the redheaded boy asked.

"The rot starts as an STD, and then it makes your dick fall off, and then other things start rotting off—fingers, toes, nose, ears." She shrugged. "Who's first?"

The boys looked at her in silence, unsure.

"Me, lady," the kid in dreadlocks said, reaching for her angrily. "I think you're a bullshit artist. Ain't nothing wrong with you!"

Her hand slapped her shoulder holster for her gun; the holster was empty. Sean was still laying on the passenger seat in the Cherokee, where she had put it for easy access when she blasted through the roadblock.

The boy yanked her to her feet. She tried to claw his eyes, and he slapped her.

"Leave her be!" a voice commanded from the tree line.

The boys froze. Four armed people—three men and a woman—stepped out from behind the trees. One of the men, a large, elderly Native American with white hair in braids and a seamed face, told the boys, "Get on back to your roadblock, boys. You might find someone who will pay you."

The woman cranked a round into her shotgun to emphasize that this was not the time to be stupid.

"What about our fee?" the redhead asked petulantly.

"I got your fee right here," a tall and slim Hispanic man told him, grabbing his crotch with one hand while pointing his AK-47 at the boy with the other.

"Come on, you guys," the kid in dreadlocks said. "We can do better than that skanky bitch." The boys began the walk back to the roadblock, making rude gestures over their shoulders.

Rebecca turned to the people who had rescued her, ready for anything, unsure of what was going to happen next.

"Relax," the old man told her. "We are no threat to you. My name is Tony Blackeagle. This is Russell Duke, Juan Strickland, and Mae Chung." Each person nodded as he said their name. "We are going to the mountains. We hear some survivalist camps are up there. We want to join one and find some peace."

"Well, thanks for being here," she told them, letting her guard down a little. "My name is Rebecca Silverstein. I'm going to the mountains, too. My husband and I have a cabin in a settlement about fifty miles east of Sonora. You can accompany me, if you'd like. I'm sure we can find room for everyone."

Tony got a nod from the other three. "Thank you, Rebecca. We accept. We have backpacks and camping gear. Can we tie them to your roof?"

"Sure—whatever won't fit inside. I don't have any rope. Do you?"

"Yes, we do. Juan, check the tire and get the car off the jack stand. We'll retrieve our stuff."

Tony, Russell, and Mae walked back into the woods. In fifteen minutes the gear was stowed in and on the Cherokee and tied down. Russell kicked out the windshield so she could see to drive. As they went up what was left of Highway 99 toward Sonora, they told her about themselves.

Russell—short, wiry, blonde, crew cut, with a soul patch and goatee—had been a computer network administrator before the Three-Hour War. He had served in the Navy during the Gulf War. Juan was tall, skinny, and clean-shaven and claimed he could build anything with wood and nails. Mae was Vietnamese and a little stocky. She had long, straight black hair she kept in a ponytail down her back and a still-healing three-inch wound across her left cheek from a knife fight in Stockton after the Three-Hour War. She was also Tony's girlfriend. Tony was pureblood Crow. He was huge—fully six feet nine. His eyes could be soft and gentle or hard as ice, as the Viet Cong fighters discovered during his three tours in Southeast Asia. His white hair, seamed face, and grace of movement camouflaged the ferociousness that hid under the surface.

… … … … … … … … …

"Flug, you got a problem doing what I told you to do?"

"Well, yeah, a little."

Ursa was a bear—a huge bear with black fur and deadly-looking claws—and was standing nose to nose with Flug. She was in charge of all combat operations on *Fair Wind*.

"How many combat missions have you been on?" she asked in almost a whisper.

"An exact number would be hard to say…maybe four, five hundred."

"And you still don't know how to take orders?"

"Oh, I know how to take 'em, Ursa. I just don't want to commit suicide. That's what you're telling us to do."

"All I told you to do was blow the gate on that hulk and enter the ship. That's why we're out here, remember? To test the refit and train the new teams."

"Yep. That's right."

"Why do you think it's suicide?"

"Because that gate is booby-trapped."

"And you would know that how?"

"'Cause I placed the charges when we abandoned it."

"You served on that hulk?"

"It wasn't a hulk then, but yeah, that's what I'm telling you. Its commissioned name was *Far Galaxy*."

"I've never seen it before. It's not on any charts. If it hadn't been for Zarqa's spiffy new search algorithm, we'd be practicing on asteroids instead of it. The hull number is listed as abandoned by the Ur thirty years ago at a point at least ten light years from here."

"Yeah, that makes sense. The captain didn't want anyone to be able to find it."

That made her pause. "Why would he do that? Abandoned means abandoned. Booby-trapping an abandoned ship is irresponsible and against Ur regulations. You could blow up a legitimate salvage operator as easily as a pirate."

He was having a little trouble swallowing what she had said. Here was the head of combat on a pirate ship, complaining about someone else not following the rules. "When the captain made us abandon it, he didn't want anyone like *Easy Wind* doing the salvage. He planned on returning for it himself, but he got killed a month later. That hulk has twenty kilograms of Graftium in its drive units. We didn't have time to pull it out. The cowlings are still intact on the drive pods, so I'm assuming it's still there and the Ur forgot about it or couldn't find it from the captain's coordinates."

"And its drives are intact?"

The hulk was on the display. "Sure look that way to me."

"Why was it abandoned?"

"We had a running fight with a pirate ship for a couple of days. They had hostages. One of them was a high-value—the daughter of the admiral of the fleet. The pirates told us, if we let them escape, they would put the hostages in a lifeboat. The lifeboat was equipped with a live feed. The admiral's daughter was on it. We stopped to pick it up and it exploded. The hull had major breaches in ten places. We couldn't stop the leaks and we were out of air. The generators couldn't keep up."

She thought about that for a moment in silence, and then asked, "If you were going to enter, how would you do it?"

He paused, staring at *Far Galaxy* in the monitors. "If it was me, I'd go in through the emergency drive and then disable the main drives from the console, so they don't blow up when we open 'em to pull out the Graftium."

"And risk a meltdown in the emergency drive Hore generator?"

"I'd vent the generator first. Without argon, it might as well be deck plating."

"We'll see. You lead your team in. I'll watch from here."

Flug led his team to the hulk. An atom laser drilled a tiny hole through the hull over the emergency Hore energy drive, and argon gas streamed into the vacuum. Once the argon stopped, he used the same laser to open a hole next to the emergency drive. An hour later, the team returned with the Graftium.

Captain Pey met them at the loading dock, floating in his water cocoon. "Flug, this is excellent! Is anything else salvageable?"

"Nah. We were out of ammunition. The captain sent our last photon torpedo at the escaping pirates, but it never exploded. Nothing was left..." He thought again. "There might be some radios, but they're all out of date. The encryptions would have long expired. The captain either destroyed or took with him everything that was valuable. He emptied the safe, if that's what you're thinking about. I'd have blown it, but he thought the Graftium was too valuable. I told him it was a bad idea."

"How about the computers? Would they still work?"

"Not a chance. They've been in vacuum for fifty years. Never heard of one working after ten years, let alone fifty. The silicone gel matrix breaks down."

"You get a thousand-Huz bonus for recovering the Graftium," the captain said. "Did you know that?"

"No, I didn't. Please split it between Ursa and my team."

Ursa started when he said that. "You don't owe me anything, Flug. I was going to get you killed. Remember?"

"We're a team, Ursa. We live together, we die together, and we get bonuses together. Next time, you can save my life and we'll be even."

Fey Pey shook his head. He'd never seen a pirate share anything. *Must be a primate thing*, he thought in amusement as he floated away. *I wouldn't have done it.*

Later that night, if *night* is what one would call off-shift, Flug met with Zarqa in the canteen. They were alone. He turned on the protein generator to make some noise to cover their conversation.

"Did you find anything?" he asked, in just above a whisper.

"Not yet, but I think I've found where it is. They haven't given me access to anything but files of ship's stores and on-board inventory. I could hack through the security into the secret stuff, but not without leaving tracks. Captain Xanny will have to wait for what I can find out about why they planted that dream and who had them do it."

"Don't get caught. Pirates aren't renowned for their compassion for people who steal from them."

"Flug, um..." She looked around and then at him and sighed.

"What is it, Zarqa?"

Finally, she blurted it out. "Are we going to do any real pirating?"

He looked at her in surprise. She was serious. She really wanted to experience being a pirate. "You mean, besides pilfering abandoned starships?"

"Yeah. I was expecting blood, guns, and hostages."

"You've been watching too many of those movies, Zarqa. Most of what these outlaws do isn't even illegal. And be grateful you *haven't* seen the other side—sometimes it doesn't turn out like you'd think."

The protein generator kicked off. He removed the slightly green, milkshake-looking drink, took a sip, and then walked back to the bunk area in silence.

... ...

The Cherokee died just past Sonora. A bullet had punctured the oil pan on the engine as they bypassed a roadblock in Groveland. The hole was high enough that the oil only sloshed out when they made a sharp turn to the left, but unfortunately, they did that a lot as they wove through the cars, debris, and roadblocks on Highway 120. Walking the remaining forty-five miles to the settlement took two days.

Rebecca's heart did a flip-flop when Jeremiah's cabin came into view. Smoke was coming out of the chimney. He had to be inside!

"Jeremiah?" she shouted, running to the door. "I'm home, baby!" The other four in her group stood in silence by the tree line. She yanked open the door, and the business end of a shotgun was shoved in her face.

"Ain't nobody named Jeremiah here. You best move on."

She could see a woman and two children behind the man. She raised her hands in defeat. "Okay, no problem. I must have the wrong house. Sorry." The door slammed shut. The rocker her husband had bought on the way up to the cabin sat on the porch. "Let's go that way," she told the group, indicating up the mountain. She walked toward the Johansson's house, nearby.

Liam answered when she knocked. He looked at her like she was something he wanted to step on. "Rebecca."

"Do you know where Jeremiah is?"

Amy walked up behind her husband. "He left to find you after the bombs fell. He hasn't come back yet."

Rebecca gasped. "Did he tell anyone where he was going?"

"He said you wouldn't survive the chaos. He was going to find you and lead you out."

"Dammit." She didn't want to think about her husband being caught up in the anarchy that was raging throughout the urban areas of California. "Did anyone go with him?"

"No. He wanted to go alone." Disapproval was plastered all over Liam's face.

Rebecca could see he wasn't telling her the whole story. "Did he go on foot?"

"He didn't have much choice after you took his car and his money."

"It was our car and our money, and he tried to take it from me first, by the way."

"Whatever." Liam turned his back on her and sat down without inviting her in.

"Who are those people in Jeremiah's cabin?" she asked Amy.

"They showed up about a week ago. His name is Jonathan something or other. His wife is Caitlin. They came up from Fresno to escape the violence. Didn't see any point in turning them out, since Jeremiah left and you were gone. They keep to themselves and haven't bothered anyone yet. Who are those people you brought with you?"

"Lost souls I met on the way up from LA. None of us would have made it up here alone."

"What was it like? What's happening out there?"

"Anarchy, just like you guys predicted. Looting, rape, murder, robbery. The police who try to stop it get killed, so most of the cops joined in with the looting. I haven't seen the military at all. People are dying everywhere—starvation, people like diabetics and critical care patients who can't get their medications, babies and children, old people in rest homes because they have no food, water, or electricity. Diseases from poor sanitation like cholera and typhoid are appearing in the cities. Prisoners have killed the guards and escaped their prisons. Psychiatric hospitals are shut down and the patients are wandering around the countryside. Hospitals have been overrun by people stealing the drugs that kept the patients alive. There's even rumors of cannibalism going on in the big cities after the food ran out. Gangs are calling themselves militias and they have created little kingdoms. They charge people to pass through and murder with impunity. The people in the cities who can are fleeing. They are coming to the country and mountains. They think we have food."

Liam and Amy were quiet for a moment while Rebecca's words sank in. "We heard a broadcast from the president last night," Amy told her.

"President Robbins? Is he still alive?"

"Yep. He's up in Canada for a while, until he gets things going in the US. He said he's reestablishing the government. In California, Fort Hunter-Liggett, Camp Pendleton, and Travis Air Force Base are creating zones of control. He ordered all surviving active duty military personnel in the state to report to one of those centers, and he activated the National Guard and Reserve units nationwide and told them to report. He also invited any retired military, ex-military, or anyone who wants to volunteer to go to one of the centers. He said they will begin to enter the urban areas and end the lawlessness. Reserve and National Guard units operating out of Travis are approaching the Bay Area around San Francisco from the north. Camp Pendleton has secured San Diego. They are beginning to work north into Orange County. Greater LA is next. Hunter-Liggett has started from east of LA into San Bernardino County."

"Do you have any idea where Jeremiah was going first? Did he tell anyone what his plans were?"

Liam chimed in from his chair without looking up from his book. "He said he left you a letter in his house in case you showed up."

"Thanks, Liam. I'm sorry I let you guys down. You were right; I was wrong."

He set his book down and stared coldly at her. "You need to say that to Jeremiah, not me. I told him you weren't worth saving. The way I see it, we lost a good man and got you in return." He picked up his book again—the conversation was over.

She started to respond and then decided not to. He was just saying out loud what she'd been saying to herself for a month. She turned to his wife. "Thanks to you also, Amy." She hesitated for a moment. "Are any of the places here empty, where the owners didn't show up after the bombs? The four who accompanied me up here are good people. We need some place to stay, and I can't turn out Jonathan and Caitlin—they have two kids."

She pursed her lips in thought. "A couple of places are available. Stan Maloney never returned, but he worked at the docks in Long Beach—he may be dead. And Jim Southerland and his wife, Maria, didn't either. He worked at Edwards Air Force Base. From what I heard before the radios quit, Edwards was flattened. I would use the Southerlands'—it's a little bigger and he put in dark energy last year. But if they show up, you'll have to leave."

"Yeah, that's fair. Thanks for your help, you two." She walked back to her companions. "We're going to use someone else's house. If they show up, we'll have to move. It's this way." She headed up the mountain.

After they had settled into the Southerlands' house and everyone took a shower, she headed back down to the cabin.

"Jonathan? Caitlin?" she called out from the tree line. "I need to talk to you."

The door opened, and Jonathan came out with his shotgun. "Whaddaya want?"

"My name is Rebecca Silverstein. My husband, Jeremiah, bought this cabin a couple of months ago. You can use it until he comes back, if that ever happens, but Liam and Amy Johansson told me he left me a letter when he went to search for me. Could I have it, please?"

"I don't know nothing 'bout no letter." He turned around in the doorway. "Caitlin, you seen a letter?"

Caitlin came to the doorway with it in her hand, walking out to Rebecca. She was pretty, in a delicate way and wore a scarf around her head that kept her thin auburn hair off her narrow face. "I knew you'd show up someday. I saved it for you." She handed the worn envelope to Rebecca. "I hope you don't mind, but I read it about a hunderd times. Someday, I hope somebody loves me like your Jeremiah loves you." She turned and went back into the cabin.

... ...

"What if it isn't the hyaluronidase?" Dr. Powell suggested in the CDC morning staff meeting. "We've spent months chasing our tails, fooling with hyaluronidase and its trigger protein. What if the problem is really in the acrosin?"

Dr. Hehsa stared at him, wondering why he hadn't asked the same thing. "What is your idea, Peter? How could the acrosin have been changed?"

"I don't know yet, but I would love to have permission to try to find out."

"You have it, but before you start, though, let's take a moment and try to figure out what else could have changed—what else we haven't examined because we assumed it couldn't be any different. We have enough people to do several research lines concurrently."

"What if the change is actually to the cumulus cells the hyaluronidase digest to access the interior of the ovum?" Dr. Stewart asked. "Maybe it's the digestion of the cells that releases the trigger to harden the exterior of the ovum and not the hyaluronidase at all."

"Terrific question. Go find the answer."

The sound of several gunshots came from outside the building. Everyone jumped.

"Just the marines keeping us safe," he told the group. "How are your families settling in?"

Of the several hundred scientists who had been stationed at the CDC in Atlanta, only sixty-eight remained on duty. The rest had left to find loved ones and not returned. Those sixty-eight either had no families or had successfully brought them into the CDC compound for safety.

"My wife wants me to ask if any spices are available," an Indian man spoke up. "We're not complaining, but the emergency food in the basement is kind of bland."

"Beyond basic salt and pepper, the facility has none," Sridhar told the group, "but my wife has many spices. We will share what we have until they run out or the greater Atlanta area returns to normal."

"Do you know when that will be, Dr. Hehsa?"

"No more than you do, my friend. We must be patient. President Robbins will bring order back to our country. Let's go back to work while we wait. Imagine his surprise when we tell him we might have found the answer."

The people in the meeting got up in silence. No one even knew if the president was still alive.

Chapter 32 – Tubs of Lard

"Hold on, old timer." Freddie held up his hands. "It's just me and two toddlers. No need for firearms. I am unarmed." The children both stared at the old man from behind Freddie without saying a word.

"Who the hell are ya and what're ya doing in the Sullivans' house?" Ray demanded.

"I am Chief Petty Officer Freddie Harris of the US Navy. If you let me put my arms down, my ID card is in my wallet. I can show you."

"What the hell's the Navy doin' in Montana?"

"I was stationed in the sterile habitat the government built on Wysnewski's ranch. We were raising children uninfected by BSV so we could send 'em to a colony in another solar system or stay inside 'til the virus died. The habitat got blown up when the bombs started fallin'. The kids and me, we was the only ones who escaped."

"So *that's* what they were doing." Ray lowered his rifle from his shoulder but kept it pointed at Harris. "No one could figure it out. I never believed that shit about research for a cure to BSV. How did they find uninfected babies?"

"The government grew them from embryos fertilized before the virus. They put the embryos in monkeys for the incubation. The Baby Machines hadn't been invented yet."

The old man laughed. "In monkeys? No shit?"

"Yes, sir. Can I put my arms down?"

"How could you tend babies without infecting them?"

"I wasn't infected, either."

The old man was suddenly suspicious. "Why weren't you infected along with everyone else? You an alien?"

"I was serving on a nuke sub when the virus hit. We was under water and never got exposed."

"Let me see your Navy ID." Freddie gingerly dropped his right arm and pulled his wallet out of his rear pocket with two fingers. He started to open it, but the old man said, "Just toss it over." Ray picked the wallet up and studied the ID. "Okay, you can put your arms down. Here's your wallet back." He tossed it to Freddie and dropped his rifle to the crook of his arm. "Well, you three are exposed to the virus now. Do the Sullivans know you're using their house?"

"No. I had no way to tell them or ask permission. I was injured and the kids was cold and hungry. I broke in. I figured the government would pay for the broken window and food we ate."

"Where was you hurt?"

"I had a piece of shrapnel in my shoulder from one a the bombs."

"Still there?"

"Nah, I pulled it out—healing up pretty good now."

"Shrapnel hurts. Still got some in my knee from Tet in '68. First Marine Division. You been living on that survival shit Sullivan had in his basement?"

"Yeah, mostly. The pantry was full of canned fruits and vegetables."

"Dolores loved to can." The old man turned to go and then stopped, looking back at them. "Well, come on. I'll be on Andrea's Dammit List for the rest a my life if I don't bring home them two babies. You the one I run off the night a the bombing?"

"Yeah, I think so."

"I'm sorry about that. Me and Andrea, we was scared shitless. You ate yet?" The old man flipped on the safety and slung his rifle over his shoulder.

"I was gonna start dinner when I got back inside."

"Well, come with me. Andrea'll fix ya something. What're them babies called?"

"Shannon McGhee and Wilson Rabinowitz."

"Shannon's a right fine name for a carrot top. Andrea always wanted a redheaded girl—any girl, for that matter. We ended up with four blond boys; they're all gone from home now. My name's

Ray O'Flynn, by the way. I used to have hair redder 'an hers, 'fore it turned white. Think she'd let me carry her?"

"What do you think, Shannon? You wanna ride with Mr. O'Flynn?"

She held out her arms. "Want you carry," she told him in her best two-and-a-half-year-old words.

Ray slung his rifle across his chest so the barrel was out of the way and pulled her up onto his shoulders. Freddie put Wilson onto his shoulders gingerly and they started walking toward Ray's house. Shannon ran her hands through the man's white hair. She'd never seen white hair. The two men walked along in silence for a few minutes.

"You kids ever had a slice a cherry pie?" Ray asked. Both children shook their heads. "Well, you're in for a treat. Andrea was pullin' a cherry pie outta the oven when I left. You ain't tasted nothin' 'til you tasted one a Andrea's cherry pies."

... ...

President Robbins left Calgary on Air Force One bound for Fort Riley, Kansas. The nearest runway to the fort capable of landing a 747 was at Manhattan Regional Airport. It had been patched enough to use. The president chose Riley because it was near the geographical center of the United States, perfect for setting up his temporary government. The fort was also the home of the First Infantry Division, known as the Big Red One. Brigadier General Harry Barstow, the ranking survivor at the fort, had repaired two warehouses enough to house the staff to run the base and support the administration of the government. Construction was underway all over the fort, fixing what they could and tearing down what they couldn't.

Troop strength of the First Division and its support brigade was up to about sixty percent of its pre-bombing numbers. General Barstow filled out the division's decimated ranks from four sources: active duty soldiers who survived at other nearby bases, activated reservists, National Guard units, and volunteers who continued to show up after the radio announcements commenced three weeks ago.

Irwin Army Community Hospital was up and running again, although in a limited capacity, as the bombing had destroyed the hospital buildings beyond use. The hospital staff who were not on duty during the attack had created a field hospital with materials from underground storage bunkers, augmented by what they could salvage from the ruins of the hospital. One Army Reserve and three National Guard medical companies had activated themselves after the president's radio announcements and were supplying desperately needed emergency and surgical facilities. They sent the patients they couldn't handle to the two civilian hospitals in Manhattan, Kansas, both of which had come through the barrage without significant damage.

As at Fort Lewis, an engineer battalion had dug large pits to bury the thousands of dead. The burial workers collected ID cards, wallets, and dog tags where possible, but many of the dead had been blown into unidentifiable pieces and the workers didn't have time to collect DNA samples or anywhere to send them if they had. The Kansas sun created a certain urgency to put the remains underground before they rotted. All the other military bases to which the Beechcraft Brigade transported a Rosy radio had begun the same effort.

Robbins was sitting in the studio constructed to record his daily radio message, which would be sent to the twenty-five surviving military bases across the nation. Those bases were the command centers for the recovery effort in each geographical region of the United States. They transmitted the president's message every hour to the areas around them on their newly installed radio stations.

"Sir, are you ready to begin?" the recording tech asked him.

"Yes, I am."

"Begin on my mark." The tech held up three fingers and then pulled them down one at a time. "Three, two, one...go."

"People of these United States, this is President Robbins. I am alive and well. I am broadcasting this message over the new

Armed Forces Radio Network. We have transmitters located at twenty-five military bases around the country.

"The government of the United States is functioning and recovering from the devastating attack that began four weeks ago in the middle of the night. Construction is ongoing nationwide, repairing the damage to our infrastructure. If we haven't reached your particular area yet, please be patient. There was a lot of damage; it will take many years to repair it all.

"Repairs are being made to the water supply, sewage treatment facilities, and power grid first. Our efforts in many areas are being hampered by lawlessness and looting. I will not put the repair technicians' lives in danger by sending them into areas where they will be attacked.

"The military bases that have survived the attack are augmenting the local and state police forces in reestablishing zones of law and order. I urge everyone to cooperate with them to the highest degree possible. I invite local, law-abiding militias to join forces with the military and police to help us bring an end to the lawlessness.

"I urge everyone to support and join their law-abiding, local militias as well. These consist of loyal Americans who are the final line in maintaining law and order. They are defending the values and ideals that we hold dear. The brilliant minds who created the Second Amendment of the US Constitution did it for just this type of situation. We have the right to bear arms and protect our homes. During this emergency, these heroes are the only thing shielding our loved ones from the anarchy that has swept our nation after the attack.

"Law breakers will be brought to justice. If you can do so without endangering yourself, take a picture when you see a crime being committed. When we reach your neighborhood, those photos will be key to punishing those who disregard everything we hold dear.

"Keep the faith, my fellow Americans. This war has not crushed the United States. We will rise from the ashes like the phoenix of old, better than before and stronger than ever. We will lead the world back from the destruction to a new era of peace and prosperity." He signaled the end of the session.

The technician stopped the recording. "I liked that part about not supplying services to areas that won't quit the looting and anarchy."

"That's about the only club we have left. Our military is stretched way too thin to begin an extended urban guerrilla battle."

"Taking pictures is going to be a sure-fire way to get into trouble with the outlaws."

"Well, this is war. You don't have safe wars—people die in wars. I hope we can take the country back before a lot of the good people, the heroes, are killed. What I'm counting on is that the militias will listen to the message and stop crossing the line."

"I hope you're right," the technician said doubtfully.

"I believe I am. The average American is a good, honest person. When all this is behind us, we will still have to figure out whom to punish and for what."

… … … … … … … … …

For the fourth night in a row, Samantha Evers waited in the parking lot. The bar where she'd met the man promising her a cloning of Kayleen was now a looted hulk, half burned down. The man hadn't shown up yet. Today was the sixteenth of April. He said he would meet her here on the thirteenth for the second payment.

A group of men approached her car, baseball bats and pipes in their hands. For the last three nights, she had watched one group after another go by as she waited in the shadows of the parking lot. No one had noticed her car until tonight. Tonight her luck ran out.

One of them shined a flashlight into the car. "Hey, it's a woman!"

"Cool!" another one said before crooning, "I'm in the mood for love."

Hey, baby! I'm coming. Don't start without me."

One of the men snickered. "If you're coming already, it sounds like you started without her."

A 9mm pistol sat in her lap. She flipped off the safety and pulled the slide back so the men could hear the round being chambered.

"Now is that any way to act, darling?" one of them. They were still twenty feet away from her car, but coming closer and spreading out on both sides of the Acura SUV.

She started the car, put it in gear, and turned the high beams on.

"I think she likes me," one of the men guffawed. "She left the lights on."

They were only ten feet away when Samantha floored it. The men jumped out of the way, but as she sped past them, pipes smashed into her windshield from both sides. Another hit the rear window as she left them behind, shattering it into the back seat. She pulled out into the street with a screech of tires and drove several blocks. She was having trouble seeing where she was going through the broken windshield, so she stopped and kicked it out from the inside. It plopped onto her hood and slid to the ground in front of her car. She drove over it and continued down the road toward her house.

As she drove around the stalled cars and debris from the looting, she thought about what had happened. Maybe the man she'd paid was dead. Maybe Kayleen's clones were dead. Maybe the whole thing was a scam and the guy had no intention of cloning Kayleen, or, worst of all, maybe Kayleen was growing in a Baby Machine somewhere and someone was about to turn it off for nonpayment.

She checked her rearview mirror for anyone following her. No one was visible. No moving car was in sight. She pressed down on the accelerator and cut left to avoid a car with its hood up. Her tires squealed for a second, and she didn't see the spike strip that someone had stretched across the lane. All four of her tires went flat simultaneously as the car passed over it. She struggled for control, but she was going too fast for the flat tires. The car swerved, went up on two wheels, and then, almost in slow motion, tipped on its side with a crunch and slid to a stop, leaving a shower of sparks and broken glass behind it.

Samantha unsnapped her seat belt, grabbed her gun, and climbed out through where the windshield had been. An arm appeared around her throat from behind and began choking her. She lifted her gun, pointed behind her, and fired. The roar deafened her right ear and left it ringing like a bell, but the arm released her. Terrified, she turned around and fired into the body at her feet until the gun stopped firing.

"Now that was pretty dumb," a voice told her. "He was already dead." She spun around and faced the voice, her gun at the ready. A man came around the side of her car. "Are you going to reload? If you'd look, you'll see you're empty."

She realized her spare magazine was on the dresser next to her bed. She pulled out a pack of hundred-dollar bills from her waistband and threw them at the man. They hit him and the band broke, spreading the bills to the wind. As he gasped and reached for them, Samantha turned to run. A second man came around the other side of her car, but she dodged him, his fingernails scraping down her back. She took off down the street as fast as her marathon training would take her. Someone was running behind her.

"Stop, lady! We're not gonna hurt you!"

Instead Samantha poured everything she had into increasing her speed, swerving from side to side. A bullet went past her ear; a second bit into her right inner thigh. The burning pain in her leg was unbelievable. She kept running, though—she had no choice. It was either ignore the pain or surrender to the people who had just shot her.

Ten minutes later, she got to the turnoff to her neighborhood and slowed to a jog. Her right leg kept trying to buckle, but she didn't hear anyone behind her anymore. She jogged slowly up the road. "I don't remember this being so steep." She slowed to a walk and then stopped, panting like a locomotive. After tearing off the sleeve of her runner's jacket, she tied it tightly around her thigh. "That should help." She stumbled as she got to her driveway; her leg wasn't working properly.

There was no light to see it in the dark. She put her hand to where it hurt and gasped; it appeared to be black in the starlight from all the blood. The jacket sleeve was completely soaked, and blood covered her leg from mid-thigh to her shoe. The world spun around her as Samantha tried to limp to her house. She stumbled and fell, dropping the empty pistol still clutched in her hand, but was able to crawl on her hands and good knee several feet closer to her house before she collapsed again.

"*SOMEBODY HELP ME!*" she screamed in desperation. No one heard her. She turned her head so she could see her house across her yard; it might as well have been a thousand miles away. The world grew blurry and nausea gripped her stomach.

"This is the end," she whispered between heaves. No one *was* going to save her—no Mounties were coming to the rescue—and Kayleen was going to arrive in a world without her! "I'm sorry, baby!" she cried out. "I tried! I love you!"

The effort of calling to her daughter made her dizzy, and she rolled onto her back. The grass on her front lawn was softer than her concrete driveway, and the sky glittered with stars. One of the stars over her got brighter and brighter, filling the sky while she watched. *Where is that light coming from?* she wondered. *The power has been off for weeks.* Then Samantha was moving toward it.

Another spirit, familiar somehow, approached and held out their hand. "Come on, Mom. I've been waiting for you. I know the way."

... ...

Even though Sergeant Bleese had modified the evacuation devices to take a much broader area than deep, it took one hundred and twenty-three devices to eliminate the radiation around Washington to a safe level. They were also able to evacuate most of the cloud on its way to Europe. The nuclear cleanup had dramatically altered the entire East Coast shoreline from New Jersey to North Carolina. Many areas no longer existed—New Jersey—south of Newark, all of Delaware, Eastern Maryland,

Virginia east of the Bull Run Mountains, down to fifty miles south of Norfolk. Trenton, Atlantic City, Philadelphia, Baltimore, Richmond, and the nation's capital and surrounding suburbs were gone as though they had never existed.

The evacuation had expanded Chesapeake Bay into what would become known as the Gulf of Columbia. The northern edge began at New York Harbor, went west to Harrisburg, Pennsylvania, and then turned south, following the eastern side of the Bull Run Mountains until it cut back to the east through Petersburg, Virginia, and out to the northern edge of North Carolina's barrier islands, at the Virginia-North Carolina border.

The twenty-one million people in and around the radioactive area were considered collateral damage by Grock and went with the radiation into the sun. The Atlantic Ocean, rushing into the void, caused a mile-high tsunami that devastated the areas within twenty miles of the new shoreline. Another million lives were lost, primarily in New York City, northern New Jersey, and southeastern Pennsylvania.

Around the world, the aliens had detected and evacuated four hundred and three fission and fusion weapons, including one hundred and twelve aboard submarines. This was all that remained of the seventeen thousand warheads on Earth before the Three-Hour War. The bombed rocket silos were not touched because the bombs had already been destroyed and the radiation in the silos was contained and not affecting the surrounding area.

The four hundred and ninety-three nuclear reactors around the world were sent into the sun; most had been bombed and were leaking contamination into the atmosphere and ground water from their meltdowns. They didn't evacuate the seventy-eight under construction—the breeder reactors that made their fuel rods had been disposed of. Without the breeders, the under-construction reactors could never be switched on. They also removed areas of massive radioactive contamination, like Hanford Reservation in Washington State and Oak Ridge, Tennessee.

… … … … … … … … …

"Anything else?" Doug asked Lily as he climbed the stairs to the bedrooms.

"No. Well...just this small carry-on bag. I'll take it."

Lily checked her hair and walked downstairs behind him. The limo was loaded with suitcases for the trip, and Lan's car seat was buckled in. Lan was scratching goodbye to Clara's horse's nose while Kevin held her up.

"If you have any trouble, call Dr. Willer at the Centre. His number is on the bulletin board in the kitchen. We don't know how long we'll be gone."

Bill chuckled. "We'll be fine, Clara. The horses will be fine. The farm will be fine. Go save the world. Mindy, Martin, and me, we got this covered." He gave Mindy a squeeze. She snuggled under his arm and smiled at them, squeezing him back. He held Martin with his other arm.

Clara returned their smile. Even though they came from such different backgrounds, they had become friends and peace settled over the farm. Then the surprise of the century occurred: Mindy and Bill became lovers! Clara shook her head again. Life had played some weird games getting those two together. Martin couldn't have been happier with Bill in his life. The man had turned out to have a side even he had never imagined: he was a terrific dad. Bill had explained it this way: "All I have to do is think how my father wouldda done it and do it the other way."

Clara went over it one more time. "If you need money for an emergency or something around the farm breaks, Dr. Willer has an account all set up. All you have to do is explain what you need it for and he will give you the money. Your pay will be auto-deposited directly into your checking accounts."

Bill shook his head, amused. They'd been over this many times in the past few days. "Clara, the farm will be fine. Are you gonna go, eh?"

"Okay then," Doug announced to the group, "let's get to the airport."

Kevin didn't move. Instead, he looked at the four with a very serious expression on his face. "Are you sure you want to do this?"

The others didn't understand. "Well the first time we did a big project together, we changed the world with Rosy. The second time we got together, World War III started. What's going to happen this time?"

Lily put her hand on his cheek and smiled. "If this works, we save humanity. Is that big enough for you?"

He thought about it for a minute and then nodded, smiling. "Yeah, that'll work. It's big enough. Let's do it." Half an hour later, the five of them climbed into the C-130 and took seats next to the one-of-a-kind transportation portal the Centre had built for a very special purpose: it was going to launch a capsule past the moon.

President Robbins had asked Edmonton Command if they would let the United States borrow Doug for the effort, and Edmonton agreed. Another scientist from Doug's team took over the portal installation duties. Clara announced that they weren't leaving her behind, so all five of them were going to Camp Pendleton, where a top secret facility was under construction for the building of the capsule and its launch.

Venkat had secured their luggage next to the portal. Lan was excited that she didn't need to be in her car seat for the whole trip; Kevin had promised her she could get down and run around after they got to cruising altitude. The fifteen-hundred-mile flight to Pendleton, outside of San Diego, was supposed to take four-and-a-half hours.

… … … … … … … … …

Gunny Silverstein leaned over the marine trainee squinting downrange. "You're consistently high and to the right. Adjust your sight one click down and one click left."

The trainee made the adjustments and fired again.

"Better," Jeremiah told him. "One more click to the left."

The next shot was a dead bull's-eye.

"Give me two more like that and I'll progress you to the pop-up range."

Two shots later the trainee was walking down the access road to the next course.

Jeremiah watched him go. "Another marine for the First Marine Volunteer Regiment."

He was in Malibu, looking for Rebecca, when President Robbins announced the activation of all Reserve and National Guard units. All he had found so far was looting, gangs, and out-of-control violence. Rebecca wasn't there, or at least, if she was, he didn't know where else to look. Maybe she was dead. Maybe she was hiding. Maybe she was a sex slave somewhere. He had no way of knowing. So, he heeded the president's call for ex-military to come back on active duty and made his way to Camp Pendleton. He didn't see any point in going back to the cabin in the Sierras without Rebecca.

He'd been a marine for five years during the Gulf War—he'd served a deployment in Iraq and two in Afghanistan. He remembered his drill instructor from ten years ago like he was speaking yesterday. "Once you become a marine, you will never not be a marine. It's a permanent transformation, ladies. Once a marine, always a marine. Oorah!"

The training command made him a drill instructor. He had to wonder at the path his life had taken—now *he* wore the Smokey Bear hat he had feared so much during his own basic training. Now he was the one making the trainees do push-ups and teaching them how to be marines. It was a little different looking down than it had been looking up. It was up to him to give these civilians the skills they needed to stay alive in combat. He was tasked with getting their fat, lazy bodies into shape and teaching them to fight, to depend on each other, and to learn that they could do more together than they ever could by themselves.

He shook his head at their failures. Surely he had been different back then. There was no way he could have been like these tubs of lard—these undisciplined, city kids who had never held a rifle, let alone learned to shoot one. Wearing of the uniforms had been a challenge to some of the kids; the marines didn't do saggy, baggy pants, and underwear was meant to be worn, not seen. Many trainees had sore arms from not pulling up their pants and putting their belt around their waist, but when you do enough push-ups, it does tend to get your attention, and no one ever does them alone. When a violation was found on one individual, the whole platoon received whatever discipline was handed out. If a marine didn't care, the rest of the platoon soon convinced him they should.

Chapter 33 – Fort Lewis Bound

"I found something," Zarqa whispered. They had been on the *Easy Wind* for almost a month, and she was waiting for a chance to tell Flug. It was hard to get alone time on a starship. The canteen was deserted for the moment, a rare condition at any time.

Flug turned on the protein generator. "What did you find?" he asked softly.

"Well, the captain gave me greater access to the ship's servers after I found that hulk with the Graftium. I needed access to the long-range scans he 'borrowed' from the Ur."

"So, what did you find?"

"I found the jump history data. It goes back ten years."

He blinked in surprise. "And it shows where they jumped before they went to Earth?"

"Yep. It sure does."

"So, where did they go?"

"They were in clear space a light year away from Earth for a week. But before that, they jumped to an asteroid in the Glycemis System and were only there for an hour."

He was even more surprised. "Really!" The Glycemis System was Fey Pey's home, the home planet for the only species of air-breathing aquatic mammal that had been admitted to the Ur.

"He jumped to an asteroid? Not to his home planet?"

"Yep, but I don't think he could go to his home planet. Glycemae has a shoot-on-sight order for him. Something about Fey Pey seducing the king's daughter and leaving her pregnant."

"That sounds about right." Nothing Fey Pey did would surprise him. "So, what was he doing at the asteroid? Who did he meet?"

"No idea yet, but I connected two dots that may or may not actually connect. Guess who else is from that planet?"

He shrugged. "No idea."

She grinned like the cat that swallowed the canary. "The envoy who failed Earth, Gart-Disp."

Flug paused to think about the implications of accusing a galactic envoy. "You'll have to find a lot more evidence than that to prosecute him. Those guys speak for the Ur itself; they make galactic policy."

"Yeah, I know. But it sure is interesting."

"But, if it *is* a conspiracy, why would the fishes want to fail Earth?" He stared off into space.

"That's the big question, isn't it?" Zarqa agreed. "At least for now, we have somewhere to look."

The protein generator kicked off. Flug took his drink, and they walked back to the bunk area together. They had to pass this information to Captain Xanny.

"Did you take that picture for your mom?" she asked when they got to her bunk. He didn't understand—his mom had died years ago. She winked at him. "I'll help you send it to her. Attaching photos to an email can be a little tricky with all the security around here."

… … … … … … … …

Rebecca reread the one-page letter from Jeremiah for the twentieth time.

My dearest Rebecca,

If you're reading this, then you made it back, safe and sound. This cabin is a good house. It's dry and warm and will protect you while I cannot. I hope you make it back, but I fear it will never happen. All I have done since you left was wish you here with me. I made so many mistakes with us. Someday, I hope I have a chance to try again.

After the bombs fell, I waited a week for you to come back. The radio stations that were still broadcasting gave horrific tales of death and destruction. I knew in my heart you wouldn't make it back on your own, but I was just as sure that, if you were dead, I would know. I couldn't deal with the image of you being hurt and helpless, so I decided to go find you. I'll try our old neighborhood in Malibu. I will search until I find you or die.

Love, Jeremiah

Rebecca read it again and came to a decision. She walked down the path to Jeremiah's cabin and knocked on the door. Jonathan answered.

"Whaddaya want?"

"I've come to make a proposition to you," she began. "I want this cabin back."

Jonathan's eyes grew hard. "We gonna fight?"

"Not necessarily. Here's my proposition. My friends and I want to help you build your own cabin on your own property. That way, no one can show up and take it away from you. You can live here until your new place is done. Then I can have this one back, and you and your family will have your own place, free and clear."

"Where would you build it?"

"Well, let's find a site you'd be happy with. There's plenty of space up here. If we build it nearby, it can share our well and dark energy generator."

"Give me a minute. I want to talk to Caitlin about it." A few minutes later, he stepped out on the porch and closed the door behind him. "Caitlin brought up some things. Just building the house ain't enough. Where would we get the kitchen and bathroom stuff? She needs a stove, a sink, a refrigerator, a toilet, a bathtub, a furnace, windows, doors, roofing, wiring, plumbing...where you gonna get that shit? What's it gonna take to build a copy of this here cabin? Caitlin's got real attached to it."

Rebecca couldn't believe she was hearing this. "Are you saying you won't leave this cabin unless we build you something just like it?"

"Yeah, that's what I'm saying. We're happy here. If you want us to move, build us something as good or better. Until then, we're staying put."

"But this isn't your cabin!" She wrapped her arms around herself and wailed, "This is all I have left of him! It belongs to me and my husband. It's in his name. I WANT IT BACK!"

She might as well have slapped Jonathan. He looked at her grimly. "Well, the way I see it, this cabin is ours now. None a that old property title shit works anymore. You abandoned it when you left your husband and went to Los Angeles. He abandoned it when he went to look for you and didn't come back. We found it abandoned and, by right of possession, it's ours now. Build *yourself* a new cabin."

"It wasn't abandoned. It was unoccupied."

He paused for a moment and then told her through clenched teeth, "We ain't movin'."

He turned his back on her and walked back inside, closing the door. She heard the lock click shut, and then the *shick-shack* of Jonathan cycling a round into his shotgun.

She turned on her heel and stalked off toward the Johanssons' house.

... ...

Jeremiah proudly watched the assembled group of marines go through their graduation ceremony. He had turned these soft, self-absorbed, undisciplined civilians into hard-bellied killing machines. He would put them up against the toughest of the recruits who had graduated with him ten years ago. They could out-shoot, out-run, out-maneuver, and out-think any marine he had ever known—except himself, of course.

This was his last day as a drill instructor. Tomorrow, he would go to his next assignment. He would be guard commander on some new super-secret project in a newly built warehouse on base. The project was so secret they couldn't even tell him, the guard commander, what his team was guarding. All they would tell him was who was allowed into and out of the warehouse and that deadly force was authorized without having to call in for permission.

After the graduation ceremony was complete, Jeremiah joined the graduates in the traditional post-graduation drunk. Every member of his graduating platoon (thirty-three men) was required to buy him a beer. He was required to drink them and buy one for each of them.

He passed out around ten o'clock, after having puked twice and fallen into it the second time. His platoon had decorated him appropriately. He woke up in a skirt and bra with makeup on and shaved legs. Someone had taped full-color pictures of the night before on every mirror in the latrine, including three copies of the picture of him lying in his puke.

He emptied his bladder and examined the makeup job in the mirror over the sink next to the urinal. The eyes were pretty well done. The lipstick was smeared, but he could have done that while he was unconscious. Private Santera came in and put a glass of water, three aspirin, and a bottle of Listerine above the sink next to the door and then left without saying a word.

Jeremiah went into his room and retrieved a towel and his shaving kit. Half an hour later, after a shower, a shave, the aspirin, and a clean, starched uniform had overcome the effects of the night before, he felt reborn. He used his towel to wipe down the shower and sink. The barracks showed no sign of the raucous celebration of the night before: the floor glowed, the mattresses were folded neatly, and the trashcans were spotless. He shook his head. Once a marine, always a marine. Oorah!

Jeremiah finished packing his seabag, folded his mattress, and walked out of the barracks. Forty-five minutes later, he arrived at the warehouse. The private at the gate in the twenty-foot chain-link fence challenged him.

"I'm the new guard commander, Private."

"I need to see your ID, sir." Jeremiah handed it over. "You aren't on my list, sir. You cannot enter."

"Who is your guard commander?"

"Gunny Merchal."

"Call him. Tell him Gunny Silverstein is here to relieve him."

"Yes, sir."

Two minutes later a grizzled, gray-haired gunnery sergeant came walking out of the warehouse with his seabag. "About damned time you showed up. I thought I was gonna have to call for a search and rescue. Private, this is your new guard commander."

"Yes, sir." The guard returned his ID.

Jeremiah felt he should explain to the sergeant why he was late. "Graduation ceremony last night. Had to do a little refit and recovery when I woke up."

"Now that I understand!" Marchal laughed. "Did you get 'em graduated?"

"They are now marines."

"Maybe. As far as I'm concerned, they aren't marines until after their first fire-fight."

"Where are you going next?"

"Los Angeles."

"Damn. I'd hate to have to shoot Americans, Gunny."

"Don't matter if they're Americans or Martians—once they aim at me and pull the trigger, they are the enemy. I know what to do with the enemy."

"What can you tell me about the warehouse?"

Merchal noticed the guard listening to every word. "Come walk with me, Gunny." When they were out of earshot, the sergeant said, "They're building a Rosy portal to send an emissary to the alien base on the moon."

Jeremiah blinked at that. "What makes them think the aliens will pay any attention to a human emissary? They haven't listened to anything we sent them so far."

"I don't know, but they're gonna send her. And wait 'til you see who it is. She's a babe! Hey, I gotta go. Watch out for Schwartz—he likes to pretend he's sick. The twelve-ounce arm curls are mostly what he has trouble with. I told him the next time he shows up drunk for duty, he's going to the brig. The other guys are green, but their attitude is good."

"Got it. Thanks. You be careful out there."

"Those guys can't be half as tough as the Taliban and I kicked their asses." He picked up his seabag and saluted. "They're all yours."

Jeremiah return the salute and walked back to the gate. "Give me the list of allowed personnel, Private."

"Right here, Gunny." The private passed him the list.

It was short, and he was not on it. "Why did you give me the list, Private? I am not on it."

"Be...because you're guard commander. Gunny Merchal said so."

"This is the last time you can make that mistake. If the person asking for entrance is not on the list, don't let them near you. I don't care if it's a frigging general—you don't let them near you. That person could have an explosive vest. Just because we have a secure base around you doesn't mean you can relax."

"Yes, sir."

"Now open the gate."

"No, sir."

"Why not, Private?"

"Because you aren't on the list, sir."

"Very good. We may get along after all. Who creates the list for you?"

"The guard commander, sir."

"And who is the guard commander?"

"You are, sir."

"Now listen carefully. As guard commander, I am telling you to add Gunnery Sergeant Jeremiah Silverstein to the list. Do it now. A new list will be generated for the next shift."

"Yes, sir." He added the name.

"Now open the gate."

"ID, sir."

"Very good. Here it is." The private verified that Jeremiah was on the list and then pressed the switch to open the gate. "Why isn't a machine gun covering you while you check IDs and allow people in and out?"

"I don't know, sir."

"Carry on, Private."

"Yes, sir."

... ...

"Are you sure you're okay with taking care of the kids?"

"I raised four boys," Andrea O'Flynn told him. "I think I can handle two toddlers." Shannon was asleep in her lap. She smiled down at the little girl as she brushed the red hair out of her eyes.

Freddie didn't have any doubt that Andrea and Ray could care for the kids; he had serious doubts about whether *he* could leave the kids with them. They had been his life for two-and-a-half years. He had raised them from newborns. They were his children as surely as if he were the sperm donor, and now the president had ordered all active duty service members to the nearest military base. He had to leave.

"No one knows you're here," Ray told him. "You could've been killed at Wysnewski's. You could stay. Andrea and me, we'd love to have you stay."

"*I* would know, Ray. That's called desertion. I'm no deserter."

The old man looked at Freddie with mixed emotions. He'd grown very fond of the man. He was proud of the responsibility the corpsman had shown with the kids and just as proud that Freddie heeded the president's call. "Them kids'll be fine. You take that old truck—belonged to my youngest son, until he graduated from college and was suddenly too good to drive a beat-up Chevy pickup. I'd give you my old deer rifle, but it's the only one I got."

"You wouldn't know how to open Sullivan's gun safe, would you? I bet he's got a couple a rifles in there."

"Tom had a worse memory than me. It has to be written down somewhere. You check all over that room? It would be four two-digit numbers. He probably wrote it on a two-by-four or the wall near the safe."

"Four two-digit numbers?"

"Yeah. I helped him move that heavy bastard down into his basement. We rigged a block-and-tackle at the top of his stairs to ease it down. Once it was in place, he showed it off to me. Took him three tries, reading the numbers off a little piece of paper."

"I think I know where that paper is," Freddie told him. "I saw one just like that in the nightstand next to his bed."

Half an hour later, they were looking into Sullivan's open safe. It contained fourteen rifles and shotguns and three pistols on the top shelf, as well.

"Well, take your pick. If Sullivan comes home and bitches, I'll tell him I told you to take one."

Freddie pulled each weapon out and checked it. They were well cared for and oiled. The rifle in the back of the safe caught his attention. "Is that a 416? How the hell did Sullivan get an H&K 416? I thought they were military only."

"Tom loved to shoot. His son was in special ops in the Air Force."

Freddie picked up the rifle reverently and cycled the action. It was a little stiff from its almost new condition. "That must be where he got it. This rifle is a personal friend of mine—I used one just like it in Iraq and Afghanistan. Could I have it? It takes the standard NATO 5.56 round. It'd be easy to get ammo."

"I doubt if Tom needs it anymore. If it will keep you safe, then take it with my blessing."

Freddie sighted through the scope and smiled. "This is beyond wonderful. I'd like the Remington .380 pistol, too, if I could. I can keep it in my pocket without anyone noticing. Let's go test fire 'em to make sure they work."

They grabbed a box of ammo for each weapon and walked out the back door. Fifteen minutes later, they were examining the scrap of plywood they'd used as a target.

"Nice pattern with the pistol, Ray." The cluster of holes was the size of a silver dollar.

"I still got the touch," the old man crowed. "Got expert with them worn-out .45's the marines made us use."

"Let's go clean 'em and leave an IOU for Mr. Sullivan. As soon as they pay me, I'll send him the money."

Freddie was ready to leave by lunch. The pickup started on the first try. Ray had kept the battery on a trickle charger and the gas tank full. They topped off the oil, coolant, and brake fluid and filled all the tires to their recommended pressure.

"Here's a can a gas in case you have trouble findin' some." He put the can in the back of the pickup.

"And here's lunch." Andrea handed him a bag.

"Where are the kids?" he asked, knowing this was going to be the hard part.

"They was in the barn, a minute ago," Ray told him. "They was playing hide-and-seek in the stalls."

Freddie walked into the barn. "Kids? Come here. I wanna say goodbye."

Shannon came out first. "You go bye, Fweddie?"

"Yep. I go bye. You're staying with Grandma Andi and Grandpa Ray for a while. Give me a hug before I go."

Shannon walked over to him and held up her arms. He lifted her and took a deep whiff of her clean baby smell. It would have to hold him until he came back. Wilson didn't come out of the stall, so Freddie carried Shannon in and set her down on a bale of hay. Wilson was hiding under the hay bunker.

"Hey, buddy. Don't you want to say goodbye to me?"

"You no go, Freddie. I want go with you."

"You can't go with me, Wilson, but I'll be back as soon as I can. The president needs my help. I have to go." He picked him up. The little boy pressed his face into Freddie's chest with his arms around his "father's" neck and tried hard not to cry. Freddie kissed the top of his head and put him down.

The three exited the barn, hand in hand. Andrea took Shannon's hand, and Ray took Wilson's. Freddie got in the pickup, started the motor, and waved. All four waved back as he turned left at the end of the driveway and headed west toward Fort Lewis.

"Goddammed windshield's dirty as hell," he muttered, wiping the tears from his eyes. "I can't see shit!"

… … … … … … … … …

The Three Hour War

Specialist Vaco pushed back from her workstation in disgust. "I have to run this report up to Headquarters, Dr. Medder. The local internet is down again. I'll be back in half an hour."

"What do they do with it?" Doug asked, looking at the report. It was a spreadsheet with the supplies they needed for the lunar module.

"They call Fort Riley and read them the items that are on it. Riley calls the other forts and bases to find out if they have any of the stuff we need. If they do, they portal it to us."

"And you have to do that by phone?"

"No other way—the internet outside of the base doesn't work anymore and the one inside isn't much better. They keep having to reboot the servers while they fix the fiber optic cables of the on-base backbone."

"And if you had an internet that would talk to the other forts, you would be able to do this faster?"

"God, yes," Vaco rolled her eyes. "I could send an email to all the quartermasters at each fort, and they could email me back if they have what we need or not. It would take minutes instead of hours."

"I think I have an idea that will help. I need to make a phone call." He reached for the Rosy phone he kept in his desk, synced to Edmonton Shipping Center, and pressed the call button.

"Sergeant McCoy, Edmonton Shipping Command. How may I help you?"

"Hello, Sergeant McCoy. This is Dr. Medder."

"Dr. Medder! How's California?"

"Couldn't say—they never let me out of this damned building during daylight. How are the portal installations going?"

"We just got Ottawa up. Toronto's next, but Edmonton won't allow us in until the army quiets everything down. There was a lot of looting."

"What happened to Quebec and Montreal?"

That got a snicker. "The Frenchies declared independence from Canada while Edmonton was trying to kickstart the government. Somehow, according to them, this war was all

Ottawa's fault. Edmonton told them, if they didn't come back into the fold, they wouldn't receive a portal. They told Edmonton to fuck off, eh. So, they don't have a portal and aren't going to have one any time soon. We started a lottery betting on how long they hold out."

"Put me in for a loonie. I bet two months."

"Okay, Doc. You're in, but most people are betting on a year or more. What can I do for you?"

"Is Warrant Officer Venkat Shaik available?"

Doug heard Sergeant McCoy call out, "Hey, Venkat, Dr. Medder wants to talk to you."

A moment later, Venkat's voice came on the phone. "Hello, sir. With what can I help you?

"Venkat, do you think you could break free from Edmonton long enough to help me create a Rosy internet backbone using those laser multiplexors you told me about? I want to connect all the American forts together via secure internet."

"And would this technology be available to Canada, as well?" The reluctance of the US to share Rosy technology was well known and resented worldwide.

"I'd have to get permission, but I can't think of a single reason why it shouldn't. Canada supplied the transportation portals; seems like sharing this is the least the US could do to say thanks. The powers that be may not allow the two internets to talk to each other, but within Canada, sure. Why would there be a problem?"

"Let me check with my command. You check with yours. I am liking the idea very much to work with you on this, Dr. Medder."

Chapter 34 – Day Care

Lieutenant Nussi pressed the intercom. "Captain Xanny, please come to the bridge."

The captain floated in a few minutes later. "What's happening, Nola?"

"Everyone please leave the bridge. This is 'Captain's Eyes' only."

The rest of the crew filed out and closed the hatchway. Nola pressed the play button. The computer read the message to them.

"Before Fey Pey jumped to Earth, he jumped to an asteroid in the Glycemis System. We have no idea whom he met or why, but he only stayed there for one hour. From there he jumped to clear space a light year away from Earth and waited seven days before he jumped to Earth. Envoy Gart-Disp is also from Glycemae."

Xanny stared at Earth in the hologram, considering the implications. "Now *that* is very interesting. Please encrypt and save that message in my personal storage." Only three people had access to that: himself, Lieutenant Nussi, and Commander Chirra.

"Yes, sir."

"How did that come in?"

"It was attached to a personal email to Sergeant Flug's mother, care of the Combat Corp. They forwarded it to us because they had no address for her and Flug had put in a forwarding order. Our firewall trapped it and notified me because Sergeant Shaia created an exit to look for exactly this before she left. The message was encrypted and packaged inside a photograph. It would be invisible to anyone examining the email. This has Zarqa's style all over it."

"What was the photograph?"

"Flug waving from space."

"Just the kind of picture someone would send to his mother. Brilliant."

He took a moment to let what Zarqa sent him soak in. "Doesn't the Ur keep travel records of envoys?"

"I don't know. Probably. The envoys would have to submit for reimbursement like everyone else, only no one questions their expenses."

"So, that should be public knowledge?"

"Depends on the trip. I'm sure secret trips aren't public knowledge, and envoys do a lot of under-the-surface stuff."

"See what you can find about the envoy's activities in the six months before he came to Earth. At least we can find out what he wants us to know."

He opened the hatchway. "Come back in, everyone—false alarm."

… … … … … … … … …

"What should we do wid 'em?" Wesley Toussaint asked his supervisor. Wesley was primary support technician for the Baby Factory in Port-au-Prince, Haiti. "We haven't been able t' contact our salesmen in de US, Canada, China, or Europe fer weeks."

The supervisor, Harold Fatton, looked at the Baby Machines dedicated to the "special requests" with contempt—contempt for the rich people who bought their way to the front of Haiti's queue, contempt for the corrupt government that ran Haiti for allowing the foreigners to bypass the native Haitians who needed and wanted babies, contempt for the leaders who made their millions from the bribes, but mostly contempt for himself that he needed this job so badly he had allowed himself to be part of it.

"The rules are quite clear. If we don' get de money, de babies get terminated."

The twenty machines were in various stages of incubation. Seven were in the third trimester. "I don' tink anyone planned fer circumstances like dese. Maybe we should try to find people on de baby waiting list, people what would want one."

Harold brought up the profiles of the parents of the babies in the twenty special request machines. Fourteen were white, three were Asian, two were black, and one was brown. All were rich, educated achievers. "The two black children we c'n place an' I expect we c'n place de brown one; its parents were Colombian and it's full term in one week. But what Haitian would want a white or Asian baby?"

"My wife would want one. Any baby better dan no baby!" Wesley gave his supervisor a sly look. "I bet we could sell 'em on da black market. Make a bundle—split it fifty-fifty. If anyone ever ask, we tell dem we terminated de babies fer nonpayment."

Harold started to say something but then stopped. Odds were they would get forty babies out of the twenty machines—each actually created two healthy babies, on average. If they were sold for a thousand dollars apiece, that would be forty thousand dollars to split between them—thirty for him and ten for Wesley. Thirty thousand dollars was twice his annual salary and he was considered a rich man in his neighborhood.

"Let's see if anyone wants 'em."

The baby names, chosen by who paid for them, were listed on the front of the machines. Would the people he placed the babies with want to know what they were going to be called? *Nah,* Harold decided, pulling the tag off the first one as he walked down the line. *What Haitian would name a girl Kayleen?*

Then he had a thought. *Since all da babies in each machine are identical twins, we could charge extra fer people what wanted twins—maybe three thousand fer de pair.*

Harold left work that evening with a spring in his step. Life was good!

... ...

Liam Johansson stood and interrupted the nervous social talk going on in their living room. "The homeowners' association will come to order," he said to the room. Twenty-three people had shoehorned themselves into his small house; about half were standing. "We decided when we moved up here that, if the government failed, we would resolve things by ourselves without making a bunch of rules. Well, now we need to see if that works.

We have an issue that must be resolved for the safety and peace of our little community."

Jonathan and Caitlin sat together. Rebecca stood by herself on the other side of the room.

"Everyone knew and liked Jeremiah Silverstein. There isn't anyone up here who wasn't helped by him in one way or another. His wife, Rebecca, was a different story. She chafed against us continuously in the short time she was here and then left Jeremiah, taking most everything he had. I, for one, said, 'Good riddance!'"

Rebecca watched him without expression.

"When Jonathan, Caitlin, and their two kids showed up as refugees, they moved into Jeremiah's cabin and kept to themselves. Now Rebecca has returned to our community and wants to live in the cabin. Given there is no government to decide the case, it falls on us to determine whether we allow her to evict Jonathan's family or not. Each of them wants to present their side of the story. Jonathan and Caitlin, you go first."

Jonathan looked down and then at his wife. She smiled at him, squeezed his hand, and nodded in encouragement. He stood self-consciously. "I'm a mechanic. I ain't used to speaking to five people at once, let alone a group like this, but here goes. The way I see it, that cabin is ours now. Rebecca abandoned it when she abandoned Jeremiah and the rest of the community. She went back to Los Angeles and gave up her right. When Jeremiah left to search for her and didn't come back, we can only assume he got caught up in the violence in LA. He may be dead or a prisoner somewhere. We found the cabin abandoned and, by right of possession, it's ours now. When she came to us and offered to build us another cabin so she could have ours back, we told her we would only agree if the new cabin had the same facilities as ours. She went ballistic, so I told her we ain't moving and that's the end to it." When he sat down, everyone's eyes went to Rebecca.

She stood slowly and cleared her throat. "I've done some really dumb things in my life. The dumbest of all was when I left Jeremiah to return to LA. After the bombs fell, it took me four weeks to make my way back up here. I met some good people and some not-so-good people along the way. Four of those good people accompanied me and are living with me in the Southerlands' house."

She turned to Amy Johansson. "Amy, when you told me we could use the Southerlands', you said my friends and I would have to move if the Southerlands showed up, and I agreed because that made sense. The house I'm living in was and still is the Southerlands' house, and we care for it like the guests we are." She took a breath. "I don't understand how Jonathan can claim possession if they came here one week before I got back. They brought nothing but their clothes and moved into a cabin they did nothing to earn. My husband paid for that cabin with money we both earned. He put in all those fixtures that Caitlin likes so much, because I told him to and I paid for half of them."

She faced Jonathan. "Another reason I agreed not to press for possession of the place was that they have two kids. I didn't want to turn them out with nowhere to go. Then Caitlin gave me Jeremiah's letter. That cabin is all I have left of him; it still belongs to the two of us as surely as the house I'm living in belongs to the Southerlands. I want my house back. I want to live in it until Jeremiah returns to me." She leaned back against the wall.

Liam stood. "Okay. Does anyone have any questions they'd like to ask these people?"

"I do." Alice Parker stood. "Rebecca, you said you didn't want to turn them out because of their kids, but that's exactly what you're doing. Where are they supposed to go?"

"Why couldn't they live in Maloney's house?" Amy Johansson suggested. "I doubt Stan is coming back."

"Because Maloney's house doesn't have dark energy," Jonathan said, his face becoming red. "It has a pump at the kitchen sink, a goddamned fireplace for heat, and a wood-fired stove for cooking. That's why we didn't settle there to begin with."

Rebecca jumped to her feet. "It also has a fully-stocked wood pile and kerosene lanterns for lighting. There is a chainsaw and enough gas to power it for years in his shed. Maybe the reason you don't want to live there is because you would actually have to do some work."

"We ain't moving!" Jonathan said, standing up. "Come on, Caitlin. We're outta here."

"I can run electrical service from my house," Jeb Quinn told him. "Couldn't be more than a hundred feet. I got a roll of direct burial ten-gauge wire that should do it."

"I'll donate my old furnace," Alan Cortney told him. "Milly's been whining at me to throw it away since I upgraded to a heat pump. It'd be plenty for Maloney's place."

Caitlin reached up to her husband, taking his hand in hers. "Jonathan, we need to move. I love where we are, but the cabin is Rebecca's house, not ours. You've worked hard since we got married, providing for us, and I love you for it. Let's move into Maloney's house and make it ours. If that means some work and sacrifices, what of it? I learned to cook on a wood stove from my mother. You and me, we've spent our whole lives working for someone else. Let's work for us this time and make a life up here where our kids can grow up and be happy."

This wasn't turning out like Jonathan had hoped. "And what happens when Mr. Stan Maloney shows up and kicks us out, like she's doing?"

"We'll deal with that when the time comes." She smiled at him gently.

Rebecca spoke up. "The offer my friends and I made still stands. We offered to build you a cabin. You could live at Maloney's until we're done. Liam, you have a pickup and flatbed trailer. Could we use it to go to Sonora to buy what we need?"

"Who'll pay for it?" Jonathan demanded. "I ain't got no money. Our life savings is in a bank at the bottom a San Francisco Bay." Money was a sore point. No one wanted to give up what little they had held on to.

"Well," Rebecca said, "The way I see it, we're a community. None of us would hesitate to jump to the aid of another who was threatened because we know they would do it for us. I don't think this is any different. I have enough cash to start building it, and maybe some other people will contribute too. Cash, supplies, labor?" A few people nodded and then a few more.

Liam cleared his throat. "I hate to be the naysayer in all this, but we have a problem. My truck is broken. The son of a bitch won't start. I am at a loss for where to begin, what with all the electronic falderal under the hood. If it had points and a distributor, I could fix it, but not with these new cars."

Caitlin gave Jonathan a nudge with her knee. He sighed. "Let me take a look at it, Liam. Ain't nothing I cain't fix."

... ...

"Washington is gone," Colonel Roberts announced as he walked into the conference room. Everyone around the table stared at him without understanding.

"What do you mean gone?" President Robbins asked.

"I mean gone—not there, missing, nothing but ocean."

"Where did it go?" Patty Kendricks, his chief of staff, asked, panicked. Her family lived in Delaware on Chesapeake Bay.

"No idea," Roberts said, trying to keep the anger out of his voice. "If I had to guess, I'd say the sun. That seems to be where anything that goes missing around here ends up. We just got word from the Beechcraft Brigade. The entire Atlantic coastline between New York City and North Carolina has been moved west about a hundred and fifty miles."

Patty gasped. "Delaware, too? The whole state?"

Robbins got out his cell phone and pulled up the calculator app. "New York City to North Carolina—it has to be three hundred miles." He typed in some numbers on his phone. "You mean the aliens sent forty-five-thousand square miles of the United States into the sun? Why would they do that? What happened to all the people who lived there?"

"I imagine they went with the dirt," Colonel Roberts told him, deadpan.

"Good God, man. There must have been twenty million people in that area."

"At least. Probably more like thirty. And the Brigade is reporting massive water damage all along the new shoreline. They said it looks like, and this is a quote, 'That God hit it with a fire hose.' Biblical damage—much worse than the Japanese tsunami that took out the Fukushima nuclear generator. The damage goes twenty miles inland. They also reported tremendous numbers of floating objects in the ocean near the new shoreline."

"Didn't we put a Rosy radio at Norfolk?"

Patty checked her notes. "Yes we did, sir."

"Try to contact them."

She left the room and returned several minutes later. "They don't answer."

"What's the nearest base to them?"

"That would be Bragg, sir," Roberts said.

"Call them and put them on the speaker phone."

She left again. A minute later, the speaker phone popped. "This is General Keynan."

"Hello, General Keynan. This is President Robbins."

"How may I help, sir?"

"I need you to send some people up to Norfolk Naval Base. We are having trouble contacting them. The Beechcraft Brigade reported large areas of the East Coast disappearing. I need someone to put eyes on it and give me a status report."

"Disappearing, sir?"

"You know as much as I do, General. They are reporting ocean south of New York City, north of the North Carolina line, and east of the foothills west of Washington."

"I will send a convoy immediately."

"Do an aerial survey as well. I want pictures. Call me back as soon as you find out what's going on."

"We did an aerial two days ago. DC was there, but horribly damaged. There was lots of radioactivity beginning around Norfolk all the way up the East Coast until we got past Atlantic City. It went west until the mountains stopped it."

"That sounds like the new boundaries. Do you think the aliens were trying to purge the radioactivity?"

"There were five separate craters in DC."

"Let me know what your new survey shows. There has to be someone alive near the new shoreline. Interview the people who saw what happened."

"Yes, sir."

... ...

"Dr. Yuan, please pass through the scanner."

"A gunny sergeant running the gate?" Lily asked as she followed his orders. "What happened to Private Swift?"

Jeremiah answered her crisply, "I'm the guard commander. I took over the security of this building yesterday. I want to do every job so I can find where the holes are."

"Just keep us safe, Sergeant"—she glanced at his name tag—"Silverstein."

"Yes, ma'am."

"Where are you from, Gunny?" Kevin asked. He was becoming comfortable with the marine vernacular.

"I was raised in Santa Barbara, lived in L.A, and then moved up to the Sierras, forty miles east of Sonora, about a month before the bombs. When I heard the president ask for all ex-military to report, I joined back up."

"The Sierras sound beautiful," Doug said, kissing Clara goodbye, and then stepping through the scanner. "I have a farm near Calgary."

"What do you raise?"

"Very expensive lawn ornaments." Doug laughed.

Jeremiah raised his eyebrows in a quizzical look, not understanding

"He means horses," Clara said, picking up Lan. "We have two of them."

"I grew up with horses." Jeremiah smiled happily at the memory. "I understand 'very expensive.' My dad kept a herd of Appaloosas at his ranch in Santa Barbara. He rented them to the movie companies."

"What fun!" Lily said. "I love to ride. I used to ride in China before I came to the United States."

"Well, we'll all have to go riding sometime," Jeremiah told her. "There's a stable on base—one of the only buildings that escaped the bombing."

Kevin snickered. "If the building full of horse manure was the only one that survived here, Washington should have come through unscathed."

Jeremiah tried not to laugh. "After the Pacific Coast Highway is reopened, we can go up to Dad's ranch. He loves to get his horses exercised."

"Have you heard from him yet? Was his ranch damaged?"

"No idea. I haven't been able to contact him yet. But he's a tough old marine—he made it through Vietnam. He'll be fine. I bet he's drinking Scotch on the front porch, wondering what the fuss was all about. I almost expected him to show up for duty when the president's call went out."

"Now all we need is time to take a day off to go riding," Doug sighed. "They keep us pretty busy inside."

"So, get to work and save the world, dear." Clara waved goodbye. "Call me when you're ready for me to pick you up." She spun Lan around, and the little girl squealed in delight. "I hear the day care calling to you, Lan." She put the little girl into her car seat and drove away.

When Doug entered the warehouse, Venkat was waiting for him, about to pop with excitement. "I got a hundred gigabit connection through the portal this morning! File transfers are so fast that they're done almost before they start. I sent *The Godfather* through. It took one second for the 2.6 gigabytes!"

"And it played?"

"Just like the original. I watched Sonny Corleone get killed again."

"How many separate channels can we put through?"

"Only one presently. The next step is to try ten at once. It's basically a hardware issue. My software will send as many data streams as the multiplexer can handle."

"How soon can Eric have the multiplexers configured?"

"He's working on it. He said he'd be ready after lunch."

"If his other estimates are any judge, that probably means by the middle of morning." Doug shook his head. Dr. Eric Baumgartner was a machine! He could make lasers sing, dance, and do back flips.

Eric joined them. He was always rumpled, like he had slept in his clothes and hadn't shaved for a couple of days. If you passed him on the sidewalk, you'd think he was a homeless wino and not one of the most brilliant electrical engineers Doug had ever known.

"I guess Venkat told you about our success?"

"Yep. How many channels do you think we can put through the beam at once?"

Eric rubbed the stubble on his chin. "Gee, I don't know—a couple thousand, maybe more. I think the multiplexers we're using are limited to a hundred and fifty."

"All with a hundred gigabit speed?" Doug was seriously impressed. That was fast enough for a small capacity internet backbone.

"I 'found' a matched pair of light multiplexer/de-multiplexers the cable companies use in their fiber optic networks. They do what we need, but we can't use their fiber optic cable interface—it won't work for us because we don't have a fiber cable between the sending and receiving sites and their LEDs weren't designed to go through clear air. So, instead of using their interface, we put the signal to our own laser, which can travel the two feet between the transmitter and the receiver with no distortion. And we have another pair to send the signal back; that way each side of the portal can transmit and receive simultaneously.

"But this is just the beginning! I figure we can bundle a hundred lasers into each send and receive head and have them automatically aim and connect with each other when the portal opens. Each laser should support three hundred channels. We should be able to get up into multi-petabit range with almost no latency! Transmission speed is only limited by the multiplexers at both ends, not the transmission itself. Venkat created a Linux service to feed the multiplexer from the server bank. It was all in assembler. He got it working in four hours. He's amazing."

Doug was more than a little envious of them. He'd been out of the hands-on development effort since they'd arrived at Camp Pendleton. All his time was taken up with planning and meetings that never seemed to end and were always followed by another meeting. "I have to give an update this morning to General Philpot. He wants this to be installed between us and Riley by the end of the week. Do you think we can do that?"

"Two more days?" Eric stared away again. "One beam, multiplexed with a hundred and fifty channels? Yeah, I think we can get it bundled up by then."

"And we're going to need twenty-four more pairs," Doug reminded him. "Once one works, the rest of the military posts are going to be screaming for it."

"Where are you going to find the multiplexers? I got the ones we're using from a friend at AT&T. They took a pretty big hit by the bombs. I don't think they're going to turn loose a bunch more."

"Let the general worry about that. He has lots more resources than we do. Let's talk for a minute about how we're going to build the network between sites. I want any site to be able to talk to any other. Each site would have a list of other sites and what order to attach to them. If one site fails, the transmitter/receiver would automatically fail-over to its next one."

"So, you want the ability to reconfigure the backbone on a moment's notice?" Venkat asked, cocking his head.

"We aren't talking about a backbone, are we? This is peer-to-peer. They will connect and disconnect with each other as needed."

Venkat shook his head. "Won't work. Each time a connection is made, the handshake takes five seconds before the portal activates. If they are doing that before each transmission, we're going to lose a lot of throughput and no one is going to want to Facetime. How about a backbone where any node can fail-over to another predefined node? It would be much more secure and, since it's active continuously, we wouldn't have any startup/shutdown overhead. Most of the software is already in the phone logic we based the portals on. If I remember correctly, you created that software. I took a quick peek. That's some beautiful code, Doug."

That made him blush. "Think it might be ready by the end of the week?"

"Never gonna happen. We'll have to roll it out with the single-beam, multichannel configuration we have now and have the other forts connect to dedicated portals in the server farm at Riley. We'll have to do the peer-to-peer thing as an upgrade. I'll let you know. Or we could delay the whole thing until we finish the backbone fail-over logic—maybe another week."

"One more week? Are you sure we can finish it by then?"

"That depends," Venkat said slyly.

"On what?"

"On whether you can roll up your sleeves and do the aiming-handshake logic. You know more about it than anyone else alive."

Doug looked down with his lips pursed—eight years of college and a Nobel Prize—now he was spending all his time explaining what they were doing instead of helping to do it. "I'll ask. They might let me off the hook for a week."

Venkat snorted and walked away, beginning to think about what he had to change to make peer-to-peer work.

"And there's Canada, too, remember?" Doug called out as Venkat disappeared around the corner. "They want eight pairs."

… … … … … … … …

"What is your business at Fort Lewis, Chief?" the MP corporal examined Freddie's Military ID. Two .50 caliber machine guns were trained on his truck while the other guards checked for bombs underneath with mirrors and another made a thorough search inside the cab.

"Active military reporting for duty," Freddie told him.

"Bremerton, Everett, or Bangor?"

"Excuse me?"

"Which base were you assigned to? Bremerton, Everett, or Bangor?"

"None of the above. I was stationed at a SHIPS in Montana."

"A ship in Montana?" the MP asked sarcastically, like Freddie was stupid. "What kind of ship is in Montana?"

"It wasn't that kindda ship," Freddie responded impatiently to the dumb-army-corporal question. "A SHIPS is a Sterile Heritage Protection Site. We were raising uninfected babies for a human colony in another solar system. It got blown up along with the rest of the world."

"What happened to the babies?"

"All but two were killed, along with everyone else. We were the only survivors. Me and two of my babies."

"Where are the babies?" The MP poked around in the bed of the truck.

"I left them with some people in Montana. After we got infected with BSV, there didn't seem to be any point in bringing them with me."

"Well, welcome to Fort Lewis. In Processing is straight ahead and to the right. They might have a position for you at the day care, Chief." He handed back his ID.

"Gee, you think so, Corporal?" Freddie asked in mock seriousness. "I guess I could do that. Someone has to take care of the MPs when they're off duty."

The corporal waved him through with a smile on his face.

... ...

"Chief Petty Officer Freddie Harris, report to the XO immediately."

He looked up in surprise at the page through the intercom. He didn't know the executive officer of the hospital even knew his name. They had never met. "What the fuck does he want with me?"

The sergeant major he was working on chuckled. "Officers got their own way of doing things, Chief. You got a nice touch. I hope you stick around for a while. You better go see what he wants."

Freddie cleaned up the trimmings from changing the bandage on the patient's injury—just one of many he'd performed since his arrival at JBLM on men who'd been injured in the Three-Hour War—and then left for the XO's office.

The "office" was a tent. "Sir, you paged me." He saluted and stood at parade rest.

Major Simmons saluted back. "Sit down, Chief." He motioned to a chair on the other side of his desk. "How would you feel about going to LA to help out the marines? They are catching hell taking back parts of the town and need someone who can patch them up. You did three tours in the Middle East. You think you can handle being back in combat?"

Freddie was taken aback. The three tours he'd served were a large part of his decision to sign on to submarine duty; he was still plagued by memories of what he'd seen and done in Iraq and Afghanistan. "Sir, if it's all the same to you, I'd rather stay here. My combat tours aren't something I remember very fondly."

"Son, I understand. They don't give out the Navy Cross for nothing. You were put in for the Medal of Honor, but it was denied. What happened?"

"A bunch of guys got killed. On both sides. I didn't."

"I read the award. You and everyone with you were out of ammunition. You treated four critically injured men in your squad and kept them alive while you took the rifles from the enemy you killed and used them to keep the bastards from overrunning your position. They attacked you almost nonstop for six hours. You held them off and kept those men alive until your unit could extract you and your injured."

"That's not something I want to do again, sir. I volunteered for submarine duty so I wouldn't have to."

"Aren't you too tall for submarines?"

"I slouched a little. They needed a corpsman."

"So do the marines. A lot of kids are getting hurt. The gangs in LA have recruited ex-military members. We're fighting people *we* trained! And they're pretty good—better than the frigging Taliban. Intel thinks the gangs actually sent members into the military to *get* trained; it's like they *knew* this was going to happen. They're armed with company-grade weapons from the National Guard armories around LA that survived the bombing—automatic rifles, machine guns, grenade launchers, TOWs, .50 cals, mortars, body armor—and they know how to use 'em."

Freddie sighed. *Combat medic again? Dammit!* "Can I think about it for a day or two, sir?"

"A day or two means more people killed that you could have saved."

He began to get pissed off. *Who the hell is this guy that he thinks he can twist my arm? He wasn't there—he didn't know what it was like. He probably sat at a desk his whole career.* Then Freddie noticed the major's combat patch: an arrowhead with a sword and three lightning bolts. Above the patch were two more tabs; one said RANGER and the other AIRBORNE. He was ex-Special Forces.

"Where did you serve, sir?"

"A bit of everywhere. Five deployments. I understand your reluctance. I'm not sure I would go, but they won't ask me." He pulled his leg out from under the desk and put it on top with a hollow *thunk*. The major had a prosthetic leg. "I'd like to tell you I got this in a big firefight—I had enough opportunities—but the truth is I lost this leg in a car wreck after I got back. I was stupid drunk. No excuses—I deserved it. At least I didn't hurt anyone else."

Freddie nodded sadly. He understood how hard returning from a war zone was. He had fought those same demons. "You're not the first one to do that, sir."

"And I'm not gonna be the last, either," Simmons said somberly. "Been sober for four years. So, will you go?"

The chief looked through the doorway of the tent at the construction of the new hospital headquarters going on about a hundred yards away. The noise of hammering and sawing filled the air. *Can I do this?* Then he asked himself another, even scarier question: *Can I not do this?*

He sighed again. "Yeah, I'll go. How do I get there? Is a plane service set up yet?"

"No need. We got this spiffy thing called a transportation portal our Canadian friends made for us. You walk in one end, you're in Washington. You walk out the other, you're at Camp Pendleton."

"Is San Diego secure?"

"San Diego was a cake walk. Everyone living there was so worried about the drug cartels coming across the border from Mexico, that they greeted us with open arms and American flags waving in the wind. The People's Republic of LA is another matter."

"What about my truck?"

"It'll be here when you return. Park it in the motor pool, so it'll be safe."

Freddie got up and saluted. "I'll go pack, sir."

The major saluted back. "I'll have your orders ready by the time you're done."

Chapter 35 –I Hope It Doesn't Take Longer

"Here's Envoy Gart-Disp's itinerary for the six months prior to Fey Pey's arrival on Earth. It says he was in Charnicon when Fey Pey was on that asteroid. Charnicon is a thousand light years from the Glycemis System. So, the person Fey Pey met couldn't have been the envoy?" Lieutenant Nussi was disappointed.

Captain Xanny studied the itinerary over her shoulder. "It would appear not. But I have an idea. Come walk with me and tell me what you think." They went to his quarters, away from prying ears.

Ten minutes later, the lieutenant shook her head doubtfully. "Do you think that'll work?"

"What do we have to lose? Do you think you can do it?"

"One of the data analysts might be a better choice." She shrugged. "Sure, what the hell. Let's see what happens." She brought up her communications hologram and connected to one of the pirate anonymity sites. From there she connected to a second pirate site to be safe. The second site allowed them to enter an address that would appear to the receiver as the real originating site.

Nola entered the address of Envoy Gart-Disp's office and then keyed in the coordinates of the Charnicon central communications receiver. The red light on the link came on, indicating they were connected to Charnicon. She keyed in a query for the connection to the hotel where the envoy's itinerary said he'd stayed. It popped up. She pressed the voice connection button on the hologram.

The voice translation programs synchronized. "Hello, Charming Charnicon. How may I help you?"

"This is Envoy Gart-Disp's billing office. I need a copy of a receipt he was charged during his stay."

"I'll connect you to our billing office."

There was a click and then, "Charnicon Billing Office."

"This is Envoy Gart-Disp's billing office. I need a copy of a receipt he was charged during his stay."

"When was his visit?"

"Four years ago. From star date 254939.245 through star date 254939.256."

"Four years ago, and you're just getting to his trip now?" The clerk sounded irritated. "For anyone else, I'd tell them to blow it out their—" (the translation program inserted "untranslatable" into the dialog). The clerk sighed. "Well, you'll have to wait while I retrieve his file; that will take a few minutes. We migrate everything to long-term storage after a year."

The line popped. She crossed her fingers. There was another pop. "I don't have a record of him visiting during that per—" The line popped again.

"This is the data supervisor for Charming Hotels. All information about Envoy Gart-Disp's visit has been classified top secret. Who is this?"

"I know his visit was top secret, moron. This is the envoy's *billing* office. But I have a question for you. If he wasn't there, how the hell could we have received a bill from your restaurant for twelve hundred Huz? Or are you trying to bleed a little money from the envoy's budget because you know how sensitive this is?"

"His billing office, huh? Let me dig a little deeper." They were on hold for several minutes. The hologram of the connection to the second anonymity site flashed green, indicating a trace had penetrated its firewall. She broke the connection.

"It keeps getting more interesting," Captain Xanny murmured. "Good job, Nola. You recorded that, right?"

"Yes, sir."

"Encrypt that whole call and put it into my personal storage along with the itinerary."

... ...

Dr. Hehsa stared out the window of his office on the top floor of the CDC building in frustration bordering on desperation.

None of the modifications they tried had succeeded in altering the function of BSV—hyaluronidase, cumulus cell, acrosin, proacrosin, and trigger gene. They knew what had changed, or at least they thought they did, but they couldn't figure out how to change it back. His team had spent three years chasing the fertilization rainbow and they weren't any closer to the pot of gold than when they started.

The sun was going down over Atlanta. Two monstrous cumulonimbus thunderstorms raised their billowy heads farther south, and lightning lit the clouds every couple of seconds.

"Jonesboro's getting hammered," he muttered, grateful for the distraction.

A faint knock sounded on the door to his office. The door inched open and his six-year-old granddaughter's head appeared in the doorframe. "Grandpa, will you read me a story?"

"Of course, Jhanvi. Which one would you like? Go choose a book."

She walked to his bookcase and studied the book backs with her eyes narrowed and lips pursed in concentration. She pulled out a thick volume. "This one."

He took the book from her hands. She had chosen *The Lord of the Rings*. His mind went back sixty years, to when his own grandfather had read this same volume to him. He was ten years old, and they were still living in Allahabad, India. The pages were yellowed with age and rereading. On the flyleaf was the message, in Hindi, his grandfather had written to him when he gave this book to Sridhar the year before he died. "To Sridhar: May you conquer your own Sauron."

"Why this one, sweetheart?"

"Because it has a volcano on the cover. I like volcanos."

"I will read you one chapter a day until we finish."

She crawled up into his lap. He opened the book to page one.

"'When Mr. Bilbo Baggins of Bag End announced that he would shortly be celebrating his eleventy-first birthday with a party of special magnificence, there was much talk and excitement in Hobbiton...'"

… … … … … … … … …

"The house is all yours, Rebeccaaaah!" Jonathan said bitterly as he opened the door and did a deep bow.

"Thanks, Jonathan. Maloney's cabin is ready for you guys to move in."

He leaned back inside the door. "Caitlin, ain't no need to clean the damned thing. It wadn't exactly pristine when we moved in."

"You can get on to Maloney's if you'd like, Jonathan. We've lived here, and I'm going to clean it before I leave. And I'll say 'thank you' to Rebecca, even if you've forgotten your manners. Your mother wouldn't believe you were her son." She went back to mopping the floor as her husband stormed off with a red face and their two kids.

Rebecca peeked inside. It was spotless. Jeremiah was a wonderful man, but he was no housekeeper. She could only imagine its condition when they arrived.

"Caitlin, the house is fine. It certainly wasn't worth getting into a fight over."

She smiled at Rebecca. "Out of all the things in here I love, the one I'm gonna miss the most is the toilet. I thought my outhouse days were gone forever."

Rebecca remembered her shouted words to her husband when he showed her the cabin for the first time: "If I have to use that outhouse in a week, I'm *outta* here!"

"We'll have to make sure your new home has a toilet."

"Could I ask you something?" Caitlin asked tentatively.

"Sure."

"Could I borra some a them books?" all the words coming out in a rush. "I never had much of a chance to read nothing, what with workin' since I was twelve. I started readin' one while we was livin' here, an' I can't stop thinking about it."

"Which one did you start?" This was a side to the woman Rebecca had never imagined.

"*Moby-Dick*. Have you read it?"

"Sure have, several times. I love that book."

"Do you think Captain Ahab was crazy?"

"As a mad hatter!"

"What about that Injun? Queequeg? Why did he stay with the ship? He knew they was all gonna die."

"I think he thought that was his destiny. Death meant something different to him than it does to us. It was more important for him to meet death bravely than it was to try to escape somehow, but he didn't want to die at the bottom of the sea. That's why he had the ship's carpenter make him that coffin."

Rebecca reached into the bookcase and retrieved *Moby-Dick*. "Take this, Caitlin. When you want to talk about it, please come back anytime. When you finish that book, many other titles in that bookcase are just as good. Wait until you read *A Tale of Two Cities, The Call of the Wild,* or *The Old Man and the Sea!*"

She clutched *Moby-Dick* to her chest, and then she hugged Rebecca.

"Are you two going to be okay? Jonathan sure was mad at me."

A soft glow grew on Caitlin's face. "Don't worry about him. He'll simmer down in a day or two. He's a good man, Rebecca. He's just lookin' out for his family. Gettin' that new cabin goin' will help a lot."

"I'm bring back the first load of materials tomorrow."

She hugged Rebecca again, and then hurried up the trail to Maloney's cabin.

… … … … … … … … …

"Mr. President?" General Keynan's strong, masculine voice came through the speaker.

"Yes, General," the president answered. "What did you find?"

"Sir, the damage is unbelievable. I went up in one of the planes to see for myself if what the pilots were telling me was true; then I went to some of the interviews with the survivors. The Atlantic Coast is gone from Newark, New Jersey, to the North Carolina border. The new coast goes due west from where Newark used to be all the way to where Harrisburg, Pennsylvania, had been. It heads south from Harrisburg along the Appalachian foothills through Bull Run to Charlottesville, Virginia, and then kind of southeast through Petersburg, Virginia, to the old coast at the Virginia-North Carolina border."

"Is there anything left of the old terrain?"

"No, sir. Everything is underwater now. I sent some people out to test the depth at several places. The sea floor goes up and down a little but mostly stays at a depth of about three thousand feet. The new shoreline is covered with debris, but none of it appears to be from the missing terrain or people. We thought the missing area had just been pushed down and might have some salvageable places, but we were wrong. It's gone. The land beneath the new ocean was removed down to three thousand feet. The floating debris is from the water wall blasting into the new shoreline and washing the resulting wreckage out to sea."

"Tell me about your interviews."

"We got some pretty far-fetched stories from the survivors. If I hadn't witnessed the damage with my own eyes, I never would have believed even half of what they said. The wall of water that hit the shore must have been at least a mile high. The Shenandoah Valley is still draining. The water wall made it all the way to the Allegheny Mountains, over thirty miles to the west. The flood damage from the rivers is biblical—bridges, buildings, cars, roads, transmission lines gone. Entire forests were knocked down with all the trees lying flat in the same direction. But this isn't all that disappeared, sir."

"What do you mean?"

"North Carolina had three separate nuclear-generating stations: Brunswick, McGuire, and Shearon Harris. I say had because all three are gone. There's nothing left but holes full of water."

"Did you encounter any radiation?"

"No. Well, nowhere but around Shearon Harris, and we figure that radiation was from the meltdown it had during the bombing. Someone put bombs right inside the condensation towers. But most of the radiation was removed with the generating station."

"Thank you, General. Please help the survivors as much as you can. They've lost everything. Tell me what you need. I'll try to find some FEMA supplies that weren't blown up. I want all the pictures and videos you've taken showing the damage."

"Yes, sir. I will put them on a plane to you within an hour." The line to Fort Bragg clicked off.

Robbins turned to his military attaché. "General Rheem, when those pictures arrive, I want your staff to prepare a briefing of the damage based on that material. I want it first thing tomorrow. Work all night if you have to. Once I approve your presentation, I want it put on DVDs and carried to the commanders of all twenty-five bases."

"Yes, sir." He turned to go then hesitated. "Uh, sir?"

"Yes, what is it?"

"Do you want me to have General Dodd at Fort Drum send some people to New York City and check out what the situation is after the East Coast disappearance?"

The president stared at the wall for a moment. "No. New York City is still in chaos and has been since this started. I don't see how this could make the situation there any worse or better. We'll start on the Big Apple after Dodd gets the rest of New York State under control. The Northeast is going to be a long time coming back into the fold."

"Yes, sir."

"Send in Patty on your way out, please."

Patty Kendricks, his chief of staff, knocked and entered.

"Hi, Patty. I need to know if all the nuclear-generating stations in the country have disappeared. Someone needs to call all twenty-five commanders and tell them to find out if the ones local to them are gone."

"Yes, sir."

… … … … … … … … …

"The first email came through," Venkat announced, studying his display.

Doug walked over. "Does it look okay?"

"Looks good to me." A digitized *Playboy* centerfold filled his display.

Doug snorted in disgust and walked away, mumbling, "The most secure, fastest internet technology in the world, and they use it to send porn."

"The next one was a request for body armor for the First Marine Division," Venkat called out.

"Did you hear that Gunny Silverstein got pulled from the security detail and assigned to them? First Division's getting pounded in LA"

"Yes, and I wish him well. I was liking him very much." There was a pause and a gasp from Venkat.

"What?" Doug asked, walking back over to see what was happening.

Venkat stared at his screen in disbelief. "The East Coast!"

"What about it?" he asked, concerned. "Has one of the routers failed?"

"It's gone" One of the pictures General Keynan had sent the president was on his monitor.

"Maybe you shouldn't be reading the president's email, Venkat," Doug said gently.

He looked up with tears in his eyes. "My mother lives in Philadelphia. She moved there last year to escape the cold of Toronto."

Doug didn't know what to say. "Venkat, I'm so sorry. Could she have been somewhere else? Maybe she escaped."

"I am not knowing where else she might have been. She had been talking about returning to Toronto to visit some friends."

"If you need to take some time off, go ahead. Show me how to run your interface."

"No. I will be staying here, doing my job. I have nowhere else to go."

Doug tried to snap his friend out of his spiral by changing the subject. "How's the topology of the backbone holding up?"

Venkat took a deep breath and wiped his face with both hands. He brought up the GUI he had built that showed the active nodes and the send/receive activity of each. "It's a little slow now."

Doug knocked over the coffee beside him in surprise. "*What?*"

Venkat was startled at the man's reaction then realized what he had said. "I don't mean slow speed. I mean slow activity. Norfolk is offline. Fort Bragg failed-over to Fort Drum, as it should have. All twenty-four bases are online, and all are sending emails. The emails are being routed to and from all nodes except Norfolk. We've got twenty-four greens and one red. Capacity is stable at about twenty terabits per second. Use is about one-half of one percent of capacity." His friend visibly relaxed. "After the initial burst of queued emails, everyone is probably reading their inboxes."

Specialist Vaco burst into the room. "Thank you, thank you, thank you!" she said, all in one breath.

"What did we do?" Venkat asked, perplexed.

"You got the internet going again. No more trips to HQ with stupid spreadsheets and no more phone calls to Fort Riley. Thank you *soooo* much."

"We didn't fix texting," he reminded her. Every time they met, she bemoaned not being able to text her friends. "And Facebook won't be running on this internet anytime soon."

"Hey, with you guys"—she laughed—"that'll be next week, right?"

He turned to Doug, about to say something, but his friend had cocked his head with a faraway look in his eyes as he stared at the poster of Mount St Helens they had taped on the wall because the building had no windows.

Venkat held his finger to his lips and motioned for her to go out into the corridor. The two left the lab in silence. He said softly to her, "The master is working. He needs quiet. He wasn't awarded either of his Nobels for pulling dandelions." He didn't mention Doug had declined his Nobel in Physics. It was still inconceivable to him that anyone would do such a thing, no matter what the reason.

Specialist Vaco left quietly. Venkat thought again about the pictures he'd seen in President Robbins's email. Philadelphia...gone. His mother...gone to his father and grandparents. "Goodbye, Mother," he whispered, trying not to be overcome. "I love you. Say hi to Dad." He checked his GUI. Fort Drum went yellow. "What the hell!" he grumbled. It flashed back green. "Let's bring up the log." He leaned toward his display. There would be time enough to grieve later.

... ...

"The oxygen will last a lot longer than anything else," Lily explained to Leann. "The dark energy supply will give you all the power you will need forever. The scrubbers will convert the CO_2 back into oxygen, almost forever."

Leann sat at the console of the capsule, trying to understand enough of the controls to be self-sufficient after the launch.

Her friend continued, "You should have plenty of water. The water from your urine and perspiration will be recycled also. What you will run out of is food. We've put ten days of food onboard. When that runs out, you will live for thirty days, plus or minus, before you starve to death."

"That should be plenty. If they don't come for me within ten days, I've already failed."

"Do you understand the radios?" Lily had gone over how to operate them many times.

"I do. And the video feed as well."

"You will have a real time feed flowing to and from the flight command center on Earth through the linked Rosy radios. You can disable the cabin cameras whenever you'd like to have some private time. The world doesn't need to witness you using the toilet. The external cameras will be on full time."

"*Okay*, I've got it." Leann was getting a little exasperated with repetition of the training.

Lily wasn't sure she did. "Leann, you are the world's last chance. I'm not sure why you were the one chosen to do this. I would have thought a pilot like Captain Marshall would have been a better choice—at least she knows how to fly. But, for some reason, President Robbins wants you. Could you at least try to listen and learn?"

Leann started to bristle but then backed off. The stress of preparing for the flight was wearing on everyone, including herself. "This isn't about flying the capsule, Lily," she said gently. "There are hundreds, maybe thousands, of people who could do that better than me. This is about getting the attention of the aliens. If I have problems or forget something about the capsule while I'm in flight, I have you and a whole staff at the flight center to call on. I'm not worried about the mechanics at all.

"I do understand how important this is, but my job isn't to fly the capsule. My job is to try to convince the aliens that humanity has something to contribute to the galaxy—things positive enough to offset the negatives that led us to be selected for elimination, and that I'm willing to die to tell them about it. President Robbins selected me because I get people's attention. I do it in ways no one else thought of. I think I can do it with the aliens, too."

Lily had huge misgivings about Leann being the correct person for this mission. The woman seemed more concerned about the goddamned cameras and how her profile appeared on the monitors than what she was trying to accomplish. But Lily was most terrified that she, herself, was contributing to the death of a woman she had come to like and admire. Every time she wondered why Leann needed the next silly thing she asked for, the president's edict jumped up in front of her. He had said she would get anything she wanted in that capsule, no questions asked.

"Let's try some dry runs. You want to sleep without the world watching. What do you do?"

She reached for the timer on the camera shut-off control, set it for eight hours, and pressed the start button. The display started ticking off seven hours, fifty-nine minutes and fifty-nine seconds, fifty-eight...

"The aliens show up next to your capsule. What do you do?"

Leann chuckled. "Smile, wave, and breathe a huge sigh of relief!"

"You might put on your protective suit," Lily snapped, irritated again that she was making light of something so vital. "They will probably move you to their shuttle. That pretty face won't be so pretty after passing through a vacuum."

"Yeah, a protective suit would be a good idea." She took a breath and closed her eyes, underlining that item on one of her many mental checklists.

"They may freeze you. If they do, let them—it doesn't hurt. You will wake up in their ship. Where is the president's greeting?"

"In the pocket of my protective suit."

"What are your goals?"

"To draw the aliens into a dialogue with the leaders of Earth."

"Have you finished your will?"

Leann still resisted completing a will. She had no siblings, and her aunts and uncles had tried to talk her out of this ever since her intentions were made public. They had used every tool in their relationship toolbox to coerce her to change her mind: guilt, cajoling, tears. She had finally said, "I love you, but this has to be done. Leave me alone. I'll see you when I return." Only her mother supported had her without question.

"No. I'll finish the damned thing today."

"The astronauts had to do it, too."

"Yeah. You've told me that before." She left out "a hundred times."

"You need to write a letter to your parents explaining why you are doing this. If the mission fails, we will deliver it to them."

"And if it doesn't? If the mission doesn't fail?" Her eyes filled with tears at the pain she was causing her parents.

"No one will ever see it, including me."

Leann blew her nose into a tissue. "I'll finish that today also."

"What are you bringing with you to take up your time while you wait?"

"I have a couple of hundred books and movies loaded into my tablet."

"Which ones? We don't want them to be too violent."

"Oh, I thought I'd bring *Alien*, *Godzilla*, *Terminator*, *Forbidden Planet*, *Predator*, and *War of the Worlds*. What do you think? Should I include *Mars Attacks, too*?" There was a twinkle in her eye. "Maybe they like country music."

Lily shook her head, trying to ignore Leann's sarcasm. "Whatever."

"I started to bring my personal favorite book but decided against it." Her eyes were still twinkling.

Lily had to ask. "What is that?"

"Chairman Mao's *Little Red Book*," she said, waiting for a reaction. "Do you think I should?"

Lily coughed a little. She had left China the night before her parents were arrested for being dissidents against the communists. "Maybe not that one."

"Alright, I'll leave it out." She grinned. "But seriously, I have some books I love and want to read again: *Gone with the Wind*, *Garden of Lies*, *Fifty Shades*, *The Thorn Birds*, and *Wormhole*."

"*Wormhole*? Really? Richard Phillips?"

"Actually, I brought his whole trilogy, *The Rho Agenda*. But I thought *Wormhole* was especially appropriate."

"Let's hope there isn't an alien army waiting at the other end of this like there was in Phillips's book."

Leann reached out to her tutor and took her hand. "Lily, thank you for being so thorough in your training. I also need to thank Kevin and Doug for the countless hours the three of you have spent telling me every detail of your interaction with the aliens and their starship. You think this mission is suicide, but I don't. You think I'm not the right person to go, but I do. I think I have a real chance of success."

Lily squeezed her hand. "I hope you're right." Then it was her turn for her eyes to twinkle. "*Fifty Shades*? You're going to read *Fifty Shades* while you're moving away from every man in the world at twenty-five thousand miles an hour?"

"It'll give me something to look forward to when I succeed." Leann giggled and then changed the subject, growing serious again.

"Do you have the two cameras inside that I asked for? Ninety degrees apart inside the capsule?"

"Yeah. No one can figure out why you want them, but Kevin put them in, like you asked."

"And the remote-control device that can fit in the palm of my hand?"

"Yep. That was the easy part."

"Great. I need to play with them for a while to get the feel of the remote control."

"Well, do it now. I have some paperwork to finish."

"Close the door on your way out, please."

Lily paused at the door and looked back inside. Leann was looking from camera to camera and watching her image in the monitor. She faded one camera and then activated the other before she started playing with the zoom and aim functions. Lily pursed her lips, wondering again why President Robbins chose her for this mission. They needed an ambassador or a head of state in that capsule, not an undergraduate more concerned about what books she was bringing than what she was supposed to accomplish. Lily closed the door and left the training room, putting aside her misgivings to focus on the reports she had to finish and her daily email to Fort Riley. With the launch date next week, the interest level of everyone had increased exponentially.

... ...

"Sergeant Silverstein, I want you to rendezvous with a local militia in Santa Clarita tomorrow." Captain Rousselot showed him where the meeting would be on the map.

"We haven't finished Reseda yet, sir. What's the hurry?"

"The Second Infantry Division used JBLM as their center of operations. They went north from JBLM and cleared the Seattle-area to the Canadian border and secured the naval bases along the way. They then started down the I-5 corridor toward Sacramento. Fort Lewis sent the Seventh Infantry Division to Travis to continue the clearing of San Francisco and south. After they cleared the Bay

Area, they went down the San Joaquin Valley to Wasco. They made it sound like the Battle of the Bulge. I don't know what they were bragging about—no one lived out there but a bunch of farmers.

Tomorrow, they are supposed to enter Bakersfield. President Robbins wants to reopen I-5 all the way from the Canadian border to the Mexican border by the end of the week. He thinks it would give us a ceremonial victory over the whole West Coast. That gives us four days to take control of Santa Clarita, Valencia, and the mountainous area between there and Bakersfield."

"There is the problem of a few bridges being blown along the way and about a million cars gridlocked on it."

"I didn't say it would be like the old days—not for a couple of years. But each blown bridge has a get-around. The Corps of Engineers and the Seabees are working as hard as we are. They have cleared the freeway all the way from the Mexican border to LA You don't wanna know what a hundred-thousand-dollar Mercedes looks like after a forklift moved it off the freeway, and the next car goes right on top. Doesn't matter if it's a Mazda or a Maserati."

"So, who do I meet? When? How will I know them? What should I bring?"

"It's all in your packet—read it. If you have any questions, I'll be in the command tent for another hour. When you execute the rendezvous, feel out the people—who will fight us and who will help us. Your contact is a guy named Carlos Sanchez. We have minimal intel on him, and what we have isn't too complimentary. I'm depending on you to decide if we should trust him, arrest him, or shoot him."

"What can you tell me about him, sir?" He got a twinkle in his eyes. "He isn't a zombie, is he?" The old Netflix series, *Santa Clarita Diet,* was popular with everyone on the base since the movie archive created by one of the navy techs had been made available at all the service clubs.

That got a laugh. "I guess you'll have to find out! If his wife looks like Drew Barrymore, I probably wouldn't go to dinner with 'em! And you have a new corpsman to replace Britt—a guy named

Chief Petty Officer Freddie Harris. He's waiting outside to meet you. Two tours in Afghanistan, one tour in Iraq, Navy Cross, washed out of Seal training saving another candidate's life. You two should get along great."

"A corpsman with the Cross?" He raised an eyebrow.

"His award text is in the packet—looks to be someone you can count on. Your rendezvous time is 0300 tomorrow." The captain saluted. "Dismissed."

"Yes, sir!" Jeremiah snapped a sharp marine salute, took the packet, and left. Freddie was waiting outside. "Hey, Chief." He held out his hand. "We'll be working together. I'm Gunny Silverstein."

"Glad to be aboard, Gunny. When's the balloon goin' up?"

"Tomorrow morning. Let's go find some coffee—gonna be a long night."

"Some things never do change." Freddie sighed. He was back on Marine Time—you slept when you could because, when you couldn't, life got pretty exciting. As they walked to the consolidated dining facility that had been set up, he wondered how the kids were doing. Andrea should be able to make them better clothes than he had.

He sipped his coffee while the gunny read the packet. After the sergeant read each piece of paper, he slid it across the table to Freddie, who was pleasantly surprised, unable to remember the last time a marine combat sergeant had treated him as an equal.

They were meeting with a local militia leader, Carlos Sanchez, in Santa Clarita. He was credited with bringing and maintaining order to the area west of I-5. There were also reports of him being violently brutal in how he brought calm to the area.

"We're going to take The Old Road instead of the freeway," Jeremiah explained. "I-5 hasn't been cleared that far yet. The California DOT lent us a big highway truck with a snowplow to remove any obstacles we encounter. We'll run it at the front of the convoy. It has armor all around the cab, windshield, and wheels."

"Can we get an Abrams to accompany us?" The M1 Abrams was the main battle tank of the US Forces.

"Not a chance in hell. There are only two left in the whole LA basin, and the people clearing Compton have both. This mission is just us in three pickup trucks and a snowplow. We don't even have Humvees. We mounted a .50 on the roof of two of them and a minigun on the third. All three got an M-60 on both rear corners."

"Any armor for the poor bastards who have to shoot 'em?"

"Kind of. There is what they're wearing, of course. We put sandbags on the floor, steel plates in the doors and sidewalls of the trucks up to about three feet, and round armor plates on the outside of all the tires. The .50s are a standard Humvee mount with integral armor."

"Better 'n nothin'."

"And they have canopies to prevent anyone from lobbing a grenade into the bed. We cut a hole for the .50 operator to use, and the rear corners are cut out for the 60s."

"So, these pickups aren't, like, F-150s, are they?"

"Well, they're Fords, but they're F-450s. We found 'em at a Ford dealer lot. I left a government IOU on the windshield of the truck next to 'em. First new rig I've ever had. They even have leather seats and air conditioning."

"Where's the team?"

"Waiting for me in our tent. Let's go meet 'em. Maybe we'll be able to sneak in a couple of hours sleep before we leave at 01:00"

"You think we'll need two hours to drive from Reseda to Santa Clarita? It's only fifteen miles."

"I hope it doesn't take longer."

The intel packet and his briefing hadn't been enough—Freddie hadn't been part of Jeremiah's team while they cleared Reseda. The gunny's comment finally made it clear to him how big of a shit pile they were wading into. "How about corpsman supplies? Sounds like I should bring a little extra."

"We have what Britt was carrying when he got hit. You can look it over. If you think we need it, there's more in the supply room and at the hospital. We're counting on you to bring enough."

"Got it." It was a typical marine operation: going into harm's way without enough people, equipment, or backup. Jeremiah was right. It *was* going to be a long night.

And I thought I was done with this shit!

The end of **Book Two** of *The End of Children Series*

If you liked this book, please do a review of it on
GoodReads.com
or Amazon.com, if you bought it from them.
It's reviews that sell books and help me fund my next
novel.
Thanks - Fred

Book One: The Beginning of the End

Book Three: The Emissary

Both titles are available on Amazon in either paper or e-book format.

Fredrick Hudgin

I have been writing poetry and short stories since I took a Creative Writing class at Purdue University in 1967. Unfortunately, that was the only class I passed and spent the next three years in the army, including a tour in Vietnam. After leaving the army, I earned a BS in Computer Science from Rutgers and struck off on a career as a professional computer programmer and amateur poet.

I find that my years of writing poetry have affected how I write prose. My wife is always saying to put more narrative into the story. My poetry side keeps trying to pare it down to the emotional bare bones. What I create is always a compromise between the two.

Short stories and poems of mine have been published in Biker Magazine, two compilations by Poetry.Com, The Salal Review, The Scribbler, That Holiday Feeling—a collection of Christmas short stories, and Not Your Mother's Book on Working for a Living.

My home is in Ariel, Washington, with my wife, two horses, two dogs and six cats.

My website is **fredrickhudgin.com**. All of my books and short stories are described with links to where you can buy them in hardcopy or e-book form. I've also included some of my favorite poems. You can see what is currently under development, sign up for book announcements, or volunteer to be a reader of my books that are under development.

Other books by Fredrick Hudgin:

Ghost Ride – Fantasy/Action-Thriller – Available as a paperback or e-book on the Amazon web site.

A novel about how ghosts share our lives and interact with us daily

David is a Green Beret medic. At least he was for thirty years until he retired and returned to his parents' home without a clue what to do with the rest of his life.

While he is trying to figure out how to recover from the violence he'd faced in Afghanistan and Iraq, he meets a woman who shows him the way then disappears.

As David rebuilds his parents' home and attempts to start an emergency care clinic in his rural town, he meets the woman's granddaughter. Together they figure out how to bring down the meth lab that has poisoned their rural town, overcome state licensing regulations preventing the clinic from opening, help their friend attempt to beat his cancer, and discover David's roots buried in an Indian sweat lodge.

Ghosts abound in this story of love, betrayal, supernatural guides, and unfaithful parents. The good guys aren't entirely good. The bad guys aren't entirely bad. Nothing is what it seems at first glance in Chambersville as the book leads the reader on a merry Ghost Ride.

School of the Gods – Fantasy – Available as a paperback or e-book on the Amazon Kindle web site.

A novel about the balance between good and evil.

The idea for **The School of the Gods** began with a series of "What if…"s. What if we really did have multiple lives? What if God made mistakes and learned from them? What if our spiritual goal was to become a god and it was his job to foster us while we grew? What if we ultimately became the god of our own universe, responsible for fostering our own crop of spirits to godhead? If all that were true, there would have to be a school. I mean, that's what schools do … give us the training to start a new career.

The School of the Gods is not a book about God, religious dogma, or organized religion. Instead, it's a story about Jeremiah—ex-Marine, bar fly, and womanizer. Jeremiah's life of excess leads to an untimely end. There is nothing unusual about his death other than he is the 137,438,953,472nd person to die since the beginning of humanity. That coincidence allows Jeremiah to bypass Judgement and get a free pass into Heaven. It also begins the story.

Jeremiah's entry into the hereafter leads to him becoming the confident of the god of our universe. As Jeremiah begins his path toward godhead, he discovers the answer to many questions about God that have confounded humanity from the beginning of time: why transsexuals exist, the real reason for the ten commandments, why the Great Flood of Noah actually happened, and where the other species that couldn't fit on the boat were kept. Along the way, God, Jeremiah, and three other god-hopefuls throw the forces of evil out of God's Home, create a beer drinker's guide to the universes, and become all-powerful gods of their own universes.

Four Winds – A collection of Poetry Available as a paperback or e-book on the Amazon web site.

A collection of poetry in two parts: Poems about love, tears, hope, and fears. Poems that are *not* about love, tears, hope, and fears. Some rhyme—some don't. Some are silly—some are serious. They encompass the beginning of my written career through my current efforts. They lay the groundwork for the prose that I have created. If you can't write about things you experience, you probably need to do something else. And like anything else, you get better with practice. I was tempted to put them into chronological order but after so many years of polishing and correcting, who knows what the actual date should be. Or I could have put them in order of my most favorite to my less favorite. But your order would be different because everyone resonates to poems differently. So I decided to make them alphabetical.

A Rainy Night and Other Short Stories – Fiction/Non-fiction. Available as a paperback or e-book on the Amazon web site.

The little girl who greets Frank on **A Rainy Night** told him about her father and uncle who had not come home from Afghanistan. But there was more to the story than she said … a lot more. Frank had already lost his wife and family. The girl's loss reached out to him until the men appeared.

In **Ashes on the Ocean**, her husband of forty-three years has died. Suddenly she was free of his strict ways. She rebuilds her life, filling the void he left with bright happy things. But she still had one remaining obligation—to get his ashes to the ocean. The temptation was to repay his years of intolerance in kind, but a promise is a promise.

Being Dad is about healing. How do you bury the memories along with your son when he comes home from the war with an honor guard instead of a bear hug?

Susannah finds out that parallel universes really do exist and that the **Green Grass** isn't always quite so green on the other side of the fence.

This collection of short stories are my favorite of the stories I have I written. Some are twisted. Some are fun. Some are sad and some are happy. Kind of like life. I hope you enjoy them.

Green Grass – Fantasy/Sci Fi – Available as a paperback or e-book on the Amazon Kindle web site.

> This is my first young adult book. My grandkids kept asking me for one of my books and they were all full of adult words, thoughts, and actions—clearly not appropriate for young readers. So I wrote this one.
>
> I'm sure you've heard the cliché about the grass always being greener. Sometimes it's true—sometimes it's not. It's usually a little more complicated than that.
>
> There are no adult words beyond what I hear tweens use every day. And no sex beyond holding hands, giving hugs, and kissing. While the book contains some violence and death, it is not graphic and I feel it is presented in a way that most young readers would understand without getting disturbed.
>
> However, being a young reader book doesn't mean that the plots and subplots are not interesting. Susannah and her friends are dropped into the middle of a civil war. There are good people and bad people on both sides of the portal. Deciding who is whom becomes a pretty important question

to figure out. After the Earthlings get cloned, things really get complicated. Imagine saying "Hi!" to yourself!

So pull up a chair and enter a world of Magic with dragons, mages, and swords. It is called Gleepth. You can only get there once a year, and only for a few minutes. But no one told Susannah that when she stepped into the portal and into a life beyond anything she had ever dreamed. And there was no way back beyond waiting a year for the next window.

Sulphur Springs – Historical Fiction – Available as an e-book on the Amazon Kindle web site.

A novel about two women who settle in the Northwest.

Duha (pronounced DooHa) is the daughter of a slave midwife. Her mother and she are determined to escape the racism in Independence, Missouri, by migrating to Washington State in 1895. But her mother dies in Sheridan, Wyoming, leaving Duha with no money, no job, and no future but working in the brothels. She meets Georgia Prentice, a nurse in the hospital where her mother dies. Georgia takes her in and, together, they begin a life together that spans sixty years and three generations.

They settle in the quiet, idyllic settlement of Sulphur Springs, Washington, nestled between three volcanoes—Mt Rainier, Mt Adams, and Mt St Helens. The beautiful fir covered hills and crystal clear rivers belie the evil growing there that threatens to swallow Duha's and Georgia's families. Three generations must join together as a psychotic rapist/murderer threatens to destroy everything that they have worked and suffered to create.

Made in the USA
Columbia, SC
28 September 2019